Praise for Denise Patrick's
Gypsy Legacy: The Marquis

Rating: 4 Angels!   "...a good...romance with all the elements you would expect...a bad guy with evil intent, mistreatment of the heroine, the bad reputation of the hero, and the twist with the gypsy...Jay is not what you would expect...and Tina is far from the demure, quiet, silly woman that is usually the darling of London society. Both of these characters are strong, intelligent, caring people and ...in a seemingly impossible situation...I particularly liked the suspense elements..If you are looking for a charming, yet suspenseful, ...romance, you will enjoy Gypsy Legacy: The Marquis. I am looking forward to the next story in the series!"

~ *Stephanie B., Fallen Angel Reviews*

Look for these titles by
Denise Patrick

Now Available:

The Importance of Almack's
Gypsy Legacy: The Duke

Gypsy Legacy: The Marquis

Denise Patrick

A SAMHAIN PUBLISHING, LTD. publication.

Samhain Publishing, Ltd.
577 Mulberry Street, Suite 1520
Macon, GA 31201
www.samhainpublishing.com

Gypsy Legacy: The Marquis
Copyright © 2008 by Denise Patrick
Print ISBN: 978-1-59998-958-7
Digital ISBN: 1-59998-693-0

Editing by Lindsey McGurk
Cover by Dawn Seewer

First Samhain Publishing, Ltd. electronic publication: November 2007
First Samhain Publishing, Ltd. print publication: September 2008

Dedication

To my first readers: Evie and Eva. Without your encouragement and patience, this book would never have been published.

To my family—who put up with me writing long into the night, on weekends, and even on vacation.

Last, but by no means least, to my Aunt Emma-Jean, whose death reminded me that "someday" will never come if you keep waiting for the perfect time. You are still missed.

Prologue

June 1843

The outskirts of London

The brightly painted wagon moved slowly by the light of the full moon. At the reins, a gypsy, her face lined with age, hummed softly to herself as the horse plodded on. Only a little farther to go. She'd left the last town's fair later than expected, but she had many coins to show for her day's work of telling fortunes.

The scent of wildflowers filled the air. Summer was upon them and nature was eager to show off. An owl hooted in the distance, but otherwise all was quiet. As the *vardo* negotiated a bend, the horse slowed and nickered, then came to a stop. Snapping the reins was met with a disdainful toss of the horse's mane. The animal refused to budge. Resigned, the gypsy clambered down to find out what was wrong.

Sprawled in the road was a young man. His clothing was torn and he lay face down at such an odd angle, that, at first, she thought him dead. The horse nudged him and he groaned. Moving quickly back to the wagon, she lifted a small skin of water from the seat, then approached and dropped down beside him. Running practiced hands over him, she found a large lump on the side of his head, and a few skinned knuckles. He'd obviously put up a fight, but she couldn't immediately tell whether anything might be broken.

Turning him over, she found herself looking at a youth of perhaps seventeen with dark hair and brows. Dried blood was smeared along the side of his face and around his mouth, but it didn't look as though his nose had been broken. Using the

9

water and her scarf, she cleaned his face. A deserted road was
no place to be at this time of night, and she debated whether to
leave him there with her water skin. She couldn't lift him
without help, but if he awoke, he might be able to walk to the
nearest village for assistance.

Just as she decided to leave him, he stirred and opened his
eyes. Dark eyes regarded her warily and she scooted backward
a short distance. Sitting up slowly, he looked around in
confusion.

"Was ye in a fight?" she asked.

He turned his head sharply and she could see that he
immediately regretted the sudden movement. Pain flared in his
eyes and he inhaled sharply.

"Here, here," she said gently. "Don't go making yourself
worse, lad."

The boy looked over at her. "Where am I? And who are
you?"

"Well, you be on the road to Lunnin," she answered. "Is
that where you be headed?"

He nodded slowly, the movement obviously causing him
pain, then started to stand. She hurried to his side to help him.

"'Tis good," she said. "Nothing broken. Come, Nona will
help."

"Nona? Is that your name?"

She nodded. "Come," she said again. "Can't stay on the
road too long. Camp not far." She appraised him for long
moments, taking his measure, then commented, "Many years
will go by before you pass this way again but you will return. It
is your destiny." He seemed not to hear her and she allowed
him to lean on her as they moved slowly toward her wagon.
"Tomorrow, Nona will take you to Lunnin."

Chapter One

June 1861

London

My father must be squirming in his grave!

Andrew James Collings, Jay to his family and friends, raised his glass in mock salute to the empty room, then downed the potent whiskey in one swallow. At the unpardonable hour of three o'clock in the afternoon, he was nearly drunk, but he didn't care.

He never thought he would set foot in this house again, yet memories assailed him the moment he had. It had taken the solicitor almost four years to track him down to inform him of his father's death. He'd heard a rumor about his brother's death, but paid scant attention to it except to briefly register that, if it was true, he was now his father's heir. Returning to find out that it was, and that his father had also died in the interim thereby making him the eighth Marquis of Thanet, had shaken him.

Now, he surveyed the library of Thane House as he poured himself another drink and smiled.

The library had changed. The last time he'd been in this room the drapes and carpet had not been royal blue. The overstuffed, wingback chairs sitting before the fireplace and the large oak desk had not been upholstered in wine red velvet. What hadn't changed was the smell of beeswax used to clean all the surfaces to a bright shine, the dreary paintings of the English countryside displayed on the walls between the oak floor to ceiling bookshelves, and the location of the whisky decanter on the sideboard.

Crossing the thick Aubusson carpet to the window, he pushed aside the velvet drapes and stared out across a nearly deserted London square at the houses standing sentinel over the small patch of green in the center without seeing any of it. A hackney went by, but he was lost in the past.

He was the ungovernable one. How often had he heard that? Wild. Reckless. Uncontrollable. Destined to end badly. First his governess, then his tutor, had said so. He'd heard it all before he was sixteen—before he left his home for what he thought was the last time.

Eighteen years. Eighteen long, lonely years. He hadn't been idle—he'd managed to amass a fortune in that time, building a shipping concern and traveling extensively, but he missed England. If it hadn't been for Brand, he might have lost his purpose long ago.

Now, he'd returned—but to what? He was not the same headstrong youth who'd slipped away in the night. He had come back a man and his father would never know, not that he would have cared.

The door to the library opened and in strolled Brand. His friend and business partner always made people look twice. He was as tall as Jay, but thin and wiry, often giving the impression of a half-starved adolescent. His light hair and pale skin only contributed to the impression of fragility, causing most people to underestimate him on first acquaintance. But he had become a master fighter in the Orient and Jay had been thankful for his skills more than once during their partnership.

"Not bad," Brand commented now. "You've done well, my lord."

Jay grinned. "Well, that's a relief. I thought perhaps my humble home wouldn't measure up to your standards."

"Considering I have no standards, that wouldn't be too hard," Brand returned. Dropping into one of the wingback chairs before the desk, violet-colored eyes watched Jay keenly from beneath a thatch of straw-colored hair. "Now what?"

Jay knew not to prevaricate. Brand understood him better than anyone. Although six years his junior, Brand had a perceptiveness about him that gave one the impression that he could see right through any half-truths. "I don't know. I suppose we wait to see what the solicitor has to say when he arrives. I sent a note asking him to come 'round as soon as possible. I suppose we will get to the bottom of this then."

Brand nodded and said no more.

"Then we get to the bottom of your problem."

Brand looked up. "Perhaps we should see what the solicitor has to say before we delve into my problems. One set of problems at a time."

They lapsed into silence once more, the crackle of the fire the only sound in what was quickly becoming a suffocatingly interminable wait. Jay moved from the window to the desk, aware of Brand's eyes following him as he prowled the room. He wasn't staggeringly drunk yet, that might come later—after the meeting with the solicitor.

He also wasn't sure he wanted to be here. There were too many ghosts for him to be comfortable. He half expected his father to come into the room any minute and demand to know what he wanted, why he was back. Returning to the desk, he settled his long, lean frame into the soft leather chair and leaned back, closing his eyes. He heard Brand rise and move to the sideboard. The clink of crystal told him Brand was pouring himself a drink, but Jay was oblivious to it as another memory assaulted him.

He was in the library at Collingswood, one of the family's estates, standing stiffly before his father's desk while his father berated him yet again. This time it was over the unauthorized riding of his father's prize stallion. But, it could have been over any number of things—from being too friendly with the servants to being sent down from school to playing some prank on his brother, Aaron. Of course, some of the pranks *had* been somewhat dangerous and, with the invincibility of youth, he never thought they'd do much damage. Unfortunately, his father often disagreed.

His mouth twisted at the recollection. Although only two years separated Aaron and him, they had not been close. Their temperaments were too different. As children they were opposites: Aaron seemingly timid and self-effacing while Jay was daring and reckless. But, there was a side to Aaron their father never saw—a devious side that only Jay had seen, and often been the victim of, which was why he was standing defiantly before his father's desk being called to account for something he hadn't done.

"Why?" his father demanded, his dark eyes snapping furiously. "You're just fortunate no harm came to him. But, why would you do something so foolish?"

"I told you, Papa, that I didn't..."

His father cut him off with a furious oath. "Bloody hell, I *saw* you. Don't lie to me, boy!" his father thundered. "If you cannot be honest about your misdeeds, then you are no son of mine!"

Goaded beyond sense and with the recklessness of a sixteen-year-old, Jay replied hotly, "Perhaps I'm not." Then, before his father had the chance to reply, he turned and bolted from the room.

As he ascended the staircase to his room, he'd heard his father roar, "You won't be when I'm done with you!"

He hadn't cared. He'd walked away from Collingswood that same night and never looked back.

Perhaps, that long ago argument was about to come true, he thought wryly. Maybe the solicitor would tell him that he really wasn't the Marquis of Thanet after all. That some quirk in the law allowed his father to disinherit him and pass the title to some long lost relative. The relative would have to be very "long lost" since Jay knew his father had been an only child, as had his grandfather before him. They would have had to trace the line back at least three generations, then back down again before they found another male heir. The title had originally come from France, but he knew there were no Thanets in the line still to be found there.

A knock on the door roused him from his thoughts. "Come!"

It was the butler, Keyes, to inform him that he had a visitor. "A Mr. Strate, milord."

Jay nodded. The solicitor. "Show him in." He was impatient to get the interview over with.

Mr. Derrick Strate was a slight man with a balding pate. A bit on the rumpled side, he reminded one of an absent-minded uncle, until you looked into his pale blue eyes and noted the keen intelligence that shone forth.

"Ah, my lord. A great pleasure to finally meet you." He

nearly tripped over his words. "I must say that I'm glad you are finally here. I came as soon as I could, as time is running out. Another two months and disaster might have struck."

Pleasingly intoxicated only moments before, Jay was suddenly stone cold sober as the solicitor's words sunk in. Introducing the solicitor to Brand, Jay bade him sit in the other chair in front of the desk.

"What kind of disaster?" he inquired in a deceptively mild voice.

Mr. Strate rummaged in his battered satchel for a few moments and came up with a sheaf of papers. "Ah, yes. Here they are," he muttered to himself. Then, putting the papers on the desk and pushing them toward Jay, he said, "I think that everything is in order. The top document is your father's will. You might want to read that first."

Jay picked up the papers warily. He thought he was prepared for anything—until he saw the contents of the will. As he read his anger grew. The wily bastard had managed to trap him after all. Flipping through the rest of the stack, he found the other document referred to. Reading it through, he could feel the beginning of a fine rage. When he finished and looked up at the solicitor, the man flinched.

"Well?" he ground out. He didn't trust himself to say more.

"I tried to talk him out of it, my lord, but he was adamant." Shifting nervously in his chair, Mr. Strate continued. "He insisted that it was the only way to ensure that you took your responsibilities seriously. Having never met you, my lord, I could not gainsay his opinion."

"I see." Jay glared at the solicitor. "So, tell me about my betrothed," he demanded in a tightly controlled voice, ignoring his partner's sharp intake of breath.

The solicitor visibly relaxed. "She is a wonderful young lady. Lady Christina is, I believe, two-and-twenty years of age and currently resides in the dower house at Thane Park."

"What does she look like?"

"Pardon, my lord?"

"Is she a hag? Does she limp? Is there something wrong with her that my father saw fit to foist her on me instead of society?"

"I do not believe so, my lord."

"Would you say she was comely?"

"I—I believe so, my lord."

"What color is her hair?"

"Black, my lord."

"Eyes?"

"I'm not sure, my lord. Blue, I think. Lady Carolyn's eyes are blue, as were her mother's."

"Lady Carolyn?"

"Your sister, my lord. She lives with Lady Christina."

"I see. And how old is my...sister?"

"I believe she is fifteen or sixteen, my lord."

Jay ran a hand over his eyes. Good God! Saddled with a wife and sister. Could it get worse?

"The earl is four-and-twenty, I believe."

Jay's head snapped up. "Earl?" he asked. "What earl?"

"The Earl of Wynton. He is Lady Christina's brother, my lord. You will find a complete explanation in the documents before you." The solicitor cleared his throat and continued. "You are his guardian until he reaches the age of five-and-twenty."

"Guardian? Me? To an earl, no less." Jay leaned his head against the back of the chair, resisting the urge to laugh, and closed his eyes. After a moment, he returned his gaze to the solicitor and sighed, "I suppose you'd better just tell me everything."

"Everything, my lord?"

"Yes. Let's start with a sister I didn't know existed."

"Ah, yes, I see."

"I'm sure you don't, but enlighten me, if you will."

"You were not acquainted with the late marchioness?"

Jay shook his head. "Not unless you are referring to my mother."

It was the solicitor's turn to shake his head. "Lady Thanet was a recent widow when she met your father. Her husband had been the youngest son of the Earl of Wynton. Major Kenton—Kenton is the family name of the Earls of Wynton—was in India when his father and two older brothers died. As I understand it, the family was very unhappy with his choice of brides, but since he was not expected to ever inherit, they tolerated her. When the Major was posted to India, taking his wife with him, I don't think the family ever expected to see him again. I am not aware of the particulars, but the major, or rather, the earl, died during the voyage back to England, leaving a four year old daughter, Lady Christina, and his six-year-old son, Jonathan, as the new earl. He did, however, leave his widow a will of sorts, and a letter asking your father to act as the boy's guardian and trustee of his estate until he was twenty-five. By the time I became involved with the family, your father had married Lady Wynton and your sister, Lady Carolyn, also called Felicia, was nearly five years old."

The solicitor paused, cleared his throat, then continued.

"As you may know, our firm has handled estate matters for the marquisate through at least three generations. When my own father died, I took over the responsibility. However, my first contact with the late marquis came when I was sent for and requested to draw up a betrothal contract between Lady Christina and your brother, Viscount Collings." He paused again, as if waiting for a reaction. When none came, he continued. "When your brother died five years later, I was instructed to substitute your name on the betrothal contract. You might be interested in knowing that your stepmother was not at all in agreement with that course of action and, had your father not mentioned it in his will, I would have followed her instructions and destroyed the contract after his death. However, I could not. Therefore, the reason for this near disaster."

"Does she know?"

The solicitor blinked. "Does who know, my lord?"

"My betrothed. Lady Christina," Jay ground out patiently. "Is she aware of the contents of the will?"

Mr. Strate considered this question for a moment. "I do not know, my lord. Certainly Lady Thanet knew, for she and I discussed it at length after your father's death, but whether or not she told her daughter of the contents, I have no idea. And, your father instructed me specifically not to reveal the contents of his will to anyone but his widow."

"I see. And the earl? Where is he?"

"He is at Oxford, my lord. He is apparently quite a serious student."

"I see. Is there anything else I should know?"

Mr. Strate was silent for a moment, drawing his thin eyebrows together in a slight frown. "I do not think so—except that you have less than two months to fulfill the terms of your father's will. Your father passed away on July 29th, 1856."

"I see."

Mr. Strate began to rise. "Well, then, will that be all, my lord?"

Jay eyed him uncertainly. What was he to do now? Then something struck him.

"You said that Lady Christina and my sister were living in the dower house?" The man nodded. "Is the main house closed up, then?"

"I don't believe so, although it may have only a small staff. Your steward, a Mr. Roderick Milton, has rooms in the house."

"And the earl? What of his estate?"

"A Mr. Lyon of Lyon and Mayer handles that estate. I believe that the earl receives a quarterly allowance through them. Mr. Lyon would, I assume, be happy to answer any inquiries. A quarterly allowance is also sent to Lady Christina through your steward. Lady Christina has, understandably, not been happy about that arrangement. A full accounting of the amounts is contained in those documents as well." He nodded toward the stack of paper resting in front of Jay.

Jay nodded. "Very good, then. Thank you for all your help." Jay rose to his feet, signaling the end of the interview.

Once he was gone, Jay sank into the chair behind the desk and put his head in his hands. What was he to do now? His father had effectively put him in a corner and he didn't know whether to laugh at the old man's audacity, or curse him for the debacle he had created. His father wouldn't have known about the gypsy, so he had arranged matters the way he wanted them to be.

"So what do we do now?" Brand broke into his thoughts.

Jay slanted him a glance. "Aren't you the least bit curious?"

Brand grinned good-naturedly, showing white, even teeth. "Of course, I am, but I am sure you'll tell me when you calm down a little. I'm sure the solicitor flinched more than once."

Jay stared off across the spacious room. He hadn't planned on anything so complicated interfering with his life. And he certainly hadn't planned on taking a wife until he was ready to. Until he found the right one. The one he was supposed to find. Perhaps he should let it go. After all, the title meant little to him. He'd never aspired to it. In fact, never expected to come into it. *And what about your sister?* a small voice asked him. *Don't you even want to meet her?*

There was the rub. After being answerable only to himself for the last eighteen years and not having to watch out for anyone except Brand occasionally, suddenly he was responsible for a younger sister, an earl, and betrothed to the earl's sister. What a tangle.

"My father revised his will shortly before he died. Probably because I never responded to any of the summons he sent during the year after Aaron's death, he decided that I was uninterested in my heritage. He had no way of knowing that I never received any of them. I suppose the will is written in the normal way, except for the last paragraph. In that one he nullifies everything left to me unless I honor the betrothal contract drawn up between myself and Lady Christina Kenton before the fifth anniversary of his death. If I don't, or refuse, then Lady Christina—not my sister, mind you, but Lady Christina—inherits everything."

His restlessness got the better of him and he paused to stand and cross the burgundy carpet to the sideboard. Pouring himself another drink, he turned to Brand and continued.

"What he has effectively done is disown me. The only way back into the family is to marry the woman he has chosen. I suspect that if he could have, he would have left her his title as well."

Brand whistled. "He thought of everything, didn't he?"

Jay took a sip of his drink, resisting the urge to gulp it down and pour another one. "He probably thought he did. He obviously didn't consider what might happen if I refused to marry her and fought the will in court." Jay was silent for another moment, before adding, "It's just fortunate that I'm not already married—something else he obviously didn't think of."

Brand grinned. "That widow in Charleston nearly snared you, didn't she?"

Jay grimaced at the reminder of an episode he'd rather forget.

"But why leave everything to Lady Christina and not your sister?" Brand asked.

Jay shrugged. "Who knows. Maybe because my sister is so young, he assumed that Lady Christina and her brother would take care of her. And he didn't leave her penniless—a substantial dowry is allotted for." He pursed his lips for a moment. "Then again, perhaps he assumed that Lady Christina would need the extensive lands and fortune behind her in order to marry well after waiting for me all these years. Twenty-two isn't really so old, though. Makes me wonder what she's really like."

"I suppose you'll just have to go and find out, won't you?"

Jay smiled, but it didn't quite reach his eyes. Raising his glass in a mock salute, a beam of sunlight caught the amber liquid, making it glow.

"I suppose I shall...eventually."

∽

Tina looked up from the herb bed she was weeding. Familiar footsteps crunched the gravel behind her and she turned to see her sister approaching. Dressed in a simple blue muslin dress, her long, dark hair tied back with a blue ribbon, Felicia was obviously a budding beauty. Of course, Tina admitted to herself, she was somewhat biased, but she thought her sister quite lovely and was positive Felicia would eventually make a brilliant splash when she made her debut.

"Mr. Milton is here," Felicia announced.

Tina sighed. "What does he want this time?" she said more to herself than Felicia, who responded nevertheless.

"How should I know? I don't trust him. So, I avoid him as much as possible."

"Yes, I know. I don't trust him either, but as long as we live here, we don't have any choice but to be civil. He holds the purse strings, after all."

Felicia made a very unladylike noise, her blue eyes darkening. "I don't see why we should be civil just because he controls what is already ours. If we up and left tomorrow, he wouldn't bother to try to find us."

Tina got to her feet, arching her back to work the soreness out. She didn't trust Roderick Milton the way her stepfather obviously had. Until their brother, Jon, took complete control of his own inheritance or until the current marquis made an appearance, she and Felicia had no place to live but at Thane Park. That meant being somewhat polite to the person who held their livelihood.

Removing the leather gloves she wore, she handed them to her sister. "Since you don't care to be cordial to Mr. Milton, why don't you finish the weeding? I was almost done, so it shouldn't take you very long."

Muttering something about preferring to be cordial to wild boars, Felicia took the gloves and Tina headed toward the house. The late afternoon sun reflected off the windows of the house, their sparkling reflection reminding Tina of the jewels her mother often wore when they entertained. On the heels of the recollection came memories of her mother and with it, a stab of pain at her loss.

Often Tina found herself wondering "Why?" when it came to her mother's death. It seemed so senseless, but she'd been taught from a very young age not to question the vagaries of life, so she kept her wondering to herself. Death was just another facet of life, her great-grandmother would have told her. We all experience it eventually. She just wished her mother had not experienced it so soon.

Stepping into the back hallway, she allowed her eyes to adjust to the dimness and smoothed down her gown. It was wrinkled and stained from gardening, but she felt no compunction to change for Mr. Milton. Moving slowly down the hall, she wondered again why he was here.

Roderick Milton stood before the empty drawing room fireplace, hands clasped behind his back, his eyes fixed on the opening. As she entered, Tina wondered if he was looking for something among the ashes. He was a tall, well-built man in his late thirties with brown hair and flat gray eyes. She'd long ago relegated him to the category of town dandy. He never seemed to fit in as a country gentleman, his style of dress and manners too foppish and smooth to be sincere. A friend of her former betrothed, Aaron, he was later hired by Aaron to help manage the properties belonging to the family when the marquis' health began to fail. Her mother had not approved of him, nor trusted him. However, since he and Aaron spent little time at Thane Park, preferring Collingswood because it was closer to London, it had not been an issue.

After Aaron was killed, Mr. Milton briefly aspired to take his place in her affections, but, due to her mother's intervention, nothing had come of it. Aaron's death had devastated the marquis such that he paid little attention to the estate, leaving Mr. Milton in place and only occasionally looking over his activities.

"Good day to you, Mr. Milton. To what do we owe this visit?"

She did not bother to sit nor offer refreshment, thereby assuring the visit would be short. It was rude to do so, but she could only endure so much of Roderick Milton's company. That he insisted on treating them like dependents irked her— especially since he was the one who should be dependent on them. He was but an employee. Unfortunately, her stepfather had given him too much control and it had gone to his head.

Turning abruptly, a grimace crossed his face as his eyes fell on her. She resisted the impulse to pat at her hair or brush her hands across her cheek to displace whatever dirt might have accumulated.

"It seems the new marquis has finally made an appearance in London."

She fought to control her expression, deliberately schooling it into calm disinterest. "What has that to do with me? I daresay Felicia will be more interested in her brother's whereabouts than I."

"Come now, let's not play games." Disbelief colored his remarks, and his posture became rigid. "You know what it has to do with you—or have you conveniently forgotten the betrothal contract?"

"It's not binding," she answered. "He was not a party to it so he should not have to honor it."

Tina wondered, as she had often of late, if the only reason he hadn't driven them away was because of the betrothal contract. If the new marquis showed up prepared to honor the contract and she couldn't be found, he might have to explain himself and his actions.

"So you plan to continue living off his charity?"

The question surprised her. "I do not consider living here charity. It is my home as well as Felicia's. At the moment we have nowhere else to go, else we would not even be here." She paused for a moment. "He is responsible for both Felicia and myself, for now. Fortunately, his responsibility for me ends upon my brother's twenty-fifth birthday."

He glanced around the room and she knew that he was taking in the faded draperies and carpet, peeling wallpaper, and worn furniture. It screamed genteel poverty. There was no fire in the fireplace, the ashes from the previous evening having yet to be cleaned out.

When he turned to face her again, she nearly recoiled from the flicker of hatred she thought she saw in his eyes. "Your brother doesn't turn twenty-five until next year. Have you given more thought to what you will do this year?"

"I have already given you my answer to your offer. Felicia and I will manage somehow. We have no other choice."

"There is always a choice, my lady," he countered with a sneer as his eyes narrowed. "As others have learned to their detriment."

"I suppose we shall have to wait and see what the marquis has to say about those choices," she countered. Drawing herself up, she said coolly, "Until then, I suggest that you continue your normal practice of ignoring us. Good day, Mr. Milton." And, deaf to Mr. Milton's furious sputtering, she inclined her head briefly, turned, and left the room.

Needing a moment to herself, she slipped into another small parlor just down the hall. The furniture in this room was rarely used and, therefore protected by dust-covers. Sinking into one of the uncovered chairs and slowly massaging her temples, she forced herself to relax and slow her breathing. She didn't know what it was about Mr. Milton that seemed to unbalance her so thoroughly, but she couldn't seem to be in his presence for more than a few minutes before she was tense and out of sorts, her perpetual calm threatening to crumble. Even a momentary encounter left her feeling shaken and disturbed.

She was too sensitive, her great-grandmother would have said. She could feel his hostility. Her mother often told her that facing up to something helped you to stay in control of it and yourself, and she had always tried to acknowledge the feelings, but not let them overwhelm her. Today, however, his animosity was almost tangible, seeming to sap the very life from her.

Choices indeed! She would not marry that creature. Two months ago, he informed her that her stipend from Felicia's father would run out at the end of July, on the fifth anniversary of his death. At that time, he stated, he would no longer allow her to inhabit the dower house. As steward of the estate, he'd said, he had to ensure the estate did not support charity cases. He had then offered to marry her, thereby allowing her to stay— and move back into the main house. She refused, but later worried that her refusal might eventually come back to haunt her.

But, no longer. After eighteen years, the prodigal had returned. She hoped it meant she and Felicia would have some protection against Roderick Milton. At the very least, she no longer needed to worry what would happen to them come the end of summer. It would be nice to move back into the main house as well, but she wasn't counting on it. Even with the marquis there, she would not feel comfortable living under the same roof as the steward.

Hearing the front door slam, she waited and listened for the sound of the curricle leaving before emerging from the room. Feeling as if a heavy weight had been lifted from her shoulders, she sighed and headed back outside into the garden. Felicia was seated in the grass, her face lifted to the sun. She turned in Tina's direction at her approach and Tina hoped Felicia wouldn't notice her agitation.

"What did he want?"

Tina didn't immediately answer, sinking down into the grass beside her first.

"Well?"

"He came to inform me that your brother is back and in London," she answered, and was startled by Felicia's squeal of delight. For a moment Tina just stared at Felicia in open-mouthed astonishment, taking in the wide smile and sparkling blue eyes. It never occurred to her that Felicia was waiting for her now-oldest brother to return. She'd never met him and barely knew of his existence.

Felicia leaned over and threw her arms around her sister, squeezing merrily. "That's wonderful! Oh, that's just wonderful. I wonder when he'll come to see me. Do you think he'll like me? He never met Mama, so he won't know I look like her, will he? Do you think he'll let me go to London for a season next year or the year after? Do you think he'll let us buy some new gowns? Should we write to Jon and let him know?"

Tina, somewhat dazed by all the sudden questions, answered slowly. "I don't know. Mr. Milton didn't say anything about him coming here, and I didn't ask. I didn't even ask how he knew. But, yes, I think it would be a good idea to write to Jon and let him know."

"It doesn't matter. He'll come anyway, won't he? Mr. Milton wouldn't have told us if he didn't think my brother might come and make him go away, right? I hope he does, too. I hope he makes Mr. Milton go far, far away and never come back. That will be just plain marvelous!" she ended with a dramatic flourish.

And, so saying, she jumped up and skipped off in the direction of the kitchen, probably to inform Cook and Milly that their fortunes were about to change.

Tina watched Felicia go with a sigh. Relieved the marquis had returned, she was still unsure of the ramifications. The betrothal contract came to mind.

She might have told Mr. Milton it wasn't binding on the new marquis, but she wasn't sure. From what her mother said, the new marquis might not want to marry her. He might resent being forced into it. If that were the case, he might not bother to show up in Devon for months, preferring London just as Aaron had. She hoped Felicia would not be disappointed.

But, if he didn't show by the end of the summer, she'd just write him and demand that he present himself. Or perhaps she'd take Felicia and travel to London. She was counting on the marquis' presence to relieve the steward of his control of the purse strings. There was so much that needed doing around the house. She glanced back up at the warm brick building. The rooms on the third floor were all closed up. It didn't matter because she and Felicia had no need of them, but they could use more help.

Tina didn't mind the gardening, or the occasional bit of housework, but Milly and Cook were loath to allow her to do much more, so many things just didn't get done.

She sighed again and got to her feet. If the marquis didn't present himself soon, she'd write her brother. It was nearing the end of the term, so Jon could go track the marquis down. For Felicia, the two of them would ferret out Old Nick himself and invite him to visit. She just hoped the marquis didn't turn out to be the devil incarnate in the end.

CR

Roderick Milton watched in astonishment as Tina deliberately turned and walked out of the room. He couldn't believe she had intentionally turned her back on him, dismissing him like she would a mere servant. How dare she?

For a few moments he allowed his furious gaze to sweep the room. It was a shame she chose to live in such squalor. But she was the one who insisted she and her sister could not share a house—no matter how large—with him. And when he refused to budge, she moved her sister and herself here to the dower house.

He scowled. She was a beautiful woman. Too bad her blood was tainted. He should have done something about her before now, but he had been enjoying himself and allowed the time to slip by. Now he was afraid it was too late. The return of Aaron's brother complicated things.

It was unfortunate his source hadn't thought to tell him whether the marquis was on his way here. Perhaps he'd better find out.

Retrieving his hat from the mantel, he turned and stalked from the room into the front hall. It was empty, not a servant in sight. The tiled floor had been swept clean, but it obviously needed a thorough scrubbing and the staircase needed polishing.

The door rattled as he closed it with more force than was warranted, but he needed to take his frustration out on something.

How dare she? He fumed as he climbed into the curricle and picked up the reins. She'd pay for that slight, he promised himself. Yes, she would pay dearly for that.

Chapter Two

The last rays of the sun fell below the distant horizon, leaving a soft blanket of semi-darkness over the countryside. The subtle fragrances of honeysuckle, lavender, and rose wafting on the light breeze tickled Jay's senses as he stood on the balcony outside the master suite at Collingswood. Breathing deeply, he marveled anew at the whim of fate which brought back the once denigrated younger son to be lord of the whole.

The previous three weeks had been a welter of activity. Between putting his household in order, establishing himself in society and making an appearance in Parliament, taking care of his financial interests, as well as familiarizing himself with the estate of the Earl of Wynton, he'd had little time to sit back and appreciate his new station in life. He wasn't sure he wanted to give it up, but he'd made a promise. The gypsy asked little of him all those years ago, but she had given him much. It was nothing less than honorable to repay it by keeping his word.

His interview with the earl a few days ago had been both interesting and informative. He found himself liking his would-be brother-in-law and, by the end of their meeting, promised the earl he could move his sisters to London or Wynton Abbey if they desired to go. Jay also promised to dispatch a letter to the earl's solicitors, instructing them to transfer all responsibility for his estates and holdings to him. A promise he had kept before leaving London.

Learning the earl's history made him curious and he had sought out the Countess of Wynton. Surprised to find she had her own home on Park Court, he knew the earl would be relieved not to have to endure her presence when he took up residence at Kent House in London. His visit to her had not gone well for she was not happy to hear he planned to turn over the running of the earldom to her grandson. Having never made any effort to meet her grandchildren, she had not gone so far as to publicly disclaim them, but she'd made it quite clear she was not interested in making their acquaintance. That explained why Lady Christina had not had a Season. Betrothal or no, there was no reason why she shouldn't have been allowed to enjoy herself until her situation was settled. The dowager, in her own right, could well have afforded a season or two for her granddaughter.

Obviously, it was the knowledge that his mother might refuse his family outright which had led the previous earl to consign his family into Jay's father's care. For whatever reason, they were now his responsibility—one that did not seem to be as onerous as he had thought it might be.

He and Brand had spent no little time insuring their shipping business was on solid ground by acquiring investors, setting up bank accounts, engaging solicitors, and hiring a manager to oversee it all. In addition, Brand hired a private detective to delve into an old family matter. The information the detective uncovered left Brand stunned, but unwilling to follow up on the information. Instead, he elected to take over the captaincy of their flagship and sailed away. Jay would miss him, but by then he had come to the decision he was ready to settle down and rebuild his life in England. Of course, what he built would depend on what materials were to be found at Thane Park.

With that in mind, he also spent time debating his options with Mr. Strate.

Suppose he didn't marry Lady Christina? The will was clear. She would inherit everything.

Suppose he fought it in court? He would have to prove his father had not been of sound mind when he created it. Mr. Strate had been straightforward about his odds for success and they weren't very good.

On the other hand, a court might be sympathetic to his situation and willing to order a compromise. Something along the lines of the ancestral estates—Thane Park and Collingswood—to him, and everything else, including the old marquis' personal fortune, to Lady Christina. Thane Park and

Collingswood were not self-sufficient. They hadn't been since the sixth marquis. The income from the other properties, which included a lead mine, kept all the properties afloat.

Jay turned over the possibilities in his head. He'd returned home a wealthy man. How large an infusion of capital would it take to make Collingswood and Thane Park self-sufficient again? He was sure the amounts would depend on new farming techniques and possibly the replacement of livestock, but what it might cost and how much was needed he had no way to determine until he reached Thane Park and spoke with the steward.

Once there, he would make his decision. Realizing the possibility, though slim, existed that he might not have to give up the ancestral lands was helpful in his consideration, but not the determining factor. What really would make up his mind, or rather who, was Lady Christina. Whether she knew it or not, she held most of the cards.

But he had always been an excellent card player.

∞

The matched team of grays ate up the distance effortlessly as the curricle traveled swiftly down the road. At the reins, Jay studied the countryside as if seeing it for the first time. The gently sloping fields undulated toward the horizon, the patchwork of greens and browns brilliant under the late morning sun. Taking a deep breath, he sought to convince himself he was actually home. It had been a heaviness in his heart for so long—the thought that he might never see home again—that he was unaccustomed to the lightness he now felt.

He'd left Collingswood yesterday afternoon. Although the two estates were only a long day's travel apart, he'd deliberately stayed overnight along the way in order to arrive at Thane Park by late morning. His spirits buoyed as he topped a rise and drew the team to a halt, spotting the estate in the distance.

Shading his eyes, he squinted, trying to make out the house and grounds. All he could see was the house in the distance, the mid-morning sun reflecting off the windows. For a few moments, he sat and looked his fill, then—with a quick snap of the reins—was off again. Fifteen minutes later, bowling up the oak-lined drive to the broad circular sweep, he savored the moment the house first came into view.

Built originally in the seventeenth century after the first keep was pulled down, the warm, golden brick of the house had mellowed considerably over the years. The center portion had once been a large manor house, but, added to over the years, it had become the sprawling H-shaped manse he now approached, the original manor house sitting perpendicular to the rest of the buildings, forming the crossbar.

Tossing the reins to his tiger, he stepped down from the conveyance as the massive front doors opened.

"Welcome home, my lord."

For a moment, Jay took in the erect figure in somber black before a large grin split his face.

"Jack Keyes? Is that you?"

"Yes, my lord."

"Well, well. Your father didn't say a word. Nor, might I add, did your brother at Collingswood. Sure makes it easy to remember names at the different houses when they're all the same."

"I would rather think so, my lord," was the formal reply.

Jay was about to make a light remark to tease the butler from his severity when a shot rang out from the small wood a short distance from the house. Taking off at a run, Jay reached the wood moments later and, taking care to move swiftly and silently from tree to tree, advanced in the direction of the shot.

Reaching the edge of a small clearing, he was brought up short, astounded at the tableau before him. To his left stood a young woman. Despite the fact that she was clad in a shirt, breeches and boots, she had not tried to disguise her status as female. He couldn't see her face clearly, but the wealth of midnight black hair hanging past her hips was intriguing. She was an unusual sight, but what truly amazed him was that she was pointing a pistol at another figure standing across the small clearing from her.

The other figure was a man. He was tall, although shorter than Jay, but taller than the young woman, possibly in his mid-to-late-thirties, dressed in an elaborate ensemble that included a bottle green riding coat over a white shirt and gold brocaded vest with an intricately tied cravat, dark colored breeches and highly polished and tasseled boots.

"Dammit, girl, you almost killed me!" the man was saying, his face mottled with outrage and anger.

She barely acknowledged him, except to say, "If I had wanted you dead, you would be."

The man's eyes widened at that calm statement. "So why did you shoot at me?"

"I wanted to get your attention," she replied. "I wanted to talk to you, but didn't want the audience we'd have if I went to the house." She was silent for a moment while he eyed the pistol warily. Jay wondered if he was considering trying to take the pistol away from her. "I've come to a decision and wanted you to be the first to know."

"About what?"

"You," she spat. "It's time for you to leave here. I have sat by for the past few years and watched you try to do everything you could to destroy us, but thanks to Jon you haven't been able to. I have even watched you strut around like the lord of the manor and try to take my brother's place. But no more. Tina might be willing to tolerate you, but I'm not. You have upset her for the last time."

The man threw back his head and laughed. "You want me to leave because I upset your sister?" he asked incredulously. "That's rich. How do you suppose this place will run? By itself?"

"I'll write to the solicitor and ask him to find someone else. Anyone would be an improvement over you."

"You cannot replace me quite so easily. Your mother tried and failed," he sneered. "Solicitors do not listen to gypsy brats trying to get above themselves."

"The last time I checked I was above you," she shot back, "regardless of my gypsy heritage. At least gypsies are honest folk, unlike the thieving, lying scoundrel you are. How difficult could it be for the solicitor to find another puffed-up coxcomb who wants to bleed someone else's estate dry? London must be full of qualified candidates."

"Why you..." the man started to move toward her and Jay automatically tensed to move to protect her, but it wasn't necessary. Another shot rang out and dirt sprayed up to shower the man's breeches, effectively halting him in mid-stride.

"The next one goes through your knee," she said patiently, the calm tone belying the aggressive stance she'd adopted. "And don't think I won't do it, because I'd like nothing more than to put an end to your existence."

Jay nearly laughed out loud as the man turned ashen and hastily stepped backward.

"What do you want?"

She sighed and Jay could almost see her eyes roll in that exasperated sound. "I *told* you. Leave here. You are no longer welcome here and, if you know what's good for you, you'll be gone before my brother arrives." She began backing toward the shelter of the trees as she continued speaking. "Don't ever come back. The next time I won't bother shooting your hat to get your attention."

"I'll report you to the magistrate," he threatened. "I'll have you brought up on charges for attacking me like a common footpad."

For a moment, she was still, then she shrugged a dainty shoulder. "I dare you to try," she challenged. "I'm sure it would make a good story—if you could get Lord Bowen to believe it." Shaking her head, she laughed lightly. "Besides, you don't want to end up in front of the magistrate with me. My brother would make sure you'd be the one to end up in the gaol."

"Your brother isn't here."

She shrugged again. "I'm not talking about the marquis."

The man's eyes narrowed. "What does the earl have to do with this?"

Her voice was cold as she replied. "To whom do you think I've been sending all my information on your activities?"

The man sputtered. "Why you little bitch..."

She cut him off with a wave of the pistol. "Tsk, tsk, such language," she chided. "And in front of a lady, too."

As she reached the edge of the trees, she let out a sharp whistle. From the shelter of the trees an enormous black stallion appeared. For the second time, Jay's jaw dropped and he watched in amazement as the animal bent its front legs, allowing his half-sister to quickly leap into the saddle. Turning her eyes on the man one last time, she said, "Remember, I don't make idle threats." Then she and her mount disappeared into the trees.

Jay forced himself to stay where he was hidden while the man collected his own horse and rode away in the opposite direction. Then he turned to retrace his steps.

As he strolled back to the house, Jay replayed the scene in his mind. So that was his little sister, he mused, a slight grin lifting his lips. A wild hoyden if he'd ever seen one. Unless society had changed dramatically in the last eighteen years, genteel young ladies did not ride about the countryside in breeches accosting men with pistols.

CR

Having refreshed himself with a light luncheon, Jay settled behind the desk in the library preparing to acquaint himself with its contents when he heard footsteps out in the hall. Moments later, the library door opened and the man from the clearing entered. He obviously had not been informed Jay was in residence because he headed straight for the decanters sitting on a sideboard in front of the windows.

Jay sat back in his chair and watched the man pour himself a drink, throw it down quickly, then pour himself another and turn toward the desk. He stopped abruptly when he realized the chair behind the desk was already occupied.

"Who are you?" he demanded in a sharp voice.

"I might ask the same of you," Jay responded blandly. "But by your actions, I must assume you are Roderick Milton."

"I am. And you are...?"

"Thanet," Jay returned and was pleased to see some reaction. The blood drained from the steward's face and he quickly put down the glass he was holding.

"Er...I apologize, my lord, for not being here when you arrived. I had not realized you were on your way."

"No need to apologize," Jay replied graciously, rising from the chair. "I can assure you that I was not sure when I would arrive. I expected my sudden appearance would upset the household somewhat. It is I who should be apologizing for descending upon you unannounced. However, that is neither here nor there," Jay noted expansively. "I am here."

"Yes, yes, I see."

"I have been reacquainting myself with the house and surroundings. It has been some time since I was last here."

"Yes, I would imagine it has changed over the years."

"Indeed it has. And, with that in mind, I would like to take the time in the next few days to go over the estate ledgers with you to see exactly where we stand now."

The steward couldn't conceal his start of surprise at the statement, but he answered smoothly enough. "Of course. They are upstairs in my chamber. I was reconciling them just last evening. And since you are here, my lord, I should inform you I was thinking of leaving."

"Leaving?"

"Yes, my lord. I have felt for some time that I should be moving on. I stepped into this position to help out your brother and when he was killed, I naturally felt I could not abandon your father at such a time. I had not planned to make Thane Park my home, but events seemed to conspire against me. The estate itself runs quite well on its own and it should not be too difficult to find another steward able to take up the reins. I had thought to write to the solicitor today."

"I see." Jay resisted the urge to smile, remembering the scene he witnessed earlier. Inviting the steward to reclaim his drink and sit, he resumed his own seat. "And how soon were you thinking of leaving?"

"Er, I hadn't thought quite that far ahead, but now that you are here, I needn't write to the solicitor, nor wait for an answer. So, it should be soon. I have family up north that I need to look in on—a, er, mother and a sister. And I thought I'd look for a position near them."

Jay leaned back in the chair and studied the steward. Although he made an effort not to show his nervousness, Jay could sense his apprehension. It made him wonder if the steward was hiding something.

"Very well, if you do not mind we can go over the ledgers

perhaps tomorrow. If all is in order, I will be happy to write you a reference to take with you whenever you wish to leave."

The steward swallowed. "Th—thank you, my lord. That is a most generous offer."

"Think nothing of it. It's the least I can do after you have done so much for this family." Jay watched Milton relax and make himself comfortable. "I would be interested in knowing how Aaron managed to get himself killed. Of course, I heard all manner of rumors in London, but I understand you were a friend of his."

The steward sipped his drink, then launched into a recitation of the events leading up to the duel in which Aaron met his demise. Jay showed little reaction to the telling, merely asking questions and making appropriate noises during the pauses. Careful not to give away his knowledge of the scene he'd witnessed, Jay managed, by the artful placement of his remarks, to learn quite a bit about the newest members of his family.

They talked through the afternoon, through a pleasant dinner and afterwards. As the steward consumed more wine and the after-dinner port, his tongue loosened. Jay was surprised to hear the dislike in the steward's voice for his deceased stepmother and betrothed, but was not shocked at the escapades the steward revealed he and Aaron indulged in before Aaron's untimely death.

The next morning, Jay was up early. Having ascertained from Keyes that the steward was not an early riser, he decided his review of the estate ledgers could take place shortly before luncheon. After a substantial breakfast, he set out to survey the area, finding very little had changed in eighteen years. Many of the tenants remembered him, but he noticed they were not as warm as they had once been. He also noticed many cottages were in need of repairs. He would ask Milton if materials had been ordered yet to do so.

As a child, he'd loved Thane Park and knew most of the families. Before his return, he'd convinced himself he no longer cared. Now, back for less than an entire day, and he was surprised to discover his affinity for the estate and its people had not changed.

He stopped at the top of a small rise and surveyed the land.

It meant more to him than he'd thought. But too much depended on Lady Christina. Suppose *she* refused to marry *him*? He frowned. He hadn't asked Mr. Strate that question. It bothered him that he didn't know whether she knew about the will's provisions. If she knew, she might refuse to marry him to keep Thane Park and Collingswood for herself. If she didn't, maybe she would prefer a season. It occurred to him that she might refuse to marry him because she hadn't met any other eligible parties. He wondered what her feelings were in regards to the betrothal contract. Again, however, he questioned how he might find out.

Lord Wynton had told him Felicia wanted a season. In regards to Tina, however, he had revealed nothing. Jay wished he'd asked outright whether Lord Wynton knew of the will. Then he might have asked if his sister knew as well.

He returned to the house shortly before luncheon and inquired about Mr. Milton.

"Mr. Milton apparently has left, my lord," Keyes informed him.

"Left? When?"

"Quite early this morning."

"How?"

"He took the carriage as far as the nearest posting inn, telling Jeb that he was going to visit relatives up north and didn't want to take the carriage the whole way."

"And why wasn't I informed of that this morning?"

"I was not aware of it until Jeb returned, my lord," Keyes responded. "By then you had left."

Jay turned toward the library. "Damn!" he swore under his breath. He wondered if he'd underestimated Milton. Despite his obvious dislike for the other members of Jay's family, Milton had spoken of Aaron as a close friend and seemed knowledgeable about the estate. Mr. Strate had reported nothing untoward about Milton's administration of the estate, so Jay hadn't taken the accusations he'd overheard his sister throw at the steward seriously. And although Milton seemed nervous, Jay had attributed it to the run-in with his sister he had witnessed. He wondered now how badly he'd been duped.

Entering the library, he was not surprised to find the desk

uncluttered by ledgers. He wondered if Milton had left them at all. A search of Milton's former rooms did not turn them up, but he did notice a large amount of ashes in the fireplace, causing him to wonder if they'd been burned.

Returning to the library, he settled down to a light luncheon on a tray and to think. What had he learned so far? Milton despised Lady Christina and his sister. He'd been Aaron's friend, but hadn't been welcomed by the previous marchioness. His sister apparently had some information on him she felt could be used to force him from Thane Park, although she apparently had been sending that information to her other brother, Lord Wynton.

He wondered about the comment he'd overheard concerning gypsies. Milton had accused his sister of being a "gypsy brat" and his sister had defended gypsies as being "honest folk". He had nothing against gypsies—one had likely saved his life eighteen years ago and he'd made a promise in return he intended to fulfill if he could.

A sudden impulse found Jay striding out of the library through the glass doors, heading for the stables. Minutes later, atop the same massive black stallion his sister had ridden the day before, he set off toward the dower house. He wasn't sure what motivated him to do so, but he needed to question his sister concerning the scene he'd witnessed. Perhaps, it would clarify some things for him.

He'd deliberately not visited the day before because he hadn't wanted to meet Lady Christina yet, but now he had no choice. He'd wondered about her last night. What kind of woman was she to allow a young girl to fight her battles for her? The last thing he needed was a shrinking wallflower of a woman.

The dower house came into view and Jay stopped for a moment to appraise it. Set amidst an unkempt lawn, it was still a beautiful structure. The warm brick had mellowed over the years—the same material used in the building of the main house, even though the dower house had not been built until almost one hundred years after the main house was finished. It was not hard, however, to note the signs of neglect it suffered.

As a child he'd spent many days here with his grandmother. She had died when he was eleven, but his memories of her lingered. Back then, the house and grounds were spotlessly kept. Now all of the rooms on the third floor were shuttered and many on the second floor were the same.

As he approached the door he noted the cracks in the stairs, the driveway fighting a losing battle to weeds, and the bellpull for the door was no longer in place. Deciding against trying the front door, he led his mount around the side of the building toward the stables.

Here he found more evidence of neglect and deterioration. It made no sense. He had read through all the documents Mr. Strate gave him and was amazed at the amounts his sister and betrothed had been left to live on. Had she been of a mind to, Lady Christina could have easily financed a season or two for herself and had more than enough left over to keep the house and grounds up. This place, however, was nearly falling into ruin.

Leaving the stallion in the only stall that looked safe enough to house him, Jay walked toward the back of the house. The rose garden, his grandmother's pride and joy, stood wildly overgrown, the roses competing with all manner of weeds for a chance at the early-afternoon sun. Hearing a noise, he turned and made his way to the low wall that separated the formal garden from the kitchen garden and there discovered a young woman working. She was humming to herself and did not hear him approach.

On her knees and bent over at her task of digging around a plant, Jay could tell little about her except that she was a woman. The drab dress she wore had seen so many better days it was difficult to tell what its original color had been. Now, however, it was gray. The battered straw hat completely concealed her face and hair from all sides. The one item she wore that made him suspicious of her identity was gloves. In his mind, only a lady would protect her hands so.

Humming to herself as she worked, Tina was unaware she was no longer alone. Giving the small plant one final pat, she reached for the watering pot beside her. It was then she felt the hairs on the back of her neck rise and turning, found herself looking up into a pair of coal dark eyes. Scrambling quickly to her feet, she looked around to see if anyone else was near.

Thankful for even the low wall standing between them, she gathered her courage as she took a step backward.

"Who are you and what are you doing here?"

The stranger sketched a graceful bow and answered in a carefully modulated voice, "Thanet, at your service, madam. And you are?"

Tina stared unbelievingly. Thanet? The marquis? He couldn't be. Aaron had been a tall, blond Adonis, but the man watching her from the other side of the wall was as dark and tanned as a gypsy. His hair was a light chestnut, the sun picking out the burnished highlights in it as he moved. Black eyes watched her from under dark, arched brows, and a straight, chiseled nose over a full-lipped mouth completed the picture. There was nothing soft about this man. From the sharply angled planes of his face, to the broad shoulders tapering down to narrow hips, muscular thighs and impossibly long legs, all superbly encased in the latest fashion, he commanded attention.

Remembering herself, she curtsied and responded. "Tina Kenton, my lord."

Looking back up, she caught the surprised expression that crossed his face before being schooled back into neutrality.

"I apologize for no one being present to greet you. I, er, we did not expect you and we rarely receive visitors."

Her stammered words seemed to bring him around.

"No need to apologize," he answered quickly. "I came on the spur of the moment. I thought to make the acquaintance of Lady Carolyn."

"Carolyn? Oh, you mean Felicia. I'm afraid it has been a long time since anyone has called her that. I'm not even sure she'll answer to it."

She was disappointed, but she did not let it show. Of course he would seek out his sister first. She grimaced.

"I'm afraid I don't know where she is at the moment. She is rarely found where she ought to be. However, if you don't mind waiting a few moments, I will ask Cook if she has seen her."

The marquis bowed again. "Shall I await you in the drawing room?"

"Y-yes," she stammered. "It is through the double doors directly behind you." Then she turned away and headed for the kitchen door.

Chapter Three

Jay watched the graceful sway of her hips as she moved away, a thoughtful expression on his face. When she disappeared around the corner, he turned and approached the double doors. The air was suddenly warmer and he had the feeling the bright afternoon sun had little to do with the rise in temperature he felt.

He hoped she hadn't noticed his astonishment. He'd caught himself enough not to let his mouth fall open, but he hadn't been able to stop himself from staring. Lady Christina Kenton was not what he had expected. Although he wasn't exactly sure *what* he had expected, he knew she wasn't it.

Small and petite, with a waist he was sure he could span with his two hands, her eyes barely topped his shoulder. Her skin appeared smooth as cream with a delicate blush tinting her cheeks. A pert nose over a perfect rosebud mouth and eyes the color of a tropical lagoon surrounded by lush dark lashes nearly made him forget the reason he had come. Suddenly he wasn't sure her grandmother hadn't done him a favor by not bringing her out. She would have been married by the end of her first season and though he might not have been out a title, he would have been deprived of an inheritance he was beginning to consider rightfully his.

Jay was standing in the drawing room, looking out over the overgrown garden when he heard footsteps behind him. He turned just in time to see the young woman from the clearing the day before hurry into the room. She stopped only a few feet away and stared openly at him through the bluest eyes he had ever seen.

Today she was wearing an old frock of an indeterminate shade of blue, trimmed in white. Although he knew her age to be sixteen, she seemed younger. Perhaps it was because she was also very small or the innocent expression of wonder on her face—or perhaps it was just that the dress she was wearing looked like a young girl's dress. But, whatever it was, it disguised her age well. Had he come upon her without knowing, he would have guessed her age at thirteen at the most.

"Felicia, don't stare." Lady Christina entered the room on her heels. "His lordship will think you gauche."

Felicia ignored her and continued to stare, finally remarking, "He doesn't look at all like Aaron. Are you sure he's my brother?"

This statement surprised them both and Tina glanced at him again before answering. "Since I have never met him, I wouldn't know if he's telling me the truth or not, but you've seen the picture in the gallery as well as I. I also suspect you've seen it more recently than I. What do you think?"

Felicia turned and walked back to her sister. "Well, he does look a little like the picture. But, his hair is darker. I don't know."

Jay nearly groaned aloud. He knew what picture they were discussing. It was one he'd always hated because the painter made a special effort to make him and Aaron look alike.

Leaning back against the doorframe, he watched them as they discussed him. They were undoubtedly sisters, both being possessed of the same fine bone structure, straight nose, delicately arched brows, and slightly tilted eyes. Felicia had a smattering of freckles across her nose, but that was the only flaw in two otherwise perfectly smooth complexions. Now that she was inside, Lady Christina had removed her bonnet and he noted her hair was the same raven-wing black as Felicia's. He wondered if it was as long and thick.

Deciding enough was enough, he cleared his throat. Perhaps it was time to take control of the situation.

"May I suggest that we are at an impasse?"

Tina looked up. "An impasse?" she asked. "How so?"

"Because I can neither confirm nor deny your identities either. If you do not wish to accept I am who I say I am, then I must believe you have some motive for not doing so. That being the case, I must conclude you may not be who you say you are."

"But everyone knows who we are!" Felicia exclaimed in wide-eyed disbelief.

"Such as...?"

"The cook, the grooms," she began.

"Servants," he replied smoothly, suppressing the grin that threatened to appear. "Of course they will vouch for you. Their livelihood may depend on it. Just as those same servants will vouch for me, despite my lengthy absence."

"What about the tenants?"

"They, too, have an interest."

They were all silent for a time before he noticed Felicia's eyes darken angrily and she said tightly, "You can always ask that toad, Mr. Milton."

"Felicia!" Tina gasped.

"Of course, he'd deny us out of spite..." she began, but was interrupted by Jay.

"Actually, that was exactly what I came to speak to you about. It seems Mr. Milton felt the need to leave the Park at quite an early hour this morning. In doing so, he neglected to leave me the location of the estate ledgers or any other financial records. I thought you might be able to enlighten me."

The silence following his announcement seemed to stretch on for minutes. Finally, Felicia let out a whoop of joy and embraced her sister. "I did it! I finally got rid of him! Oh, Tina, now we don't have to leave."

Tina did not seem to share her enthusiasm. Disengaging herself, she bent narrowed eyes on her sister and demanded, "And just what did you do to him this time?"

Jay watched in fascination as Felicia turned mulish, crossing her arms over her chest and staring defiantly back before answering. "I threatened to shoot him."

Tina's eyes grew wide. "You what?"

"You heard me. And it was a threat I was prepared to carry out."

"Felicia!" Tina was obviously shocked. "You should know better than to annoy him. Do you remember what happened the last time? How could you?"

"Of course I remember. But, you heard him," she indicated Jay with her hand, "this time he's gone."

"How can you be so sure?"

"Didn't you hear Jay?" Felicia turned large blue eyes on him. "May I call you Jay? Papa always did when he spoke of you."

Surprised, he replied without thinking. "Of course."

"Felicia, you don't understand—" Tina began.

"I understand more than you think." Felicia's agitation was obvious. "It's you who has no idea what you're talking about. Mr. Milton was nothing more than a liar and a thief—and a coward, too."

Tina must have noticed it too. "Calm down, Felicia. It's fine. We'll discuss this—"

"Oh, I give up!" Exasperated, Felicia turned to him. "Maybe *you* can explain it to her." And with that she turned and stalked out of the room.

Tina watched her go, shock written all over her features, before turning to Jay, worry clear in her aquamarine eyes. "I'm sorry. She has blamed Mr. Milton for so much lately, I don't think she can think about him rationally." He watched small, white teeth worry her bottom lip as she glanced back and forth between him and the door.

"Perhaps she has reason," he answered, remembering the tenants' reactions to him earlier.

He also noted the shabbiness of the dower house now that he was inside. While clean and tidy, it nevertheless needed some refurbishing. There were no knick-knacks on tables or the mantle and the color of the drapes and carpet in this particular room were so faded as to be almost unrecognizable, although he knew once they had been a nice shade of blue.

Why had no repairs or redecorating been done? She surely wasn't spending her allowance on herself, he thought, noting she was wearing the same drab colored dress she had been gardening in. Nor was she spending it on her sister. The dress Felicia had been wearing was at least a size or more too small. And he knew the earl had been sending his sisters part of his quarterly allowance to help make ends meet.

He looked at Tina, realizing she had been watching him as he studied the room. Casting about for a suitable topic of conversation, he said, "I spoke with your brother before I left London."

Tina glanced one last time at the door then moved further into the room. "I'm sorry about Felicia's outburst, but that's no reason to have misplaced my manners. Please, have a seat. Would you like some refreshment? I'm afraid we only have tea."

Jay crossed the room to the two chairs placed before the fireplace. Declining the offer of refreshment, he watched her sink gracefully into one of the chairs.

"I haven't heard from Jon in at least a fortnight. How is he doing?"

"He is preparing to take over the reins of his inheritance. He assured me you and your sister would not be adverse to joining him either at Kent House in London or at Wynton Abbey."

"That's wonderful news for Jon!" she exclaimed, then asked, "But, how? I thought the solicitors said he could do nothing without his guardian's permission, or until he turned twenty-five."

Jay took the other chair. "As I understand it, my father promised him independence at age twenty-one. Unfortunately, my father did not live that long and left nothing in writing to confirm it, so the promise was never kept."

"That's true," she concurred. "But now...?"

"I have decided I do not need to spend the next six months or more learning about an estate only to turn it over to someone else. Ergo, I wrote to his solicitor instructing them that from now on they should consult him on any matters concerning the earldom. I felt it was past time for him to shoulder his responsibilities. He, coincidentally, agreed with me."

"Jon has been at such a loss these past few years. He's had too much and not enough to worry about. I know he has worried about Felicia and me here at the Park, but there just wasn't much he could do about it. He tried to help us as much as he could, but the only other thing he could have done would have been to come back here to live—and that would have driven him mad. Jon is not one to be idle."

Jay watched the joy suffuse her face. Her expression inexplicably warmed him.

"How has he been helping you?"

She blushed. "He has been sending us part of his quarterly allowance to help make ends meet." For a moment she looked disconcerted, almost embarrassed. "I—I don't mean we didn't appreciate the amounts left by your father, but we always seemed to need more, and Jon insisted he didn't need all he received."

Jay was astounded. "You mean to tell me you exceeded the amount of your quarterly allowance on a regular basis?" he asked, keeping his voice even.

Tina looked down at her hands in her lap, now clenched tightly together. She seemed so uncomfortable Jay nearly took back the question.

"We—we have tried to live as frugally as possible, but it was such a small amount and there is much to do to keep up the house," she revealed in an embarrassed whisper.

Jay sat back in the chair in incredulous silence. He didn't know what to think. He had seen the documents. She had a bloody fortune to live on each quarter, but she thought it was a small amount! She couldn't make ends meet most quarters and had to rely on her brother for help. He glanced around the room again—what was she spending it on? And, did Roderick Milton approve of those expenditures?

The thought of Roderick Milton brought him up short. Maybe that was the key. If, as Jay was beginning to suspect, Felicia's words from the day before hadn't been so wrong...?

"How much is the quarterly allowance?"

Tina looked up at him for a moment. Then she named a figure that had him grinding his teeth in pure frustration. "It has been gradually decreasing," she told him. "It is due to run out at the end of July as it is. Although I still do not understand why Papa put such a clause in his will."

Jay was still in shock at the paltry amount she named, but the next statement propelled him out of his chair to pace the room. He wished Roderick Milton was standing in front of him— he'd like nothing more than to throttle him.

"And just what, may I ask, did he think was to happen

then? And what about Caro—er, Felicia?" he demanded.

"I asked him that once, but he never really answered me. Of course, there is no doubt Jon would not have refused her. He has already promised her a season." She watched him pace a few moments longer, then asked, "Is there something wrong, my lord?"

"Hmmm?" He looked up from his pacing for a moment to pin her to the chair, a look of pure frustration on his face. "Oh. Wrong? Of course, there is something wrong! I am wrong! You are wrong! My father was definitely wrong! And Aaron, bloody idiot that he was, was the worst of all when it came to wrong, because it was he who introduced that leech Roderick Milton into this family!"

She was clearly taken aback by this sudden tirade. He felt her eyes on him as she watched him resume his pacing, then ventured, "You mean Mr. Milton was...is...?"

"Mr. Milton, I'm afraid, was exactly what Felicia claimed him to be. There are any number of possibilities for why he and Aaron became friends, but it was no doubt a windfall for him." Jay brought himself up suddenly, realizing he was taking his frustration out on a complete innocent. Shaking his head to clear it, he turned to Tina, "I apologize. It has suddenly come to me that the whole family—with the exception of Felicia it seems—has been taken in by what may well have been a common thief. Roderick Milton has not only deprived you of the very generous allowance my father left you and Felicia, but I would hazard a guess that he has managed to siphon off amounts from the estate as a whole. That, however, remains to be seen as I will need to have Mr. Strate do a complete accounting as soon as possible."

"I see." His mention of Felicia caused her to glance at the door again and he wondered if she expected Felicia to return. Apprehension surfaced in her eyes as she turned back to him. "I didn't know. Once Papa turned over the running of the estate to Aaron, I was not allowed to be involved, except to visit the tenants. Even that became difficult after Mama died. Whenever I visited a tenant, something untoward befell them not long afterward."

"Such as?"

Tina looked up at him, and he knew she was wondering if

he had asked the question merely to be polite, or if he really wanted to know. But he did want to know so he waited. After a moment during which she watched him with wide, unblinking eyes, she answered the question.

"Well, when I visited the Barnes a few months after Mrs. Barnes had their third child, I noticed their roof was leaking. I mentioned it to Mr. Milton and the next day the cottage caught fire and burned down, killing their baby girl." He noticed a suspicious sheen to her eyes as she related the incident. "Then there was the time Mr. Staple's plow horse got hold of some bad feed and nearly died, right after I visited Mrs. Staple." She rubbed her forehead and closed her eyes, her distress obvious. "There were many things that seemed to happen right after I visited someone or another that Mr. Milton had the tenants thinking I was cursed. I stopped going to the village because the tradespeople wouldn't do business with me. Cook has had a hard time getting supplies or help because people are afraid of any one that lives here. Even the vicar refused to come when I asked him to tutor Felicia."

"Why?"

Tina looked up. "Why? Oh, why wouldn't the vicar come?"

"No, why do you think Mr. Milton was so intent on driving you away? That is obviously what he was trying to do."

Tina shook her head. "I don't know. Perhaps he was trying to get back at Mama. For some reason he hated gypsies and Mama's grandmother was a gypsy. Mama never denied it and, after she died, he used it to turn most of the people in the area against us."

Jay was not surprised. Too many people had irrational feelings where gypsies were concerned. It surprised him that Aaron would have allowed such a situation if he was to marry Tina. Of course, it was likely this side of Mr. Milton had revealed itself only after Aaron's death.

"She would not let him live at the house, you see," Tina continued, staring into the empty grate. "She didn't trust him. Mama had a good sense of people and she didn't trust him at all. She told me not to trust him, either. That's why I moved Felicia and myself here after Mama died. I couldn't keep him from moving into the house after that. The servants tried to help, but they were afraid for their jobs after he dismissed the cook and housekeeper. Many of them were too old to look for new positions."

"What happened to the cook and housekeeper; Mrs. Liston, wasn't that the housekeeper's name? She would have been quite old—she had been there since my father was a boy."

She turned back to him. "Yes. They both came here with Felicia and me, but Mrs. Liston died last winter. So, now there's just Martha, the cook, but she's getting on in years, too."

"I see," was his only comment. And, indeed, he had seen, and heard, enough.

Tina studied the marquis as he spoke. It was obvious their circumstances had come as a shock to him. Perhaps now was the time to bring up the betrothal agreement and ask him what his intentions were. Now that he was back, the agreement loomed large in her thoughts. She wondered what he would do if she refused to marry him. Her mother had been of the opinion that she might not have a choice in the agreement, if he chose to honor it.

Tina was aware her mother had asked the solicitor to destroy the agreement, but he had refused. Why, Tina had not been told. After all, as her mother said, the present marquis knew nothing about the agreement, so if it didn't exist, what would it hurt?

She had to admit to herself though, he was undeniably handsome. He didn't seem at all like Aaron. She had to catch herself to keep from visibly shuddering at the thought of what marriage to Aaron might have been like.

Jay had stopped pacing before the doors leading out to the overgrown garden, staring at something in the distance. He seemed lost in thought for a very long time before turning back to her.

"There is still some unfinished business that you and I need to discuss, but first I must make sure the marquisate is still on solid ground. It worries me I can find no financial records at all, and this information of Roderick Milton's perfidy where you and Felicia are concerned only serves to heighten my unease. I need to return to London as soon as possible and speak to Mr. Strate."

"I understand," she said nervously, understanding that the unfinished business was, in all probability, the betrothal agreement.

"However, while I am gone, you and Felicia will move back into the house and I would like you to put the household in order. It has obviously been allowed to lapse somewhat and will need a skilled chatelaine to do so."

Tina stared at him. "Move back into the house? But, why?"

He seemed surprised by her question. "Why?" he repeated. "Because that is where you and Felicia should be living. As Felicia's guardian, I cannot permit the two of you to continue to live here. This place is nearly falling down around you." A hardness crept into his voice as he continued. "Roderick Milton has gone and the servants will be instructed not to admit him to the house again, should he reappear. I will also leave word giving you authority to make any changes you wish concerning the house, household, and any other estate matters requiring immediate attention."

He was obviously used to having his orders obeyed instantly. It made her wonder what he'd been doing for the last eighteen years. But, if he could assure her that Mr. Milton wouldn't return, she was more than happy to move back into the home she'd grown up in. Felicia would be, too.

"I see," she replied. "Very well, we will move this afternoon."

He smiled and his eyes softened. She caught her breath at the transformation of his features.

"Excellent."

CR

The Marquis of Thanet and the Earl of Wynton sat before a roaring fire, the small table between them sporting two glasses and a decanter of brandy. Deep in their own discussion, they were marginally aware of the curiosity of the other club members partaking of the hospitality to be found at White's.

Jonathan Richard Kenton, the Earl of Wynton, "Jon" to his family and friends, had arrived in London earlier in the afternoon. He presented himself at his solicitor's and was immediately shown into the spacious office of Mr. Quentin Lyon where he spent the next two hours being given a thorough accounting of his holdings, interests, and finances. Then he had been handed the keys to Kent House and informed it had been fully staffed and aired. He was also advised the Marquis of Thanet was in town and had requested he call upon him at Thane House as soon as possible. Concerned something had happened to his sisters, he had gone straight there from the solicitor's office.

Once there, over a slightly more substantial tea than usual Jay filled him in on the activities of one Roderick Milton. Now he understood why it had been necessary for him to supplement his sisters' allowance. Unfortunately, he blamed himself for not paying more attention to his stepfather's interests. Had he done so, he might have discerned there was something wrong with the allowance his sisters had been given to subsist on.

"There's no use kicking ourselves over it now," Jay was saying. "I'm just relieved the damage wasn't worse. I, for one, am thankful my father had enough sense not to allow the steward to sell any of the property. While most of the properties have been so poorly neglected it will take some time to put them to rights, at least they are still part of the holdings. I suspect I will have to do a personal inspection of the mining properties to determine what is happening there."

Jon nodded in agreement as he continued.

"And you are fortunate he was not able to have a say in the running of your estates. From what I have discovered, his hatred of your mother might have led him to destroy whatever inheritance you had."

"Thank God for small favors," Jon agreed. "And, I can help you piece together some things he's done merely because of Felicia."

Jay's head snapped up. Smacking himself in the middle of his forehead with the palm of his hand, he groaned aloud. "I forgot. *That* was the reason I went to the dower house in the first place. To ask Felicia what she knew and whether she knew where the ledgers were. But we started out on the wrong foot when she wasn't inclined to believe I was who I claimed to be. It wasn't until she stormed out of the room and I spoke with your sister that I discovered Milton's duplicity. I came straight to town from there, only stopping to have my curricle brought round and give orders regarding the two of them moving back into the house. I wasn't sure what I might find."

Jon grinned. "Felicia can be disconcerting, can she not?"

"That is an understatement," Jay replied and related the scene he had witnessed between Felicia and the steward.

When Jon's laughter finally subsided, he said, "If I had known what the little baggage was up to, I wouldn't have stayed at Oxford so long. Who knows what he might have done in retaliation if you hadn't shown up."

"True. But it is likely that my appearance was the real reason he left."

They sat in silence for some time, each sipping their drinks. Then Jay spoke again.

"Tell me what you know of my father's will."

"Not much, I'm afraid. I was only 19 and Mother seemed to have things well in hand. I left it to her to manage. Your father left the care of my estate to my solicitors, so there was nothing for me to do. As for the contents of the will—Mother told me before she died. Her words to me were, 'If he hadn't already been dead when I found out, I would have wrung his neck'. But Tina doesn't know. Mother didn't want Tina to feel obligated to marry you."

Jay shook his head although a grin lightened his features. Now he knew who his stepsister inherited her spiritedness from. "What a tangle. So, how am I to marry her without deceiving her? I don't know what my father thought he was doing, but he's put her in an impossible situation."

"Actually," Jon told him, "he did exactly what he promised. It's the manner in which he chose to do it which is unfortunate."

"What do you mean?"

Jon closed his eyes for a moment as thoughts of his stepfather crowded his mind. He still missed him. Opening his eyes, he found Jay watching him, curiosity in his dark gaze. "Your father promised Tina when she was a little girl that Thane Park would someday be hers. He told her if she learned to manage the household and worked hard to become a proper lady, she would be the next Marchioness of Thanet. Mother was, as far as I'm aware, not privy to this promise. Tina only happened to mention it during a conversation she and I had after Mother died."

"I see."

"After Aaron died, he apparently told her if you didn't return, she'd have to manage the entire estate." Jon paused for a moment, then continued. "Unfortunately, she was never able to involve herself in the running of the estate because she couldn't get rid of Milton. Mother tried to dismiss him once, but he laughed at her and refused to leave. And the solicitor said since your father had left nothing that would allow Mother to have any say in appointing a steward and he was satisfied with Milton's administration, he could stay."

"So, what happened then?"

"I'm not sure. Mother couldn't get rid of him, but she did something that kept him under control somewhat. To this day, I don't know what she did, but it was another reason he hated her so much." Jay looked up sharply. "You didn't think I knew he hated her?" Jon asked, noticing the movement. "Yes, I knew. He wasn't obvious about it when I was around. He never made any overt moves, but I was aware."

Jon glanced around the dimly lit room. There were only a few other men in the same room, and he wondered if they were listening to their low voiced conversation.

"I have a detective looking into Milton's background," Jay said, "but I'm not sure he's going to find much. It could be Roderick Milton was a fictitious name."

"We could do some asking ourselves. I have a few friends I knew at Oxford who might have known Aaron and his associates. Perhaps they could shed some light on our Mr. Milton."

"And even if it turns out Roderick Milton was a fictitious name, it had to be fictitious from the beginning, since Aaron introduced him to the family that way and I would hope Aaron wouldn't have deceived our father by deliberately introducing someone into the household under an assumed name." Unfortunately, the Aaron Jay had known was perfectly capable of doing just that.

"True. And I know Aaron met him here in town, so someone else had to have known him. There might have even been someone around who was present at the duel in which Aaron was killed, although whoever he dueled with has probably left the country."

"I wonder if we could find out more about this duel? Someone else had to have known about it. Perhaps I'll get another detective to look into it. The *ton* likes to gossip, but they do tend to protect their own so our best bet might be to try to find out if there was a doctor present."

"'Pon my word! I don't believe it. Jon, is that you?"

Jon turned in the direction of the voice to find himself being approached by a flamboyantly-dressed young man.

"Well, well, Teddy. I see that town life agrees with you," he returned, rising from his seat, hand outstretched.

Teddy pumped his hand vigorously. "What has happened to unearth you from Oxford? I thought you were going to molder away in that stuffy old place. Don't tell me you've finally decided to get a little town polish."

"Actually I finally decided it was time for me to leave."

Jon turned to Jay and introduced him. Jay stood and found himself shaking hands with a young man in his early twenties with bright gold hair that any matron would envy and shrewd gray eyes. He might look like a dandy with his brightly striped pink and yellow waistcoat over dark trousers, but there was an intelligence in his expression that stopped Jay short of writing him off as fluff.

"Lord Teddy Hartwell, Lord Thanet."

"A pleasure, sir," Teddy said genuinely.

"Hartwell? You wouldn't by any chance be related to Gerald Hartwell, the Earl of Weston, would you?"

"My older brother. D'you know him?"

"I did. We were at school together for a while," Jay replied. "He was a year older than I, but a year younger than my brother. How is he doing?"

"Fine, fine," Teddy answered. "Got leg-shackled last year and settled into happy domesticity. Wife expecting their first child any day now."

Jay groaned. "Makes me feel old, somehow."

"Shouldn't, y'know. Both very happy, just hope they don't do something rash and name the baby after one of them."

Another chair was brought up and Teddy joined them. "Why is that?" Jon asked as a waiter brought another glass.

"Brother's name is Gerald, wife's name is Geraldine—both grew up answering to Geri. A damned nuisance at family gatherings," Teddy grumbled. "Oughta be a law against people marryin' with the same or almost same name."

"Interesting," Jon agreed, splashing some brandy into the new glass and handing it to his friend.

The three spoke of mundane matters for a time, Teddy filling them in on the latest gossip, then Jay asked Teddy whether his brother had been in town at the same time as Aaron's duel.

"Don't know, but I'll ask. Even if he wasn't, still might have heard something. Of course, Mama might have heard something, too. She knows everything about everyone. A more interfering busybody you'd never want to meet, but if there's something you want to know, she probably knows it."

"Someone had to know with whom he dueled and why. There had to be seconds and a doctor," Jon noted.

"Not necessarily," Jay responded. "If they really wanted to keep it mum, they might have dispensed with any number of the normal accouterments. I would guess our nemesis, Roderick Milton, would have been Aaron's second and maybe the only one."

"Probably true. And, even if there was a doctor, and we could find him, he might not admit it," Jon said. "I do remember Milton was the one who brought Aaron's body home. The old man was never the same after that."

"I thought you were away at school?"

Jon shook his head. "I couldn't have been, now that I think of it. It was late summer, probably late August." For a moment, Jon seemed to look backward, then he grinned. "Tina and I weren't paying too much attention at the time—we were too busy spoiling Felicia, although Tina reacted strangely."

Jay chuckled. "You did a good job."

"About the only thing I've done well," Jon commented wryly.

"Not true," Teddy chimed in. He turned to Jay. "Was the best in the class at school. Could do anything."

There was a long silence, then Jon leaned back in his chair and sighed, "Anything except protect my mother and sisters from Roderick Milton, that is."

Jay wanted to ask what he meant about Tina reacting strangely, but he wasn't sure he wanted to know. Having seen her, he could imagine his brother would have been proud of her beauty. They would have been a perfect foil for each other— Aaron, tall and golden, while she was petite with lush, dark hair. The image plagued him.

In the three days since he'd returned to London, he'd relived again and again the scene in the dower house drawing room. But he dwelt less and less on what was said and more and more on remembering Tina—and memorizing her every move, gesture, and expression.

"You did what you could at the time," Jay told Jon now. "But you cannot continue to dwell in the past. We will both ensure past mistakes are not repeated, and old debts are settled for good. Then we will move on."

Chapter Four

"Maybe today?" Felicia asked as she took her seat opposite Tina at the table in the sunny breakfast parlor.

It was a rhetorical question. Every day since the marquis left two weeks ago, Felicia began each day with the same question.

And each day Tina answered, "Possibly," because she didn't know either.

She knew Felicia felt she'd ruined her chance to make a good impression on her brother, but Tina disabused her of that notion by explaining the conversation that had taken place after she stormed out. Tina had been surprised to learn Felicia suspected Mr. Milton of cheating them all along, but was frustrated because she could not prove it.

Picking up her teacup, she sipped the fragrant brew. Moving back into the main house and picking up the threads of their former lives had been easier than she thought, but not without some bumps.

The cook was a woman from the village who, upon learning that she and Felicia were returning to the house, declared she wouldn't work for gypsies, then packed up and left. Thankfully, Martha was willing to step into the position, but it left her searching for a housekeeper as she'd planned on Martha taking that job.

Keyes had few recommendations for a replacement. Mr. Milton had caused enough trouble in the nearest village that few women were willing to work at the house. It was too bad, Tina reflected, that Mrs. Keyes had died a few years back, although the confusion might have been too much. That particular family had served the Collings family for so long there were a few in each establishment.

The staff treated her as mistress of the house, and she had to insist she be moved into her old room rather than one of the larger suites. She suspected Keyes thought she should have moved into the marchioness' suite.

Wasn't that what Papa promised? a voice in her head whispered. Despite Aaron's death, everyone seemed to expect she was still to be the next marchioness.

Tina was not so naïve. She knew that while Jay's appearance meant things were looking up for her and Felicia, it leant a new uncertainty to her situation. One she couldn't ignore.

Her stepfather wanted her to marry one of his sons—it hadn't seemed to matter which one, and because she was eager to please him, she had agreed. After all, Aaron spent most of his time in the city, so she would have had free reign at Thane Park, and Jay, well, his father hadn't known whether he was even alive, so he promised the house and estate to her.

"What about Felicia?" she'd asked him once, but he waived away her concern.

"You will be the marchioness," he told her. "Felicia will be well taken care of."

But not everything worked to her stepfather's order. Aaron died, and Jay returned. Now, she wondered if the betrothal agreement would come back to haunt her. It bothered her more than she would admit, even to herself. Almost as if it meant she had no choice. Of course, there was the rub—she didn't have any choice if she wanted to be mistress of Thane Park. And she did want to be. It was, after all, what she had been brought up to be. She sighed and looked up, noticing Felicia watching her expectantly. She blinked.

"You were daydreaming again," came the accusation.

"I'm sorry, did you say something?"

"Madame said you need to have another fitting this morning. She told me not to let you forget it."

"Oh."

Another sign their lives had taken a turn for the better. A week after the marquis' departure, a coach laden with Madame and her girls arrived. Sent by Jay and Jon, Tina was informed Madame had been hired to completely outfit them both with new wardrobes. Felicia had been ecstatic, Tina, wary.

"And who is paying for this?" she inquired.

"I was told ze marquis was responsible for ze young miss and ze earl was responsible for ze young lady," Madame answered, as if expecting the question.

Tina relaxed upon learning Jon was paying for her wardrobe. She might have been more concerned had she known of the argument which ended with the compromise. Madame actually didn't care who paid—she had been given carte blanche to dress the two young ladies and she intended to see it happen.

As it turned out, Madame was pleasantly surprised and delighted to dress two such lovely young women. She was also cautious. Both gentlemen warned her they would not pay for anything outrageous, and she had been warned that the young one was a bit wild and might need guidance. The older one, she discovered, was determined not to dip too deeply into what Madame was sure was a very deep pocket.

CB

Tina endured her fitting later in the morning while mentally reviewing what still needed to be done. There were still two cottages needing new thatch, and she would have to look in on Mrs. Wills and her new baby. At least the Wills would still speak to her. She'd get Martha to pack a basket.

"M'lady, *s'il vous plait?*" Madame's plaintive voice interrupted her thoughts, bringing her back to the present.

Tina looked down at the dress she was wearing. The shimmering aqua color of the overdress almost perfectly matched her eyes, and the underskirt, revealed by the scalloped edge, was trimmed with deep flounces of white lace. The off-the-shoulder bodice and white-lace bertha should have been indecent, but Madame assured her it was all the rage in London. Tina had never had anything quite so lovely before.

"And how is Felicia's wardrobe coming?" she asked the

modiste as she stepped down off the stool.

"All zat can be finished will be done by ze end of ze week, zen we will leave. Ze rest will be shipped as soon as possible." Madame pursed her lips for a moment, then continued. "Ze young miss, she does not want a riding habit, but ze marquis said she must have one."

Tina smiled. She knew the last thing Felicia wanted to do was ride like a demure miss, but she also knew it was necessary. And, she also knew just how to get Felicia to cooperate.

"Then you may tell her no more dresses will be finished until the habit is done. She has a few, so she will have to make do with them."

After one of Madame's girls helped her out of the aqua creation and back into her day dress of peach muslin—another new one—she added, "I will inform her brother of my decision. I think he will agree."

Madame nodded.

Tina left the room and headed down to the kitchen. Martha beamed at her as she entered. "Luncheon will be ready shortly, my lady."

"Lovely. Would you prepare a basket for me to take to Mrs. Wills and her new baby this afternoon? I will leave right after luncheon."

"Of course, my lady. Would you like anything in particular in the basket?"

"Perhaps some bread, cheese, and a meat pie or two. And, if you can manage it, a couple of fruit tarts." The cook nodded and turned back to chopping vegetables as Tina left.

Tina strolled back toward the front of the house, wondering as she went where Felicia had gotten to. Her thoughts reminded her she meant to ask the marquis about employing a finishing governess. It was time Felicia settled down to learning the basics required for entry into the *ton*. She was sixteen now and already clamoring for a season. Although Tina had taught her sister all she knew, she'd never had a season and did not know all the ins and outs of such an undertaking. And, because they had no close relatives on whom to depend—she was sure her paternal grandmother would not even acknowledge them, much less help them—they would have to hire someone. Perhaps she should write to the marquis and ask him to contact an agency, provided he didn't return within the next day or two.

Glancing into the drawing room, she noted it was empty and sighed again. Where had Felicia gone now? The luncheon gong sounded and she headed for the dining room. Felicia entered through the front door as she was crossing the foyer. Dressed in a sunny yellow day dress, Tina smiled at the bright picture she made. With her dark hair tied back with a ribbon the same color as her dress, Felicia looked every bit the demure young miss Tina knew she was not.

Over luncheon, Tina told Felicia of her decision regarding her wardrobe and the finishing governess. As she expected, Felicia was not happy regarding the habit and Tina steeled herself for another explosion of temper.

"I don't see why I have to wear a habit and ride sidesaddle just to please a brother who I only laid eyes on recently," she grumbled.

"Perhaps it's because he specifically requested you have one. Or," Tina persisted, "perhaps it's because he is aware you cannot ride astride in London."

"And why not? It's perfectly sensible. Everyone should ride astride." Felicia argued.

Tina smiled in response. "Maybe someday you will start a new fashion. Until then, you will have to live within the confines of the current fashion which requires women to wear habits and ride sidesaddle."

Felicia continued to complain, but Tina knew the habit would be ordered. The subject of a finishing governess, however, was a different matter.

"Why would I want some old harridan making my life miserable under the guise of teaching me manners?"

"What makes you think she'd make your life miserable?"

"She wouldn't let me ride Midnight," Felicia declared, "or help Martha in the kitchen, or go fishing with Mick, or help Ella with her babies, or..."

"Felicia!" Tina cut short her list. "She's to come and help you, not lock you in your room."

"And how do you know that?"

Tina rolled her eyes heavenward for forbearance, then fixed Felicia with a hard look. "Do you really think Jon or I would employ someone we knew would be unkind to you?"

Felicia had the grace to look sheepish. "I know you wouldn't deliberately, but suppose she's nice to you but not so nice to me?"

Tina wondered where Felicia dredged up such imaginings. "You would just have to tell me, then, wouldn't you?"

"I suppose."

Tina watched her sister push her food around her plate. Finally, she put down her fork and asked, "Felicia, what's wrong? You have finally gotten rid of Mr. Milton, your brother has returned, we've moved back into the house, and it looks like you're going to get your season. So, why aren't you happy?"

Felicia put down her fork and looked up with a sigh. "I suppose it's because I know things are beginning to change and I'm not sure I want them to after all."

Tina sipped from her water glass. "So you want Mr. Milton back?"

"Of course not! Of all the things that have started to change, that's the only one I would not want reversed."

"Only that?" Tina teased. "You mean you really don't want any new gowns, after all?"

Felicia made a very unladylike sound of annoyance. "Of course I want new gowns. We both need them. That's not at all what I meant."

"Then explain it to me."

"I—I'm not sure I can. I just have this feeling things are going to change even more than any of us could have anticipated."

"And your part in all this will be...?"

Felicia let out a very large sigh. "If I knew, I wouldn't be so worried."

Having no answer, Tina resumed her meal, giving herself time to think. Maybe she just didn't understand, but they still had to make a decision.

"So, what do you want to do about preparing yourself for a season?" Tina asked again. "You know I'd love to be able to help you through it, but I don't really know all that is necessary."

Felicia toyed with the stem of her water glass. "I thought maybe," she hesitated, concentrating on the liquid in the glass, then continued in a low voice, "maybe I could go to a young ladies' academy."

If Felicia had declared that she was going to fly, Tina wouldn't have been more astounded. She wanted to go away?

"It would be the same as hiring a finishing governess," she rushed on, "but I'd just be somewhere else. You wouldn't have to find someone who we all like, and maybe I'd make some friends my own age, and I promise to be really good. I'd even leave my breeches at home. I wouldn't—"

"Felicia!" Tina interrupted the stream of words. "Felicia, are you serious?"

Momentarily silenced by Tina's exclamation, Felicia merely nodded.

"And when did this idea surface?"

"I've been thinking about it for a while, but before Jay returned, I just didn't think it was a possibility." She rushed on before Tina could speak again. "Oh, Tina, I know everyone around here thinks of me as a undisciplined hoyden and worse. I suppose I have just let them all think that because it hurt so much otherwise, but I really want to learn to be like the other girls. I know I read too much, and riding on Midnight in breeches scandalizes and scares everyone in the area, but I can learn to be proper, so I don't embarrass you, or Jon, or Jay when I finally make my come-out."

Tina sat and listened. It never occurred to her that Felicia was so wild and defiant because she was hiding behind a wall of hurt. The pain in her sister's voice brought home to Tina just how much the last few years had changed her carefree little sister and she wondered why she hadn't noticed it.

She had been so busy trying to keep them afloat, she had neglected Felicia terribly. There had been so many other problems, she hadn't taken the time to see Felicia longed for something more. And the isolation they experienced hadn't helped. How had she missed seeing her grow up?

"Oh, Felicia, you should know you could never embarrass me. I just wish you had said something before," she said in dismay.

"What would have been the use? Mr. Milton held the purse strings, and Jon wouldn't have been able to send me to school and send you money, too. I knew Mr. Milton was trying to dispossess us by keeping money from us, but he couldn't completely cut us off or the solicitor might have found out. I just couldn't prove anything because I couldn't find any papers, but I tried to copy parts of the ledgers he kept in his rooms thinking Jon might be able to do something. It's just—it wasn't enough." She took a deep breath. "But now he's gone, and Jay has returned, so all should be well. Maybe he'll let me go to a finishing school."

Tina watched her sister, feeling as if her heart would break. She had failed her. She should have spent more time with her. When Felicia's father died, their mother seemed to withdraw from nearly everything. Perhaps it had been the shock of losing a second husband, or maybe she had been unable to cope with her grief and Mr. Milton too. Whatever the reason, she seemed to have no interest in running the household, so it had fallen to Tina, at seventeen, to manage. And Tina had been managing things ever since—at Felicia's expense.

Tina rose from the table now and going to her sister's side, hugged her fiercely. "I will talk to Jon and the marquis."

For Felicia, it was enough. Hugging her sister back, she responded, "Thank you. Oh, Tina, thank you. I promise to be better from now on. I'll even go up this afternoon and discuss a riding habit with Madame." Then she skipped out of the room, her face alight.

Tina watched her go with a sigh, then headed to the kitchen to pick up the basket from Cook for Mrs. Wills.

As she walked to the Wills' cottage, she replayed her conversation with Felicia. "Maybe I'll make some friends my own age." Felicia had said. It should have occurred to Tina that Felicia might be lonely. She had some friends among the tenants—and Tina knew she had been careful not to let Mr. Milton find out. But she wanted friends of her own age and from her own class.

Their mother had not been class conscious. In fact, she had been quite proud of her gypsy heritage—and she had passed that pride on to her daughters. But, Tina knew, sometimes that heritage came back to haunt them.

While her stepfather had been alive, the local families had no choice but to acknowledge them. They were the ranking family in the district. She, Jon, and Felicia had been invited to the birthday and holiday celebrations of many local families. And reciprocal invitations had been regularly accepted. Her mother had never thrown the knowledge in anyone's face, but if it came up, she hadn't prevaricated. And, of course, it occasionally did.

Lady Bowen, the wife of the local magistrate, had been particularly displeased to find the marquis considered Tina fit to be Aaron's viscountess over either of her girls. And when Aaron died fighting a duel, she had been particularly nasty in spreading rumors throughout the district claiming Aaron preferred another woman over his own betrothed. A woman he had been willing to fight a duel over.

Then there had been the unique problems Jon had to endure. He'd come into his title so young that during his teens he was often a target for the local matrons with daughters. Fortunately for him, the marquis had been there. Lady Bowen might think Tina and Felicia were beyond the pale but Jon was an earl and wasn't to be dismissed so easily. Tina often wondered if the old marquis hadn't been there, if Lizzy Bowen wouldn't now be the Countess of Wynton. She shuddered lightly at the thought as the Wills' cottage came into view.

Mrs. Wills was awake and delighted to see her. It had been a difficult birth, but Tina could see she would be fine. After exclaiming over the baby and singing her praises, Tina and the new mother settled into a discussion of the small family's immediate needs.

"I heard his lordship is back," Mrs. Wills remarked. When Tina nodded, she continued, "I hope he'll be stayin' put for a while."

"I think so," Tina tried to reassure her. "But, he's already gone to London because he can't find any of the estate ledgers."

"Ledgers?"

"Mmm, hmm. He said when Mr. Milton left, he didn't leave the ledgers for him. So he doesn't know what expenditures have been made on the property."

"T'ain't hard to see nothin's been spent. Whenever my Bobby asked if'n there was money for repairs, Mr. Milton would say he was waitin' on his lordship's approval. An' it never came."

"I see," Tina murmured. But she wasn't sure she really did. If Mr. Milton hadn't been keeping up the estate and helping the tenants, then what exactly *had* he been doing all this time?

"Well, now he's back, I have been trying to take stock and see what needs doing." Looking around the small cottage, Tina could see where some repairs could be made. Making a mental note to add the Wills' cottage to her list, she turned back to the woman.

An hour later Tina left, satisfied Mrs. Wills was being well taken care of by her neighbors and husband.

As she walked back to the house, Tina allowed her mind to wander. Today was a warm day, the sun bright in a cloudless sky. Insects buzzed around her as she entered a small stand of trees absently swinging the now empty basket. Carefully picking her way around tree roots and flowering bushes, she soon found herself across the drive from the house. Stopping for a moment, she merely contemplated the house as if seeing it for the first time.

The afternoon sun struck the western facade of the house, warming the golden-hued brick. The formal gardens between the two wings, Tina knew, would be a glorious hive of activity with flies, bees, and butterflies flitting from flower to bush to tree, the melodious gurgle of the fountain in the background. Farther behind the house, the duck pond would be alive with activity as well. There had been seven new ducklings hatched in the spring and she had seen them parading around the pond behind a proud mother duck before tumbling back into the pond for a swim.

The house itself beckoned like a comfortable friend. Gazing at the house, Tina was conscious of a sense of being home—of security—she had not felt since her stepfather's death. This was her home. She knew no other. And, she loved it. She might eventually move to Wynton Abbey with Jon, but she knew she would leave her heart here.

It wasn't just the house and its warmth she would miss. It was the countryside as well. The rolling hills, the meandering streams, and the people. For her, this was a magical place. The old marquis had told her many stories about those hills and streams—of dragons slumbering peacefully under the hills, of fairies in the tall grasses around the streams, of sprites and pixies playing in the various stands of trees. Jon scoffed at the stories of sprites, pixies, and fairies, but he was always ready to slay the dragons, sometimes climbing the small hillocks and jabbing his toy sword into the top in triumph. She could still see the old marquis' dark eyes, so like his youngest son's, and hear his booming laugh as he warned Jon against waking the beasts.

She and Jon couldn't have asked for a better guardian and stepfather. He had been as kind and loving as if he had been their own father. For Tina, he was the only father she had ever known and she still grieved his loss.

When her own father died on the way home from India, she hadn't understood. Because her mother felt she, at age four, was too young to understand death, she'd told Tina nothing except her father was gone. It was Jon who had told her he was dead, and, therefore, gone forever. Confused and lost, she had been initially frightened of the marquis, but he had gently coaxed her from her shell, and she grew to love him.

Leaning back against a sturdy oak, Tina's thoughts wandered to Jay. Could she marry him? She had no experience with men except with Aaron and Roderick Milton, but if Jay was more like his father and less like Aaron, perhaps she would feel comfortable with him. She knew she'd been attracted to him the day he came to the dower house to see Felicia. It might have been more difficult to hide, if other things hadn't commanded their attention.

It was surprising, she thought, that, having grown up with Aaron, she could not now recall his face, but, having met Jay once, she could see him clearly whenever she closed her eyes. She wondered if he remembered her.

If she married him, could she love him? Her mother had loved both her husbands and Tina found it curious. The true love she read about would have only paired up two people forever, yet her mother had found a deep and abiding love twice in one lifetime. She had no idea what he might think of love, but her short acquaintance with Jay gave her hope it might be possible. She hoped so. A marriage was forever. Life with Aaron would have been hell on earth.

Sighing, she pushed away from the tree and continued up to the house. As she entered, she was surprised to hear Beethoven floating down the hall from the music room. It had been a while since Felicia bothered with her music even though there had once been a time when she would have been found nowhere else. Their mother had been an accomplished pianist and taught all three of them to play. As she headed toward the music room, she wondered if Jon ever played anymore.

Felicia was lost in the music as Tina entered the room. Her eyes closed as her fingers tripped over the keys, an expression of pure contentment on her face. As the music flowed, Tina allowed herself to be carried away as well. Sinking onto a small settee, she leaned back, closed her eyes, and allowed the notes of the "Moonlight Sonata" to wash over her.

Felicia was a gifted player. After their mother's death, she had continued to teach herself, learning piece after piece until she had exhausted their store. Since then, with no money to buy any more pieces, she played very little, but when she did, Tina found herself in awe of her sister's ability. She knew she was a good player, but her attempts seemed to pale in comparison.

The music stopped and, opening her eyes, she found Felicia watching her, smiling. "It's been much too long since I last played," she said. "I just felt drawn here today for some reason."

Tina smiled at her. "We will have to make sure your young ladies' academy has plenty of music. I should write to the marquis this afternoon."

"Maybe we should find out which school Lady Bowen sent her daughters to," Felicia offered helpfully, "then make sure I don't end up at that one," she added with a grin.

"Felicia!" Tina admonished. "You should not say such things," she told her, vainly trying to smother her amusement.

"I know," she returned, unrepentant. "But there's no one here to hear, and we both know what I mean."

Tina did know. Before Lizzy had gone off to some young ladies' academy, she had been bearable, even nice sometimes. When she returned, she'd become vain, smug, condescending, and had developed a mean streak which was often turned on Tina. Her sister, Evelyn, had been even worse—if possible. She and Felicia considered themselves fortunate when those two had gone off to London for a Season and not returned, both having made acceptable matches.

Keyes appeared, bearing a silver salver with a note upon it. Presenting it to Tina, he informed her it had been brought to the kitchen by an urchin who insisted it was urgent and should be answered the next day.

Tina took the note and thanked Keyes, who then left the room.

Felicia left the pianoforte, unmistakably curious. Tina glanced at the note, then handed it to her as she sat down. Felicia looked down. There was nothing on the small piece of paper but a roughly drawn symbol—a circle with a star inside, its points extending slightly beyond the outside of the circle—but both knew what it meant.

"Nona's back," Felicia breathed. "I wonder how she knew."

Tina wondered as well, but she knew the fruitlessness of speculation, so she merely said, "It doesn't matter how she knew. What matters now is that we see her. Which we will do tomorrow."

Felicia looked at Tina, a mischievous glint in her eyes, "My habit won't be ready by then."

Tina just shook her head. "But mine is, so you can wear my old one—it will fit you."

Felicia snorted, but agreed. It meant leaving Midnight home since he refused to allow a sidesaddle on his back, but there were other horses in the stables—one of the few places Mr. Milton hadn't stinted on.

CR

Tina and Felicia sat at the crest of the hill, looking down at the copse of trees nestled in the small valley. From this distance, they could barely make out the plume of smoke rising from the middle of the trees and disappearing into the cloudless summer sky. Picking their way down the side of the hill, they soon found themselves in the shade of the trees and, moments later, in the clearing in the middle.

A man and a woman sat on a log in front of a small fire in the center of the clearing. The woman noticed them first.

"Tia?" she queried, rising to meet them as they dismounted. "Good, you have come. Nona has been restless."

The woman was small with lush, rounded curves clearly displayed by her loose-fitting blouse and bright, multi-colored skirt. Small, trim ankles flashed as she walked, revealing a slim gold anklet. Her arms were bare, but gold coins dangled from both ears, tinkling as she moved.

"Mira!" Tina rushed into the woman's arms. "How good it is to see you again. You are looking well." Mira had been close in age to Tina's mother, but Mira's life as a gypsy was etched on her face in the lines around her eyes and mouth. Laugh lines, she called them, although there was sorrow there as well. Tina had last seen her shortly after her mother's death. She didn't seem to have aged much since then.

"And you? You are looking well, too. You have grown even more beautiful since then." Mira's kindly brown eyes rested on Tina affectionately, then turned to Felicia. "And you, Caro....oh, my!" Mira's eyes widened at the sight of Felicia. Turning back to Tina, she said, "Nona will think she has seen a ghost."

Tina smiled. "She does look like Mama, doesn't she?"

"You do not know how much since you did not see your mother at the same age, but they are nearly identical."

Obviously pleased at the compliment, Felicia asked, "Really? I truly look that much like Mama?"

"Yes, you do." The man had come to stand beside Mira, speaking for the first time. He was only slightly taller than Tina, but compact and well-proportioned. His white, loose-fitting shirt was tucked into dark breeches, which were tucked into black boots. Around his waist, a bright red scarf was the only splash of color. Dark-haired and dark-eyed, he had the weathered, slightly swarthy skin that identified him as a gypsy.

"It is good to see you as well, Carlo," Tina said. For the first time she looked around the small camp. There were only two wagons, or *vardos*, as the gypsies called them. "Where are the others?"

"They are staying further north. Nona did not want them to come. She has said her goodbyes and only wished to see you." Mira's voice lowered almost to a whisper. "She has been in frail health for some time and wanted to see you before, but last week she finally said it was time."

"Time?" Felicia asked. "Time for what?"

"Time to see you, little one," Mira replied with a smile, but Tina noticed the sadness in her eyes.

"May we see her now?" Tina asked.

"I will see if she is awake," Mira replied, turning toward the *vardo* Tina recognized as belonging to their great-grandmother.

Tina watched her go, unsure whether to follow. A hand touched her shoulder and she turned to find Carlo beside her. "Go," he said. "I will keep Caro out of mischief." Tina looked up into his eyes. They were somber, a trace of regret in their depths.

Tina knew he was thinking of her mother again. Once Carlo thought he should have married her mother, but Nona had forbidden it, declaring her mother was not destined to become part of their way of life.

"Go," he said again. "She has been waiting to see you."

Tina turned and followed Mira into Nona's *vardo*, while Carlo went back to the fire where Felicia had made herself comfortable on the log.

Chapter Five

The interior of the *vardo* was dim, the aroma of herbs and wildflowers hung in the air. Tina hesitated for a moment, allowing her vision to adjust, while taking in the familiar surroundings.

On her left was a bench covered with brightly colored cushions. High above it, two shelves ran completely around the interior, crowded with gaily-colored jars filled with potions and herbs. Nona had tried to teach her what each one was used for, but she had not been interested. Jon had, and spent hours with Nona, learning what she had tried to teach Tina.

A small chest sat at the front end of the interior, its intricately-carved surface depicting a variety of animals and birds. Above it, the small panel through which the driver could speak to whomever was inside while they traveled, allowed light and air into the small space. To the right was the small bunk Nona occupied. Mira sat on a small stool in the middle of the floor, leaning over Nona and stroking her hand. She looked up as Tina entered.

"She is awake," Mira said in a low voice. "She says she has been waiting for you." Rising from the low stool, she motioned for Tina to take the seat as she moved toward the door. "I would tell you not to overtire her, but I do not think you will have any control over that. But, call me should she need anything."

Tina nodded and took the stool as Mira slipped out into the sunlight. Turning back to the still figure on the bed, tears sprang to her eyes at the sight. Despite her age, three years ago Nona had still been a vibrant and commanding force among her small band. Time, however, seemed to have caught up with her, reducing her to little more than a very old woman. Her hair was completely white now and very thin, the lines in her face etched deeply. Her dark eyes, sunk deep into their sockets, regarded her clearly. Picking up the hand lying on the coverlet, Tina held it gently between both of hers.

"Good day, Nona," she said softly, trying not to allow her voice to break. "How are you today?"

Nona smiled briefly at her. "I am as well as a dying person can be. No," she interrupted when Tina would have said something, "do not deny it. I have lived long enough—more than eighty years upon this land—and I have seen many things. Fate has smiled upon me many times. Not many live long enough to see their great-grandchildren wed and while I will not be able to witness your marriage, I will not breathe my last until after 'tis done. It is enough."

Tina's eyes widened at Nona words. "But, how...?"

"How do I know this?"

Tina nodded, unable to speak.

"I have seen it in the cards and the cards do not lie."

Tina was silent at this pronouncement. She would not gainsay Nona, but she wondered if Nona knew of the betrothal agreement. Perhaps her mother had said something. "I will miss you," was all she finally said.

"Yes, but you will be happy." Nona smiled at that. "That is what is important. Now, help me to sit up, so that we can talk. I have much to tell you."

Tina did as she was bid, using the cushions from the bench to help prop up her great-grandmother. When Nona was settled, she asked Tina to open the chest beside the bed and retrieve a small casket. Moving a small cup of water, Tina opened the chest and found the casket, setting it in Nona's lap. Nona opened it and searched the contents. Eventually, she removed a gold chain, on which hung a gold and diamond starburst pendant approximately the size of a pocket watch, with a star-shaped opening in the center. She held it out to Tina.

"I have waited to give this to you because you have not needed it until now, and I worried you might lose it. But now it is time. Wear it with pride and do not remove it until you have found its mate."

"Its mate?" Tina asked. "But how...?"

74

"You will know and recognize it when the time is right. The wearer of the mate is your destiny. You must not accept any other."

Tina stared in amazement. Unable to find words for a moment, she slipped the pendant on to cover her confusion.

"But how am I to find him?"

"He will find you."

Tina sighed. It just didn't seem right to base her future on finding a matching pendant. There was still the betrothal agreement to be dealt with. What was she supposed to do about that?

"You need not worry so, little one." Nona said, as if reading her thoughts. "All will be well. You will see. My Shana did not think so, but all was well. Her Felicia worried, but all was well, and you, too, will see." She closed her eyes, but continued to speak. "I will tell you a story."

Nona settled back against the pillows and Tina picked up her hand again. It was little more than skin and bone. The skin was soft, the pads of the fingers calloused, but Tina held it lovingly.

"I was sixteen when I met Richard. He was strong and handsome, with a laugh that caused my heart to stop. He was also already married. I was infatuated as only a sixteen-year-old could be. I disregarded the cards and pursued him all the same. It was the only time I have ever ignored the cards." She was silent for a few moments, then continued. "I soon realized the error of my ways, but not before I was with child. But Fate was kind to me and I bore a girl. I had twelve years with her before Richard learned of my Shana's existence."

Nona shifted against the pillows. "Shana was a kind and trusting soul, but longed for something different. Despite having been born into our way of life, she did not fit in. When Richard offered her the chance to live with him, she took it. By then the cards had warned me her destiny no longer lay with our people so I did not protest. I did not see her again until after her marriage to a baronet. And it was many years after that before I learned she had married the baronet because her half-brother cast her out after their father's death. Although he was much older than she, the baronet doted on her and when your mother was born, his delight knew no bounds."

Tina helped her to sip from the small cup of water before Nona continued. "Your grandfather was very tolerant of us. He allowed us to camp on his land—and allowed your mother to spend months at a time with us. It was good for her and she learned much. At one time, I thought she would marry one of us but, once again, the cards said it was not to be. Before she went off to London for her debut, I knew she would not return for many years. Not long after your parents sailed for India, my Shana and her husband perished in a fire. We have not journeyed to that area since."

Nona closed the casket and set it aside as Tina spoke. "I do not know what we would have done without you, Nona. Perhaps Felicia is destined to join Mira and Carlo, and the others."

"Certainly she is spirited enough, but it is not to be. You, JoJo, and little Caro will fare well, the cards have said so. That is enough. But there will be no more contact between you and our people. It is as it should be. You are members of the nobility and none will cast slurs upon you."

"But Nona, our own grandmother despises us—Jon and I— for our blood. It does not matter to her we are two generations removed."

"She does not matter." Nona waived away her objections. "The cards have not said whether she will ever come around, but it is clear she will not matter."

Tina considered her words. She knew better than to question Nona's belief in her cards. They had directed her great-grandmother's entire life, but Tina found her unquestionable reliance on them unnerving. She, frankly, did not believe consulting the cards or a crystal ball, or anything else could take the place of reasoned logic. The cards might be helpful when wrestling with a matter requiring some thought, but they should not be relied upon to the exclusion of all else, and when it came to action, reason and practicality often won out.

Practicality was the reason the old marquis taught her to shoot and Jon, in turn, taught Felicia. It was the reason she and Felicia could not live under the same roof as Mr. Milton. And, she was forced to admit, it was probably the reason she would marry the current marquis if he asked—regardless of Nona's edict.

"Do not do anything rash," Nona said as if sensing her

thoughts. "I know you do not always believe the cards, but do not jump without making sure you will land softly."

Tina regarded her fondly. "I won't, Nona. I will not make a move without thinking about it first."

Nona regarded her patiently. "You will go your own way whether I wish it or no, but things will eventually make themselves right, so I am content. Now where is my wild little Caro today?"

Tina laughed. "Felicia is outside with Mira and Carlo. She is trying very hard to become a demure young lady, so I do not think she would be very pleased to hear you call her that today."

Nona nodded. "As she should be. She has a good heart and a pure soul. She will also do well. Call her. I am beginning to tire and would speak to her before I rest."

Tina took a moment to study her great-grandmother one last time, wondering if she was in pain or discomfort. Before she could ask, however, Nona reached up and stroked her cheek with a gnarled finger.

"Remember what I have said and all will be well."

Tears sprang to Tina's eyes and she blinked to hold them back. She leaned over and kissed the weathered cheek, then stood. "Good bye, Nona."

"Good bye, little Tia. We will not meet again, but you will remember?"

Tina held back the tears, but her voice nearly broke as she replied. "Yes, Nona. I will remember." Then she fled before she disgraced herself.

Felicia looked up as Tina emerged from Nona's *vardo*. Her smile of greeting disappeared at Tina's expression, but Tina managed to summon a weak smile of her own.

"It's your turn. Nona wishes to speak to you now."

Tina could feel Felicia's eyes on her, but she said nothing before continuing into the *vardo*.

Tina sat down on the log vacated by Felicia and faced Mira and Carlo. "Nona said we would not meet again."

"I know," Mira answered. "Once Nona is buried, we will go further north to meet up with our children. We will probably not return this far south again."

"I see. I will miss all of you, but I wish you well." Pulling her handkerchief from her pocket, she wiped her eyes. "You will send word when...?"

"Yes," Mira answered. Leaning over, she squeezed one of Tina's hands. "We will send word."

They were quiet for a few moments, then Mira noticed the medallion. Reaching over, she picked it up from where it lay against the front of Tina's habit. "Nona gave you this?"

"Yes. She said I should find its mate." Tina was silent while Mira examined the pendant. "But I have no idea where to look. You know Nona, she merely said it would come to me. I do not even know what I am looking for."

Mira smiled and picked up a stick. Scratching in the dirt for a few moments, she turned to Tina. "You do not recognize this?"

Tina looked down. Mira had scratched a design consisting of a circle with a star in the middle.

"But of course, I recognize it. It is Nona's sign. Because she never learned to write, she has always sent the sign to let us know when she was near. But what does it...?" Suddenly Tina slipped the pendant off and held it up to see it better. A ray of sunlight caught the diamonds and brilliant fire burst from it.

Mira nodded as understanding dawned in Tina's eyes. "The mate to it, if I remember well enough, is a solid disc, with a small raised diamond star in the center. The star fits into the center space of your pendant. Nona showed it to me once when I was small. She told me that once the two pieces were locked together, it would be difficult to separate them again. It has been many years since I have seen the other piece."

"Many years?" Tina asked incredulously. "How many years?"

"I do not know," Mira answered. "I was not much older than Caro the last time I remember seeing it, but she could have given it away any time."

"Given it away?" Tina said in dismay. "But you have been all over England. She said the person with the mate was my destiny. How am I supposed to find him? For all I know, whoever she gave it to sold it years ago."

"Do not alarm yourself unnecessarily," Carlo consoled her. "Knowing Nona, she told whomever she gave it to never to part with it. That it would bring them good fortune or something like that. She would have been insistent enough that, whoever has it, probably has never let it out of their sight."

Tina didn't believe it for a moment. The pendant Nona had given her was worth a small fortune. If she gave something comparable to someone who needed money, they would have sold it as soon as possible. *But what if the person she gave it to didn't need money?* a voice asked. *And, what if she told them the same thing she told you?*

Tina didn't have time to continue to ruminate on these thoughts, for Felicia came out of Nona's *vardo* visibly upset. She managed to get to her feet just as Felicia threw herself into her arms, bursting into noisy tears. Tina looked over at Carlo in dismay as Mira went in to check on Nona.

"Nona says she is dying. She says we won't see her again," Felicia cried.

"I know," was all Tina could manage. First, her oldest brother, then her father, then her mother, and now Nona. All within six years. How much death could a young person take? Knowing there was nothing she could do, Tina waited until Mira returned to say their farewells, then she and Felicia took their leave. It was painful, knowing this was a final goodbye but Tina knew she needed to help Felicia cope with the loss by staying calm. Even Carlo was not unaffected, Tina noting a hint of moisture in his eyes as he embraced the two of them for the last time.

They did not look back until they reached the top of the hill, turning to gaze one last time at the tiny plume of smoke rising up through the trees to disappear into the clear summer sky.

CR

The next morning Tina entered the breakfast room to find Felicia already at the table, her face a study in despair. She did not have to ask why—taking in the riding habit Felicia wore, she knew Felicia had already been out to see if the campsite was still there.

"They're gone," Felicia announced.

"You knew they would be," she reminded her gently, "but I don't blame you for checking all the same."

Felicia waited until Tina helped herself from the sideboard and sat down. A footman entered carrying a fresh pot of tea and set it down beside Tina. He turned to leave the room, only pausing to nod when Tina asked him to close the door.

"They must have left last evening. The fire was completely out—everything was cold."

Tina nodded. "Nona may have wanted to head north as soon as possible. I know you will miss her—and I will too—but it is what she wanted and we must accept it."

"Why?"

Tina looked up as she picked up the teapot. "Why?" She poured herself a cup, then returned the pot to its place. She could feel Felicia's distress, but remained silent.

"Yes, why? Why must we accept it? Why do you always just accept it? Don't you ever want to say 'no'?" Her voice rose in agitation. "Don't you ever want to scream in frustration?"

Astonished at Felicia's outburst, Tina merely gazed at her for a moment, a fork full of eggs temporarily suspended between her mouth and plate. Slowly she put the fork down and straightened in her chair.

"Sometimes," she answered carefully. "But screaming won't help."

"How do you know?"

Tina blinked, unable to come up with a single reply.

"How do you know?" Felicia repeated with more force. "Have you ever said 'no'? Have you ever screamed and kicked when something didn't work out? Haven't you ever just wanted to rage when it seemed that life was unfair?"

Tina started to say something, but was cut off.

"It's not fair!" she cried again. "And, you don't even care!" she accused. "Why can't we do something to help? Why couldn't we have brought Nona here? We could have helped or done something. Instead we just let them go. She won't even get to see Jon again. It's just not fair! Why do we...?"

Tina was not unsympathetic. At an age not much younger than Felicia, she might have indeed raged against fate, destiny, and anything else that didn't go her way. But she'd learned her lesson. A marchioness did not throw tantrums.

"Throwing a tantrum is not the way to handle problems. Life is not fair, Felicia!" Tina finally interrupted her tirade. "If it was, you wouldn't exist and we wouldn't be having this conversation!"

Felicia's eyes widened. Tina was aware she'd wanted to provoke a reaction from her usually calm, unruffled older sister, but she hadn't expected a direct attack. Tina's temper abated as quickly as it had arisen at the hurt look on Felicia's face. What had she done now?

"I'm sorry, Felicia. I didn't mean to say I didn't wish you were here, or didn't want you around. It's just that, I too, spent last night thinking about Nona and dwelling too much on the past."

"Why?"

"Why, what?"

"Why wouldn't I be here?"

Tina paused again, this time her teacup halfway to her mouth. Taking a sip to give herself time, she put the cup down and looked at Felicia.

"Because, if life was fair, from my point of view that is, my father would still be alive." She sighed. "Not that I didn't love yours—truly, he was the only father I have ever known, but I would have preferred my own," she finished with a small smile.

"Oh."

They finished breakfast in silence, each lost in their own thoughts, the atmosphere subdued. Felicia excused herself shortly, and Tina watched her go, rising not much later and retreating into the study to check her list of repairs.

Roderick Milton had apparently done very little during his tenure as steward except live off the estate. Since there were no ledgers to determine what expenses had been made, Tina was left to ask the tenants and piece together the state of things. Of one thing she was sure, the estate was not in good shape. Too many things had been allowed to fall into disrepair and Tina dared not authorize large expenditures until the marquis returned. She wasn't sure of their financial footing.

The marquis would understand she'd had no choice. There was no reason to believe he would blame her for the steward's dealings but she worried nevertheless. She hadn't been allowed to have a hand in the running of the estate. She hadn't even realized she was being cheated when it came to her stipend. Perhaps she was too naïve, too trusting. She had allowed Mr. Milton to do as he pleased, without any questioning from her. She should have known better, but once the period of mourning ended, all the supposed accidents began to happen after she inquired about a tenant or visited one. In that situation, it became increasingly difficult to keep track of what was going on around the estate. It might have been simpler if Mr. Milton had gone to Collingswood or London, but he hadn't. And he had deliberately ensured she and Felicia were isolated from the rest of the area.

Despite it all, they had survived.

Unfortunately, now she was left to try and reconstruct and rebuild. There was so much to do to put the estate back together. And, looking at the state of Thane Park caused her to worry even more for Collingswood and the other holdings. There was no telling what condition they were in.

Her mind drifted back to her interview with Felicia's brother. He had been furious, but not at her—at Aaron. She could still see him clearly as he paced the drawing room in the dower house, frustration and anger flowing from him like a tangible force. What surprised her was that those emotions had not disturbed her as Mr. Milton's anger always had. It was as if she knew the marquis' anger would never be directed toward her in a negative way.

Nona would have said it was a good sign that her future husband's moods did not disturb her, however Nona also would have said it wasn't enough—she was to wait until she found the other half of the pendant. But Thane Park needed her now and Felicia did too. Being honest with herself, she knew she was attracted to the marquis and, therefore, not adverse to getting to know him better before deciding whether she would consider honoring the betrothal contract. It would have been a much easier decision if Nona hadn't complicated it by giving her the pendant.

CR

The sun was just sinking below the horizon when Jay arrived at Thane Park. It had been a long day but he was glad to be home and eager to be inside by a warm fire and a large tray of food. He also wanted to see Tina. Her image popped into his thoughts unbidden. His thoughts had been of little else on the ride down. Trying to decide how to approach the subject of the betrothal agreement had come to naught. Her brother's advice had been succinct—tell her the truth.

Jay was less than agreeable to that particular course of action. The few times in his past he'd told a woman the unvarnished truth, it caused more trouble than was necessary and ended the same way it would have had he not bothered. Unfortunately, except for an incident in Charleston, none of the situations involved a possible marriage or the loss of his family's heritage.

He'd nearly believed the young widow's claim that she was pregnant with his child, until Brand discovered through her maid that she was at least five months along and needed to marry quickly. The two of them had been in Charleston for almost three months by that time. The negotiations on some very lucrative contracts were concluded and had already been signed by the time the truth came out. An important and well-liked member of the community, the widow had been furious when confronted. He had been lucky to get out of Charleston alive after the furor she created, making him wish he'd said nothing at all.

With that experience as background, he now questioned the soundness of giving Tina another card to add to her hand, if, as Jon had assured him, she knew nothing of the will.

Keyes opened the door as he reached the top of the steps. "Good evening, my lord."

Jay shook his head. Butlers must have a sixth sense about these things. "Good evening, Keyes. Have the ladies retired yet?"

"They are in the library, my lord."

"Thank you." Heading in that direction, he threw back over his shoulder, "Would you see if Cook can find something for me to eat? It has been some time since my last meal."

"Of course, my lord."

Tina and Felicia looked up from their contemplation of the chessboard as he entered, surprise written on both faces.

Lamps placed strategically around the room to provide light, a cheerful fire burning in the grate, and the women sitting near the fire, suddenly convinced him that this was right. This was where he belonged—and the two women in the room belonged here, too. Unwilling to further explore his feelings on the matter, he continued into the room.

Felicia was the first one to recover. "You're back!" she cried, jumping up from her seat. "I was afraid you might stay away permanently." She took a step toward him, but stopped abruptly and turned to look at Tina.

He smiled at the artless comment. "Not likely, minx."

"Then why were you gone so long?" she demanded as he settled himself on a settee near their chessboard.

"Felicia!" Tina gasped. "You are being rude."

"I am not," she shot back and resumed her seat. "I just want to know what took him so long to get back."

"Felicia, I told you what happened." Tina turned, looking at him directly for the first time. "You must tell her, my lord, that you needed to check with the solicitor."

Jay was tempted to tease Felicia, but he could not resist the appeal in Tina's eyes. For some reason she felt Felicia needed the explanation, so he gave it.

"She is right," he told Felicia, "I needed to see how badly our previous steward had defrauded the estate."

"Oh," was Felicia's only comment.

"As I told Jon, your Mr. Milton seemed to fool everyone except you when it came to what he was up to. How is it you suspected he was unscrupulous when no one else seems to have?"

"He wasn't my Mr. Milton," Felicia replied with a shudder. "And, it wasn't just me. Papa did too, but he died before he could dismiss him."

Jay had been surreptitiously watching Tina, but now swung his gaze toward his sister. There were obviously many things about the steward's activities she was aware of. Perhaps she was the only one aware of them. "And how do you know that?"

"I heard Papa tell him. Papa said he knew Milton was taking money, but because he had been a friend of Aaron's he wouldn't prosecute if he left within the week. But Papa died a day later and no one knew about it but me."

"Why didn't you tell someone?"

Felicia didn't answer. For a moment she looked from Tina to Jay then back to Tina, worry clear in her eyes, before turning toward the fire.

The silence was broken by the arrival of Keyes bearing the requested tray of food. Putting it down on a table near Jay, he asked if the marquis required anything else.

"No, that's all."

Keyes departed and closed the door behind him. Jay helped himself from the tray before turning to Felicia. "Felicia?"

Startled, she turned tear-filled eyes toward him. "I—I just didn't," she replied weakly, then jumped up and ran from the room.

"Felicia!" Tina was on her feet, preparing to follow her, when Jay's voice reached her.

"Let her go."

Tina turned toward him, confusion written all over her face. "I—I, she's upset. I need to go..."

"Leave her. She'll talk when she is ready. She was probably eavesdropping when she heard the conversation and is loath to talk about it."

Tina glanced at the door one more time and sighed before resuming her seat. "I suspect you're right, but I'll check on her before I retire."

Silence descended again. Tina discovered that, without Felicia in the room, she was nervous. She glanced toward the door as if expecting Felicia to return. Studying the chessboard was a useless thing to do, but it kept her occupied—and her eyes from straying to the man carelessly lounging on the settee.

There was something about him that made her very aware

of him. A sense she could not describe, but recognized. He was all male in a way Aaron had never been. A potent force that could not be ignored.

A log fell in the grate, causing her to jump. Then Jay's deep voice startled her again.

"You were about to lose."

"Wha—what?"

"The game," he said, indicating the chessboard. "If you were white, you were about to lose."

Tina turned and looked down at the chessboard as if she'd never seen it before. Shaking her head to clear it, she looked back up at him.

"I know." She looked down at the board again. "I wasn't concentrating well tonight. Not that Felicia isn't a good player, but tonight I wasn't as focused as I should have been. I'm afraid I wasn't much of a challenge for her this evening."

Silence again.

"Would you like a glass of wine? Keyes brought two glasses."

She didn't want to look up at him again. She was too drawn to him—too aware of him. He seemed to fill the room. But manners won out and she found herself looking into his dark eyes. For a moment she completely lost her train of thought. What had he asked her? Wine.

"No—no thank you."

"Jon asked me to bring you his greetings. He said he would write soon."

"When did you see him?"

"In London. He and I spent quite a bit of time trying to find out as much as we could about Roderick Milton."

"And what did you find out?"

"Not much. A number of people remembered Aaron and him as being friends but no one seemed to know where they met."

Tina tried to recall the first time Aaron had brought Milton home, and whether either had given any hint of how they had met. "Did Aaron have other friends who might have known?"

"Actually, that's what Jon stayed behind to try and find out. Then he is headed to Wynton Abbey to get his first look at his country seat."

"That's wonderful," she sighed. "I hope he is able to settle in with no difficulties."

Jay did not respond. He seemed to be studying the painting over the fireplace. Tina looked up, noticing that it was of a house on a cliff overlooking the sea. Kenwyck Manor, if she remembered it correctly.

"Have you been there before?" she asked him.

Jay turned in her direction. "Once, when I was a small boy. And you?"

She shook her head. "Papa and Mama went there sometimes during the summer, but Felicia, Jon and I were usually with our great-grandmother then."

There were so many questions she wanted to ask, but uncertainty kept her quiet. If he and Jon were looking for Mr. Milton, maybe things were more serious than she supposed.

"I should thank you and Jon for sending the *modiste* to us. Felicia was ecstatic."

His eyes traveled over the deep green gown she wore. Was that light in his eyes approval? She hoped so.

"You're welcome. It was Jon's idea."

"I hope we didn't spend too much." She smiled. "I had to resort to threats to get Felicia to order a riding habit. She wouldn't have done so otherwise."

"Did you now?" he murmured. "And what did you threaten her with?" Something flickered in the ebony depths and her pulse leapt in response. The room was suddenly close, the fire brighter. His voice seemed almost tangible in its gentleness.

"I told Madame not to finish any more of her dresses until the habit was done."

Jay put back his head and laughed. For a moment, she merely stared at the change his humor wrought in his features. His dark eyes seemed to glitter and the lines around his eyes and mouth softened. Mira called them laugh lines and now Tina knew why.

"I can see you and Jon have her well in hand."

Her pulse returned to normal and she chuckled. "Well, we have been watching over her since she was born."

The silence that fell seemed awkward. She was at a loss for anything else to say. She knew they needed to discuss the contract, but she'd promised herself she would not bring it up.

"I-it is time for me to retire." She was suddenly shy, and rose from her seat. "And...and, I need to check on Felicia."

Jay rose to his feet as well. He towered over her and she cursed her petiteness as she dipped him an elegant curtsy, then moved toward the door. "Good night, my lord."

She was at the open door before he responded. His voice was low and tinged with...disappointment? She almost didn't hear the softly spoken words. "Until tomorrow, then."

CR

He hadn't wanted to let her go, but could find no suitable topic of conversation with which to keep her in the room other than the contract and, goodness knew, he was not up to a discussion of that tonight.

Jay knew she thought his reactions odd. He had forced himself to look at almost anything other than her—except when she addressed him directly and seemed to need an answer. Staring at the painting of Kenwyck Manor reminded him he needed to do a tour of the family holdings. Unfortunately, he and Tina had some decisions to make before it could happen.

Perhaps he should have said something. If he had, he might not be sitting here, alone, wondering what her reaction would be. It was too late now. He'd give himself a little time first. He would wait a few days to see what happened, then decide.

Resuming his seat, he poured himself another glass of wine, and turned to contemplate the fire. The flames were beginning to die, but it mattered not, for all he saw were twin pools the color of a tropical lagoon framed by lush dark lashes.

Chapter Six

Tina was still wrestling with the marquis' effect on her as she headed toward the breakfast room the next morning. Late—and still a bit groggy from too little sleep—she was looking forward to a strong cup of tea. The night had consisted of a useless excursion into the realm of *What If*, which kept her awake into the early hours.

She was feeling much better a short time later when Felicia and Jay entered the room. Felicia was laughing, her eyes alight as she looked up at Jay to answer a question. Tina's heart warmed at the look of happiness on her sister's face.

Dressed in her new habit of sapphire blue, the color reflected in her eyes, her cheeks flushed from being outdoors, Felicia looked as if she hadn't a care in the world. Yet she had been morose and uncommunicative the night before when Tina had looked in on her.

"He's very well trained," she was saying to the marquis. "But you were fortunate—he usually doesn't let anyone but me ride him."

Jay's voice, deep and well-modulated, drew Tina's eyes to him. Dressed for riding as well, his hair windswept, she caught her breath as he smiled down at Felicia, showing white, even teeth between perfectly molded lips.

"Of that I am no longer in doubt."

Felicia looked up and noticed Tina. "Good Morning, sleepyhead," she teased. "I'm glad I didn't wait for you this morning."

"Did we have plans?" Tina asked. "I don't remember."

Felicia laughed again as she picked up a plate and began to fill it from the array of dishes on the sideboard. "No, I was just teasing. In fact, I decided to go riding only because I woke up early and felt restless, but I didn't want to disturb you."

She finished filling her plate, then took her seat across from Tina and added, "But I should have awakened you. You would have enjoyed it."

Tina smiled. "Tomorrow will be soon enough. I see you didn't ride Midnight this morning."

Jay looked at Tina as he took the seat at the head of the table. "And how did you know that?"

"Because Midnight will not allow a sidesaddle on his back," she answered. "He is very well trained, but for that one thing."

"So I discovered. Perhaps too well trained," he said with a lift of an eyebrow, his glance directed toward Felicia.

Felicia's peals of laughed echoed around the room. "You should not have implied he was too much horse for me."

"I felt eminently qualified to make that statement, considering I was riding him at the time."

"Oh dear," Tina interrupted. "I don't suppose she challenged you to a race."

Jay, who had just put a fork full of eggs in his mouth, merely nodded—but there was a question in his eyes

Tina laughed out loud, her eyes sparkling with glee.

"She did the same thing to Jon just last year when he told her he thought Midnight had grown too strong for her. He, too, was riding him when he said so. She promptly challenged him to a race—although the mare she was riding could barely keep up with Midnight. A short distance before the agreed finish line, she whistled. Midnight came to a dead stop and nothing Jon could do would get him to move."

"I see," Jay commented.

"And to add insult to injury, she walked her horse over the finish line, then returned to reward the beast for being a good boy. It was the last time Jon rode him." Tina finished. She took a fortifying sip of her tea, raised eyes brimming with amusement to Jay's face, and asked innocently, "Is that what happened to you?"

Jay did not answer, although he seemed to be listening. For a few moments, Tina's eyes locked onto his and Felicia vanished. She was suddenly intensely aware of him. The outdoor freshness permeating his clothes and hair tickled her nose, and she restrained herself from taking a deep breath.

"Of course." Felicia's matter-of-fact statement shattered the mood, dragging Tina back with a vengeance. Dropping her eyes to her plate, she put her teacup down and picked up her fork.

Silence reigned for a few moments, then Felicia addressed Tina. "Jay has agreed to let me go to a young ladies' academy."

Tina looked up at Jay. "Was that before or after the race?"

"Before. But after, I concluded it was a necessity."

Felicia giggled. As she tucked into the food on her plate, she asked Tina about the Wills' new baby.

Tina was conscious of Jay's interest as she described the small family's situation. "And they aren't the only ones," she explained in response to Felicia's questions. "The Seevers and the Carters also need some help."

Felicia nodded. "The Larrimores and the Rileys also could use a little help. Their cottages are fine, but one of the Riley's cows took sick last week. I don't know how she's doing now."

"I'll add them to my list," Tina said as Felicia finished her food and rose from the table. Bidding them good day, she breezed from the room.

Tina watched her go, suddenly at a loss for a topic of conversation. Jay unwittingly came to her rescue.

"Felicia told me you were trying to reconstruct the books as well as see to repairs around the estate. Would you mind showing me what you've done?"

"Of course," she readily agreed. "I have been using the study. Everything is in there."

"Excellent. Shall I meet you there, say, in a half hour?"

"That will be fine."

"Until then."

Then he rose and left, and she was once again alone, but not quite. His essence lingered and she took a deep breath of the mingled aromas of the outdoors and horse, mixed with a soapy scent. Not the most romantic of fragrances, she thought, but it fit him.

Precisely thirty minutes later, a freshly-bathed Jay joined her in the study.

"I have been trying to reconstruct what has been done over the past five years," Tina said as she watched him take the seat behind the desk. A small room just off the library with shelves filled with ledgers and account books, the study was supposed to be used as an office by the steward, yet she had her doubts about how much time Mr. Milton had spent in it.

She moved a chair in position to face him across the polished oak surface and laid out a number of handwritten sheets for his inspection as well as the ledger she had been working from.

The most recent ledger she had been able to find was from seven years prior and she had begun her reconstruction from it. In addition, after visiting the Wills, she had begun asking questions about the rest of the tenants and discovered the neglect was extensive.

"I don't know what Papa and Aaron thought they were doing, hiring Mr. Milton," she commented now. "I haven't been able to find that he did anything at all."

"My guess is they were doing nothing at all."

Tina was surprised at the criticism in his voice.

"I'm sure they didn't think Mr. Milton would do nothing at all."

"I would wager neither of them cared."

Tina stared at him for a moment, noting the lines around his mouth. His features hardened as he spoke, settling into grim determination.

"Why would you think that?"

"Why wouldn't I?" he countered. "I know what my father and brother were capable of." He began flipping through the last few pages of the ledger, then took up one of the sheets she had written figures on and began comparing the entries. "Neither of them cared for anyone other than themselves. I'm not surprised Milton was able to wile his way into their good graces."

Tina couldn't conceal her shock at his assessment. She might believe that of Aaron, but not her stepfather.

"How do you know?" she asked far more sharply than she intended.

He looked up from the ledger. "What?"

"How can you say that about your father?"

"Quite easily, actually."

"It's not true!"

Jay stared at her as if she'd lost her mind.

"And how would *you* know?"

"Because Papa cared about everyone at Thane Park—and Collingswood, too. He would have never kept Milton on if he knew he would be so neglectful."

She saw the patronizing amusement lurking in the ebony depths and felt her hackles begin to rise. How dare he think she didn't know what she was talking about!

"You heard Felicia say she heard Papa tell him that he was to leave. Why would Papa do so if he didn't care?"

Jay shrugged. "Probably because he didn't like harboring a thief. Even people who don't care, care when it's their fortune being wasted—or stolen."

Her carefully cultivated calm saved her from saying something she might have regretted later. Tamping down her rising indignation for the moment, she forced herself to pick up one of the sheets, take a deep breath, then launch into an explanation of what she had done in the last two weeks.

Jay said nothing further on the subject of his father and brother, accepting the change of topic, and allowing her to guide them onto neutral ground.

It was a productive, yet unsettling, morning. Tina felt as if her nerves were on edge. Even her resentment at his attitude toward his father did not stop her from being aware of him. His mere presence disturbed her. Her thoughts strayed, concentration was non-existent at times, and she had the uneasy feeling she was being tested.

There was nothing overt in his manner, nothing untoward in his questions, nothing wrong in the information he asked for, or the tenants he asked about, but the thought, once introduced in her head, would not go away.

Despite her uneasiness, Tina was elated. Her stepfather

had taught her and Jon how to manage an estate—Jon, because he said it was something he would eventually need to know, and she because she always tagged along after Jon (at least that was the story he told her mother). He had prepared her well for what she'd tackled in the last two weeks, and she was justifiably proud of what she'd accomplished. Jay seemed surprised, and pleased, at her knowledge, which buoyed her spirits even more.

She didn't stop to analyze her feelings too closely. The excitement she felt heightened her awareness of Jay in ways she never considered and the awareness was magnified with every brush of a hand as they studied the figures she had come up with. The note of approval in his voice over her decisions as she explained what was needed, what she accomplished and authorized, and what decisions she left for him to make left her content in a way she had never felt before. Her contentment was underscored by the ease with which they interacted and worked, and the knowledge that for both of them the land, the people, its culture and traditions, were important enough to devote the time and energy to ensuring they stayed intact.

CR

Jay was flabbergasted. When he had given Tina the authority to begin to put the house and estate to rights, he expected she would take the servants in hand and hire more if needed, perhaps inventory the linens or order the cleaning of some of the unused rooms in the house. He had not expected her to begin a complete accounting of the estate and its needs. He had returned from London expecting to begin the task himself—only to find she had already determined and outlined what needed to be done.

He watched her now as she explained why the home farm should be planting one of the fields with wheat instead of barley, then justified her recommendation that one of the fields be left to lie fallow. The pale blue dress she wore set off her dark hair and intensified the blue in her eyes. Long, tapered fingers pointed out figures and numbers. She was small and delicate, raising the protective instincts within and he wondered again at Aaron's stupidity in getting himself killed in a duel.

The door to the study opened as they were deciding what to do with the last two cottages on Tina's list.

Felicia stood on the threshold, eyeing them suspiciously. "Still working?" she asked, a hint of disbelief in her voice.

"We are almost finished, I think," Tina replied without looking up.

"What have you been doing all morning? You've been in here for hours!"

Tina, who had her back to the door, turned as she spoke, her voice sharper than usual, "Felicia, it takes time to...oh, hello, Liza, Jim."

"We have been waiting for you for a while," Felicia spoke as the brown-haired imp at her side ran to Tina, arms extended.

Jay watched in fascination as Tina picked up the grubby little girl, who gave her a hug and a wet, noisy kiss on the cheek, then settled comfortably in Tina's lap. He knew of no lady who would have allowed the little girl near enough to touch her, much less have picked her up to sit in her lap.

"We have been waiting," Felicia repeated, "but since it is so close to luncheon, I decided to interrupt before they went home. Liza has been asking for you."

Tina looked down at the little girl, who was staring through wide gray eyes at Jay. "What have you and Jim been doing all morning?" she asked her.

"Play," was the tot's retort, but she never took her eyes off Jay.

"And what did you play?"

"Horsies."

Felicia came further into the room, accompanied by a boy of about six. Small and sturdy, he had the same brown hair and gray eyes as Liza. He, too, watched Jay with curious eyes.

"Jim," Felicia said to him, "make your bow to his lordship."

Dutifully, the little boy made a small bow, then straightened as Jay stood and walked to his side. Dropping down to eye level with the little boy, Jay said to him, "It's very nice to meet you, Jim."

Before Jim could answer, Liza scooted off Tina's lap and came and stood by her brother. "Me, too?" she demanded.

"And, you, too," Jay agreed, casting a smile which encompassed both children. Liza smiled back, but Jim did not respond.

"Very good," Felicia told them, "now come along or your mama will be leaving without you."

The two children skirted around Jay to give Tina quick hugs, then departed in Felicia's wake. Jay straightened, but did not return to his seat behind the desk. "I suppose this might be a good time to stop," he commented.

Tina stood with a smile. "Felicia doesn't know the meaning of subtle," she responded. "Cook's daughter, Daisy, always brings the littlest ones with her when she comes to help in the mornings. Felicia and I have been entertaining them since Liza was an infant. Before you arrived, she would drop them at the dower house before arriving here. Felicia has been doing most of the entertaining these last two weeks."

"Then I must apologize for keeping you from them."

Tina shrugged. "There is no need. There were things that needed doing." She turned to look up at him.

In the space of a heartbeat, Jay was back on a tropical island. He could feel the warmth of the sun, hear the water tumbling over the cliff into the clear pool below, smell the scents of the jungle around him, and feel the softness of the breeze on his face. Her eyes took him to another world. A world of sunwashed, white sand beaches, eternally blue skies, lush tropical jungles, rippling brooks, and clear still pools. Pools so clear, yet so deep that the blues and greens reflected on the surface darkened to black in the center. The perfect pool for cliff diving, where a man could drown in the center if he wasn't careful.

For a few breathless moments, Jay was one of those cliff divers, drowning in the depths of a bottomless pool. He forgot to breathe, the blood pounded in his ears, his muscles tightened, and from somewhere he heard a single drumbeat. The pool shifted, moved, then suddenly he was back in the study, and Tina was turning away. He had to stop himself from reaching for her and pulling her back.

"There is the luncheon gong," she said briskly. "We'd better go, or Felicia will start without us." She was at the door before he moved.

"Oh, yes. I'm sorry, I was thinking of...er...something else."

She smiled, but did not respond as he strode toward her. They left the study and made their way to the dining room in silence.

CR

What just happened? Tina wasn't sure, but something had. That moment in the study when Jay looked down at her had shaken her. For a moment his eyes had become distant, yet focused on hers, and she was able to see herself clearly reflected in the polished ebony of his. A rush of warmth sped through her body, nearly causing her to lose her balance. Yet, she had been unable to tear her eyes away from the mesmerizing effect of his gaze. Her breath caught and she had nearly acted upon a sudden, impulsive need to touch him—to run her hands over the hard muscled planes of his chest, and up over his shoulders to thread her fingers through the chestnut silk covering his head. What was wrong with her? She barely knew him!

The luncheon gong had startled her from her thoughts, yet, the craving still remained and she curled her hands into fists to prevent herself from making a rash move as they walked down the hall.

After lunch Felicia suggested that the three of them ride over the estate to reintroduce Jay to the tenants. Jay readily agreed and Tina fell in with the plans. She knew that Felicia was feeling left out as she and Jay attempted to piece together the mess left in the wake of Roderick Milton. She also understood that Felicia was trying to protect her as well.

Tina was aware that the incidents with the Barnes and the Staples, coupled with all the rumors, had made many of the tenants wary of her. With that history, she and Felicia never knew how the cottagers would react to her presence. Felicia had befriended some of those who refused help from her sister, so Tina felt comfortable that they'd kept track of most of the families. Even with their concerted effort, however, there were still a few families Tina knew little about, and some she had lost track of completely.

The afternoon was bittersweet. She had not ridden in a very long time, keeping to the dower house in an effort not to cause anyone else harm and to stay out of Mr. Milton's path. She instinctively knew that she, more than Felicia, had been the specific target of his mischief-making.

She and Felicia regaled Jay with stories of their childhood. She told him of the times his father and taken her and Jon on jaunts about the estate. Of the stories he told them, of the people they met.

She still sensed Jay's earlier cynicism concerning his father, his disbelief that his father had been anything other than an unfeeling monster. And she, unconsciously, tried harder to change his mind by relating incidents which demonstrated his father's gentler side.

◌ℛ

"And then there was the time Papa took Jon fishing. I was supposed to be upstairs napping, but I slipped away from Nurse and followed. He didn't realize I was there until Jon made him stop and wait for me." Tina smiled sadly. "He should have sent me back," she admitted, "but he didn't. He just put me on his shoulders and took me along. By the time we returned, Mama was furious."

"Why?" Jay couldn't help himself. Very few of their anecdotes sounded like the father he left behind. In fact, he had to remind himself more than once that they were talking about his father. The same man who could not be bothered to listen to his youngest son explain a situation. The same man who insisted boys had to be tough and shouldn't be molly-coddled. The same man who had driven his youngest son away from home because he refused to see any deficiencies in his oldest son.

She grinned up at him. "First, because she thought he should have sent me back with the footman he sent to let her know where I was. And, second, because Papa and I were soaking wet. I fell into the river and Papa had to fish me out. Papa said I was fine and she wasn't to worry. Of course I wasn't," she laughed. "I caught a chill and had to stay in bed for a fortnight. I would have been miserable but Papa came to check on me every day and read me stories."

Felicia giggled and he turned to look at her. "Mama told me Papa even smuggled you out of the house one morning so you could go visit your pony."

Tina's laughter filled the small glade they were passing through, the melodious sound falling softly on his ears. "He did, but it was supposed to be a secret."

Jay tried to reason away the differences in his father. Tina and Jon had only been his stepchildren. Tina was a girl—and, therefore, not to be held to the same rigid standards set for his boys. Jon was not his heir, so could be given some latitude. Felicia was not only the youngest, but also a girl to be indulged and spoiled. Unfortunately, none of them rang true. Perhaps he had softened as he had aged.

He had trouble believing that as well. The man he once knew had grown harder with age. He, too, remembered a father who had taken his boys fishing when they were seven and nine. But, he also remembered a father who, when his sons went off to school at ten, seemed to forget their existence. In fact, once Aaron had been sent off to school, he seemed to have forgotten there was one still left at home.

And once Aaron began to torment his younger brother, causing Jay to retaliate, his father had only proven to him how inconsequential he considered the second son to be.

They visited and talked to a number of tenants before they reached Daisy's cottage on the outskirts of the village. It was late afternoon, although the sun was still high overhead, and hot. As they approached the cottage, Felicia cantered ahead and dismounted before Tina and Jay reached the gate. Jay, noticing her actions, turned to Tina as Felicia hurried up to the front door.

"Is she planning to warn them?"

"In a way. Daisy's family is quite large. This is one of the cottages I thought should be expanded to better accommodate all of them."

"I see." Jay dismounted and helped her off her mare, careful to not let his hands linger. While the afternoon had been informative, it tried his control severely. Lifting Tina on and off the mare's back with each stop had become more difficult. She was so small and light that very little physical effort was required. So...why was he short of breath each time he did so? And why did his hands itch to remain on her waist after she was solidly on the ground?

"Tina!" The childish voice interrupted his thoughts and he stepped away just as Liza launched herself into Tina's arms. Tina hugged the little girl for a moment before turning to Jay.

"You remember Liza, my lord?"

He responded with a smile. "Of course."

"Mama has the twins," Liza told her. "Come see." Taking Tina by the hand, she pulled her toward the cottage.

Tina laughed. "Very well."

He had to duck under the low overhang of thatch to enter, but once inside could easily stand upright. Despite the windows, it was dim inside and most of the corners were in shadow. The smell of wood smoke and cooking stew reached him.

Felicia was sitting on a low bench holding an infant, a boy of about six standing beside her. They both looked up as Tina and Jay entered. For a moment, Jay thought he saw Aaron in the sandy-haired, gray-eyed little boy, but dismissed it as a product of his imagination conjured up on the heels of the conversation the three of them had shared. Recalling some of the scrapes from his and Aaron's childhood must have left him feeling maudlin.

A woman was standing before the fireplace, stirring a pot. She, too, looked up as they entered, a smile lighting her rounded face under a white cap. He recognized her as the Cook's assistant and daughter, Daisy. "Good afternoon, my lord. What brings ye to me cottage this fine afternoon?"

"The ladies do," he replied gallantly. "I have been informed it needs some work, so I thought I might look around a bit to determine what needs to be done."

Contemplating the clean and neat interior, Jay could see more room was needed. There were four small pallets stacked neatly in a corner. A curtain partitioned off part of the room, open now to reveal a large bed with another infant lying in the middle of it. Off to another side of the room was a large table, its scarred surface testifying to its years of use. Another bench, similar to the one Felicia sat on, stood near the fireplace and two chairs sat against the wall beside the table. A large chest sat off to the side of the fireplace, crockery dishes neatly stacked on top.

"Would ye like somethin' to drink?" Daisy asked.

"I would love a drink of water from the well," Tina answered, turning to Jay. "Daisy's well is famous. It has the best tasting water for miles around. I think it's her secret for making the best cider in the district."

Jay wondered if it was something he'd known before, but couldn't recall.

Daisy blushed at the compliment. "Why thank you, my lady. Davey, fetch a pitcher of water for her ladyship."

The boy standing beside Felicia moved. Taking up a pitcher from the table, he was out the back door of the cottage in an instant. He returned a few minutes later, the pitcher brimming with clear water. Carefully filling two mugs, he offered them to Tina and Jay, then resumed his place beside Felicia. She looked up and smiled at him, then whispered something to him that made him giggle. It was an eerie moment as the child's amusement brought back memories of Aaron again. Jay shook them off and sipped his mug of clear, cool water.

The infant on the bed stirred and began to cry. Putting her mug down on the table, Tina crossed to the bed and picked him up, leaving Jay standing awkwardly in the middle of the room. Felicia looked up and noticed him.

"Jay, come and sit. Davey, fetch his lordship one of the chairs. I'm afraid the bench is too low for him to sit comfortably."

Davey moved to do as he was bid but was forestalled by Jay. "Not right now. I think I'll go outside and look at the side of the cottage. If we are to expand it, I need to see which side it would be best to expand it from."

Tina approached at that moment, carrying a now quiet, but wide-eyed, infant in her arms. "You mustn't leave before you meet Jed."

Jay looked down at the bundle she held in her arms. Large gray eyes stared up at him, two tiny fists waving in the air.

Having never had much experience with babies or children, Jay wasn't sure how to react.

"He's beautiful, isn't he," she said softly, brushing a soft kiss across the baby's forehead.

Jay suddenly felt as if he had been punched in the gut. His whole body tightened, blood rushed into his lower parts and he was suddenly lightheaded. The rest of the cottage and its occupants faded. For the moment he, Tina, and the infant were the only ones present. Reaching up, he allowed one of the tiny fists to wrap itself around a finger as he watched Tina's features soften, and replied, "Yes."

He wasn't speaking about the child. It suddenly occurred to him this could be his future—watching Tina holding his child, love shining from her eyes. The yearning that arose was unexpected. Jay could not have formed a single, rational thought as to why this woman suddenly mattered so much. For him the reasoning should have been simple—he needed to keep the marquisate and its holdings intact. The easiest way was to marry Tina. That she was beautiful, intelligent, accomplished at managing an estate, and devoted to the tenants were merely added benefits.

There was also the physical reaction he experienced in her presence. A reaction which seemed to get stronger with each contact. He had been back at Thane Park for less than a day and he was fighting to keep his hands off of her. There was much to be said for desiring one's wife and little to recommend the alternative.

His own parents' marriage had been a disaster. Clearly not suited to each other, his parents seemed to be able to agree on only one thing—they should each go their separate ways while maintaining the pretense of a harmonious marriage in front of their sons. It might have succeeded if a ten-year-old Jay had not inadvertently discovered his mother and her lover in the hayloft of the stables one afternoon. They had not seen him, and he never told a soul, but the effect on him had been profound.

He resolved then and there to be a better son to his father, thinking his devotion could make up for the loss of his wife's. But Jay had been doomed to failure in this as well, for it was only a year later he and Aaron discovered their father was carrying on an affair with the wife of the local magistrate. Not knowing about their mother, Aaron had taken it in stride, seeing it as proof of his father's prowess with women. When their mother died in a carriage accident with her latest lover when Jay was fifteen, he had been unable to mourn her.

The door to the cottage burst open, jolting Jay back to the present. Jim scampered in, followed closely by a young girl of about twelve. He was introduced to Nan, who relieved Tina of her burden while staring at Jay. Moments later, Jim and Davey disappeared out the back door and he and Tina headed out the front.

"Just how many children does Daisy have?" he asked once they were outside.

"Mmmm, six altogether. Ella's the oldest, but she's married to the blacksmith's son. They are the parents of the twin infants, Jed and Ned. Then there's Nat—he's eighteen; Eddie is fifteen—he works in the stables at the Park; Nan is twelve; Jim is six; and Liza is three."

Jay walked slowly around the side of the cottage, examining the foundation and walls as he went. "You forgot Davey."

He crouched down to examine a place where a chunk of the plaster had separated from the wall and the crack leading upward toward the roof from it. Standing, he followed the crack until it disappeared under the low-hanging thatch.

"This wall already has some damage. It might suit to build the expansion here and take it down. Or put in a door to make the expanded area another room." He stood there for a moment longer, then turned to her. "What do you think?"

Chapter Seven

Tina stood against the wall staring out toward the fields. For a moment she had forgotten his presence. Her own thoughts had gone back to the moment when they stopped before Daisy's cottage and he had turned to ask her about Felicia.

She had felt her heart somersault in her chest at the sight of the lopsided grin which accompanied his question. The teasing light in his eyes warmed her and suddenly, the jacket of her habit had been too tight. She'd responded calmly, but not without effort.

"Tina?"

Startled, she turned toward him to find he now stood inches from her, his dark eyes hooded and unreadable. He was close enough that she caught a whiff of the spicy scent of his soap, mingled with the scent of horse and sweat. The combination was intoxicating and she allowed herself to unbend. The afternoon warmth engulfed her, the hum of insects surrounded her, drawing her into a cocoon of contentment which cast a dreamlike quality over the moment. Relaxing against the sun-washed wall of the cottage, she tilted her head up and watched as Jay bent near.

He was going to kiss her. She knew it with every fiber of her being—and she was going to do nothing to stop him. She hadn't realized it until now; she had been waiting for this moment since she first laid eyes on him two weeks ago. She wasn't sure she had fantasized about his kiss, but she had subconsciously compared him to Aaron ever since the first meeting.

He'd already overshadowed most of her memories of Aaron, just by his presence. But, the last time she'd seen Aaron, he had kissed her, so she considered it only natural she wanted Jay to overcome that memory as well. Her eyes drifted shut and her whole body went completely still at the first touch of his lips on hers.

The touch was featherlight, his lips firm against the softness of hers. But as he pressed deeper, she parted her lips on a sigh and his tongue swept in to taste. The invasion startled her and she raised her hands to his chest. Instead of pushing him away, her hands curled around the lapels of his riding jacket as his arms banded around her, pulling her away from the wall and pressing her close.

For a moment, Tina regained her sanity as Jay's mouth moved from hers to trail light kisses along her jaw and down the side of her neck. But it did not stop the thrumming of blood in her veins, or the warmth that pooled low in her belly. Nor did it give her anything but a glimpse of reality before it was snatched away again as Jay reclaimed her lips in a searing, soul-searching kiss.

Her hands crept up to his shoulders, impossibly wide and incredibly strong, the only thing solid in her increasingly disembodied world. It was frightening to think, she would tell herself later, that a kiss could so completely obliterate reality. But for the moment she was lost in an unfamiliar world with only Jay as her guide—and she was content to follow his lead.

Jay raised his head and she heard him drag in a breath. Slowly opening her eyes, she looked up into his. She did not know him well enough to read what she saw there, but it did not frighten her. Straightening at the sound of voices, Jay dropped his arms and turned away just as Felicia came around the corner of the cottage.

She was speaking to Liza. "We'll see you tomorrow, but now it's time for us to return to the house. Cook will give us a scolding if we are late for tea."

Liza giggled. "Nana not 'cold.'"

"Maybe not...oh, hello, there you are...but we still should not be late." She glanced between Tina and Jay, "I think it's time to go. It's almost time for tea."

"Oh, is it that late already?" Tina queried, turning to Liza to hide her heated cheeks.

Jay nodded in response. "I think we're finished here."

Felicia took his arm, seemingly oblivious to the tension in the air, and the two of them followed Tina and Liza around to the front. Davey and Jim were standing near the horses, having obviously given them water. Jay gave each boy a coin for his trouble, lifted Felicia and Tina into their saddles, then mounted himself. The children waved as they left.

"You didn't answer my question," Jay turned to Tina.

"What question?"

"Davey."

"Oh, Davey is Ella's oldest child. He's six."

"Ella was away helping Myra Wills this afternoon," Felicia added. "That's why the children were there, although she often leaves them with Nan."

Felicia chatted about the babies and children all the way back to the house, leaving Tina to her thoughts. She relived the moments before and after the kiss. Had she actually invited Jay to kiss her? Why hadn't she stopped him? How much longer would it have lasted if Felicia hadn't arrived?

Dear God, what if Felicia had seen them! Her cheeks flamed at the possibility. She had behaved like a loose woman. What did Jay think of her now?

She stole a peek at him out of the corner of her eye. He rode between them, his head turned toward Felicia as she recounted a story about one of the children. He seemed unaffected by what had been, for her, the most thrilling experience of her life. Did it mean so little to him that it could so easily be forgotten? Her spirits plummeted at the thought.

She was sure that was how it had been for Aaron. She had fought her way out of Aaron's arms the one time he had kissed her. She recognized his need to master, not woo, her. He might have hidden that aspect of himself from her had he not stolen that one kiss. The disgust she felt when he put his lips on hers and invaded her mouth with his tongue had made her physically ill. He had pressed her against the wall and rubbed his body against hers until she thought she might faint. He had taken what he wanted with no regard for her feelings—she might have been anyone.

"You will not fight me the next time," he'd declared. "When I return, I think I will talk to Papa about our wedding." His eyes had roved boldly over her budding sixteen-year-old body, causing her to shiver with dread. That night she had cried herself to sleep, the memory of his kiss turning her dreams to nightmares. The day Roderick Milton brought his body home she'd hidden in her room, sick with fear, until her mother had come to tell her Aaron was dead.

Her relief quickly turned to guilt. She hadn't wished him dead, had she? Wishes like that didn't come true, did they? Had she truly been so selfish? Aaron's death had destroyed the stepfather she knew, leaving a shell in his place. A shell that never laughed again, rarely smiled again, and mourned the loss of his son until his own death barely a year later.

And she'd lived with the guilt ever since. A guilt that mocked her for wanting to be happy, and persuaded her she didn't deserve to be.

She owed it to her stepfather's memory to honor the contract. If Nona hadn't given her the pendant, she would have done so without a qualm. After Jay's kiss, she might have even looked forward to it. Instead all she had was a decision to make that would require her to go against the wishes of one of two people who had given her so much.

CƳ

Over dinner, Felicia drew Jay out by asking him about his ships and the places he had been and seen. Tina found herself in awe of all he had experienced in the space of a lifetime for her. He was a gifted storyteller and the evening passed quickly until Tina found herself yawning and glanced at the clock on the mantle.

Felicia seemed to realize it was late as well and, getting to her feet, bade Tina and Jay good night and left the room. Tina rose to follow her and Jay stood as well. Taking her arm in his, he walked with her out of the salon, stopping at the bottom of the staircase. Although she stood on the bottom step and he on the floor, she still had to look up at him.

"Thank you for sharing your adventures with us this

evening," she said politely.

The crooked grin returned and mischief glinted in his eyes. His scent surrounded her. "And thank you for this afternoon," he replied. Bending his head, she thought he would kiss her hand. Instead he surprised her by brushing his lips against hers. "Good night, Tina." Then he turned and strode toward the library, his hair gleaming in the lamplight.

CR

Tina awakened in good spirits after a restful night. She felt carefree and light while getting dressed. Hurrying downstairs, she glanced at the clock as she entered the breakfast room. Trying not to begrudge the possibility Felicia was out with Jay again, she instructed the footman to bring her some tea and went to fill her plate.

Felicia entered the room just as she was finishing her first cup of tea. Dressed in a white sprigged muslin dotted with yellow and green flowers, Felicia looked exactly like a young girl on the verge of womanhood, her future bright and untroubled.

"Oh," Felicia blurted, "I didn't expect to see you."

"Oh? And why not?"

"I thought you might be out riding with Jay. I didn't wake up early this morning, so I thought maybe I'd take Midnight out later. He will probably need the exercise."

Tina smiled. "After yesterday, you are assuming Jay won't want to ride him again?"

Felicia grinned, taking her place across from Tina at the table. "Something like that."

They were nearly finished when the butler entered the room, a silver salver in his hand, on which rested a folded note, and presented it to Tina. "His lordship requested that you receive this, my lady."

Tina picked up the paper. "Thank you, Keyes."

After he left, Felicia looked at her, curiosity evident in her expression. "What does it say?"

Tina glanced down at the short note.

Gone to Exeter on errands. Will try to be back by supper, but if not back by eight, do not wait.

It was signed with a single, bold, letter "J" at the bottom. Tina passed it to Felicia.

"Exeter!" she pouted. "We should have gone, too."

Tina understood her disappointment. When their mother was alive, they made annual trips to Exeter on large shopping expeditions. It was often a highlight of the summer.

"Perhaps he had business there," she said consolingly. "He might have just needed to go and come back—after all, it is quite a distance. Remember, we used to have to stay overnight whenever we went with Mama and Papa, but he says he'll try to be back for supper." Rising from her chair, she added, "Besides, if he just wanted to shop—which I doubt—he could have gone into Bideford or Hatherleigh. They are much closer." Heading for the door, she continued, "I'd better let Cook know we will need to hold supper until eight."

Felicia rose and followed her. "I'll go with you and see if Daisy's here with Liza and Jim yet."

Tina spent the rest of the morning going over menus with Cook, and checking supplies with the housekeeper. Making lists of things needing to be ordered or repaired kept her mind busy. But during those times when she moved from task to task, she could not stop her thoughts from wandering back to the day before.

The events of the day before left her more unsettled than ever. She feared if the marquis refused to honor the betrothal contract, she would be forced to leave Thane Park. If Felicia went off to a young ladies' academy, there would be no reason for her to stay. What would she do then?

And how could she leave him behind?

There was the crux of the matter. After only one full day in his company, she feared she was already developing feelings for him. Knowing she wasn't repulsed by him or his attentions lifted her spirits, but conversely weighed them down. What would she do about the pendant if he chose to honor the contract? She wished she knew how to read him, how to tell what he was feeling or thinking. It would be heartening to know he was as off-balance as she in this. Of course, he knew nothing about the pendant, so what would she say if the contract came up?

CR

Jay did not return until the next afternoon, but Tina would have been gratified to know he had considered foregoing finishing his business in order to return the same day he left. The delay, however, yielded unexpected information and assistance in his search for Roderick Milton.

By chance, he happened upon Gerald Hartwell, the Earl of Weston and heir to the Duke of Westover, who was in Exeter to make arrangements for the christening of his new son and heir. He and Gerald had attended Eton together. Knowing the ducal seat was closer to Salisbury, Jay couldn't resist asking why.

"The Bishop is my wife's great-uncle," he explained with a grimace. "He's also a likeable old curmudgeon and often requested by the family to officiate at weddings, christenings, and funerals."

They spent a profitable evening catching up, re-living Eton, and discussing Aaron.

"I was sorry to hear about his death," Gerald told him. "But, I must confess, there was no story of a duel being batted about. In fact, most people were surprised when word got back. No one was invited to pay their respects and I know of no one who went to the funeral. Everything was kept quiet and very private. It seemed odd because Aaron had many friends besides Milton."

"Were you one?"

"Not a close one, no. If you remember, even at school we did not get along. Aaron's crowd was a bit wilder than normal. They frequented the worst gaming hells, brothels few others would enter, and generally kept to themselves. They remained on the social scene, though, appearing at balls, parties, and soirees, but they tended to be a law unto themselves."

As they caught up on each other's activities and families, Jay was reminded that Gerald had two sisters. Raising Felicia's interest in a young ladies' academy garnered an offer of help.

"Geri and both of my sisters went to young ladies' academies—I'll ask her—and Mama—for recommendations for your sister. As for Milton—I still know a few of the crowd he and Aaron were part of. I'll make some inquiries. Perhaps another avenue to explore might be your stepmother's background. Maybe there's a connection there."

Jay smiled wryly. "Now, why didn't I think of that? I just assumed he was a friend of Aaron's who used the excuse of hating gypsies to cover his activities. Felicia told me she'd overheard my father telling Milton he knew he was embezzling funds from the estate and he was to leave, but my father died soon after and no one knew Milton had been dismissed."

They sat in comfortable silence for a while, each applying himself to the excellent fare before them. The innkeeper cleared the dishes, then left them to continue their conversation.

"There was a rumor Aaron was engaged or betrothed, but no one was able to confirm it," Gerald mused.

Jay looked up from his contemplation of the ruby liquid in his wine glass. "Any idea how it started?"

"According to one of my sisters, Aaron started it—or at least a comment he made was the genesis of it."

"How?"

"It seems that, after being singled out for pointed attention at a soiree of some sort, Aaron apparently informed the hostess her efforts were wasted on him since he was already betrothed. One of my sisters overheard the comment, but heard no more."

"How long ago was this?"

"Hmmm. At least seven or eight years ago. Although, I could be mistaken in the time period since I don't even remember which of my sisters overheard the remark."

Jay warred with himself over whether to confide in Gerald. They had once been fairly close, although Gerald was a year older. He'd even spent a holiday with Gerald's family during his teen years. Out of his parents' and brother's orbits, he'd enjoyed himself immensely.

There was still the question of the validity of the contract. He and the solicitor had gone over and over the possibilities and ramifications until he had finally given up and shoved it to the back of his mind. He knew he had to address it eventually.

There were only about three weeks left. Of course, Mr. Strate had informed him the will only required he honor the terms of the contract—which, for him, meant he indicate his intention to marry Tina. It did not require—although he was sure it was what his father intended—he actually marry her by a specific date. Nevertheless, it was the reason he was in Exeter—to inquire about a special license from the Bishop just in case.

Belatedly, he wondered if the act of procuring the special license alone would serve as indication of his intent. He would write to Mr. Strate and ask him. In the meantime, he looked across at Gerald and made up his mind.

"The rumor was true," he told him. "The Earl of Wynton has a younger sister, Lady Christina. Aaron was betrothed to her. However nothing came of it since she was only sixteen when he died."

Gerald was intrigued. "So what happened to her?"

"Nothing. She is still at Thane Park taking care of my sister. We actually have quite a tangle on our hands but as far as I can tell she is unaware of her part in it." Jay went on to tell Gerald of the substitution of his name on the contract and the provisions of the will. When he was done, Gerald looked at him in amazement.

"And you say she knows nothing of the will?"

"Not as far as I can tell."

"So, are you planning to marry her?"

"I haven't decided yet. Certainly, it would be no hardship. She is beautiful, intelligent, accomplished. What more could one look for in a wife?"

Gerald chuckled as he raised his glass. "You, my friend, have never been in love."

Jay grimaced, but did not respond. It was true he'd never been in love and, if he had any control over it, he never would.

CR

Tina sat in one of the rose-covered arbors in the garden feeling decidedly decadent. She hadn't had this kind of time on her hands in so long she knew she should feel guilty for sitting outside just doing nothing. Yet, the idleness felt good. Since the marquis hadn't returned the night before, she had little to do concerning the estate because there were still decisions for him to make. As for the house, there were no large-scale projects needing attention at the moment and the smaller tasks could wait another day. So, she found herself outside in the garden, a book lying unopened in her lap, the kitchen tabby purring loudly beside her, enjoying the warm, rose-scented late-afternoon breeze.

Felicia found her a short time later. "It's nearly time for tea," she announced, "but it's so nice out here it seems a shame to go back inside."

"We can always have it on the terrace. Remember? It was one of Mama's favorite places during the summer for tea."

"Of course! I should have thought of it. Shall I go order it and meet you there?"

"If you wish," Tina replied, smiling as Felicia dashed off.

Her enthusiasm was infectious and Tina rose to follow at a more sedate pace. She reached the terrace just as two footmen were setting up the table and chairs under Felicia's direction.

The terrace ran the full length of the lower floor of the house, the low wall intermittently broken by stairs leading down into the garden. Doors leading to the music room and large salon on the north side and the ballroom and two smaller, private parlors on the south side could be opened to allow guests to move freely from one wing to the other. It was a nice arrangement that allowed for the use of the garden during summer parties.

Tina joined Felicia at the table and Keyes arrived with the tea service. Instructing him to place the pot before Felicia, Tina thanked him as Felicia asked, "Shall I pour now?"

"Yes, please."

Felicia was obviously delighted to be allowed to perform such a grown-up function and Tina was reminded how often her mother had indulged her when she was the same age. It was saddening to realize all Felicia had missed out on when their mother died.

Felicia talked over tea about the families she had visited recently.

"The Burroughs won't ask for help, but they could use some. On the other hand, the Milfords are doing well, even little Timmy. The Vicar is doing poorly—I think it's time he retired. Maybe we should speak to Jay about it?"

"Speak to me about what?"

Tina turned at the sound of the deep voice to find Jay standing in the open door. How long had he been standing there? So intent on their conversation were they, neither had heard him approach, and, facing the garden as they were, they had not seen him either.

"Jay! Did you just return?" Felicia exclaimed. "Come join us."

Another chair was brought, another pot of tea sent for, and Jay joined them at the table. For the moment, Tina could not keep her eyes off of him. Felicia asked him a question about his trip and Tina heard his answer without listening. His voice washed over her, soothing nerves she hadn't even realized were on edge. The sun suddenly seemed brighter, the sky bluer. And all was right in the world—at least this particular corner of it.

"A duchess? Really?" Felicia's squeal of delight startled her out of her reverie. "Tina, did you hear that?"

"I'm afraid not," she answered with a smile. "I'm sorry, I was thinking about something else."

"What?" Felicia asked.

"Oh, nothing really. Just...just about the Burroughs," she fibbed.

Jay seemed to study her closely and she dropped her gaze to avoid meeting his.

"Oh," Felicia said. "Well, Jay said the duchess would recommend an academy."

"Duchess? What duchess?"

"The Duchess of Westover," he answered. "As it happens, I went to school with the Earl of Weston. I ran into Gerald in Exeter and while we caught up on each other's news, he offered his help with selecting a young ladies' academy for Felicia. Or, at least, he offered the help of his wife and mother. We will probably hear from them soon."

"Oh, how wonderful for you, Felicia!" she echoed Felicia's

enthusiasm. "Any academy we write to will certainly look favorably upon you if they know the duchess recommended them to you."

Jay laughed at the comment and both women turned to look at him quizzically. "What's so funny?" Felicia demanded.

Jay bestowed a benign smile on both of them before answering. "While I won't underestimate the consequence of a duchess in the mix, I don't think any young ladies' academy worth their salt would dare consider Felicia unfavorably."

"Why not?" Felicia asked, her mood changing suddenly. "They might not want some nobody with gypsy blood in their fancy school," she commented sourly.

Tina looked at her in dismay. "Felicia, that's not true. You are the daughter of a marquis. The school won't know about the other."

Jay watched Tina as she calmed her sister down. Dressed in a light blue and white striped muslin day dress, she looked cool and comfortable. Watching her, however, he was anything but. The day was quite warm and her closeness made him warmer still. He'd hurried home, pushing his team more than was needed, to see her again. He told himself it was because he didn't have much time to decide what to do about the contract, but an inner voice mocked him, reminding him he had thought of Tina almost constantly since the afternoon before he left.

That kiss had rocked him. It had taken what he thought was a well-ordered existence and turned it upside-down.

Jay considered himself a normal red-blooded male. He valued and admired the female of the species for their many pleasing attributes. He couldn't remember the last time he'd paid for a female's company. He enjoyed what they offered and went on his merry way and had yet to find one capable of touching him in a meaningful fashion. Previous liaisons had been mutually satisfying, but quickly forgotten when he moved on. In all his travels, he hadn't found a woman he could have considered marrying. Until now.

Blue-green eyes turned toward him, but Felicia's comment made him think. Glancing from Felicia to Tina he wondered if it was truly possible they did not completely understand their status in the world. Having never been to London, it was conceivable their view of the world had been colored by the prejudices they had encountered here in Devon. The servants in the house were devoted to them, but from the people living beyond the borders of the Park they had been alienated.

What had Jon told him? They had been effectively isolated by the deaths of their parents. While Jay had no doubt Tina had been schooled by her mother in manners, deportment, courtesy, and other social requirements, she had had very little practice in a social setting. Tina had passed much of her learning on to Felicia.

"You do know," he interrupted, sensing Tina's expectation of support, "that you are amazingly unique."

"Being different is not always good," Felicia shot back.

"True, but you are unique in a good way. Even without the Duchess of Westover to recommend you, Jon and I together can wield a considerable amount of influence. The likelihood of any establishment aware of your connections refusing you is about as remote as you teaching Midnight to fly."

For a moment, Felicia and Tina stared at him, speechless with shock. Then a smile blossomed across Felicia's face and her sister and brother watched the knowledge dawn in her eyes as laughter bubbled up out of her, flowing over them until they both began to smile.

"Oh, Tina," she gasped in the middle of a breath, dabbing at her eyes with her napkin, "I never thought of it quite like that before."

Impulsively, she reached over and gave Jay a hug. "Thank you, thank you, thank you," she wheezed. Then she was up and out of her chair, heading into the house. "I can't wait to tell Cook how important I am," she threw over her shoulder as she skipped away.

Tina watched her retreating figure, then turned back to face him.

He was frozen in time. He didn't know why, but Felicia's hug had opened the door on his childhood a little wider. Her actions brought to mind happier days spent with his grandmother in the dower house. Those memories had been locked away for so long he had nearly convinced himself they had been the product of wistfulness.

His parents had shown little affection. Touching had been strictly forbidden. His father hadn't wanted to make his sons soft and his mother had been afraid they would muss her hair or dirty her gown. The only person who had given affection freely, unconditionally, had been his grandmother.

"I think Cook probably already knows," Tina commented, startling him from his thoughts.

"I would hope so," he replied automatically, still marveling at the warmth Felicia's hug had wrought.

Chapter Eight

Silence fell. Birds chirped, the water gurgled and splashed in the fountain, flies and bees buzzed. In the distance a dog barked.

Tina wanted to ask him about his trip to Exeter. What errands had been so important he had gone off after only one full day in residence? And, had he accomplished them?

She wondered if it had anything to do with finding Roderick Milton. Jon had written to her and Felicia, informing them he was leaving London to inspect his holdings. It sounded like a grand adventure and she wished she could go with him.

"I don't think Felicia and I have ever considered Jon, and now you, as more than brothers. I think we both tend to forget that in the wider world an earl and a marquis might have some influence."

He seemed distracted, but her comment caused him to turn sharply toward her.

"I hope you do not consider me your brother," he said bluntly, "because I definitely do not consider you my sister. In fact, in light of the events of two afternoons ago, I would say the likelihood you and I should consider each other in that vein is truly far-fetched."

Tina felt the blood rising in her cheeks at his reference to the kiss.

"I was speaking of brothers in general," she said more tartly than she intended.

Jay's eyebrows rose at her tone. "I see."

"I was just thinking of Felicia."

"But I wasn't," he replied tersely. "We seem to be speaking at cross purposes, but perhaps it is because there are things between us needing attention." He rose from his seat and held out his hand. "Shall we go into the library where we can speak privately?"

Tina was suddenly worried. What now? She didn't want to discuss that silly contract now, but she knew she had little choice. It would have to be discussed sooner or later. *But why not later?* a little voice asked. *Suppose there are other things he wants to discuss?* the voice tempted. *Suppose he wants to kiss you again?* She shouldn't let him.

Tina's cheeks suddenly grew warm and, to keep her hands from straying up to them, she put her hand in his and allowed him to draw her to her feet.

The interior of the house was cool after the warmth of the terrace, the dimness hiding the red flags she knew stained her cheeks. Tina felt a measure of calm return. Did he even know about the betrothal contract? He had to—it would have been part of his father's papers.

The library was one of Tina's favorite rooms. Large and airy with floor to ceiling bookshelves interspersed with floor to ceiling windows allowing in sunlight no matter the time of year, she and Felicia spent many of their evenings here. Because it faced north, during the winter this room was particularly inviting, catching more of the weak winter sun than the parlor she preferred during the summer.

Jay seated her in one of the overstuffed chairs facing the desk and retrieved something from one of the desk drawers. Returning, he handed her a document, then leaned back against the desk, arms crossed over his chest, and watched her unfold it.

"Recognize it?" he asked.

She nodded, not trusting herself to speak. The betrothal contract sat before her, her name and Jay's written across the top.

"I'd like your opinion on it."

She looked up at him then, eyes wide in a face she knew had gone suddenly pale. "What kind of opinion?"

"Is it valid? Enforceable? Should it be honored?"

Tina's hands shook. "I—I think you should ask a solicitor those questions," she responded, trying to keep her voice from trembling.

"I already have," he retorted, "but I would like to know what you think."

"Wh—why?"

"Because you are affected by whatever happens to it. Whether it is honored—or discarded—you are primarily affected by it."

"And you are not?"

"I am," he agreed, "but not in the same way you are."

"Oh." She looked down at the document again. She was slowly calming down and now thoughts raced through her head. What should she tell him? The truth, of course. She rarely backed away from a problem and prevaricating, or telling a half-truth, would make her a coward. If he took her advice and threw it out the window, then what? There was only one way to find out. "I'm not sure it's enforceable," she told him, "at least, in regard to you, that is."

"Why?"

Taking a deep breath to steady herself, she looked up at him again, and nearly forgot what she was going to say. "Because you were not a party to it. Mama didn't want Papa to add your name, but he did it anyway. Then, after Papa died, Mama said she couldn't destroy it—we had to wait for you to return to do something about it."

"And what did she expect me to do?"

"I don't know. She never said—just that we had to wait."

"Is that why you never had a season?"

Startled by the sudden change in topic, she answered, "No. Papa died in the summer and by the time I would have been old enough to be presented, we were still in mourning. The next year, Mama was not well and the doctor said it would not be good for her to go to London. Then she died that winter, so the next opportunity we were in mourning again. After that Mr. Milton refused to provide the funds for a season. Not that I knew anyone who could have sponsored me."

Jay abruptly turned and strode to the sideboard and

poured himself a drink. Throwing it down, he turned back to Tina, his discomfort obvious, a dark scowl marring his handsome features. She wondered what he was thinking.

"So, what should I do with it?"

Tina licked suddenly dry lips. "Whatever you want to do with it."

"And if I choose to honor it? Then what?"

Tina felt as if she'd been kicked by a horse. "Why would you do that?"

"Perhaps because I'm a man of honor. Or, perhaps because it suits my purposes to do so. Why does it matter why?"

For a quick moment, Tina wondered if it really did, but she knew the answer. "Of course it does," she responded with more heat than she intended. "Why would you be willing to marry someone you've never met before, someone with whom you have only spent one full day in their company? Certainly not to please a father you obviously disliked."

Jay winced as his words came back to haunt him. Perhaps letting Tina know of his feelings regarding his father and brother hadn't been such a good idea. Still, she had no idea of the importance of the betrothal contract in the larger scheme of things.

"Betrothal contracts were once commonplace. They are still used to cement alliances. There's nothing untoward about this particular one which would make a solicitor think it wasn't valid." He tried not to wince as he said the last, but Tina refused to let it go.

"Of course there is," she responded, obviously annoyed at his attitude. "Such contracts were normally entered into by the fathers of infants or children. Those are indeed binding, but the thought of a father forcing a grown son into marriage by such a thing is ludicrous in this day and age. I doubt I could renege on it. After all, I actually signed it, although I was all of eleven at the time. And...there is a little matter of not going back on a promise once made, but you—you weren't even aware I existed!

"Any solicitor worth his salt should question the validity of it after ascertaining by its date that you were an adult when it was entered into. He should be suspicious of the fact you did not sign it. Mr. Strate *knows* you were unaware of its existence and had not agreed to it. I, personally, would not blame you for refusing to honor it. You could toss it into the fire and be done with it and no one would be the wiser except you and I—and maybe Jon, but he would understand."

He listened to her in silence. A promise is a promise. She'd promised to marry him and she meant to keep that promise, regardless of what it meant. He should be glad she was willing to do so, but she wasn't making his task any easier. One thing was for sure, she certainly did not expect his next words.

"That is all well and good, but you did not answer my question. Suppose I choose to honor it?"

Tina stared at him in consternation. He wished he knew what she was thinking, but waited for her response. It wasn't what he expected.

"Why?" she demanded.

He was speechless. What happened to the calm, quiet woman he was acquainted with?

Why indeed, he thought, remembering the will. Perhaps there was the need to reclaim his ancestral holdings without a court fight, he thought grimly. Or, perhaps, he was letting his body rule him because goodness knew it would be no hardship married to her. For a moment he let his imagination run riot, imagining her in his bed—naked, soft, warm, willing.

For the second time, he was at a loss for words. "Why?" he repeated, wondering if he had truly heard her right.

"Yes, why?" she echoed. "Why would you do such a thing?"

"You are repeating yourself."

"Do not avoid my question, then."

A brief smile flitted across his features. "Perhaps because I find you beautiful and intelligent. Perhaps because I think it would be the right thing to do after you have waited all this time for me to come home and make a decision. Or, perhaps because you intrigue me as no other woman ever has."

Tina's expression bounced between outraged and flattered. "Because I waited?" she burst out. "You think I was waiting for you?" she asked incredulously. "What makes you think that?"

There was something in her voice that warned him he was on dangerous ground here. A wrong step and everything would blow up in his face. Suddenly, he wasn't sure he was in control of this conversation any longer, if he ever had been. He looked down into a tropical lagoon turned stormy and wondered what he should do next.

Retreat. "I'm not sure I think that, exactly," he conceded. "It's what Mr. Strate seemed to think. He said you'd waited to honor the contract."

The habitual calm he associated with her reasserted itself.

"I was waiting for Jon to be able to move to his estate, then I had planned for Felicia and I to join him there."

Jay returned to his stance before the desk. "I see."

"I'm not sure you do. Mr. Milton made it clear to me I would no longer be welcome at Thane Park by the end of this summer. Although Jon will not turn twenty-five until next year, I had already begun to make plans to find a place for Felicia and I to live until then."

"Why by the end of this summer?"

"Because the allowance was to run out five years after Papa's death. That would be the end of this month. I still do not know what he expected to happen to Felicia, but you may be assured I would not have left her here." Tina suddenly halted, a frown appearing to wrinkle her brow. "Mr. Milton was lying, was he not? The allowance was much more than he was giving us all along—and it would not have run out at the end of the summer."

Jay nodded, unable to voice his thoughts. Such comments were not made in polite company. He would be very satisfied when the detective found Roderick Milton. Quite frankly, he hoped he found him already dead—it would save Jay the possibility of hanging.

"Oh," suddenly deflated, Tina sat back in the chair.

"He told you you had to leave by the end of the summer?"

"Yes."

"He did not offer to allow you to stay here—for a price?"

Tina looked up, surprise and something else in her eyes. "How did you know?" she blurted.

"Know what?"

"That...that...he might have...off...offered to allow me to

stay?"

Dread. That's what he read in her eyes. Dread of what? "Because it's what most scoundrels would have done," he replied smoothly, then continued on a hunch. "His offer didn't, by any chance, include marriage as part of the bargain, did it?"

Tina's eyes widened, and he knew her response even before she gave it voice. "Yes, but how...?"

Her response confirmed what he'd suspected all along. Not only had Roderick Milton known of the will, but he had tried to force Tina's hand.

"It's a common ploy," he shrugged, hiding his rage behind nonchalance. "By marrying you he may have thought he could have assumed guardianship of Felicia and openly siphoned funds from the estate. Until I made an appearance, Felicia would have been considered the heir to the estate." He warred with his conscience over the half-truth. If not for the will, it would have been completely true.

Tina's eyes widened in shock.

"I never understood why he would want to marry me," she said now with a shudder, "especially since he hated me because of Mama." She was silent for a moment, obviously mulling the information over. "But I would not have married him. I would have just moved Felicia and myself to Oxford and joined Jon."

"Had you told Jon of this?"

"No. I didn't want him to worry."

Jay stared at her in alarm. "Not want him to worry!" he nearly shouted. "The two of you were living here literally at the mercy of that scoundrel and you didn't want Jon to worry! Just what did you think he was doing up in Oxford?"

"Studying," she answered calmly. "What else would he be doing?"

For a moment, Jay felt frustration so keen he thought he would burst. She didn't understand the magnitude of the danger she and Felicia had been in. In his experience scoundrels like Roderick Milton never gave up with a simple "no" from their victims. He would bet one of his ships Milton would not have allowed her and Felicia to simply walk away when the time came. But, how far would he have gone to get what he wanted? That was the question, the answer to which would tell him whether he was merely dealing with a thief—or a possible murderer.

Taking a deep breath to still his churning thoughts, he brought himself back to the matter at hand. Having asked her twice in a roundabout fashion, he decided to approach the issue head on.

"I have given this quite a bit of thought since first being presented with it some weeks ago and I have decided I should honor the betrothal contract. So, what say you?"

Having thrown down the gauntlet, he waited for the explosion he was sure would come.

Tina stared at him for a very long time. Her eyes registered varying degrees of astonishment, disbelief, doubt, and a cautious hopefulness before she looked back down at the document still sitting in her lap. It was the last emotion that he hoped would win out. After all, she had been promised Thane Park and he was now offering it to her.

It had only taken one morning in the study reviewing what she had accomplished in the two weeks he had been gone for him to realize she loved this place as much, if not more, than he did. That, to her, this place was home—and always would be. The people on the estate were dear to her, despite their treatment of her at Milton's instigation.

And it had only taken the afternoon for him to realize he wanted her. One kiss had been enough. Enough for him to realize that too much time spent in her company without touching her and he would surely go mad. Enough time to realize she was already in his blood. Enough time to realize he wanted more than a stolen kiss or two.

"You do not have to do this. I wouldn't force you to..."

He swore. "No one is forcing me to do anything."

Tina's startled gaze fastened on his face. "But, the contract. You wouldn't..."

Jay reached down, snatched the contract from her lap, and stalked toward the fireplace before he realized there was no fire burning there.

"Blast!" he muttered. Striding back to the desk, he opened a drawer, threw it inside, and slammed the drawer shut. She flinched. Returning to where she sat, he looked down at her.

"Forget the contract. I'm asking you to marry me. How difficult is that to comprehend?"

Even as he said the words, he knew they were the wrong thing to say. It wasn't so much what he said, but how he said it. She could not have missed the thinly-veiled sarcasm he had put into the words, nor could she have missed the frustration and condescension in his tone.

Tina rose from the chair to stand before him, and he knew her heart must be pounding furiously, because he could see the vein in her neck throbbing. The scent of roses wafted around him.

"It is not difficult at all," she responded in a voice that told him she was barely holding on to her temper. "However, I have only been in your company for less than two days and I will not decide my future upon such a short acquaintance. Nor will I allow you to throw away yours upon some misguided notion of honor."

"Misguided notion of honor," he sputtered. How dare the chit throw his offer back in his face! He'd thought long and hard about this. He was about to renege on a promise made eighteen years ago in order to regain what should have rightfully been his with no strings attached. And she had the nerve to label his actions a misguided notion of honor! If he wasn't afraid of what might happen should he touch her, he'd strangle her.

Tina stepped closer and put her hand on his chest, as if restraining him. "I did not mean it the way it sounded," she told him in a gentler tone. "I am honored by your offer, but I—I don't know you at all—and you don't know me. Perhaps..."

At her touch, Jay felt as if a brick wall had fallen on him. Her hand burned through his jacket and shirt and he was positive when he undressed he would find a brand the exact size and shape of her hand on his skin. He forgot to breathe; his blood turned to liquid fire. He watched her lips move, but heard only the last word before he covered her lips with his, his arms enfolding her slight frame and crushing it against the hardness of his.

Their first kiss had been a gentle exploration. The second had been a mere salute. But neither prepared Tina for the sudden conflagration that ignited between them this time. It was overwhelming, overpowering, and threatened to consume them utterly. Jay's mouth took complete possession of hers, slanting over hers, his tongue penetrating her lips, seeking her inner secrets. A moan rose in her throat, its sound muffled by an answering groan from his.

Her hands rose of their own accord, sliding up the muscled planes of his chest, winding around his neck, fingers threading through the hair at his nape. Her eyes closed, she responded purely by instinct, gasping for breath when his lips left hers to travel along her jaw and down her neck to the pulse beating at the base of her throat.

Another low moan escaped her as his hand moved up over her rib cage and caressed the underside of a breast through the thin material of her gown. Something told her she should stop him, that she should not allow him such liberties, but it was overridden by the sheer magnitude of emotions roiling through her body.

Jay's mouth returned to hers and she gave herself up to the sheer wonder of it all. There was no way to explain to herself—or anyone else, for that matter—why. She only knew she didn't want him to stop. He could ravish her mouth forever and she would never be satisfied.

His hands speared into the curls at the back of her head, scattering the pins holding them in place. Ebony waves tumbled down her back and his hands sifted through the dark tresses. Lifting her off her feet, he pivoted and sat in the chair she had just vacated, settling her in his lap, as his mouth continued to plunder hers.

His hand cupped her breast and she felt her nipple tighten against the material. She gasped as his thumb grazed the sensitive peak, feeling an unfamiliar warmth begin in her lower belly and spread downward. As she began to recognize the hunger coursing through her veins, she registered the proof of his own burgeoning desire against the back of her thighs. She was suddenly aware she was sitting in his lap, and belatedly wondered how she got there.

Lifting his mouth from hers, Jay stared down into eyes glazed with untried passion and marveled at her unconscious ability to excite him. No woman had ever affected him the way she did. She touched a protective and possessive streak he didn't know he had. And while she had no idea of her allure, of the temptation she presented, he did. And he knew he would do almost anything to claim her, to protect her, to save her. He would save her from the Roderick Miltons of the world.

He nearly laughed out loud. At this moment, the Roderick Miltons of the world were the least of her worries. He should be asking who would save her from him. Because right now he wasn't sure of his own ability to resist her. Until she agreed to marry him, he had to keep his distance. A near impossibility living under the same roof.

Jay watched her carefully. He should say something, but what? He wondered if she would be embarrassed or discomfited by her current position. As he slowly managed to bring his emotions under control, he knew he wasn't up to hysterics, and hoped he had accurately assessed her disposition was such that she was unlikely to fall into them. She did not disappoint him.

Moving slowly, she slid off his lap, smoothed her dress down, and began trying to restore some order to her hair, all the while not looking at him. "I was going to say," she began, her breathing still strained, her body rigid with acute embarrassment, "that perhaps we should spend some time getting to know one another, then I will give you my answer."

Then she turned and, moving slowly, left the room without a backward glance.

CR

Tina had regained a measure of composure by the time the gong sounded for dinner. It had taken much reflection and speculation, and a lot of arguing with herself to recover her outward appearance of calm.

She still wasn't sure how it happened, except she knew she had instigated it. She wasn't aware of consciously wanting to touch him, but looking back on her actions, she was convinced she had somehow manipulated the situation in order to compel him to kiss her again. Perhaps she had wanted to experience the first kiss all over again or see how close she needed to be to get him to react. Maybe she wanted to know if he really wanted to marry her, or if *she* really wanted to marry *him*. The kiss, however, had destroyed everything she thought she had learned from the first kiss.

So now what? She wasn't repulsed by him. Aaron's kiss had filled her with revulsion, making her physically ill. She had spent long hours wondering how she was going to survive marriage to someone who repelled her. She was drawn to Jay like a duck to water—she wasn't sure she absolutely needed him for survival, but she knew life would not be as complete without him.

She'd learned her feelings could be fully engaged in a pleasurable way. Pleasure, however, was too tame a word for the sensations Jay aroused in her. She lost her mind completely when he kissed her. It should annoy her, but it didn't. Kissing was merely a prelude to the more intimate side of marriage and, as Mira had told her, if she enjoyed the kissing the rest would be just as satisfying.

Jay was not unaffected by her. He seemed in total control, but it was belied by the fact that she had felt the rapid beating of his heart under her hands, could see the barely leashed passion in his eyes, and had noted his agitation even before he had touched her. He desired her, she knew. Did he feel anything more than lust for her? That was what she wanted to know. She did not think a marriage based on lust could last a lifetime.

The pendant on her dressing table upstairs seemed to accuse her. She hadn't bothered to put it back on since the day Nona had given it to her. No one was likely to see it here, anyway. Despite that she hadn't given Nona her promise, she felt guilty for not making an effort to find the person with the other half.

What would Jay do if she insisted on a season first? Did she even want one? When it was accepted that she would marry Aaron, there hadn't been a need for a season. He'd promised, instead, to take her to London to see the sights after their marriage. But the charming young man who'd agreed to the terms of the betrothal contract and the man who'd assaulted her were two different people. If they'd married, she wondered if he'd ever have taken her to Town.

Felicia, unaware of the currents flowing between Tina and

Jay, chatted about various topics and people through most of dinner. Tina noticed recently she was more cheerful than she had been in the years since their mother's death. It was good to see her enjoying herself again, and Tina derived a measure of happiness from her sister's obvious contentment. If only she could be so easily satisfied.

Her guilt over Aaron's death pushed her inexorably toward agreeing to marry Jay. It was what her stepfather wanted and, contract or no, she'd promised.

After dinner, Felicia offered to play for them so the three of them trouped off to the music room where Felicia performed an impromptu one-person concert. Tina pleaded tiredness when Jay asked if she played, but promised to reciprocate another time.

All in all, the evening managed to pass quickly and soon Tina found herself back in her room, undressed and crawling between cool sheets. She hadn't prevaricated. Tonight she was exhausted, more emotionally than physically, but tired all the same. She was asleep before her maid left the room.

CR

Jay spent the next day closeted in the study, emerging only for meals. He seemed preoccupied and barely acknowledged her presence at luncheon, although he bantered with Felicia as if he hadn't a care in the world. Tina found his behavior puzzling and tried not to dwell on it too much. But that was not to be.

Did he regret his hasty proposal? Was he disgusted by her response to his kiss? She worried he thought the worst of her— that she was free with her favors. After all, wasn't that what many men thought of gypsy women? Mira had warned her once English men considered gypsy women to be of easy virtue. She had told her English women were cold and unfeeling and English men expected such aloofness from their wives.

"But you will not be so, little one," Mira reminded her. "You have the fire in your blood."

Tina hadn't wanted to have fire in her blood. She wanted to be a lady—and ladies did not have fire in their blood. She had carefully cultivated a calm demeanor and serious disposition.

She would be the perfect marchioness.

Once she had been as easy and outgoing as Felicia, impulsive and with a temper. But she ruthlessly squelched it, burying all those emotions beneath layers of self-control. And she had succeeded. Roderick Milton had not been able to rile her. Even Lizzy Bowen had not been able to goad her into losing her temper. No one besides Felicia had ever been able to ruffle her feathers, until now.

She wondered what Jay thought of her outbursts yesterday. Had he been surprised? Shocked? She had certainly astonished herself with her reaction. It had been many years since she reacted in a purely emotional fashion to anything.

When Aaron died, she had initially cried tears of relief, but they had quickly turned to guilt. Rationally, she knew she hadn't caused his death, but a part of her *had* wished he would never return and that part taunted her with the knowledge her wish had been granted.

Aaron's death had nearly destroyed his father and the old marquis had died not knowing whether his second son was even still alive, leaving his wishes for his holdings in limbo. He had wanted her to have them, but if Jay hadn't arrived, Felicia would have inherited them.

All that no longer mattered. One of his sons would inherit— she had the chance to be marchioness as he wished—and she was not repelled by marriage to this particular son. Everything seemed to be falling neatly into place. So why was she making more out of this than seemed called for?

Because she would be letting Nona down and Nona was her own flesh and blood. Shouldn't that count for something?

CR

Jay sought Tina out the next afternoon and asked her to accompany him into the village. There were some repairs to the stables that needed to be made and he wanted to consult the blacksmith. He also wanted to gauge the state of the village and look in on the vicar. Furthermore, it might be a good opportunity to speak to her alone and repair some of the damage he might have done. She seemed to hesitate before she agreed.

The afternoon was hot, with barely a breeze stirring the air, the sky a cloudless blue. The bays were restless as Tina descended the front stairs, tying her bonnet beneath her chin. Dressed in a light-green muslin with touches of white around the puffed sleeves and hem, Jay was reminded as he waited for her to reach him he owed the Dowager Countess of Wynton a note of thanks. He smiled at the thought. The dowager might not understand, nor appreciate it, but he might write one all the same. Maybe it would pique her curiosity.

"Ready?" he asked.

"Yes."

He lifted her to the seat, releasing her reluctantly once she was settled. Moving around to the other side, he climbed up into the seat and took up the reins. Eddie released the horses and they were off. He set an easy pace down the drive and waited until they had turned onto the road to the village before turning to her.

"I must apologize for neglecting you these past two days. I have been trying to finish up the matters we left in the study before I ran off to Exeter."

"It is not necessary to apologize, my lord. I have not felt neglected."

"Jay."

"Pardon me?"

"Jay. I think we have gone beyond the formalities by now. Do you think you could call me Jay?"

Tina blinked. "I—I see," she said nervously. "Well, yes, I suppose I can."

He flashed her a broad smile. "Good." Then turned to concentrate on the horses.

Jay was aware of her tension, and relieved when she finally relaxed. He wondered if she was concerned over his driving, or just nervous in his presence? He could allay any fears over the former, but wasn't quite sure what to do if it was the latter. The scene in the library had replayed again and again in his head over the last day and a half and he wondered again if there had been a better way to handle the matter of the betrothal contract.

Telling her the truth wouldn't have hurt, his conscience nagged. But he had discarded that notion. The time to tell her the truth had been before he asked her to marry him. Now she would just assume he had wanted Thane Park all along. And that wouldn't be completely true.

Just as he shied away from telling her of the will, he refused to acknowledge to himself he wanted her—and not just because Thane Park, Collingswood, and his entire patrimony came with her.

Chapter Nine

Parkton lay a short distance from the Park. It was a typical village with small whitewashed cottages, an open green, a few shops, and a small church. The local tavern and inn, the Hill and Dale, sat on the outskirts of the north end of the village while Daisy's cottage sat near the south end. Tina noted there seemed to be no one about when they passed Daisy's cottage, but knew the smaller children would be napping because it was right after luncheon.

Tina had not been in the village beyond Daisy's cottage for well over a year. She was, therefore, astonished at the state of some of the buildings and the general aura of dilapidation that pervaded the area. During the last few weeks she had concentrated on the state of the Park's tenants, but had given very little thought to what might have been happening in the village. It had not occurred to her the area had become so depressed.

The vicarage was a large ivy-covered cottage sitting beside the church on one side of the village green. As they approached, Jay turned to her.

"I thought I'd check on the vicar. If I remember correctly, Felicia thought he was in ill health. I'm assuming Mr. Farthingale is still here?"

"Yes."

"Then it might be true. I remember him as being quite old when I was a young boy, or so it seemed."

Tina did not let her nervousness show. She'd had no contact with anyone from the village beyond Daisy's family since her mother's death. Her last contact with the vicar had been shortly after she had come out of mourning, when she had asked him to tutor Felicia. At the time, he informed her he would not do so unless the rumors currently making the rounds in the village were addressed. When she asked him what he meant, he had told her there were rumors in the village that she and her sister were consorting with gypsies and casting spells. He had then told her unless she repented publicly, he could not condone such practices by tutoring Felicia.

His disbelief when she told him she would not apologize for something she hadn't done told her all she needed to know. The situation was made worse when he'd made them unwelcome at Sunday services.

The housekeeper met them at the door and showed them into the parlor. The vicar arrived a few minutes later. Moving slowly into the room, he extended his hand.

"My lord, it's good to see you again."

Jay shook the thin hand, then took a seat as the vicar seated himself. Tina hoped Jay would merely discuss his concerns with the vicar, and not bring attention to her, but it was not to be. Turning to her, he said to the vicar, "You remember, Lady Christina, do you not?"

The vicar looked up and pinned her with his mud brown gaze. "I do, my lord," he responded curtly, and turned back to Jay. "Now what can I do for you?"

Jay was clearly astounded at the deliberate snub. "Rudeness does not become a man of the cloth, sir."

The vicar, surprised at the reprimand, peered closely at Jay. "And why would I wish to extend my hospitality to that person or her sister?" he replied indignantly. "T'would be unseemly."

Jay would have moved then had Tina not reached out and laid a hand on his arm. "No, my lord. Please, do not do anything rash." He turned to look at her then. Her eyes pleaded with him for calm and he responded. "I will wait outside." And with that, she rose to her feet, nodded to the vicar, and left the room.

Once outside, she took a deep breath. So much for hoping things would have changed. She now questioned the soundness of continuing on with Jay. He may not have thought there was any reason why she shouldn't go into the village, but she knew she probably should not have come. It had been hard to pass up the opportunity to get to know him better by watching him interact with the locals.

There were only a few families in the entire area who disbelieved the lies Roderick Milton had told them. Having convinced the vicar, then coupled with a few unfortunate accidents, Milton managed to convince most of the villagers she and Felicia were little better than devil-worshipers.

Jay came out of the vicarage some minutes later, a scowl on his handsome face. It was clear whatever he had come to discuss had not been completed to his satisfaction. Lifting her to the seat, he joined her from the other side and took up the reins.

"You have not been to the village in some time, am I right?"

"No," she answered, startled by the curt question. "Not for over a year, perhaps two."

"Why?"

"After Mr. Farthingale refused to tutor Felicia because of rumors circulating through the village, I felt it was best not to."

"And Felicia?"

"I told her she should probably avoid the village, but I doubt she did. She loves Daisy and her family, and they—and perhaps one or two others—were not inclined to believe the rumors."

"I see," he said grimly. "Should I expect the same reception at the blacksmith's?"

"I don't know, although Daisy's daughter, Ella, is Mr. Smythe's daughter-in-law. Perhaps not." She shrugged her shoulders. "Either way, it doesn't matter. I have done nothing wrong, so I have left it at that."

He said nothing as they came to a stop before the blacksmith's. Tina held her silence as Jay helped her down. He would have steered her toward the dark interior from which came the sounds of metal striking metal had she not balked, saying she preferred to wait outside. She could tell he did not want to leave her, but short of forcing her to accompany him, there was little he could do. Promising to be brief, he left her sitting on a bench underneath a small tree and strode into the shop.

Tina sat in the shade of the tree for a few minutes until she began to feel conspicuous. There were relatively few people outside at this time of day, so no one came by as she sat there, but knowing it would only be a matter of time, she didn't want to wait for a possible disaster to happen. Rising to her feet, she spied the dressmaker's shop across the way. It had been so long since she had been here she no longer knew who owned the little establishment.

A nagging voice warned her she should stay where she had been left.

But, it was hot and dusty outside. What would it hurt to take a peek? Perhaps she could provide some business. She had a few coins in her reticule. A ribbon or two wouldn't be amiss. The gowns made for her and Felicia by Madame were nice, but a few locally made ones would be better for everyday chores around the estate.

She should stay put, the inner voice reminded her. Jay expected to find her here when he returned.

In the end, curiosity won out and she crossed the street to the small shop. The interior was cool and dim, the only light coming in through the front window. Bolts of fabric lined a wall to her right, many beginning to fade around the edges, and a small table to her left held unadorned straw bonnets with ribbons and other decorations displayed around them. She was examining some of the ribbon when a woman came from behind the curtain hung behind the counter.

"Can I help you?"

She looked up and knew she had made a serious error in coming inside. Mrs. Barnes stood there, smiling, until she realized who had entered the shop.

"You!" The accusatory tone told Tina all she needed to know. Mrs. Barnes had not forgiven her for the death of her baby girl two years ago.

Retreating was not an option. "Good day to you, Mrs. Barnes."

Greta Barnes considered herself a good Christian woman, and she knew adversity often befell small children. But, she had not been able to get out of her head that the fire had happened the day after Lady Christina had visited her, especially considering the rumors. And that oh-so-nice Mr. Milton had been so concerned over her loss. He ordered a new cottage built, but their grief had been ignored by the ladies of the manor. The last straw, however, had been when the new cottage had begun to deteriorate and Mr. Milton informed her and her husband there was no money to make repairs. He had been forbidden, he said, by Lady Christina to make any more expenditures on repairs until they could be personally inspected by the marquis.

"I never thought you'd have the cheek to come here, of all places," she replied to Tina's greeting, outrage in every word.

Puzzled, Tina regarded Mrs. Barnes for a moment. She had been sorry for the baby's death—had even sent over a basket with Mr. Milton and her condolences. But, after realizing Mrs. Barnes blamed her, she had stayed away, not wanting to exacerbate her grief.

"I don't understand," she said. "Why would I..."

Another woman entered the shop. Tina automatically took a few steps into the center of the room to allow her to enter. She turned to greet the woman, and discovered Mrs. Pettigrew. *Could it get any worse?* she asked herself as Mrs. Pettigrew gave her a freezing look and turned away to speak to Mrs. Barnes.

Of course it could, was the answer as another woman entered the shop. She was again subjected to a disdainful perusal, before the newcomer also turned away.

"Wot's she doing here?" the newcomer asked Mrs. Barnes.

"Just walked in," was the answer. The woman, one she did not recognize, looked her up and down, then left the small shop. Mrs. Barnes and Mrs. Pettigrew pointedly ignored her while they conversed in low voices.

Deciding she had best leave while they were otherwise occupied ignoring her, she headed for the door. It opened again, this time to admit Mrs. Staple. Good God, was everyone in the village going to enter this one small shop?

Mrs. Staple took one look at her and stopped dead in the doorway, effectively blocking her way out.

"I never thought I'd see the day," she declared loudly.

Tina knew she had to get out of the shop, now. It was a small space and becoming quite crowded. There was outright animosity in the three faces around her and she wondered if they would resort to violence. Trying not to allow her trepidation to show, she lifted her head.

"Excuse me," she said in her loftiest voice, "I was just leaving."

"Too good for the likes of us," came Mrs. Pettigrew's voice from behind her.

"Hmmph," a voice she recognized as belonging to Greta Barnes intoned, "more'n likely she ain't good enough for us. Better let her through, Wilma. She ain't wanted here anyway."

Mrs. Staple came into the shop to allow her to pass. Unfortunately, there were others behind her and Tina's way was still blocked. Angry and hostile faces stared at her. The women behind her whispered amongst themselves, and a buzz circulated through the growing crowd before her. The mumblings became a rumble, then a dull roar that reverberated through her head.

Oh, God! They hated her. Tina's thoughts scrambled for a reason and found none. What had she done? Or, worse yet, what had the steward done? How had he managed to turn the entire village against her? There must have been more than the rumors concerning gypsies.

Tina had no doubt this situation was Roderick Milton's doing. Somehow he had managed to dupe the whole village into believing who-knew-what about her. She knew many in the village refused to do business with her household, but it had never occurred to her the general dislike extended to her personally. Certainly, Mr. Milton had done nothing to gain their approval. *Nothing except turn them against you*, a small voice reminded her.

They wouldn't win, she thought. She would not let them know how much their animosity affected her. Stiffly, she faced the crowd, tamping down her fear of possible violence. So lost in her thoughts was she that she didn't register the force that parted the crowd until Jay was standing before her.

"I thought I might find you here," he said evenly, "but it's time to leave. Are you ready?"

She nodded, unable to speak. Ready? She was more than ready. At this moment, she wanted nothing more than to get back to Thane Park where it was safe. Where she was safe. Where no one looked at her with accusation in their eyes. Where no one assumed the worst without consulting her first. Yes, she was more than ready to leave this place.

Jay turned and directed a freezing glare at the throng-filled doorway. A moment later it was empty and he and Tina were crossing the small street to his curricle where he lifted her onto the seat. He spoke for a moment with the blacksmith, who had come outside as they crossed the street, then joined her and they were off.

As they left the village behind, relief poured through Tina, causing her to tremble violently as she tried to relax. She took deep calming breaths in an attempt to still her trembling limbs. It was no use. The harder she tried to calm herself, the more she trembled.

Jay recognized the signs of shock. He should not have left her alone outside. He knew, after the words he exchanged with the vicar, she probably wasn't safe in the village. Although he worried she might be snubbed, or subjected to a scathing comment or two, it hadn't occurred to him she might be in physical danger.

He glanced over at her as he maneuvered the team onto a small track leading back to Thane Park and circumventing the village. She was shaking visibly now and he wanted more than ever to stop the curricle, pull her into his arms, and comfort her, but he couldn't, not yet. Berating himself again for allowing her to stay outside, he turned to give the road his attention. The last thing he needed right now was for them to overturn.

Just a little further and they would be out of sight of the road and any passersby. Then he could stop. Until then he silently willed her to be strong. She had withstood so much already, it might have broken someone weaker. He knew of no woman who might have endured the scene with the outward calm she had managed. Another might have resorted to threats to get out of the situation, but not Tina. She had merely stood there quietly, chin held high, refusing to be cowed. What had she said earlier? "I have done nothing wrong."

It might be true, but even in this modern age, old superstitions died hard. And they took the longest to die in the smallest villages. With old superstitions came old fears, and old fears were invariably irrational. People who clung to such old superstitions were often easily duped into believing the unbelievable. Such was obviously the case with the inhabitants of Parkton village. The question to be asked was *Why?*

Why had Roderick Milton gone to such lengths to destroy her? Stealing her quarterly allowance, Thane Park, or even Collingswood was one thing, but he had gone beyond that. He had tried to completely destroy her—as if he was driving her...away? Did he expect her to just up and disappear? What could he possibly have hoped to gain? Jay had thought Milton was trying to marry her to get his hands on the fortune and holdings, but if the steward had gone to such lengths to rid himself of her, maybe he'd planned something much more permanent.

They topped a rise and descended into a small depression. Jay halted the team beneath a spreading oak and glanced around the area, concluding they were far enough from the road and possibly prying eyes. Quickly securing the reins, he turned and gathered her shaking form into his arms. She did not resist. Stroking her back and speaking soothing nonsense in a low voice, he waited for the storm to pass.

He knew she had not registered the progress of the curricle or that it stopped. She was still breathing deeply, trying to reclaim her composure. Very slowly, the tension eased and gradually she became soft in his arms.

Eventually, Jay felt her body go limp against him and realized she had slipped into a doze. For long moments he sat still, wondering if she would wake if he shifted. He was not uncomfortable holding her, but he knew they should not stay out in the heat for very long. She would be more comfortable back at the Park, yet he could not help but wish to continue to hold her against him as if protecting her from the rest of the world.

Lifting her gently, he shifted her across his lap. She made a small, soft sound and snuggled closer as he settled her against him and reached to take up the reins again.

It was a long, slow drive back to the house. The jostling of the curricle caused her body to slide against his chest. The silk of her hair beneath his chin sent his imagination into a full gallop. His body reacted like a spark on dry tinder and turned his blood to liquid fire. He would not have changed anything, except the incident which led to her being in his arms. She was small and trusting, soft and warm, and she smelled faintly of roses. The light, delicate scent filled his nostrils and he knew he would forever associate her with that particular flower.

Upon reaching the house, he managed to get down from the curricle and carry her inside without waking her. Reaching the room he knew to be hers, he laid her down on top of the coverlet and removed her bonnet and shoes. A light blanket lay over a chaise before the doors to the balcony. Retrieving it, he covered her lightly and glanced around the room before turning to leave.

Reaching the door, he took one last look at her sleeping peacefully amid the pillows then left, closing it softly behind him.

Expelling a breath he hadn't realized he was holding, he shook his head to clear it, then headed back down to the study. He had people to talk to and work to do.

CR

Tina was awakened a short time later by her maid, who informed her Felicia was looking for her and it was almost time for tea. For a few moments, she looked around, trying to remember how she came to be in her own room. The last thing she distinctly remembered was being in the shop...Mrs. Barnes...Mrs. Pettigrew...the crowd...and Jay. Oh! Jay had rescued her from the shop. But how had she gotten here?

"Milly," she addressed the maid who was pulling a sky blue dress from her wardrobe.

"Yes, m'lady?"

"How did I get here? I mean, who...?"

"Oh, his lordship brought you in. Carried you in himself, he did. Said you weren't feeling well and should rest until tea time."

"Oh."

Tina allowed Milly to help her change her dress and redo her hair. Still feeling slightly disoriented, she left her room and headed downstairs. She found Felicia and Jay in the large salon facing the front of the house. Felicia ran to her as soon as she entered the room.

"Tina! I heard what happened. How are you?"

Somehow Tina found herself holding a distraught Felicia and looking at Jay in accusation. Jay shook his head.

Disengaging herself to look at her sister, she asked, "What did you hear? And who told you?" Steering Felicia to a settee, they sat and she waited.

"Nan was in the village visiting Ella. I was at Daisy's when she came in to tell her what happened. I would have come, but by then she said Jay had taken you away."

"Felicia!" Tina was horrified at the thought.

Keyes entered with the tea trolley. Leaving it in front of Tina, he withdrew, closing the door behind him.

As Tina began to pour, Jay said, "I, for one, am glad you didn't. I would not have wanted to rescue you both."

Felicia turned a bright smile on him as she answered, "Oh, you wouldn't have had to rescue me. The villagers never bother me."

"And why is that, minx?"

"Because they are all afraid of Midnight," she replied as Tina handed her a cup.

Jay stared at her, consternation written all over his handsome face. Tina had to struggle not to laugh and managed to hide her grin by looking down and pouring another cup.

"Afraid of Midnight?" he repeated, wonder in his voice. "I should have guessed. Does this have anything to do with how well trained he is?"

Tina handed him a cup and saucer. Warmth sped through her as their fingers brushed.

"Well, yes, I suppose it does. But it doesn't hurt that he's all black, too," Felicia answered innocently.

"Explain."

Felicia looked over at Tina then shrugged in resignation.

"After those absurd rumors started, I went into the village one day to see Ella. It was not long after we were officially out of mourning for Mama. As I was leaving to come home, there were some boys playing in the street. I guess one of the bigger ones decided to be a show-off."

She stopped to take a bite of the lemon cake on her plate, then continued. "He tried to grab me as I untied Midnight. Even though I pushed him away, another one joined him and took Midnight's reins and started to lead him away so I couldn't mount. So, I whistled Midnight to stop, then called him to come back."

Another bite of lemon cake went the way of the first. "The boy who had his reins got tangled up in them, so Midnight dragged him back, too. Then the first boy tried to grab me again, but I ducked and Midnight hit him."

"Hit him?" Tina asked.

"Actually, he butted him with his nose." Tina heard the shrug in Felicia's voice. "It was an accident, but I think they thought I told him to do it. After all, I was a gypsy witch. I should be able to command animals—especially all black ones," she grinned. "Once I mounted, I had Midnight raise up on his hind legs and I think the boys thought I was going to trample them so they ran off."

"Why didn't you ever tell me?" Tina asked worriedly.

"Because it was just silly little boys acting even sillier. There wasn't anything you could have done about it. I'd heard all the rumors, so I knew what they were thinking, but since Daisy didn't care, I didn't either. And Eddie helped by telling everyone how fierce Midnight was. The villagers don't bother with me when I'm on Midnight, so I always ride him when I go."

"In your breeches? Oh, Lord, Felicia!" Tina struggled between being appalled and laughing.

"Well, actually," Felicia began sheepishly, "I usually wear my breeches under one of my old dresses, so I don't look quite so scandalous."

Tina shook her head woefully. "I wish I'd known. You could have been hurt."

"But I wasn't, and there wasn't anything you could have done, except worry all the more. You had enough to do without worrying about whether I was safe, and I couldn't have borne it if you wanted me to stop riding Midnight, or going to visit

Daisy's family." Felicia's tone begged her to understand.

Jay, who had merely listened up to this point, now spoke up. "Well, there is something that can be done about it now." Putting down his cup with a snap, he said, "We leave for Collingswood day after tomorrow, so make whatever arrangements you wish before then."

Sapphire blue and aquamarine eyes turned to look at him in astonishment.

"Leave?" Felicia found her voice first. "But, why?"

"Because until we find Roderick Milton and get to the bottom of this, Tina is virtually a prisoner here. From what I was able to learn this afternoon, Tina has been the main target of the animosity engendered by Mr. Milton."

Jay refused to reveal how much the afternoon's incident had scared him. He had never felt such panic in his life as when he emerged from the blacksmith's shop and discovered what was happening across the street. It had taken all of his self-control not to wade into the crowd, fists flailing and not caring who he hit—man, woman, or child—in order to get Tina out of there and safe. He never wanted to see her feeling so helpless and frightened again.

For now, he knew the best way to get them to leave would be to convince Felicia that Tina's safety was at stake. Despite Felicia's outwardly indifferent attitude toward their situation, he could see she was upset by the afternoon's events. She had dealt with their situation in the past the only way she knew how, but that method would not protect Tina and he was aware she would do anything to protect her sister.

"Will I be able to take Midnight?"

"Of course," he agreed. "However, you may not ride him along the way. If you wish to ride, you may ride one of the mares from the stables."

Felicia acquiesced and said no more. Minutes later, she excused herself, hugged Tina, and left the room.

"Is it really necessary for us to leave?" Tina asked after she was gone, and he wondered whether she would balk at his orders.

"Yes, I believe so."

Tina sighed and took another sip of tea. "I did not realize

Felicia's attachment to Midnight had such a practical side to it. It seems, however, as if we are leaving under duress."

"I had planned to go to Collingswood either next week or the week after. The Park is doing better now, and I need to inspect the rest of the properties. I thought I'd start with Collingswood."

"Oh."

"I thought to tour the rest of the properties, but I would have waited until you made your decision before I proposed the idea. We are running away from nothing—the incident this afternoon merely gave me a reason to move forward my original plan."

He watched her put down the delicate cup and look up as he rose to his feet. "If you will excuse me, I have a few things to finish up before we leave as well."

Tina jumped to her feet. "I didn't thank you for rescuing me," she began.

"It is not necessary." He waived away her thanks and moved to stand before her. "I knew when I left the vicarage I shouldn't have taken you into the village, but, foolishly I assumed you would be fine for what I thought would be a short visit to the blacksmith's to discuss some repairs. I wanted to grant your request, you see, but I discounted what Mr. Farthingale said about the villagers."

"My...my request?"

"That we spend some time getting to know one another." He paused for a moment, then continued. "You were right when you said we did not know each other very well. I thought we could spend some time this afternoon...talking."

Tina was taken aback by his admission. She had not thought he'd given her suggestion any credence. After the last time she had spent in his arms, she was convinced he thought her free with her favors and had developed a disgust of her.

"Perhaps on the way to Collingswood," he said now. "But, I suspect we will have to keep it innocuous or Felicia might guess our intent."

"Do you not want Felicia to know?" she asked. "She has always known I was to marry Aaron—and probably knows about the exchange of names on the betrothal contract."

"I had not thought much about it," he admitted. "You know her better than I—how do you think she would react?"

Surprised by the question, she replied, "I'm not sure I know." She was silent for a moment, then continued, "There was a time when I would have predicted her reaction, but I'm not sure any more. She has been somewhat detached over the past few years. We are still close, but I wouldn't hazard a guess as to her reaction."

"Will you tell her?"

"Of course," she responded instantly. "But not until after I make my decision. I think I will be able to give you my answer after we reach Collingswood." Trying to sound as if she discussed marriage proposals every day, she continued, "I think by then I should have thought it through enough to make a decision. As for Felicia, if nothing happens soon, she will likely come right out and ask."

℣

True to his word, they left Thane Park shortly before dawn two days later. Collingswood and Thane Park were a long day's ride from each other, so there was no need to worry about where to stop for the night. Felicia and Tina began the journey riding in the coach, but Jay promised later they could ride in the curricle with him if either of them wished. Felicia was also wearing her habit, intending to take Jay up on his promise of letting her ride one of the mares being led by Eddie.

About mid-morning, Jay took Tina up in the curricle, while Felicia mounted the other mare. Understanding he needed to concentrate on the road, Tina was quiet and relaxed, enjoying the countryside as it went past. Felicia rode beside the curricle for a short while, asking Jay questions, then moved to ride beside Eddie.

For Tina, the day had a near magical quality about it. She found comfort and ease in Jay's company. Although they talked little, she discovered her reticence around him vanished when he wasn't concentrating solely on her. Watching him handle the ribbons, she was especially impressed with his skill because she knew he had spent most of his time away from England at sea.

She also found herself wondering whether he truly wanted to marry her—or whether he was sacrificing himself for the sake of his father. It seemed odd to her that, after leaving home originally to get away from his father, he would return to do his father's posthumous bidding. Nothing seemed to add up except, for some unexplained reason, Jay was willing to honor a contract to which he had not, legally, been a party.

So, how did she feel? She'd told him she was honor bound to respect the provisions of the contract, although it could be argued she had not consented to its provisions either. She had agreed to marry Aaron when he was standing before her and she had, in essence, grown up with him. But, she had not agreed to substituting Jay's name on the contract. In fact, she had not been consulted, so had neither agreed nor disagreed. Perhaps she had accepted the change by not speaking up when she learned of it. Perhaps the old marquis assumed she would agree simply because she had been groomed to take her mother's place as marchioness.

And perhaps, a small voice taunted, you didn't argue because you felt guilty over Aaron's death. It had been very hard to watch the old marquis, her beloved "Papa", deteriorate as he had. Perhaps she had acquiesced because it seemed to make him happy—or at least content. Whatever the reason, she had not opposed the substitution and, after her stepfather's death, felt obligated to abide by its terms.

For that reason alone she decided, regardless of Nona's edict, she would agree to marry Jay. She felt mostly comfortable with her decision—only a small twinge of guilt remained when she looked at the pendant. If someday, she found the other half, she wondered if the owner would understand.

Chapter Ten

Collingswood sat in a wooded valley bisected by a wide river, hence its name. At one time it had been a royal hunting lodge, later bestowed upon one of Jay's ancestors along with the title viscount for services rendered to the Crown. The ancestor had promptly renamed it Collings' Wood, and over the years the name had been shortened to one word instead of two. Originally the family seat, the family had decamped for a new and larger, recently acquired estate when the Marquisate of Thanet had been conferred upon the family through a distant French cousin. When the French branch died out, leaving the title wholly in England's realm, the third English marquis named the family seat Thane Park.

The original manor at Collingswood had been torn down during the reign of Elizabeth and a new manor built of Cotswold stone in the shape of the letter "E". Smaller than Thane Park, Collingswood was nonetheless a handsome property, perfect for staging hunts and country parties. The old marquis had given it to Aaron to manage upon attaining his majority. Since it was also much closer to London, they had not seen much of Aaron during those years.

As far as she knew, the old marquis had no complaints about Aaron's management, but she knew her mother had been concerned over some of the activities she'd heard about. The grapevine between the servants at all the Thanet properties was strong, especially since the butlers who presided over both the major estates and the town house were all related. Little went on at one property that wasn't known to the others.

Although they arrived in darkness, they were expected. A late supper was served in the dining room, after which Felicia excused herself and went off to find her bed, leaving Tina wondering how she should broach with Jay the subject of his proposal.

Once again, he came to her rescue. "Have you reached a decision?"

Tina looked up at him and felt as if her heart turned completely over in her breast. Leaning back in his chair, his chestnut hair gleaming in the lamplight, he was beyond handsome. The shadows in the room seemed to emphasize the sharpness of his features, yet managed not to make him look dark or sinister. His long, slim, fingers toyed with the stem of his wine glass as his dark gaze rested on her.

"Yes." The tension in the air became a tangible force, almost overwhelming her in its intensity. Carefully folding her napkin and laying it on the table, she slowly got to her feet. "My answer is yes." She was trying for nonchalance, but could feel the color creeping into her cheeks. "Now, if you'll excuse me," she said as she turned to go, "I'm tired as well."

Jay seemed to recover himself as she reached the door. "Wait!" he called, scrambling to his feet and hurrying toward her.

"Thank you," he murmured, taking one of her hands in his and bowing over it. Tingles shot up her arm at his touch. For a long moment, he stared into her eyes and she refused to put a name to what she thought she saw in the ebony depths. Then he brushed a kiss across her knuckles and let her go. "Until tomorrow, then."

"Tomorrow," she repeated softly, then opened the door and slipped out.

Long after she lay in her bed in the darkness, her heart continued its rapid tattoo. Had she read exultation in his eyes at her answer? Or was her mind merely playing tricks on her? She had been afraid to look at him, expecting only to see relief. After all, she'd told him originally she felt honor bound to abide by the contract. Shouldn't he have expected her answer? Yet, he hadn't expected it at all. In that moment when he thanked her and kissed her hand, she had known he had not expected her to agree. Why? Perhaps she should ask him.

CR

There are days in a person's life when so many things happen at once the person vows never to forget it. Tuesday, the twenty-third day of July, in the year of our Lord, 1861, was such a day for Lady Carolyn Felicia Collings. For it was on that day she received her first letter from a duchess, her brother, the Earl of Wynton, appeared at Collingswood, a shipment of dresses and gowns arrived from Madame's establishment, and she learned her older brother, the Marquis of Thanet, was to marry her sister, Lady Christina Lorraine Kenton, in four days.

"Four days!" She stared at Tina and Jay in stunned amazement. "Are you mad? We can't put on a wedding with only four days notice."

"Of course, we can," Tina answered. "After all, who is there to invite besides you and Jon?"

Felicia shook her head. "I suppose you are right, but it just doesn't seem right that it should happen so fast," she conceded. "At least wait until Jon comes. We'll have to write to him and who knows where he is at the moment."

"On his way here, I hope," Jay offered. "I wrote to him a few days before we left the Park."

"Before we left?" Tina asked. "But..."

"I did not mention a wedding," he said. "I only asked him to join us so he and I might compare notes on our investigation of Roderick Milton. And, I thought you'd be glad to see him."

"Oh." Tina's cheeks pinkened as he explained himself.

Felicia watched the two of them closely. If they weren't already in love, she thought, they were pretty close. Of course, neither would probably admit it. But, four days? Why such a rush? She had the distinct feeling something else was going on she knew nothing about. She hated being in the dark about anything, but short of coming right out and demanding an explanation, she knew she'd learn nothing at this juncture.

"Jon can give you away," she said now. "He'll like that. And I can be your bridesmaid. But what will you wear?"

"I haven't given it much thought," Tina answered her. "I'm sure there is something suitable among all those clothes Jon ordered from Madame."

Jay was pleased she didn't seem to want a large wedding. Nor did it seem to matter to her what she wore. Of course, what she wore mattered little to him—he had already jumped ahead to when she would be wearing nothing at all.

He had also been fortunate she accepted his reasons for not bothering to wait any longer. Informing her he already had procured a special license had been tricky inasmuch as he was unable to predict her reaction. He had been pleasantly surprised, however, when she accepted that he had only wanted to be prepared should she agree.

She had also provided him with another reason why the nuptials should be soon. She was aware Felicia might be leaving for a young ladies' academy soon and mindful of her reputation should that happen before the ceremony. Besides, she wanted to have both of her siblings at her wedding.

For now, all was right in the world and he was content with his lot. As he watched Felicia get up and hustle Tina out of the library, he wondered what she was up to, but not enough to ask. Knowing Felicia, right now it probably would involve going through Tina's wardrobe for something suitable to be married in. He was not needed there.

℞

The Earl of Wynton arrived shortly after luncheon, driving a curricle and followed closely by a coach loaded down with trunks and boxes from Madame's establishment. After the initial excitement of Jon's arrival, he and Jay adjourned to the library to talk while Felicia and Tina directed the unloading of the coaches and supervised the unpacking of numerous trunks and boxes.

"We couldn't possibly have ordered so much," Tina told Felicia, as she opened yet another trunk filled with clothing. "I know I told Madame I didn't need much. And, how did she get measurements for all the rest—slippers, boots, gloves, and bonnets." She sighed. "I suppose I'll need them now, although I'm not sure I needed quite this much."

Felicia smiled as she watched her sister marvel over

everything as it was unpacked. It was good to see her happy. For too long, Tina had worried over the two of them—what would happen to them, how they would survive until Jon could take over their support, what to do about Mr. Milton, whether Cook and her family, and the other families at the Park, were doing well. It was time for her to be pampered and indulged. She had earned it after all she had been through. And Felicia didn't mind using a little subterfuge to ensure it happened.

For that reason, she had spent hours with Madame, going over fashion plates, examining fabric swatches, matching colors and various shades, and adding to Tina's order. She was sure Jon would not mind and she had decided, after that first morning ride with Jay, he wouldn't mind either. She had been right. Neither had blinked at the numerous trunks and boxes unloaded from the carriage.

"Felicia," Tina intruded into her thoughts. "What are we going to do with all of this?"

"Wear them?" she answered mischievously.

"Felicia!" Tina tried for a scolding tone, but missed entirely as she dissolved into giggles. "It's too much," she gasped. "I don't think Jay and Jon could possibly have ordered so much."

"Tina, stop worrying. Those times are behind us now. I'm sure Jay and Jon both would have given Madame a limit," she said as she drew out another tissue wrapped parcel from the bottom of the nearest trunk. She was still looking for something really special. Something special enough to be married in.

"I know," Tina replied, "but it is still hard to think we need so much after doing with so little for so long. It seems extravagant. But, I suppose..." Her voice trailed off as she realized the room had gone totally silent.

Turning, she found Felicia standing at the end of the bed, a look of complete awe on her face.

"Felicia? What is it?"

"Your wedding gown," Felicia barely breathed the words. "Tina, look! It's perfect."

Tina approached the bed and looked down. There on the bed lay the most exquisite gown she had ever seen. Even the aqua gown Madame had fitted on her back at the Park could not compare. The off-the-shoulder bodice was of white satin, overlaid with a fine white and silver lace. The overskirt was made up of layers of white gauzy lace over an underskirt of silver tissue, revealed by a dramatic slashed opening down the front of the skirt. There were no sleeves, but, upon lifting the dress, they found elbow-length gloves made of the same whisper light silver and white lace found on the bodice.

Tina stared, speechless, at the dress before her. It was the stuff of dreams. Of knights in shining armor and fairy princesses. Of magic and enchantment. Of love and happily ever after. It was the embodiment of all her girlhood dreams and wishes and, suddenly, she couldn't wait to wear it—hoping it would prove the perfect catalyst.

Felicia, shunting aside her protestations that she hadn't ordered such a gown, delved back into the trunk and lifted out the last package. In it she found a pair of white slippers embroidered with silver thread, a pair of sheer white silk stockings, and an extra length of the white and silver lace. "The perfect thing for a veil," she pronounced.

"As long as I don't have to wear it over my face," Tina allowed.

Leaving Milly to finish putting away Tina's new wardrobe, the two left for Felicia's room to see what delectables were to be found in her trunks and boxes. There were plenty of items to exclaim over, but none as stunning as the silver and white gown.

СЗ

Downstairs in the library, a different sort of discovery was being made.

"Nowhere to be found? You're sure about this?" Jay was staring at the detective's report Jon had just passed to him.

"It's as if he just vanished into thin air. The detective tracked him all the way to London, then nothing."

"People don't just vanish into thin air," Jay mused.

"I know," Jon agreed. Silence, then, "Do you think he might have changed his name again?"

"Again?"

"I think it stands to reason Roderick Milton was not his real name. No one knew him before he was seen in Aaron's company. No one knew where he came from and the Duchess of Westover insists the name doesn't ring a bell."

"So you think he may have changed his name again—or even back to what it was formerly?"

"I suppose anything's possible."

"Have you had a chance to follow-up on the suggestion I sent you from Weston?"

"Sort of. I sent the detective up to the north country to do some checking. My mother's father was Sir Ralph Tindale, a baronet. After my grandparents' death in a fire not long after my parents left for India, the estate passed to a distant cousin. As for my grandmother's family, well, you already know they were gypsies, although I also have the detective looking into my great-grandfather's family. I know very little about them because my great-grandfather died well before my mother was born and after his death, his family cast my grandmother out."

"Where did she go?"

"According to my mother, she was traveling south to meet up with her gypsy family when she met and fell in love with my grandfather. They were married at Gretna Green and settled at North Road Manor—a small holding up near the Scottish border."

Jay leaned back in the chair behind his desk and stared up at the high ceiling of the library. They couldn't have possibly run into a dead end. He had to find Roderick Milton. There was more to this than met the eye—something they were overlooking.

"There's something we have missed," he said now. "I'm sure of it. But, what?"

"I wish I knew."

CR

Felicia was in high spirits by tea time. She thanked Jay profusely for her new wardrobe and informed Jon he had done well by Tina.

"I thank you for your approval," he responded with a grin. "In the future, I shall make sure I consult you before I buy anything else."

Undaunted, Felicia replied, "No you won't. In the future you won't be buying Tina anything."

"Ah, yes. In, what is it, four days? I lose the privilege forever. Who shall I order Worth gowns for after that?"

"Not forever, silly," Felicia began, but stopped mid-sentence. "Worth gowns? Tina's gowns came from Worth?" she stared at her brother in awe-struck fascination.

"Not all of them," he allowed. "Just one."

"Which...?" Felicia began, then turned to Tina. "The white one," she breathed. "No wonder."

Tina, too, stared at her brother. "Jon? Worth?" she questioned. "How did you...?"

"That's my secret," he told her smugly. "But, Madame was quite helpful on that front. It seems she once worked with him in Paris."

Jon's emerald gaze rested on the older of his two sisters with watchful intensity. It had been a heady feeling knowing he now could shower her with nearly anything on a whim. And a whim it had been, when he visited Madame's shop in London and the two had discussed the orders Madame had received.

He had been saddened, but not surprised, to learn Tina had insisted on ordering very little, until Madame had revealed what she and Felicia had done. Amused that Felicia had taken it upon herself to supplement Tina's wardrobe, he had ordered Madame to make up everything Felicia had suggested, then asked her opinion about something special. It was then Madame mentioned her connection to Worth.

Charles Worth had taken Paris fashion by storm a few years earlier and now was the premier dressmaker in Europe. It was fast becoming the fashion, even in England, for young ladies to travel to Paris to have their trousseaus made by the famous couturier.

Jon could not supply Tina with a Worth trousseau, but he could supply her with at least one gown. The cost had been exorbitant, but he could well afford it now, and he didn't mind paying for a few fripperies to see his too-serious sister smile.

As expected, Tina took him to task after tea was over. They were walking in the gardens behind the house, Felicia having wheedled Jay into taking her into the nearest village so she could consult with the vicar about the wedding. The heat of the day was waning and a light breeze had come up.

"You shouldn't have," she told him now. "I know it must have been frightfully expensive."

"I know," he grinned, unrepentant, "but I did anyway. I made a promise I haven't been very good at keeping of late. But, now I have the chance, before I lose the opportunity forever."

"What promise?"

"To Papa. I promised I would take care of you and Mama."

"Papa?" she asked. "Felicia's father?"

"No. Ours."

"Ours?" She was confused.

Jon was suddenly serious, staring off over the gardens, a distant look in his eyes, before turning back to her. "Before he died, Papa wanted to see us both, but Mama wouldn't allow you to see him. She said you were too young and wouldn't understand."

Tina started to say something. "You should know Mama regretted that decision for the rest of her life," he explained. When Tina said nothing, he went on. "Papa told me because I was to be the new earl, it would be my responsibility to take care of you and Mama. It was not something I would recommend telling a six-year-old, especially one who knew very little of what was happening.

"Unfortunately, I took my role too seriously and when I was ten, Mama let me know in no uncertain terms that she did not need me to look after her. By then she had Felicia's father to do that."

He was quiet for a moment. "She softened the blow a bit by telling me I should always look out for you. *She* might not need me to be her champion, but you would. And when she died, she made me promise I would do whatever was necessary to ensure yours and Felicia's well-being." Tina remained silent beside him as they continued walking. "Unfortunately, I haven't done a very good job."

"Of course, you did," she said impulsively. "It wasn't your

157

fault Aaron brought home that awful Mr. Milton. And, it wasn't your fault he tried to run us off. I'm sure he was just trying to get his hands on Thane Park somehow, but as long as Felicia and I were there, he would always be just the steward, and not a very good one."

Jon's smile was more of a grimace. "I meant the gown to be my way of bringing you out. When I ordered it, I knew Jay was going to propose, so I thought it could be either a wedding gown or a coming out gown. If you didn't want to marry him, I had planned to ask Teddy's mother if she would sponsor you."

"Teddy?"

"Teddy Hartwell. A friend from Oxford. His father is the Duke of Westover. And, having just recently met his mother, I discovered she knew Mama. She indicated she would be more than happy to sponsor you, if you wished it. I have a letter from her to Felicia. And she recommended a young ladies' academy."

"Felicia will be thrilled."

"I thought so."

They walked in silence for a while longer, then turned back toward the house. Shortly before they reached the edge of the garden, he asked, "Are you sure you want to marry Jay?"

Tina stopped and turned to look up at her brother. He might not realize it, but he had been her source of strength for most of her life. She had relied on him when things seemed at their worst—and he had never let her down, despite what he might think.

"Yes," she answered softly. "He is everything his father was, and more. He is kind, considerate, and gentle. He cares deeply about the land and the people, and has even developed a brotherly affection for Felicia."

"And you?" Jon asked. "Has he developed an affection for you?"

"I—I think so," she answered as the blood rose in her cheeks and she looked off over the riot of color that was the garden. "But I suppose only he can actually answer that."

"And what about the pendant Nona gave you?"

Her eyes snapped back to his face. "How did you know about that?"

"Nona told me." Seeing the question in her expression, he went on. "I don't know how, but she found me at an inn on the way to Wynton Abbey."

"She...?"

"Well, actually Carlo did. He said she knew I was nearby and sent him out in search of me." His expression turned as sad as his tone as he related the last conversation he had with their great-grandmother. "She told me of the pendant she had given you and insisted I not allow you to marry anyone except the holder of the mate."

"And did you agree?"

He grinned. "Sort of. I promised to try, but I wouldn't force you if you wanted to marry someone else."

"So, is that why you are not stopping me from marrying Jay?"

He shook his head. "No. The truth is that I would prefer you marry someone you know and care for, rather than trying to find a perfect stranger. And, I like him."

Shock registered on Tina's face at his words. Was she that transparent? She was only beginning to accept her feelings for Jay were more than friendly. This afternoon she had actually asked herself if she was falling in love.

"How do you know I care for him?"

"Because I know you better than you think," he replied. "At tea, I noticed the way the two of you watched each other when you didn't think anyone else was paying attention. I would guess his feelings are also engaged, but I wouldn't risk guessing how far." Amusement lurked in his eyes as he added, "You, however, are an easy read. I just hope you don't regret the step you are about to take. Are you sure you wouldn't prefer a season to try and find the other half of your pendant?"

"I don't think I'll regret it," she answered quietly. "But thank you for your concern. And, I can't explain why, but I just feel as if this is the right thing to do now. I suppose it's possible I may find the other half of the pendant eventually, but I'm too old for a season now and I want to honor the promise I made to Papa."

"Marriage is a big step. You should be sure."

"For now, I am. Someday, I might feel guilty for not

searching out the person with the other half of my pendant, but for now, I think this is the best course for me."

She thought he would say more, but he didn't. Instead they continued into the house.

CR

Over dinner, Felicia told Tina and Jon about the village church and the vicar.

"It's a beautiful little church and the vicar was so nice. Just perfect for a small wedding."

Tina giggled. "By that you mean, perfect for me, but not for you."

"Of course," Felicia agreed. "One does not marry a duke in a country church."

Jon nearly choked on his wine. "What duke?" he demanded.

"The one I'm going to marry," Felicia replied smugly.

Jay, who was fast learning how Felicia's mind worked, asked, "And is there such a person on the horizon?"

"Not yet, but there will be by the time I'm eighteen," she answered breezily.

Jay leaned back in his chair and eyed her thoughtfully. "And if there isn't?"

Tina erupted into laughter. "Oh, Jay, don't encourage her. You'll only make it worse."

"I'm only trying to determine whether I should be out scouring the countryside for appropriate candidates to bring to heel—or if she already has someone in mind. Dukes are quite hard to find these days. Especially ones who are not already married." He turned back to Felicia. "Will an heir do—or must he have already acquired the title?"

Felicia thought for a moment. "I suppose an heir will do."

"Very well. I will keep my eyes open."

Tina was disconcerted. "You should not make promises you cannot keep, my lord," she told him. "And, Felicia, you cannot possibly intend..."

"Of course, I do," Felicia cut in. "But, it's at least two years away—who knows what will happen in two years."

"Who knows, indeed," Jay concurred, thoughtfully.

After dinner, the men followed the ladies into the drawing room, insisting there was nothing they needed to discuss that couldn't be put off until tomorrow. When the tea trolley was brought in, Jon excused himself, returning a short time later.

"I almost forgot," he told Felicia, handing her an envelope. "This is for you." Dropping into a chair across from her, he watched her open the missive. "It's from the Duchess of Westover."

As Felicia opened the missive and began to read, Jon and Jay exchanged glances. Jay stood, drawing Tina to her feet as well. Although curious as to the contents of Felicia's letter, she allowed Jay to lead her from the room and into the library. Seating her on the settee in front of the fireplace, he lit two lamps on nearby tables, then crossed the room to the desk in front of the windows. Retrieving something from inside the desk, he returned to sit beside her.

"I asked Jon to stop and pick this up on his way here. I thought it would suit you."

He opened his hand to reveal an elegant ring. The slim gold band was topped by a large diamond surrounded by smaller emeralds, which were in turn, surrounded by sapphires.

"It's beautiful," she whispered.

He picked up her left hand and slid the ring on the third finger. A tingling coursed through her fingers and up her arms.

She stared down at the ring in wonder, then lifted luminous eyes to his face. "It fits," she said in surprise.

His smile appeared and she was mesmerized. "I thought it might," he said softly just before his lips covered hers.

Tina went boneless in his arms, her mouth parting beneath his in complete surrender. As before, she was not prepared for the rush of sensation that invaded her body, nor could she deny the simple feeling of rightness she felt being in his arms. Her breathing stopped, her heart sped up, and a dull roar sounded in her ears. For long minutes, she was lost, then Jay raised his head and she was able to breathe again.

She knew she should not be embarrassed, but she could

feel the heat rising in her cheeks. Dropping her gaze to his shirt front, she missed the carefully controlled fire burning in the depths of his. His sigh teased the tendrils of hair at her temple.

He leaned against the back of the settee and moved his hand upward, dislodging the mass of curls styled at the back of her head—and was rewarded with a shower of ebony silk tumbling over his hand and arm. A sense of contentment surrounded them both as he threaded his fingers through the soft curls.

Tina rested against his broad chest, half lying, half sitting on the settee. His heart beat strongly against her ear and she found herself wondering, not for the first time, if Nona might have been wrong. Her feelings were in turmoil. If someone else was her destiny, then why was she falling in love with Jay?

She had agreed to marry him, but only because it was the most logical choice when looking at all of her options. It made sense for her to honor her promise. It made sense for her to marry him, as his father had wished. But logic had nothing to do with her moods lately and she found herself alarmed at times at the intensity of her feelings where he was concerned.

"Is there somewhere in particular you'd like to see or go?"

Jay's deep voice startled her from her thoughts and she lifted her head. Their eyes met and she lost her train of thought. What had he asked her?

A ghost of a smile hovered around his mouth as he took in the bemused look in her eyes. He had surprised her. Good. It seemed only fair considering the shocks she regularly delivered to his system, the impact she was having even now on his system as he took in her wide eyes and kiss-swollen mouth framed by a soft cloud of raven curls.

"I asked if there was anywhere you'd like to see or go?" he repeated.

"Why?"

"I thought perhaps you'd like to take a trip somewhere. I do own a small fleet of ships."

"Oh." She sat up. "I haven't given it much thought," she admitted. She seemed to be scanning the room, as if looking for something, but he wished she'd turn back to him. "I thought we were going to tour the properties."

"That is purely business—something we need to do, regardless. But I thought you might like to take a pleasure trip—a honeymoon, if you will."

"I—I don't know, I'll have to think about it."

He slid his hand up her back, tangling it in the shining mass. He was tempted to tug on it, pull her back into his arms and continue where he left off, but thought better of it. When she moved her head, shaking the silky fall, he had to bite back a groan. At that moment, he wanted nothing more than to bury his face in its softness and inhale its sweet scent—and try his damndest to disregard the clamoring of his body.

He knew he shouldn't get too attached. She was only a means to an end. It was too bad he hadn't reminded his heart of that *before* he kissed her. Before he tasted pure innocence. He could count on one hand the number of times he had tasted her, but he was already addicted.

Tina allowed her eyes to wander the room, trying desperately to look anywhere but at the man seated beside her. Her heart was still beating entirely too fast, making her breathless and a little lightheaded.

A lock of hair fell over her shoulder and she lifted her arms to push her hair behind her, shaking it out and unaware of the effect it was having on her companion. She heard a small sound, and turned to look at him. Sprawled carelessly on the seat, his booted feet crossed at the ankles, he looked cool and composed. Why was it she felt anything but?

She began gathering her hair to put it back into some order when he moved. Sitting up, he caught her hands and drew them down. "Don't," he said gently. "I like it this way."

"But..." He shushed her with two fingers over her lips. She only just restrained herself from pursing her lips and placing a kiss on those fingers.

"There is no one here to see but me," he told her, his hands continuing to sift through the long, heavy tresses.

Tina watched his hands in fascination. The long fingers gently combed through the thick mass and she found herself imagining those hands stroking over her body in the same manner. They would be tender, yet sure, soothing any

163

apprehensions she might have before he claimed her body with his own.

The blood surged into her cheeks as she realized what she was thinking, yet she smiled to herself all the same. Mira had been quite explicit in her explanation of marital intimacy. Tina had been somewhat mortified by what seemed to her to be an uncomfortable act, but Mira had told her someday she would understand—and welcome—the knowledge. And Mira had been right. If not for Mira, she knew right now she would be horrified by her body's reaction. Understanding it was natural made all the difference in how she felt.

Raising her eyes to his again, she said, "I suppose it is time to retire anyway, so no harm done."

Reluctantly Jay rose to his feet, pulling her up with him and into the circle of his arms. She felt so good against him, he didn't want to let her go. Nevertheless, he had tortured himself enough for one night.

"Thank you for my ring." Her voice trembled slightly.

"You're welcome."

Impulsively, she lifted up on her toes and brushed her lips against his lower jaw, that being as high as she could reach. Slipping out of his arms, she was at the door before his brain registered anything other than her touch. Opening the door, she turned back. Her eyes glowed as she gazed at him from across the room.

"Good night."

Then she was gone, the music of her voice remaining to tease him long after she had departed.

Jay fell back onto the settee, his hand going up to the spot on his jaw where she had kissed him. What the hell just happened? He glanced again at the closed door, seeing only a black-haired siren with blue-green eyes staring back at him, a smile on her lips. He felt as if he'd just been sucker-punched. And he still had to endure three more days!

Chapter Eleven

The next three days might have dragged for Jay, but for Tina they flew by. The house was cleaned from top to bottom and menus decided upon. Felicia had taken charge, leaving Tina little more to do than help supervise. It was a good move. More often than not, Tina was distracted, staring off into the distance, a dreamy look on her face. Felicia watched her with mild amusement, often sending her off to sit in the garden gazebo with a non-essential list of things to do. Felicia was enjoying the role-reversal, delighted to finally be of some help rather than the burden. Having decided she should be the lady of the house until Tina married Jay, she savored her newly assumed role.

Jay and Jon spent most of the time riding the estate and surrounding countryside, checking on tenants and local villages which relied on Collingswood. Word had spread and Jay found himself welcomed and congratulated many times during the days. As he and Jon catalogued repairs needing to be made, Jay often found himself thinking of Tina and the day he had ridden Thane Park with her and Felicia. Invariably, his recollection of the day centered around the kiss they had shared outside Daisy's cottage.

The evening before the appointed day, Tina and Jay discovered another reason for all the frenzied indoor activity of the prior two days as three carriages came rumbling up the drive shortly before dinner. Felicia, obviously on edge since tea time, fairly flew out of the front parlor where she and Tina had settled with last minute lists, Tina following at a more sedate pace. Jay and Jon came out of the library to investigate as the carriages disgorged their occupants.

The first to disembark was a tall, distinguished-looking gentleman with reddish-blond hair graying at the temples. Behind him, he helped out a woman. Golden blond hair styled in the latest fashion framed an arresting face inhabited by sharp blue eyes.

Jay stared in shock as Tina moved to his side and asked, "Do you know them?"

Sliding his arm around her waist, to give her support he told himself, he replied, "The Duke and Duchess of Westover."

She turned to Felicia in a panic. "Felicia! What have you done?"

Flashing them a brilliant smile, she replied, "Nothing, really," then turned and headed out the front door being held open by Keyes. Jay squeezed Tina's waist in assurance, then followed, leaving her with Jon.

"Did you know?" Tina asked her brother.

"No, and had I guessed she might do something like this, I would have waited until today to give her the letter from the duchess."

"She has no fear, you know," Tina told him. "It would never occur to her she shouldn't write to a duchess to whom she hadn't been formally introduced."

"Unfortunately, I suspect the duchess gave her the opening in the letter I delivered." The group outside, which had grown now to two others—obviously the occupants of the other carriage—was moving up the front stairs and into the black and white marble tiled entryway.

"I did not know if you would actually come, but I had rooms made ready just in case," Felicia was saying to the duchess as they came through the front door.

Introductions were made and Tina found herself thoroughly scrutinized before Felicia shepherded the ladies off to their rooms. Tina watched her sister in wonder, turning to Jon after the crowd had passed. "When did she grow up?"

Jon shrugged, unable to answer. With Felicia, one was never sure, so it was best not to speculate.

CR

The knock on her door came just as Milly was putting the final touches on her hair. Dressed in the aqua and white dress Madame had created for her, Tina felt a bit bare around the neck and shoulders, but beyond the pendant Nona had given her, which needed a good cleaning, she had only a set of pearls which she concluded would not do with the dress.

Milly answered the door and came back with a velvet case in her hand. Putting it down in front of her, she said breathlessly, "His lordship sent these—and he's waiting to escort you downstairs."

Opening the case, Tina found a necklace, bracelet, and earbobs obviously made to go with her ring. The necklace and bracelet were each triple strands of gems—diamonds, emeralds, and sapphires—set in a delicate lacework of gold, the earbobs a diamond surrounded by alternating emeralds and sapphires. As Milly fastened the necklace on, Tina wondered how he knew which dress she would be wearing this evening. Glancing in the mirror, she felt less bare than before, and was inordinately pleased with the result. The prospect of dining under the watchful gaze of a duchess set her stomach to fluttering.

Jay turned from the contemplation of a small landscape as she opened the door. For a moment, he merely watched her, causing her to worry all the more.

"Do I look all right?"

Raising her gloved hand to his lips, he hastened to satisfy her doubt. "You are beautiful," he rasped. "So much so that if there were any other unmarried men in the house, I would insist you dine in your room." His words were softened with a smile and a light brush of his lips against hers.

She smiled in return and allowed herself to relax as he escorted her toward the staircase. They were the last to enter the drawing room, making their entrance all the more conspicuous and bringing color into her cheeks.

Felicia rushed forward. "Oh, Tina, how lovely you look," she exclaimed. Looking up at Jay, she said, "The jewels are beautiful and perfect with the gown."

Jay chuckled as he relinquished her arm. "I'm glad you approve."

He didn't let it show, but he was amazed as well. Not by Tina, but Felicia. At sixteen, his sister was already a beauty. Thinking ahead two years, he was afraid it would take both he and Jon to keep her out of trouble when she finally made her debut. Remembering his speculation of the *ton*'s reaction to Tina, he wasn't sure he was equipped with an imagination vivid enough to predict their reaction to Felicia.

Felicia linked her arm in Tina's and ignored his comment. "Don't pay any attention to him," she told Tina, leading her toward a chaise where the duchess and her daughter-in-law, the Countess of Weston, sat. "You still have tonight to ignore him, but I suspect after tomorrow it will be impossible to do."

Tina did not correct her, but she knew it was already impossible for her to ignore Jay. She felt his presence whenever he was near, knowing even without looking, when he entered or left a room she happened to be in.

As it turned out, the countess was near her own age and the two became instant friends. She had the ability, Tina discovered, to put people at ease around not only herself, but her formidable mother-in-law as well.

"You must call me Geri," she told Tina, "but not too loud or Gerald will answer, too." Her brown eyes twinkled merrily as she turned to locate her husband across the room.

The men all stood in a knot at the far end of the room, sporting drinks as they chatted. Turning as well, Tina's eyes met Jay's and for a moment, the rest of the room vanished, until Jon said something and Jay turned to answer him.

After dinner, the women left the men to their port and gathered back in the drawing room to chat.

"I hope you don't mind that Felicia invited us," the duchess drew Tina aside for a moment. "As I told your brother, I knew and liked your mother. I wished we had stayed in contact after she left London."

"I have to admit I was apprehensive at first. Because we have spent all of our lives in the country, I suppose I worry excessively over whether I will fit," Tina confessed. "I realize Jay, I mean, his lordship, will have to spend some time in London, but I'm not sure I'm looking forward to it."

The duchess patted her hand comfortingly. "The *ton* can be

daunting at first, but I don't think you are likely to have any trouble. Geri and I will be delighted to help."

"Of course, it will be our pleasure," Geri agreed, joining them. "Besides," she declared, "I want to be there when the *ton* gets their first look at you and his lordship together. You'll be the talk of the town."

"And Lorry will not be able to ignore it this time," the duchess said gleefully. "Yes, my dear, you and that handsome husband of yours will set the *ton* on its ear."

"Who's Lorry? And what would she want to ignore?"

"The speculation, of course. Lorry, actually Lorraine, is the dowager Countess of Wynton—your grandmother," the duchess informed her. "She and I came out together, I won't tell you how many years ago. Unfortunately, she has grown into a bitter old woman after losing her husband and sons."

Tina greeted this revelation with stunned silence. "I never knew," she whispered.

"Knew what?" Geri asked.

"That I was named for her. It never occurred to me to ask where my second name came from."

The men joined them shortly afterwards and Felicia presided over the tea trolley. Jay lounged on the arm of Tina's chair, his hand absently toying with her curls. On the surface, Tina seemed oblivious as she conversed with Jon, the duchess, Geri, and anyone else who commanded her attention, yet she was acutely aware of his presence beside her.

In the middle of a discussion of young ladies' academies, Keyes entered and announced a late arrival.

"Teddy!" Jon exclaimed, greeting the young man as he crossed the room. "What brings you here?"

"Curiosity," Teddy answered. Approaching the duchess, he explained. "I arrived at Westover this morning, intending to make the acquaintance of my nephew, only to be informed you had all packed up and headed for Collingswood for a few days. How are you, Mama?" he asked, raising her hand to his lips.

The duchess wagged her finger at him. "I'm doing just fine, you naughty boy, but you'd best make your bows to your hostess or you might find yourself without a bed tonight."

Teddy straightened and surveyed the assembled group. Jon came to his rescue, presenting him to both Felicia and Tina, ensuring he understood Felicia was his hostess.

While Teddy was engaged in charming Felicia, Jay leaned over and whispered in Tina's ear, "Come for a walk with me."

She rose from her seat. "I think I will turn in," she said. "I will bid all of you a good night." She curtseyed to the duchess, then left the room on Jay's arm.

"I can imagine what they are thinking," she told him as they crossed the hall and entered a smaller salon, which they walked through to exit the french doors into the garden.

Jay shrugged his impossibly wide shoulders. "I'm sure you can, but the question is, do you care?"

The scent of roses and honeysuckle met them as they emerged onto the terrace. Crickets chirped and she could hear the small fountain gurgling.

She flashed him a sparkling smile. "At the moment, no. But there may come a time when I might."

Jay closed the doors behind them, shutting out the gathering inside. As he came up behind her, she felt his warmth engulf her. His hands settled on her waist and she leaned back against him, resting her head against his chest. She felt his chin come to rest on the top of her head.

"The duchess has agreed to take Felicia under her wing after tomorrow. She says she has been in contact with the same academy the countess attended and it has agreed to accept Felicia. One might say it was a little presumptuous, but Jon and I are quite happy to leave such things in her hands," he said.

"I hope it has a good music teacher. Felicia loves music."

"I will mention it to Her Grace."

"I was hoping she would not think Felicia presumptuous."

She felt the movement of his chest against her back as he chuckled. "The duke assured me she did not. In fact, she was expecting an immediate answer. When Felicia responded, she came immediately because she assumed we would not want to leave Felicia alone after the wedding."

"Jon would have been here."

"But not for very long. He only came so we could discuss our investigation. He is planning on leaving the day after. Remember, he knew nothing about a wedding until he arrived."

The conversation she'd had with Jon the day he'd arrived came back to her and she realized Jay was right. Jon arrived shortly before the gowns had, but said he'd ordered the gown she planned to wear tomorrow as a debut gown or a wedding gown—he hadn't known which.

"And how does the investigation fare?"

"We've hit some dead ends, but Jon will be pursuing some new avenues."

She nodded and vainly tried to smother a yawn.

"You must be tired," he said. "Tomorrow will be a long day."

She was comfortable leaning against him. Unfortunately, it was the comfortably relaxed feeling which was making her drowsy.

She smiled. "You're right. I should retire."

They reentered the house and ascended the stairs. Reaching her room, she turned to look up at him. In the deepening gloom, his eyes glittered with passion held severely in check. Awareness snaked down her spine. Tomorrow, they promised.

"Thank you for the jewelry." She hoped she didn't sound as breathless as she felt.

Jay did not move. Indeed, he wasn't sure he could at the moment. Nor did he want to. He could stare at her forever and not get his fill. Would he ever stop thanking his lucky stars for her grandmother's intransigence? The combination of innocence and passion drew him like a lodestone. The jewels around her neck and in her ears twinkled in the lamplight, but seemed dull against the brilliance of her eyes. He was going to drown, he decided. And he didn't mind in the least.

Moving closer, she put her hands on his chest, sliding them upward to rest on his shoulders. When she raised her face to his, he accepted the invitation and bent his head as she rose up on her toes. Their mouths met and his arms closed around her. Heat flooded his body, skittering through his veins, and setting him afire. Tomorrow couldn't come fast enough.

She didn't move when he raised his head. For the space of

a heartbeat, he stared into her eyes, then reached behind her and opened the door. "Tomorrow," he promised. Then he turned and headed down the hall.

CR

Tina awakened the next morning with Jay's promise still ringing in her ears and a vague sense of mortification. What had come over her last night? How could she have so brazenly kissed him? In the hall, no less. Perhaps she had become too comfortable in his presence. Of course, she speculated, it might have something to do with the fact that she was marrying him today. Maybe becoming comfortable also meant becoming bolder. Whatever it was, she wondered if she would be able to face him today, remembering her actions of the night before.

A knock on the door heralded the arrival of Milly, followed by two footmen carrying a large copper tub. Tina watched from beneath her covers as Milly directed the filling of the tub and added her rose fragrance to the water. Once the footmen left, Milly ushered her out of the bed and into the warm water, leaving her there to soak while she went for a tray for her breakfast.

Two hours later, dressed in the white and silver dress, her hair perfectly coiffed, the piece of lace attached to it at the top to drape down her back, she was ready to leave the room when Felicia entered, a velvet case in her hand.

Dressed in a light blue watered silk gown decorated with small white rosettes along the scalloped lower edge of the overskirt, the underskirt of white lace peeping through the scallops, Felicia reminded Tina so much of their mother she had to blink away the tears which sprung unexpectedly to her eyes.

"Jon asked me to give this to you and ask you to wear them. They go with the gown, he says." She handed the case to Tina and waited expectantly for her to open it.

Inside Tina found a double strand necklace of diamonds with earbobs to match. "Perfect," Felicia declared. "Stand still." An order. And, once the jewelry was on, "Let me look at you."

Felicia inspected her sister from all sides. The dress of

silver and white fit Tina perfectly, the skirts draped over numerous petticoats to give them definition and girth, while her shoulders rose out of the lace bertha of the top. With the addition of the jewelry, her neck and ears flashed with brilliant white fire.

Felicia also noted the shimmering anticipation in Tina's eyes. For today, there were no doubts, no insecurities, and no trepidation. *Good,* she thought, remembering Jay had already left for the church, impatience emanating from him in waves.

"Jon is waiting," she said now. "It's time."

℣

The Earl of Wynton watched his sisters descend the staircase. Their parents would have been proud of them, he thought. Tina and Felicia had grown into beautiful, apparently self-assured, young women. He knew Tina suffered bouts of self-doubt and had become especially introspective since meeting Jay. He expected her natural self-confidence would reassert itself once she was married and comfortably settled. Felicia, on the other hand, seemed to have no insecurities at all, and he didn't know if he looked forward to her debut with anticipation or dread.

Today, however, was Tina's day. He would worry about Felicia when the time came, but for now he would concentrate on seeing that today was as perfect as possible for Tina.

The whole village turned out for the wedding. An open invitation had been extended to the villagers and tenants of Collingswood and the tiny church was packed. Felicia entered the church first, stopping in the small entryway to wait for them to join her.

The local sheriff's wife had been enlisted to create the flower arrangements and Jon knew by Felicia's expression she had exceeded expectations. The scent of roses filled the small space, causing him to wonder if there was a rosebush left in the county which hadn't been denuded. The woman handed Felicia a small bouquet of forget-me-nots, peonies, and violets tied with white, silver, and blue ribbon.

Tina was handed a larger bouquet of the same flowers with

white roses added in, and tied with white and silver ribbon. Smiling her thanks, she turned to him as the music began and Felicia started down the aisle.

"Our parents would have been proud of you," he told her. "And I know they would have approved of Jay. Even Mama, who was unsure what he would be like."

"Thank you," she whispered. "And I'm sure Papa knows you kept your promise."

Then she turned to face the front. Jay stood alone in front of the altar. Felicia had decreed Jon was to perform double duty today. He was to give the bride away and stand up with the groom. Once the Westovers arrived, he and Jay had discussed asking Gerald to stand up with him, but Jay was content with the way Felicia had it all arranged. It was unusual, but so was nearly everything else about this wedding. Felicia reached the front of the church and turned to face the burgeoning pews. That was their cue, and he and Tina started down the aisle.

ᴄᴙ

"Superb!"

"Wonderful!"

"Well done!"

Such were the accolades Felicia received from their guests as the day wore on. Tina agreed they were well-deserved. Her sister had accomplished much in four short days.

After the ceremony, they had returned to a banquet set up on the expansive front lawn. Tables had been set out for the villagers and tenants, a large covered dais erected for the wedding party and their honored guests. The set up and atmosphere reminded Tina of a description she had read once of a medieval fair.

Even the weather cooperated, providing a light, cooling breeze in the afternoon when it could have been unbearably hot.

Jay rarely left her side for the duration of the celebration. As the two of them circulated among the guests, tenants and villagers alike congratulated them and wished them happy. It was a wonderful feeling for Tina, who had not been able to talk to anyone around Thane Park for more than a year. Although she had never spent much time at Collingswood, she found herself more and more at ease among its people. It also reminded her that she and Jay had to decide how to handle the animosity of the villagers around Thane Park. She did not want to feel uncomfortable in her own home when they returned in the fall.

Later in the afternoon, she sat with the duchess and countess beneath one of the various canopies erected as shade from the afternoon sun. The third carriage, it transpired, had contained the newest member of the earl's family and his nurse. William Michael Gerald Hartwell was barely a month old. Light blue eyes regarded the world around him with intense interest when he wasn't sleeping or clamoring to be fed. Naturally both parents and grandparents doted on him and he took it all in stride as his due.

Jay was crossing the lawn toward the small group when he abruptly stopped, seemingly turned to stone. His mouth went completely dry for a moment and his heart stopped as he took in the scene before him. His brain told him to stop staring and move, yet he remained, rooted to the spot. Frozen in time, he watched the group before him until a large hand fell on his shoulder, jolting him back, and he turned to find the duke's blue gaze twinkling at him.

"I remember the first time I saw my wife holding an infant, too," he explained, nodding toward the tableau before them where Tina sat on a rug, her white and silver skirts billowing around her, holding the baby in her arms. Her laughter rang out and Jay felt the sound settle in his chest. "It does strange things to a man to realize the possibilities, does it not?"

Jay managed to find his voice. "Yes, I suppose it does." It didn't matter that this wasn't the first time. He still felt the same way he had when she approached him holding Daisy's grandson.

The two men joined the group, Jay dropping onto the rug beside Tina. "He's almost the size of the twins already," Tina informed him, "and they are near four months."

Jay took in her animated features and looked down at the infant in her arms, before looking back up to make a suitable reply. The duchess spoke instead.

"I suspect his lordship is not necessarily interested in babies this day."

He turned to the duchess, mischief in his eyes. "On the contrary, your grace," he replied smoothly. "I find I am very much interested in babies these days. Especially the manner of their conception."

"Jay!" Tina blushed to the roots of her hair, as the others around her erupted in laughter.

A short time later as they walked away from the group, Jay apologized for his remark. "I did not embarrass you, did I?"

"No," she replied. "I was just surprised is all. But you were attempting to shock Her Grace, weren't you?"

He tried to remain somber, but a fleeting smile touched his lips. "Yes, I was. Not that it worked, mind you."

"She will be exactly what Felicia needs. Someone who is not shocked easily, but will not hesitate to take her to task if she needs it."

He agreed.

The rest of the afternoon and into the evening sped by. As the light waned, the locals all wandered away to their homes and soon, everyone else wandered indoors where an early dinner awaited.

"I suggest," Jay murmured to Tina as they went in to dinner, "that if you do not wish to bring attention to yourself later, you slip away right after dinner."

Tina looked up into eyes that could have devoured her on the spot. A rush of heat spread through her body, and she nearly melted into a puddle right then and there. Unable to speak, she merely nodded.

All throughout dinner, she felt Jay's gaze on her, the barely restrained passion almost physical in its intensity. She half expected to find burn marks on her skin from the fire she knew burned just beneath the surface. It was exciting and exhilarating all at once. And she thought dinner would never end.

As the ladies left the dining room, she turned, prepared to excuse herself, but the duchess did it for her. "Now is your chance, my dear. Hurry on upstairs before that husband of yours makes even more of a spectacle of himself."

There were general chuckles all around as she headed up the stairs, but Felicia had to have the last word. "Don't forget to turn left rather than right at the top," she called after her, and Tina wondered if one really could hang for strangling a younger sibling.

The master suite took up the whole of the bottom line of the "E". Tina approached the massive double doors as she had nearly everything else—pragmatically, but she could not help the frisson of anticipation that streaked through her body as she did.

Milly was waiting for her, and quickly stripped her of her finery and helped her into a nightgown of the finest white silk. The material slipped sensuously over her skin, clinging to every curve. Sitting passively while Milly brushed out her hair was difficult and when she started to braid it into its customary rope, Tina stopped her.

Trying not to blush, she said, "You may as well leave it, his lordship prefers it loose." Milly's smile of approval lit up her face and Tina knew the comment would be repeated to the delight of the rest of the staff. Despite her own misgivings and doubts, there was no doubt among the servants, tenants, and villagers that theirs was a love match. If only she could be so certain.

Rising to her feet, she dismissed Milly, knowing the maid was anxious to join the rest of the servants below stairs to continue their celebration. Milly had been disappointed over her refusal to wait in the large bed in the other chamber, however, she put her foot down at seeming too eager for Jay's arrival.

The suite was a knot of connecting rooms, consisting of two sitting rooms, two dressing rooms, a bathing room, and only one bedchamber containing a massive four poster bed of carved oak. As she wandered the suite, she noted one of the sitting rooms was nearly as large as the bedchamber, leading her to wonder if it had actually been another bedchamber at one time. The whole suite was decorated in white and gold with small touches of blue, except the bedchamber, which contained oak paneling with burgundy drapes and bedcovers. All in all, it was a beautifully and tastefully decorated suite.

Jay entered the bedchamber from his dressing room and

was not surprised to find the bed empty. He grinned in realization. Crossing the room, he paused in the doorway to the large sitting room.

It had once been another bedchamber and, until Keyes pointed it out to him yesterday, he had not realized it was no longer one. In answer to his query, he had learned that the previous marchioness, Tina's mother, had converted it because she never used the bedchamber. He remembered smiling at the thought. His father had obviously fallen hard if he had allowed that to happen. Reminding himself of what he knew of his own parents' marriage, he wondered if they had ever shared a bed again after his conception.

Tina knelt on a cushioned window seat, leaning slightly out of the open casement, staring up at the night sky. The outline of her derriere, clearly visible through the thin silk gown she wore, had him catching his breath as his lower body stirred. Leaning against the doorway, arms crossed over his burgundy brocade covered chest, he watched her for a few moments. Just as he had convinced himself she wouldn't turn, she did.

Her gaze trapped by his, she scrambled down off the seat and stood before it for a moment. Uncertainty chased across her features as she scanned his face, then she moved toward him. As she neared, he straightened and opened his arms. Without hesitation, she stepped into them, relaxing against him as he closed them around her.

"I was glad to see you took my advice and escaped."

Tina giggled and looked up at him. "I didn't have any choice. Her Grace all but ordered me up the stairs."

Jay scarcely heard her reply, so captivated was he by her animated face and sparkling eyes. He should be a candidate for sainthood for having resisted temptation all day. Either that, or he should be committed. Only now he no longer needed to worry about either. He could yield to the temptation she presented and indulge them both. After all, they had all night.

Lifting her in his arms, he carried her into the bedroom, kicking the door firmly shut behind them. The lamps had burned low, leaving the room in shadows. Yet even in the dim light, he could see her clearly. Putting her down on her feet beside the bed, he slipped the thin straps of the nightgown from her shoulders and watched as it slid into a shimmering puddle at her feet. She did not move. The only sign of her nervousness was the delicate blush that dusted her cheeks.

He lifted a handful of midnight silk and let the strands flow through his fingers. "Beautiful," he rasped. "So beautiful." Gathering her back into his arms, he bent his head and took possession of her mouth.

Tina's mind went blank. A jolt of pure sensation went through her from head to toe and her hands climbed to his shoulders, gripping them tightly, as a soft moan escaped her. The kiss was thorough and passionate, demanding complete surrender in a way that left her breathless with anticipation. One hand moved upward to cup a breast, his thumb moving lightly over the peak and causing her to catch her breath as he raised his head. The nipple hardened under his touch and she unconsciously leaned into him even more, pressing her breast completely into his hand.

The eyes staring down at her glittered in the meager light and Tina felt a surge of possessiveness shoot through her. He was hers. She had fulfilled her promise, and was glad it didn't feel like a duty. So far it had been nothing but pleasure and she expected the rest of the night would only bring more wonders.

His hand left her breast to brush the fall of her hair back from her face as he placed feathery kisses on her forehead, down the side of her face to her cheek and jaw.

"Soft, sweet, perfection," he murmured, his head dipping to her shoulder.

Tina gasped as she felt his tongue move across her collarbone, the feeling sensual, yet soothing. She could feel a peculiar tightness building in her midsection and slowly moving downward. Her knees were turning to water—a few more moments of this and they would no longer hold her. As if he read her mind, Jay scooped her up and deposited her in the middle of the bed.

Tina felt bereft for a moment as she watched Jay shrug free of his dressing gown. Lifting her arms in open invitation, she had no idea she had just fulfilled one of his fondest fantasies. She only knew he reacted to her invitation with surprise and delight, joining her hastily and taking her mouth in a kiss that heated her blood to boiling.

Time no longer existed for the two of them. Attuned only

one to the other and the responses they elicited from each other, they were submerged in a sensual haze that completely shut out the rest of the world.

Tina barely recognized the tiny whimpers of pleasure that issued from the back of her throat as Jay's hands and mouth alternately explored and ravished her body. Her restless hands explored the muscled contours of his back, and threaded through his hair, all the while wishing she was bold enough to touch him as familiarly as he touched her. She could not stop the startled cry that was wrenched from her as Jay touched her more intimately than she had ever touched herself.

She was burning up. Once unleashed, Jay's passion engulfed her, the flames licking along her skin like a slow spreading blaze that leisurely consumed everything in its path. Yet it gathered momentum, dragging her with it toward an unknown peak, magnifying the pleasurable feelings such that she barely noticed the slight twinge which accompanied his possession of her body. Quickly forgotten amid the new sensations surging through her, she gave herself up, allowing Jay to take her wherever he chose.

CR

It was sometime later when Jay remembered the moment she had come apart in his arms. Her cry of release had invaded his soul. He could not say how he knew, just that it had. And it unconsciously worried him. She had touched a part of him he had not known existed—or if he had suspected it existed, had thought long dead. She had given herself completely and unreservedly and he had uncovered a passionate nature beneath the calm exterior. But, it had come at a price. For, unknowingly, she had exposed a well of emotion within him. A well he did not want to acknowledge was there.

He could not possibly fall in love with her. He was incapable of the emotion. He felt possessive, protective, proud, and a host of other emotions toward her, but love? He would not give her that kind of power over him. Yet, at the moment, with her warm body softly draped over his, her breath delicately ruffling the hairs on his chest as she slept, he wondered if it truly mattered.

Of course, it would fit nicely into his plans if she fell in love with him. At least then, he could be certain of her forgiveness when she learned of the will. Jon had not been pleased to learn he had not told her, but had been persuaded to let him tell her in his own time. Yet, now that she was his wife, did she need to know at all?

Chapter Twelve

Could anything be more glorious than being kissed awake each morning? Or being stroked, caressed, and loved thoroughly before breakfast? How about opening your eyes only to find a dark, adoring gaze above yours?

Such were Tina's thoughts as she finally emerged from the master suite near teatime the next afternoon. Jay had warned her he was only letting her go because he knew Jon and Felicia were leaving with the Westovers the next day. After that, he told her smugly, delighting in the blush that rose in her cheeks, the servants might not see them for days on end.

She would learn later he had nearly exhausted himself in the days before the wedding, riding the estate and surveying the surrounding villages to determine what needed to be fixed or repaired. Likewise, Felicia had taken the household in hand while planning the wedding to ensure Tina would not need to give much thought to it for a while. It would, therefore, allow them days of uninterrupted time together before they left to inspect the mines in the wilds of Northumbria.

Hearing music coming from the direction of the drawing room, Tina entered to find Felicia entertaining the duchess and countess. They both welcomed her warmly. The men did not join them for tea, so they chatted about young ladies' academies, fashion, households, and other topics. Felicia was excited to be leaving with the duchess but the duchess insisted it was entirely her pleasure, having missed her own girls once they all married. It was an enjoyable afternoon that passed all too quickly.

CR

It was quite a different story for the men. Ensconced in the library, they pooled their collective information on Roderick Milton and came away with more questions than they had answers.

"No duel?" Jay asked Teddy. "Are you sure?"

"I tracked down a few of Aaron's old crowd. Grantham insists he would have known, but he says he knew of no one who might have challenged Aaron to a duel." Teddy's tone was grim. "And he says he's sure he was one of the last to see Aaron before he and Milton left London. Says Aaron said he was headed home to get leg-shackled. According to him, Aaron boasted the next time they saw him, he'd have the prettiest little thing on his arm."

"So, now what?" Jon asked. "If there was no duel, then how did Aaron die?"

"You said you were home on a holiday when Milton brought Aaron home. Did you see Aaron's body at all?" Jay inquired of Jon.

"No, not that I recall. But Mother told me he'd been shot through the heart."

"Hmmm." Weston steepled his fingers under his chin. "It just may be possible we are looking for a murderer—not just an embezzler."

"But why would Milton kill Aaron—if that is indeed what you are thinking?" his father questioned. "What would he gain?"

"Perhaps he wanted to stop Aaron from marrying," was the reply from Jon. "But why? He couldn't have possibly thought Tina would marry him instead."

"And this was a year before my father's death; the will did not exist yet. So, the question is—what would Roderick Milton gain by Aaron not marrying Tina?"

"That may, indeed, be the pivotal question in all of this. But, until we track him down, I'm not sure we will find the answers." Jon's statement had them all nodding in agreement.

"Did Grantham know anything else about Milton?" Jay

asked Teddy after a short silence.

"Not much. He said Aaron met him at some gaming hell. Apparently, Milton won a packet off Aaron one night and by the next evening they were fast friends. Said he thought he was from somewhere up north. Spoke once of a couple of older brothers. Never heard him mention any place in particular, though."

"What about Aaron's other friends?" This question came from the duke. "Grantham, as I recall, ran with a pretty wild crowd at one time." He turned to his oldest son, "Weren't Martindale and Jamison part of his crowd?"

"Hmmm, now that you mention it, yes. And there was a regimental officer who often tagged along with them. I met them once at a mill. What was his name? He and Milton had known each other before they came to London. It was a name close to Milton's. Millen? No. Molden? No. Milden. Yes, that was it, Milden! I remember even though everyone else called him Milton, this friend called him "Rod". Said it was an old nickname."

"Rod would be a short version of Roderick," Jay agreed. "Perhaps the assumption his name was fictitious is where we are failing."

"Milden?" Jon queried. "You're sure?"

Weston nodded. "Why?"

"I don't know. The name is very familiar, though. As if I should know it for some reason."

"We can have the detective see what he can dig up. Perhaps he can find this officer. You don't happen to remember which regiment he might have been part of?" Jay's voice carried a hint of hope. At least they had something more to go on.

"No, not at the moment. But, I will think on it. Perhaps it will come to me."

CR

Watching the coaches rolling down the drive, Tina felt as if a chapter of her life was closing. This would be the first time in her life without Felicia. Jon had been in and out since he started school many years ago, but since Felicia was born sixteen years ago, she had always been there. Now she was gone, too. For a moment Tina felt empty, then Jay slipped his arms around her waist, pulling her back against his hard, muscled body.

"It won't be the same without her," she whispered, resting her head against him. "We have never been separated."

"Think of it as an adventure," he suggested. "I would wager she is."

She turned then, looking up at perfectly molded lips that last night had taken her to previously undreamed of heights. She would miss Felicia, true. But she also looked forward to being alone with Jay. There were so many things she had yet to learn about him—and he about her.

The next fortnight was as idyllic as they come for Tina. She and Jay spent hours riding and walking the countryside, having picnics, fishing in the river, talking, reading, and, of course, in each other's arms.

While Jay ordered and began overseeing some badly needed repairs, she inventoried and took stock of the house. There were parts of the house needing refurbishing and she wrote copious notes and made sketches of possibilities. In addition, she tried to remember what needed doing at the Park as well. Consulting with Jay turned out to be a waste of time once he determined the extent of the changes she wanted to make.

"But, this will cost quite a bit, my lord," she told him. "At least let me know which ones I should pursue in some sort of prioritized fashion."

Jay looked up from the ledgers on his desk to his wife of less than a fortnight and wondered how he had managed before without her. She was a fount of information on general estate management, a talented musician, well-read, an engaging conversationalist, and a master pupil in bed. Every time he looked at her, his temperature rose, yet he was learning she could be tenacious when working on a project. The small changes she wanted to make to Collingswood and Thane Park had become such a project.

Her rose silk gown reminded him of the scent she wore, which somehow reminded him of how she had looked this morning shivering deliciously in his arms, which, in turn, caused his blood to heat.

"Tina," he said now, exasperation in every word, "unless you plan to tear down and rebuild both houses completely, I do not think these small changes will bankrupt us."

"Not all of these changes are small," she defended. "I would like to do some major remodeling at the Park and completely refurbish the dower house as well."

That got his attention. "Refurbish the dower house? Why?"

"Because it is nearly, to quote you, my lord, 'falling down around us'," she returned smugly.

"I agree it needs work—but not right now. If you must do it eventually, put it at the end of your list."

Tina cocked her head to one side and appeared to consider this for a moment. "Very well, my lord," she agreed and made a notation on the list she held.

Jay found a smile tugging at his lips as he watched her. She had been trying to provoke him, he now realized. They had been sitting in the library for most of the afternoon, each working on their own separate projects. She wanted his input, but he had been a grudging participant. Looking down at the ledgers he was trying to decipher concerning the family's mine holdings, he decided they could wait another day.

Rising, he strode around the desk and scooped her out of the chair.

"Jay!" Pad and pencil went flying as her arms latched onto his neck and held.

Carrying her over to one of the long couches positioned in front of the fireplace, he lowered the two of them onto it, covering her mouth with his as he did so.

Tina instantly forgot that she was annoyed with him. Her blood began to simmer, and her body turned to warm wax. The top of her gown was quickly opened, Jay's hand sliding inside seeking the softness of her breast.

"I'm glad you don't wear a corset," he had told her only a few days before. "Those things are a menace."

"If we go to London, I will have to," she had told him primly. "But they are uncomfortable, so I don't see any reason to wear them while in the country."

She was glad she had never cared about being fashionable. There were some things not worth the discomfort.

Jay's hands seemed to be everywhere. She wondered at times if he had three or four, yet she knew he only had two. She had checked. Her gown was quickly stripped from her as his hands caressed and stroked her intimately. The familiar excitement vibrated through her and she reached for the fastenings on his shirt.

"Oh, God, Tina," he rasped as her hands slid inside and over the lightly furred skin of his chest.

His mouth moved to her breast, nibbling, teasing, sucking, until she thought she would explode. Nothing could have prepared her for the instant passion that unerringly erupted between them each time Jay took her into his arms. Mira's descriptions had been tame in comparison.

"Jay," she whimpered. Her hands tangled in his hair and she arched her back, pressing her body closer.

"In a moment, sweet," he murmured, then his mouth claimed hers in a deep, drugging kiss that blotted out all but the two of them.

ᘓ

Sometime later, Jay roused himself sufficiently to look down at his wife nestled partially beneath him in the cushions of the couch. Soft, sweet, and oh, so giving, he wondered what he could possibly have done to merit such perfection. He had done too many things in his life of which he was not proud. And there were times when marrying Tina counted as one of them. He should have told her of the will. But at times like now, as he watched her lashes lift to reveal tropical pools still glazed with passion, he was convinced he had chosen the right course.

He wasn't sure he believed in fate or destiny, but the old gypsy who had helped him as a lad of sixteen had. It was she who had warned him he would be restless for many years, but would return to eventual peace and happiness. He had not believed it then—and he wasn't sure he believed it now. But, the truth was unmistakable. With Tina, he seemed to be at peace—and happy.

Tina stretched sinuously and his body stirred again. Rolling further onto his side, he gathered her into his arms. "Was I crushing you?"

Tina smiled. "Of course not." Looking over his shoulder, she surveyed the clothing littering the surrounding pieces of furniture. "We had best make sure we find everything this time. I don't know that Mrs. Harper's heart would survive finding another article of clothing in here."

His rumble of laughter had her giggling in response.

"Perhaps," he chuckled, "if you didn't wear so many layers, you wouldn't lose them all."

Tina gasped in pretended outrage. "Perhaps, my lord," she returned cheekily, "we should confine these activities to our bedchamber—where the servants might expect such things to happen."

Jay grunted. "I think not. The servants are paid well enough not to be offended by a little sex. If there are prudes on the staff, they should be confined to the kitchen."

"Which is probably the only room in the house you don't consider fair game for such activity," she quipped.

Jay's eyebrows rose at her impudent statement. "On the contrary, madame," he told her with an exaggerated leer, "any room I find you in is fair game."

Tina had no reply to the outrageous statement, but moments later all was forgotten as Jay took her mouth in a long, tender kiss that left her lungs gasping for air and enveloped her body in a sensual fog.

CR

Growing up in Devon with only occasional trips to Exeter, Tina was unprepared for the sprawling metropolis that was London. Gazing out the window of the carriage as they entered the suburbs of the city, she was amazed at the streets, people, buildings, carriages, and general chaos which seemed to inhabit the thoroughfares of the capital. Dusk was beginning to settle as they reached the quieter section of the city where the very wealthy lived.

The door to Thane House opened as the carriage drew to a halt in front. As Jay helped her alight, she looked up at the large, but plain, three-story brick-fronted house. It looked much like the houses on either side of it with its large windows looking out over the square in front. The wrought iron gate leading to the steps was being held open by a footman, and Jay ushered her through. Entering the house, she didn't have time to look around the vast entryway as the entire staff had been assembled to meet its new mistress.

Jay introduced her to the butler, Keyes, who also happened to be the father of the butlers at Collingswood and Thane Park, and the housekeeper, Mrs. Greaves, who, in turn, introduced her to the rest of the staff. Mrs. Greaves beamed as Tina spoke a few words to each person.

"I know we will only be here for a week this time," she told Mrs. Greaves as the housekeeper escorted her upstairs, "but I will need to visit a few shops to pick out some samples for some refurbishing that needs doing at the Park and Collingswood. Since this is my first trip to London, I'm hoping you will be of assistance in suggesting shops and businesses."

"Of course, my lady," Mrs. Greaves answered, obviously honored to be looked to for such advice. "I still have the swatches and sketches from the last time some changes were made to this house. The late marchioness was very pleased with the tradesmen she did business with then."

"Wonderful," Tina replied enthusiastically. "I'm sure those will give us someplace to start."

The housekeeper opened an ornately carved door and stood back to allow Tina to enter. "This is your ladyship's room," she said, following her in. "There is a sitting room through there," she pointed to her left, "and his lordship's chamber is through that door," she pointed to her right.

Tina looked around. The room was large, bright, and airy, decorated in white and blue. At the moment, the large four poster bed was covered with a rainbow of fabrics, as Milly was already present, in the process of unpacking.

Mrs. Greaves left after informing her his lordship had requested dinner be served at eight.

"The house is beautiful," she told Jay over dinner. "Especially the entry hall. The staircase is quite magnificent."

Indeed, she had been awed by it as she descended to the drawing room before dinner. The entryway rose two stories high, a large gold and crystal chandelier hanging in the center. But, by far, the centerpiece of the hall was the staircase. Gleaming white marble, with highly polished mahogany banisters, it rose to a landing halfway to the second story, then split into three separate sections, each leading to the three separate wings of the house. It would be the perfect staircase to stage a grand entrance upon.

"For that you must thank some distant ancestor," he replied. "But, for your suite, I understand you must thank your mother."

"Mama had exceptional taste. At least Papa, I mean, your father, always said so."

Jay chuckled at her slip. "You need not worry about how you refer to my father. I understand that, for you, he was the only father you really knew and, therefore, you felt close to him."

"And you did not, my lord?"

Jay shook his head. "No, I did not. But, you saw a side to him I still have trouble believing existed."

"Why is that?"

Jay thought for a moment, wondering whether he would destroy her memories if he answered her truthfully. Then he wondered why it mattered if he did. After all, marrying her had been the means to an end. Having accomplished that, did he care whether she believed in fairy tales?

"Because the father that I knew was an embittered old man. He never laughed, unless it was at someone else's expense. He was a philandering husband and an unyielding father who felt showing affection to his sons would make them soft." His voice had become hard and his eyes grew cold. "In short, he was the exact opposite of what you and Jon have told me he was."

Tina's astonishment at the depth of hurt and anger in his response was obvious. "Perhaps he changed after you left," she said encouragingly. "People do, you know."

Jay did not answer. He knew people changed. After all, he had. He had walked away from Collingswood an angry boy, not caring whether anyone would wonder what had happened to him. He had only wanted to get away. He had deliberately stayed away, even after he had learned of Aaron's death, not wanting it to be true, but perversely wanting to make his father suffer and wonder about the fate of the family holdings. It had never occurred to him—and no one he met in his travels from England had ever mentioned it—his father might have remarried. He wondered briefly if his father would have bothered trying to locate him after Aaron's death if Felicia had been male.

"Mama always said love changes people for the better," Tina continued cheerfully. "Perhaps that is what happened. I know he and Mama loved each other deeply."

Her words brought him back. "What about your father?"

Tina blinked at the seeming change of subject. "What about him?"

"Did your mother care for him?"

"Yes," she sighed. "She loved him very much. But," she continued, "as she told me once, it was different."

"How so?"

"She said people see things differently at different stages of their lives. She told me once that had she met your father during her season, she would have considered him too old and not given him a second thought. At eighteen, she said, someone with already half-grown children would not have seemed exciting enough."

"But at what, six and twenty, a man twice her age was acceptable?" There was patent disbelief in his tone. It had crossed his mind more than once that his father's second wife might have been little more than an adventuress. Yet, from all accounts it did not seem to be true.

"She was seven and twenty," Tina responded, "and I suppose from another's point of view, it might have appeared as if she married merely to provide security for herself and her children."

That wasn't all it looked like, he thought. It also occurred to him that his father might have married her just to get her into his bed. After all, if his stepsister truly was the mirror image of her mother, his father might have been willing to tie the knot again to possess her—especially if she wasn't amenable to an affair.

"But Papa's gentleness won her over."

Jay had to suppress his snort of disbelief over the last statement. Gentle? His father? Not bloody likely! More than likely it was a facade designed to get her into his bed, and if he had to take a trip to the altar to do it, so be it. After all, he hadn't been faithful in his first marriage, what difference did it make whether he married her or not?

⚭

Jay was off the next morning to the offices of his shipping company. Spending the morning checking bills of lading, checking on and signing purchase orders, he was surprised to find the time fairly flew by. Knowing it would take the better part of the rest of the week to finish catching up, he left, promising the manager he would return the next morning.

Tina also spent a profitable morning getting acquainted with the house and staff. Mrs. Greaves, she discovered, was a fount of information and, having lived all of her life in London, knew the city intimately. And so it was that by luncheon, Tina had a list of those shops her mother had previously employed in refurbishing some of the rooms, and had looked over her mother's notes.

In addition to her own suite, her mother had redecorated the dining room and a small private parlor at the back of the house for herself. She had left sketches and suggestions for redoing the large drawing room and the ballroom. After inspecting both rooms, Tina decided to carry out her mother's plans.

Over luncheon, Tina chatted excitedly about her morning and afternoon plans. She had instructed Mrs. Greaves to send round to some of the shops to request the proprietors send over some fabric swatches and samples, so she might begin to discuss her plans. Some had agreed to do so, but others had requested appointments to personally show their wares.

Jay didn't understand the strange disappointment that came over him at learning her afternoon was scheduled. He had thought she would spend the day settling in before getting down to business. But he was learning Tina rarely spent time being inactive.

Still oddly disappointed, he set off after lunch to see if Mr. Pymm had uncovered anything yet. After spending a fruitless hour at the detective's office while a clerk checked on Mr. Pymm's whereabouts, he was discouraged to learn Mr. Pymm was still "up north" somewhere, having been asked to check out some new possibilities by Lord Wynton. Leaving a message for the detective to contact him if he returned within the week, he set out for his club.

Because most of the nobility vacated the city during the summer, White's was virtually deserted. He thought Jon might have returned to town, but a trip by Kent House revealed the knocker still off the door. Settling in a comfortable chair, he spent a quiet afternoon perusing the Times, and catching up with the few patrons who happened by.

Not wishing to repeat the inactivity of the day before, the next morning before leaving for the docks, Jay left a message for Tina informing her that after luncheon he would take her out to see some of the sights of the city. He told himself he shouldn't be surprised she had a list of places she wanted to see, including the Tower of London, a number of museums, and the Crystal Palace, site of the Exhibition of 1851, but he had been, nevertheless.

All in all, it was a productive, if unsettling, week. Had anyone asked him before they arrived in the city, Jay would have predicted Tina would have stayed at home and waited for him to escort her whenever she wanted to go somewhere. Instead, his seemingly shy and somewhat retiring wife suddenly blossomed. With her maid in tow and Mrs. Greaves as a guide, Tina spent hours shopping. Looking over fabric, wall coverings, upholstery, mouldings, furniture makers' sketches and designs, Tina seemed tireless in her pursuit of the perfect materials with which to accomplish the refurbishing she wanted to do. By the time they left at the end of the week, she had commissioned a number of items to be made, and the large drawing room and ballroom to be redone by their return.

Jay was astounded. What happened to the young woman who had gone into shock in Parkton? What happened to the cautious woman who worried over Milton's retaliation after Felicia gloried in driving him away? What happened to the seemingly biddable woman he thought he married? More than once, he found himself rethinking his reading of his wife. And worrying more and more what she would do if she found out about the will.

∝

Tina fell in love with Kenwyck Manor on sight. Situated on a small promontory overlooking the sea, the small brick dwelling boasted only twenty rooms in all. Mr. Green and his wife, the caretakers, were pleased to see them, having expected them for the last few days.

"Tis glad we are you made it, my lady," Mrs. Green said as she showed Tina to her suite. "We was hopin' you was merely delayed. But you never know."

Tina was touched by the concern. They had left London two days later than scheduled because of some plan changes, then had taken their time sailing up the coast. The duke had put his yacht at their disposal and Jay pointed out not only was it a much quicker trip by sea than by road, but during the summer, it was a very pleasant voyage. Tina had been fascinated by the sea and spent hours standing at the railing watching the coast roll by.

Disembarking at Newcastle, Jay hired a coach to take them to Kenwyck Manor. Tina was enchanted on sight.

Now, settling in, she smiled at Mrs. Green and assured her they had, indeed, only been delayed.

They spent three nearly perfect weeks by the sea. Part of the time was taken up with traveling into Newcastle, then further inland to inspect the mining properties near Hexham. All was in order and Jay spent a couple of days conferring with his foremen over improvements.

Tina found the countryside around Newcastle beautiful.

From the heather covered moors around the mines to the rolling countryside around the city, thence to the sandy beaches of the coast, Tina found something new and interesting everywhere she turned.

"I hope we spend more time here," she told Jay one afternoon as they walked along the sandy beach below the manor. "It is so beautiful and peaceful."

Jay chuckled as he watched her gaze out to sea. The gulls flying overhead screeched at each other, occasionally landing on the shore to pluck something out of the sand. She had removed her shoes and stockings, lifting her peach skirts just enough not to get wet as she allowed the water to wash over her toes. With her hair tumbling down her back past her waist, she looked like a young girl frolicking in the waves.

"You might not think so were you to be here when a winter storm blows in."

"Surely, they can't be *that* bad. Mrs. Green informs me Kenwyck Manor has stood for well over a hundred years. If it has withstood winter storms for that long, I would feel safe enough."

"You are not afraid of storms?"

"No. In fact, I find them fascinating. Mama used to have to remind me not to stand too close to the windows when we had storms back at the Park," she told him. "Felicia never liked them, though, but she would sit with me sometimes even though she was afraid. She never wanted anyone to know she was."

"Somehow that doesn't surprise me."

There were letters waiting for both of them when they returned to the manor for tea. Felicia, now firmly settled at Miss Ridley's Academy for Genteel Young Ladies, was a tireless correspondent and Tina found herself looking forward to her letters. They were often full of interesting tidbits she was learning, as well as funny incidents involving her new-found friends. In short, she was enjoying herself, which put Tina's mind at ease.

Jay, on the other hand, received two missives, only one of which could be said to have had any good news in it.

Chapter Thirteen

"How would you like to take a short trip?"

Tina looked up from her poached salmon. "To where?"

"North Road Manor."

Tina was puzzled for a moment, then comprehension dawned. "Where Mama grew up?"

Jay nodded.

"But isn't it a distance away?" she asked. "It's near the Scottish border."

"Yes, it's near the Scottish border, but so is Newcastle—nearly. As it turns out, it is near a small hamlet called Byrness, just northwest of Newcastle."

Tina sat back in her seat in dazed wonder. "Somehow, I always pictured it on the western side, near the road to Gretna Green. I suspect the name had something to do with that."

"To be sure, I had suspected the very same thing. However, I suppose since there is also a road there, it, too, could be considered a north road. I'll do some checking on how to get there tomorrow, then perhaps the next day we can go."

Two days later, they set out in a coach for North Road Manor. It was a warm day, a cooling breeze making it more comfortable than it might have been. Jay warned her it would be a long drive—and they might have to make the drive back if their reception was inhospitable. Tina hadn't cared. The opportunity to see where her mother had been born and raised was an irresistible lure.

The rolling hills were green and lush, dotted with heather, a purple flower more commonly associated with Scotland than

England. Along the way, they noted pasture upon pasture of grazing sheep and cattle—with the occasional farmer's field thrown in. The bucolic scenery reminded her occasionally of the Devon countryside, minus the heather, of course.

They stopped at a small inn along the way, enjoying a surprisingly good meal, then, assured by the innkeeper they were headed in the right direction, continued on their way. Jay was heartened by the cleanliness of the inn, noting to Tina after they left, if necessary, they could spend the night there on the way back. The concern was for naught, however, as they were greeted warmly at North Road Manor by Sir Ralph Tindale and his wife. Jovial and warm, the two insisted they stay the night after their long trip.

Unfortunately, they were of little help in Jay's search.

"Hmmm. A young man did come by here looking for my cousin and his wife some years back, but I don't recall his name," Sir Ralph told Jay after dinner. "He was disappointed to learn they were dead and we did not know the whereabouts of the daughter."

"Did he talk to anyone else? Is there anyone else still here who might have known your cousin and his family?"

"Well, my housekeeper was here before I came. She probably knew somethin'. Old Martha prob'ly knew them as well. She's older than the hills. But, I don't know if that young man talked to either of them."

"As a matter-o'-fact he did," the housekeeper replied after being summoned. "Said t'were important he find my little Felicia. Course, I only knew she had married and sailed off to India. Married a soldier, she did. That was all I knew, my lord."

"He didn't happen to mention his name or where he was from, did he?"

The little old woman shook her head. "He did say if'n he didn't find her, he might be back to see if I 'membered anythin' else. But, I'm supposin' he found her, 'cause he ain't been back."

"He didn't say why he was looking for her, did he?" Jay pressed.

The housekeeper thought for a few moments. "No, m'fraid not."

"Anything else you might remember about him?" Jay asked hopefully.

But the housekeeper shook her head sadly. "No, my lord."

They spent another whole day in the area talking to very old people who remembered the previous baronet, his lady, and their daughter, but learned nothing except the young man who had come asking had been from "somewhere south".

"Considering the location of this place, 'somewhere south' is the whole of England," Jay remarked to Tina as the coach rumbled down the drive away from North Road Manor.

Tina giggled. "I suppose it is." Settling back against the comfortably padded squabs, she sighed, and turned to contemplate the countryside rolling by. "But it was nice to see where Mama grew up. It truly was a beautiful place, if a little remote."

"It's too bad no one remembered more about your mother."

"Old Martha told me I resembled my grandmother more than my mother, except for my eyes, of course. She told me stories about my mother growing up, but I'm not sure any of them will help you to find Mr. Milton." Turning from her consideration of the scenery outside the window, she raised her eyes to his. "Do you really need to still find him?"

"Yes, we do." Startled, Jay's answer was curt, brooking no argument. Tina was not deterred.

"Why?"

"Why?"

"Yes. Why?" she echoed. "Why is it so important you find him?"

"Because he must be made to pay for his crimes." Jay's tone seemed to imply she should understand this.

"Because he embezzled money from the estate?" she asked. "After all, he didn't murder anyone, so why...?"

"We aren't so sure he didn't."

Tina stared, uncomprehending. "Didn't what?"

"Murder someone."

Tina was speechless. "But, who...?" Then, understanding. "Aaron?"

Jay watched her closely. He still wasn't sure of her feelings for Aaron. He had admitted to himself he was afraid to ask and, until now, they had only discussed him in reference to the betrothal contract.

"According to Lord Weston and his brother, who questioned some of Aaron's friends, one of the last ones to see him alive— besides Milton—was a chap by the name of Grantham. He insisted Aaron was in high spirits the night before he was supposed to leave London. He even told Grantham he was heading home to get married. In addition, Grantham could think of no one who might have challenged Aaron to a duel. Aaron, he said, just wasn't duel material."

Tina couldn't think. She was immobile with shock. Aaron had been murdered? Had she brought it on? She couldn't have—could she? Nona would have said she set the wheels in motion. She had told her once before when you wished hard enough for something, you create conditions which make it possible for it to happen. But, how would she have made Mr. Milton do it? She wished she had confided in Nona and asked her about it. Now, she only had the guilt and what ifs. Looking down at her hands clasped tightly in her lap, she took a slow deep breath to calm her racing heart.

Jay watched the series of emotions pass through Tina's eyes before she dropped them to her lap. From horror, to guilt, to anguish. An anguish so deep she seemed to be tearing herself apart. Had she really felt so deeply for Aaron?

"Tina?"

She raised tormented, tear-filled eyes to his. "It's all my fault," she whispered, pain in every word. Then, as the tears spilled over, she buried her face in her hands and her shoulders began to shake.

For a few moments, Jay was frozen in shock. All her fault? Of course, it wasn't her fault. How could she think that? She hadn't introduced Roderick Milton into the family. She'd been just as much of a victim, perhaps more so if you didn't count Aaron. After all, Aaron had been the person who had made friends with Milton. He had possibly sealed his own fate by doing so. How could it be her fault?

Reaching out, he scooped her off the seat and set her in his lap, cradling her close. The tears were running rivulets down her cheeks, but she made so little noise if he hadn't seen her, he would not have known she was crying. Fishing his handkerchief out of his pocket, he pressed it into her hand.

"It's not your fault," he soothed. "Of course it's not your fault."

"But it was," she insisted between sniffles. "I—I wished it."

"Wished it?" He was clearly perplexed. "Wished what?"

"That he wouldn't come back," she gulped. "I was so frightened. And it was so horrible, I was sick. I didn't want..." her voice trailed off.

Jay waited for her to continue. When she didn't, he prompted her. "Didn't want what?"

"Him to come back. I wished he would stay away and forget about me." Completely lost in her thoughts, she continued. "Nona said if you wish hard enough for something, it somehow comes true, but not always in the way you want it to. And I wished so hard he would never come back," she sobbed. "But I didn't mean it that way. I never meant for him to die."

The realization exploded in his head. She was talking about Aaron! She hadn't wanted to marry him! For some reason, his spirits soared. He suddenly wanted to shout with joy. But, he had to quell the emotion. Tina needed him at this moment. Time enough later to savor his triumph.

"I didn't want him to die!" she cried. "I just wanted him to stay away."

She was shaking uncontrollably now and he could feel her tears soaking through his shirt.

"Tina," he tipped her face up to his, "Tina, listen to me. You had nothing to do with Aaron's death. It was not your fault. You cannot wish people away."

"I know," she whispered. "I know logically, it couldn't happen. But, I wanted it so badly, you see. I shouldn't have wanted it so much. I should have just told Mama and Papa. They wouldn't...they wouldn't have forced me." The words seemed to just tumble out, one over the other. "But, I—I was so afraid. I didn't want to disappoint Papa. And I had liked him before. I tried to convince myself that...that after we were married he would...would be nice to me again. That he might not mind I wasn't beautiful. That..." she hiccupped. "That I could be a good wife to him. That..."

And the revelations went on as he held her, the tears continuing to seep from beneath her lashes. How Aaron had, at first, been a fun companion, and someone to look up to. How he had begun to change after he went off to London and made friends with Mr. Milton. How she had thrown herself into becoming the perfect marchioness so he wouldn't be ashamed of her. And on and on, until she revealed the last time she had seen him when he had kissed a frightened sixteen-year-old into submission and promised more upon his return. And, lastly, how she had been physically ill for days after he left, but afraid to tell her parents what had happened.

Rage burned in his chest over what she had suffered. He had been so fixated on finding out what Milton had done and why, and discovering he might have actually killed Aaron in cold blood had bolstered his determination to find him no matter what the cost. He had not looked carefully enough at Tina. He hadn't wanted to ask her outright about Aaron, merely supposing she had been looking forward to marrying him and becoming mistress of Thane Park. And she had at first.

Aaron had stripped away all her dreams in an unnecessarily cruel moment. What could have possessed him to intimidate a child in such a way? He wondered, now, if his father would have allowed Aaron to marry Tina at sixteen. Would his father have been so eager to secure the next generation for Thane Park had he known? It infuriated him she had been subjected to such abuse and left with a promise of more. Then to have lived with the guilt over Aaron's death.

Jay didn't want to examine too closely his feelings when it came to Tina. It was easy to chalk it up to protectiveness, now she was his wife. But, a niggling doubt in the back of his mind and a simmering anger in the region of his heart, caused him to question even that rationalization.

Tina was subdued for the rest of the ride home and he was relieved when they finally reached Kenwyck. He had left her to her thoughts, not knowing what else to do, although he had held her in his arms for most of the trip. There seemed to be nothing else he could say to convince her she hadn't wished Aaron dead.

After a late dinner, he retreated to the study to look over

some papers and write a letter while she headed upstairs.

He would leave her alone this night, he told himself as he climbed the stairs much later. She had received a shock today and needed her rest. She was probably asleep anyway. He did not doubt she would be in better spirits tomorrow. Yet, he knew he would miss her warmth. He had become used to waking up beside her every morning.

He was lying in bed, still awake, an hour later when the connecting door opened.

Tina approached the massive bed quietly. She had not been able to sleep and had waited for Jay to join her. She acknowledged to herself she needed his continued reassurance. But when he hadn't appeared, she began to worry he had been repelled by her admission this morning in the carriage. He had firmly told her she couldn't possibly have wished Aaron's death, but he had been politely solicitous the rest of the day. Perhaps he wished he hadn't married her now he knew. Every logical and rational fragment of her brain told her he didn't believe she had anything to do with Aaron's death, but the emotional part of her—the part of her that loved him—told her otherwise.

And love him she did. Completely, absolutely, overwhelmingly. So, now what? She wanted to know. Now. Before her courage deserted her, she decided. She needed to know if he had developed a disgust of her.

She knew he was still awake. Even though he hadn't moved, she could sense it. She wasn't sure what to do. Suppose he wanted to be alone? Should she intrude on his privacy? It was too late to turn back, however. He knew she was there and if she turned and left, would he let her? Indecision kept her immobile for a moment as she warred with her thoughts, but impulsiveness won out in the end and she lifted the covers and slid into the bed—and into Jay's waiting arms.

She had never felt so relieved in her life when he asked no questions, but merely settled her beside him. A soft sigh escaped her as she relaxed completely against his large, warm body. She was asleep in minutes.

CR

"The Marquis of Thanet, my lady," the butler announced as Jay strode into the drawing room at Number 19, Park Court. Seated on a sofa upholstered in dark green velvet, the dowager Countess of Wynton looked up from the cup of tea she had just poured herself. A fashion magazine sat open in her lap, but she put it aside as she set down the cup and rose to meet him.

"I don't suppose you've come to tell me that you changed your mind and are still nominally in charge of the earldom," she said in greeting.

He raised her blue-veined hand to his lips. "I'm afraid not, my lady."

Frowning at his answer, she motioned for him to take a seat and resumed her own as he settled on a matching sofa across from her. "Then to what do I owe this visit, this time?" she asked. "Tea? Or would you prefer something stronger?"

Jay declined the offer, aware he probably would not be there above a few minutes once he relayed his information.

"I have merely come to ensure you were aware of our new relationship," he said cryptically. "And to, shall we say, request your cooperation."

She had once been a lovely woman. Not beautiful in the accepted sense, her features were too strong. But the wide-spaced green eyes and pale blonde hair would probably still be striking if it wasn't for the bitterness permanently marked on her expression. Her eyes narrowed at his comment and he knew she understood that his request was a mere formality.

"What kind of cooperation?"

"The kind which requires you do nothing to cause my wife discomfort in public."

She pressed her lips together in a straight line, her hand going to a locket suspended from a delicate chain about her neck. "And why should I bother with your wife?"

"You shouldn't," he stated. "You have made it clear to me you have no interest in your grandchildren, and the *ton* is aware you will not receive the current earl. Once they learn my wife is his sister, the rumors will fly all on their own."

"I cannot control that."

Jay inclined his head in acceptance. "I'm aware of that. However, you can refuse to add to them."

"And what will you do for me in return?"

"I, or rather we, will not presume upon the connection. You may continue to nurse your own bitterness over something you cannot change in private, but if it spills over and causes Tina embarrassment or a moment's uneasiness," his voice hardened as he continued, "you will answer to me."

Her eyes widened at his tone and a flicker of uncertainty appeared in the emerald depths. "I see."

He studied her for a moment, then spoke before he could stop himself. "I wish you did."

Her eyes hardened at the comment. "Pardon?"

"My wife and her brother are the only family you have left, yet you continue to live in the past, holding them responsible for a situation over which they had no control. Even so, Tina would welcome you with open arms should you take the first step. I, on the other hand, do not have the same generous capacity for forgiveness. You would do well to remember that."

Confident his message had been understood, he rose from the sofa. "I am grateful to you, by the way," he said as he did so.

The countess continued to stare up at him, her green eyes glittering. "Grateful to me? For what?"

"For ignoring your granddaughter, of course."

She had no retort to that comment so he continued.

"Had you acted the part of a caring grandmother and brought her out once she was out of mourning, she would have been the toast of the town and could have had her pick of anyone. As it was, she settled for me, but I consider myself extremely fortunate on that score, as you will see tonight at the Westover ball. So you see, I am in your debt."

Then he bowed to her and exited the room, leaving her speechless. Collecting his hat and cane from the butler, he stepped out into the crisp early evening air.

Mission accomplished.

CR

The Earl of Wynton stood chatting with a group of friends in the midst of the ballroom at Westover House when a sudden hush fell over the crowd. It wasn't just your average lull in the conversation which occasionally happens at such gatherings. For the span of at least two heartbeats, you could have heard a pin drop in the room. Then the whispers began anew, this time with an urgency only new gossip could carry.

Next to him, Teddy chuckled. "Mama got more than she bargained for this time. I hope she's satisfied."

Jon turned from watching Jay and Tina descend the wide staircase to his friend. "She knew they would cause a sensation. And she was right."

"Egads!" one of the other young dandies in the group exclaimed. "I must have an introduction."

"As long as it is only an introduction," someone else replied. "I suspect Thanet would not take too kindly to poachers."

"Never say she's already taken," the first voice groaned. "Did someone say she had a sister?"

"'Fraid so," was the reply. "And the sister's much younger," the second voice said as the two moved off.

Jon and Teddy looked at each other, mirth gleaming in their eyes, and headed for the couple.

Tina knew she would not remember any of the names tripping so easily from the duchess' tongue as she and Jay were introduced. She had been initially excited at the prospect of attending her first ball, but now she was here, apprehension had reared its ugly head. Looking up at yet another old gentleman who professed to know her mother and Jay's father, she wondered if she would survive the experience.

A waltz started up and Jay led her onto the floor. She was quiet for the first part of the dance, finding her feet and absorbing the rhythm of the music.

"So far, so good," Jay spoke above her.

Looking up, she noticed he was smiling. "I hope so," she answered. "I just hope I don't embarrass myself by forgetting some important person's name."

"Don't let it worry you. We'll both muddle through. I have been gone so long I remember few people myself."

"Oh." Her eyes widened. "I had forgotten." Then she smiled and she knew eyes glowed in the light of the chandeliers. Dancing with Jay was a wonderful experience.

"We should have stayed home," he grumbled.

"Why?"

"Because I'm selfish. I'm not up to sharing you just yet."

Her smile widened and she glanced around them. "Very well," she responded. "If you don't have to share, I won't either." She hadn't missed the hungry female eyes following him. A small twinge of jealousy was quickly replaced by a feeling of pride that he was hers. She'd chosen to wear the aqua gown with the accompanying jewels tonight just for him. The light in his eyes when she'd descended the staircase had given her confidence.

The set ended and Jay escorted her back to where the duchess stood. Her eyes brightened at the sight of her brother and his friend standing with the duchess. She and Jay had only been in town two days and this was the first she had seen of him. She hadn't had a chance to tell him about their trip to North Road Manor.

"I am the envy of every woman here," she told him as he led her out for a country dance.

"And why is that?" he asked.

"Because I have been here for less than a half hour and have already danced with the two most handsome men in the room."

Jon's smile flashed. "Where did you learn to flatter?"

She looked at him from under her lashes, a mischievous sparkle in her eyes. "It's not flattery, it's the truth. But, if you wish to categorize it with all the other flummery you hear, you may do so."

He laughed outright then. "Who am I to contradict such an unbiased source?"

"You shouldn't."

The evening was an unqualified success for Tina. By the

end of the evening, she had thoroughly enjoyed herself. Although she was present, Tina asked the duchess not to present her to her grandmother. She did not want to mar her first occasion with a possibly uncomfortable scene.

Jay kept her in sight from his perch by a pillar. Usually talking with Jon, the Earl of Weston, or the duke, he still managed to keep an eye on her and whomever she danced with. At one point, he noticed the dowager Countess of Wynton sitting on a chaise surrounded by her cronies. She was watching Tina.

Jon followed his gaze. "I wonder if she suspects?"

"She doesn't need to," Jay answered bluntly. "She knows."

"Knows? How?"

"I paid her a visit this afternoon."

"And she actually received you?"

"Of course. I suspect she was curious." Jay took a sip from the glass he held. "By the time I left, however, there were no illusions."

"What did you tell her?"

"I merely made it clear we would not presume upon the connection as long as she did not attempt to publicly disclaim or humiliate Tina in any way. She understood once people found out Tina was your sister, the connection would be made and questions would be asked. She was quite amenable."

Now, as he watched her watch Tina, he knew a sense of satisfaction. The duchess had pulled off the social equivalent of a *coup* with her presentation of him and Tina to the *ton* and the dowager countess knew it. That she had passed up the opportunity through her intractability and bitterness, would grate on her at least for the rest of the short season.

Tina found popularity tiring. As she was already married, she considered most of the young men she danced with harmless. Instead, she wondered whether any of them would do for Felicia in a couple of years. Unfortunately, she weighed each of them against Jay and Jon and found all of them wanting. There were a few who wandered away once they discovered she had a brain, but she knew Felicia wouldn't want them anyway.

"I'm afraid Felicia is going to be disappointed if she encounters the same group of young men I encountered tonight. Not one of them would hold her attention for longer than the duration of a dance."

Jay laughed as he slipped an arm around her in the confines of the carriage. "Felicia will have to choose her own, but I did promise her a duke, remember?"

Tina giggled even as she tried for seriousness. "That was too bad of you."

"Not really. There is one out there."

"An unmarried duke?"

"Well, an unmarried heir, at least. The Marquess of Lofton is heir to the Duke of Warringham."

"I don't remember him."

"You didn't meet him. He wasn't there tonight."

"Would they suit?"

Jay shrugged. "Who knows? But, I will keep him in mind just in case."

Tina shook her head in disbelief. "And I thought Jon and I spoiled her."

Jay leaned back against the comfortably padded seat. "Enough about Felicia. What about you? Did you enjoy yourself?"

"Oh, yes. It was a truly wonderful evening. Mama's descriptions didn't do it justice. Her Grace said I should consider having a soiree. What do you think?"

Actually, Jay could not think of anything he might like less, but for Tina, it would give her confidence and enhance her social standing to host a fete.

"If you wish, I have no objections. The ballroom is nearly finished."

"You do not sound very enthusiastic, my lord," she said as they reached Thane House.

"I'm afraid enthusiasm for such things escapes us poor males," he countered as he helped her to alight. "They are a necessity we do not always enjoy."

"Did you not enjoy yourself this evening?" she asked as they entered the house. By mutual consent, they entered the library.

"I enjoyed watching you enjoy yourself," he confessed, his dark eyes twinkling. "It has occurred to me you have not had a chance to be part of the social whirl and I would remedy that for you. Sherry?" he asked as he headed for the sideboard.

"No, thank you," she answered, settling herself on a settee near the fire. "I'm afraid I'm not used to so much champagne and I will not be able to negotiate the stairs if I have any more to drink."

Jay couldn't help the chuckle that escaped him as he poured himself a brandy, then turned to look at his wife. Seated on a small settee, her aqua skirts spread about her, emeralds, diamonds, and sapphires flashing at her neck and ears, she looked like a water nymph.

"You find that amusing, my lord?" she queried, eyes narrowed in consternation. Reaching up, she began to pull the pins from her hair.

For a moment, he wondered if she knew what she was doing to him as he watched one silken curl after another tumble down around her shoulders and back. Then she gave him a look calculated to make his blood boil and knew she did.

"Of course," he responded blithely. Finishing his brandy, he set down the glass and stalked toward her. Plucking her off the settee, he looked down at her, a roguish grin on his face, his eyes devouring her. "When was the last time you negotiated the stairs before bed?"

Tina blushed to the roots of her hair, but Jay was undaunted as he carried her out of the library and up the stairs.

"If it were not for the fact that they see you during the day, the servants, especially Milly, might think you unable to walk on your own."

Burying her face in his neck, he felt the movement of her lips when she smiled. Milly had been instructed not to wait up for her in the evenings. Tina would ring if she needed her—something which hadn't happened since the evening they returned to Kenwyck from North Road Manor.

Chapter Fourteen

Tina threw herself into the social whirl of the small season. With the duchess and Lady Weston as her guides, she gradually found her feet in the sometimes treacherous waters of society, and thrived. Between sightseeing, at homes, balls and parties, rides in the park, and shopping, her days were full to bursting.

There were the occasional remarks made concerning the dowager countess, but she managed to turn them aside without confirming or denying the existence of a feud in the family. At the same time, she found herself being befriended by a host of matrons with eligible daughters, their eyes on Jon.

"I couldn't believe she would say such a thing," Lady Weston remarked to Tina.

It was late afternoon and the two ladies were ensconced in the gold and white drawing room of Westover House, discussing the latest *ton* antics over tea.

"I wasn't quite sure what to say," Tina responded. "She took me by surprise, you know. If Jon hadn't shown up right then, I might have outright embarrassed her."

Geri shrugged her shoulders. "It would have served her right if you had. As it is, everyone knows Lady Wilkins and your grandmother are good friends, so it's no wonder she would say what she did."

Tina nodded. "Thankfully, when Jon suddenly appeared, I was able to ignore the comment by drawing him into the conversation."

"Did you tell him what she said?"

"Heavens, no! He would have been furious. And he might have said something to Jay. I know Jay would not have let it pass."

Geri grinned in response. "No, I don't suppose he would have."

"Luckily, I do not let such boorish comments annoy me. After some of the things that were said about me and Felicia in Devon, very little bothers me anymore."

Once in her carriage on the way home, Tina went back over the conversation with Geri. She had told her new friend she no longer took offense at the snide or off-handed remarks made concerning her background, and she meant it. No one knew she had carefully developed an outward immunity to the side-long, often sly, glances sent her way.

Her grandmother's neglect still hurt and no matter how often she told herself it didn't, she knew it did. More than once in the last week, she had caught her grandmother watching her at some soiree or ball. But each time, the countess had turned away once their eyes met, and Tina knew she could not approach her. She would just be turned away and the *ton* would never let her forget the humiliation. Regardless, she held on to the hope that someday she would be accepted by her father's mother.

There was a sudden sharp sound, like that of a snapping twig, and the carriage came to a jarring halt. Tina put out her hands to keep from falling against the side as the conveyance tilted sharply toward one side. A moment later, Carter, the coachman, opened the door.

"Beggin' your pardon, m'lady, but we have a problem."

"Does it have anything to do with the fact that the coach seems about to tip over on its side?"

The coachman nodded.

She looked over at Milly. "I think we should alight," she informed the maid. "Help me out, Carter, if you please."

The coachman looked around nervously. "I don't think you ought to be standin' around on the street, m'lady. I can send Sammy, here, back to the house for another carriage."

"Nonsense," Tina responded. "It would probably be best if you flagged down a hackney. Inside the coach does not seem like a good place to remain, considering its position. What happened?"

Helping her down, the coachman answered, "It looks as if one of the carriage wheel pins has broken." He scratched his head beneath his cap. "I don't know how it coulda happened, though. There was nothin' wrong with it yesterday."

"Hmmm. Perhaps it's just worn," she answered. "Regardless, it is not going to get me home right now."

"It's a good thing we wasn't goin' faster," he said. "'Twould have caused a terrible accident for sure."

"Then I'm grateful we were merely on the way home and in traffic which would not allow for speed."

Flagging down a hackney, the coachman saw her and her maid safely inside and insisted on sending the footman along as well.

Tina thought no more about the incident. She supposed that parts of carriages and other equipages wore out all the time. Carter would ensure it was repaired and they would have no further problems.

Jay was already waiting for her by the time she reached the house. Explaining quickly about the carriage, she hurried upstairs to change. They were due to dine at the Enderly's tonight and she did not want to be late.

Lord Enderly had been a school chum of her father's. One of only a few members of the *ton* who would speak of her father to her and Jon, she enjoyed his company for that simple reason. His wife was nice enough, but if not for her husband, she probably would not have made any effort to cultivate Tina's friendship.

"It's shameful, you know," Lord Enderly said to her at dinner. "Just shameful. Your grandfather would never have acted thus had it been the other way around."

"Why do you say that?" Tina could not resist asking. "I thought all of my father's family disliked my mother."

Lord Enderly's balding pate shined brightly under the chandelier as he shook his head. "No, no. Alan—he was your father's oldest brother—was delighted. I distinctly remember a conversation between him and Jonathan in which he told Jonathan he should follow his heart. I remember thinking it was a strange thing for his brother to say. But, Alan was smitten with his own wife, so I suppose it really wasn't all that strange."

As the last course was being removed, Lady Enderly rose and Tina reluctantly followed suit.

"I hope you do not mind I am forever asking your husband questions," Tina ventured as they entered the drawing room. Decorated in robin's-egg blue with touches of rose and cream, it was a restful environment and Tina immediately felt comfortable.

Lady Enderly did, in fact, mind, but she knew better than to respond so bluntly. "It seems to be all he talks about these days," she responded cryptically. "How he and your father were such good friends."

"Did you know my father at all?"

Lady Enderly shook her head, causing the soft brown curls to dance about her rounded face. "I did not marry Harry until after your parents left for India. I think Harry would have liked to have gone, too, but as an oldest son, he had too many responsibilities here."

Tina glanced around the room and noticed a pianoforte before the large windows. Gesturing toward it, she asked, "Do you play at all?"

"No. I'm afraid I haven't the talent. My Mary plays a little, but she never had the patience to practice."

"My mother loved to play," Tina said sadly. "She taught all three of us to play, but my sister is definitely the better player."

The men joined them shortly after that and the rest of the evening passed quickly. As they were leaving, Lord Enderly handed Tina a letter.

"I do not know why I saved this particular one, or if it was just not disposed of, but I thought you might like to have it. Your father and I corresponded regularly."

Tina stared at the envelope in awe. She had never thought to receive such a precious gift. Raising tear-filled eyes to Lord Enderly, she could barely speak past the lump in her throat. "Thank you, sir."

In the carriage on the way home, she leaned against Jay and stared at the slightly yellowed envelope in her hand.

"Are you going to read it?" Jay's voice startled her, and she looked up, searching out his face in the dim light.

"I think when I get home," she replied, tracing the writing lovingly with her finger. "I'll have to let Jon read it, too."

Jay said no more, but, as he watched her handle the letter as if it were the most delicate and fragile of items, a warm feeling stole through him. He had wondered, at first, if Enderly's interest was a sham. It wouldn't be too hard for someone bent on seduction to worm their way into Tina's affections with stories of her father, so he had checked to be sure. He wasn't jealous, he told himself. He just wanted to make sure she wasn't being deceived.

But Enderly checked out. He *had* been at school with Jonathan Kenton, and had been considered a particular friend. Jay hadn't known what to expect when he realized he and Tina had been the only dinner guests tonight, but the letter had been an unexpected surprise.

He had known a moment's uneasiness when Enderly had handed Tina the letter. For a moment, Tina looked as if she might have impulsively embraced Lord Enderly and his blood ran hot. He'd had to ruthlessly quash the sudden emotions in the wake of her polite, but emotional, thank you.

He wasn't sure he liked the feeling of being on edge, of watching every man in a room and wondering if any of them had designs on Tina. It made him feel out of control. At least, he told himself, he wasn't jealous.

ি

"Has Tina told you of our visit to North Road Manor?"

Jon turned from watching the game in progress at the table. The shadows in the room made it difficult for Jay to see Jon's reaction.

"No," was the reply. "When did you go there?"

The two men moved away from the card game and found a small unoccupied table in the corner of the room. The Loughton ball was in full swing, but Tina and the Countess of Weston had yet to arrive. It was rare that Jay arrived at a function before she did, but they'd decided to meet at this particular one although he knew she and the countess were going to drop in at a smaller event being given by the Darnells in honor of their daughter's engagement.

"I received a letter from our investigator while we were at Kenwyck. He'd tracked down your grandfather's family and suggested that if I was in a position to do so, I go and ask some questions. As it turned out, North Road Manor was not far from Newcastle.

"We were both surprised. Tina even remarked that she'd assumed it was closer to the border near Gretna Green."

"I suspect we have always thought that because our grandparents were married at Gretna Green." Jon waived at a footman circulating through the room. "So, did you find out anything interesting?" he asked as the footman set two glasses on the table.

"Unfortunately not. But it wasn't a wasted trip." Jay sipped from his glass. "A few years back, someone—no one could remember the man's name, but I'm sure it was Milton—came up there looking for information on your mother's whereabouts. Since your grandparents never returned after she married, there was very little to be learned. Tina, however, spent the time talking to people about your mother and grandmother. Even though we learned nothing new about Milton she was glad to have gone."

Remembering the trip back and Tina's revelation caused him to be angry all over again at what his brother had done. With Aaron gone, there was no reason to tell Jon, but Jay wished he felt comfortable doing so anyway. What held him back was knowing that Tina hadn't confided in her brother. Understanding how close Tina was to her brother made him think she hadn't done so for a reason, so he kept silent.

"She's been busy lately and I haven't really had time to talk to her much. Maybe I'll drop in for tea and ask her about it."

"Ah, you *are* here." They both looked up at the sound of the Earl of Weston's voice. "Geri wondered if you might have arrived before them."

He joined them, seeming in no particular hurry to return to the ballroom.

"Have you been playing escort tonight?" Jon asked.

The earl grinned. "Of course. And I must say, Thanet, you have outdone yourself this time. My wife is green with envy over your wife's necklace."

"And which necklace would that be?" Jay hadn't given her any jewelry other than the set that matched her ring. Now that he thought about it, he wondered if the family jewels were still in the bank vault.

"A diamond starburst. I'd be interested in knowing where you found such an unusual piece."

Jay had no idea what Weston was talking about, but Jon came to his rescue.

"I'm afraid you're out of luck," he told the earl. "That particular piece was given to Tina by our great-grandmother, and she's dead. But I'm surprised Tina's wearing it. I would have thought she'd put it away and not bother with it anymore."

"Hmmm. I'll have to have a look at this piece, but thank you for reminding me that I haven't even thought about the family jewels. I hope they are still resting comfortably in the bank vault."

Again, Jon spoke up. "Actually, they aren't—in the bank vault, that is. At least not in yours."

Confused, Jay looked at him. "Not in mine?"

Jon's grin over his confusion disappeared as he explained. "After your father died, Mama didn't trust Milton, so she had me move the Thanet jewels from your box in the bank vault to mine. She was afraid he might steal or sell them."

Jay didn't let on that the same thing had occurred to him just then. Instead he said, "It seems that I am more in your debt than I thought."

"Any new developments in the search?" Weston asked.

"No, but Pymm is due back sometime in the next week or so. Hopefully with some news." Jay said nothing about Tina's carriage mishap.

After speaking with the coachman, he was sure the broken pin was not an accident. Carter had shown him the piece in question and it had obviously been tampered with. What neither of them could figure out was when it had happened.

Getting to his feet, he suddenly had an urge to find Tina.

He refused to allow himself to think he needed to see her to ensure that she was fine. She'd been with the Weston's for most of the evening. Nevertheless, he excused himself and left the two earls in the card room.

Scanning the ballroom as he entered, it didn't take him long to find her. From his vantage point on the edge of the floor, all he could see was that she was wearing a deep pink gown trimmed with white ribbon. Dancing with Lord Crofton, she smiled as they moved through the steps of the quadrille.

The dance ended and he moved to intercept them as they left the floor. Tina's smile brightened when she saw him.

"Good evening, my lord. Have you just arrived?"

He accepted her hand and acknowledged Crofton. "No. Jon and I have been here for some time. We were just catching up."

As Crofton left them, Jay glanced down at the jewelry she wore and abruptly lost his breath. The pendant sparkled with brilliant fire, but he was suddenly cold. The room tilted and the sound of a gale force wind echoed in his ears. He was rooted to the spot—hypnotized by the glittering jewels. Unable to tear his eyes away, Tina unwittingly came to his rescue by turning to speak to someone behind her. Dazed, he blinked to clear his head, and watched her laugh at something Lady Weston said.

What had Jon said about the pendant she wore? It had been given to her by their great-grandmother. His head swam with the implication and he refused to consider that the improbable had happened.

The opening strains of a waltz floated out over the crowd and Tina turned to him. Taking her in his arms, he fought to keep control of his thoughts as they scrambled for a way to ask what he wanted to know without arousing suspicion.

"Did you enjoy yourself at the Darnells?"

"Yes. Although Lady Darnell went on and on about Cecily so much that I think the poor girl is hoping for a very short engagement."

He chuckled as he spun her through a turn. "Let us hope she gets her wish, then."

She laughed. "Geri said the very same thing on the way here."

"Speaking of Lady Weston, Gerald informed me that she

covets your necklace. He even asked where I acquired it. I was hard pressed to answer him until Jon came to my rescue."

"Oh." Wariness crept into her expression and she regarded him nervously.

"He is right, though, in that it is an unusual piece. Jon says your great-grandmother gave it to you."

"Yes. Shortly before she died."

"How long ago was that?"

A shadow passed through Tina's eyes and silence fell around them. "I'm not sure when she died," she finally answered, "but she gave me the pendant right after you returned. She actually came to visit while you were in London."

The dance ended and he escorted her off the floor. "It's unfortunate she didn't show up sooner. She might have been able to help you and Felicia."

"I don't think so. Nona seemed to always know when we needed her most, and that's when she would arrive. I don't know how she knew, but she always did. Besides, it probably wasn't safe for her to come when Mr. Milton was there. He would never have allowed them to camp on the estate and I hate to think what he might have done had he found them there."

"I see."

He responded automatically, but his thoughts were years away in the past. Back to a warm June night when a sixteen-year-old runaway had been set upon, robbed, beaten, and left on the road to London. To the gypsy who found him, bandaged his wounds, then took him to London. And to the promise he'd given when she left him at the docks the next day.

"Someday you will return," the gypsy had told him. Then she had put a chain around his neck on which hung a gold medallion with a diamond star in the center. *"As long as you wear this, Fortune will smile upon you."*

"But, I can never repay you," he'd protested.

"You will."

"How?"

"I have great-grandchildren I have yet to see, but their happiness will depend upon you someday. One is your destiny."

"How do you know?"

"My cards have said so."

"And, how will I find her?"

She'd smiled and produced another piece of jewelry—a diamond starburst pendant on its own chain.

"She will be wearing this."

At sixteen, he'd readily believed her and, in gratitude, promised to do whatever was necessary to assist the unknown great-grandchildren. As a second son who never expected to inherit, it hadn't been difficult to promise to marry one of them sight unseen.

಄

Tina was out the next afternoon when Jon dropped by to deliver the jewelry.

"I expect her back shortly," Jay told him, "if you want to wait. She promised to be back in time for tea."

Jon availed himself of one of the comfortable chairs before the desk in the library. "That's why I came by now, instead of sending a footman around with them earlier." Settling himself, he looked at Jay with a question in his eyes. "Did you ask Tina about her pendant?"

"Not really. I mentioned that you told me your great-grandmother had given it to her. She just confirmed it and said she'd been given it just before your great-grandmother died. I found it interesting that she didn't know when she died, but knew that she had."

"That's because I wrote her while you were at Kenwyck Manor and told her. I suspect she said nothing thinking that it wouldn't matter to you."

"I did ask her why your great-grandmother hadn't come sooner."

"What did she say?"

"Only that Nona—that's what she called your great-grandmother—would come when she was needed."

"Sounds like a spirit or something, doesn't she?" Jon

quipped. "But, the truth is that Nona probably would have been burned as a witch two hundred years ago. She just seemed to know things that the rest of us didn't. I saw her shortly before I arrived at Thane Park for your wedding and she gave me strict instructions regarding how to go about finding my destiny, as she called it. I suspect she did the same with Tina and Felicia."

Taken aback by this revelation, Jay was about to ask another question when Tina burst into the room.

"Jon! I'm so glad you're here. I've wanted to tell you all about North Road Manor and everyone we met."

Jon rose to greet his sister with a hug. "I've come bearing presents, but I've turned them over to Jay for now, so you'll have to apply to him for them."

Tina looked at Jay. "Presents?"

He smiled and indicated the jewelry cases piled on his desk. "You are welcome to go through them to find anything you wish to wear, but I suspect now you'd rather spend time regaling your brother with stories about your mother's childhood."

He was right, of course, and soon he was alone in the library again with his correspondence. Unfortunately, it no longer held his attention.

"*...she gave me strict instructions regarding how to go about finding my destiny...she did the same with Tina...*"

If her great-grandmother had given her instructions, why had she married him? She couldn't possibly know he had the other half of her necklace.

He leaned back in his chair and closed his eyes.

She'd been promised Thane Park since she was a little girl. Once Aaron was dead and she knew nothing of the will, she could have married anyone. Instead she waited for him.

No. She'd waited for Thane Park. Unaware that she was her own security, she'd married him to follow through on a promise—a promise of security. Why else would she have bothered to marry him when she could have come to London and had her pick? It would have never occurred to him that she would be like every other young woman of the *ton*. That she would be out to marry a title and fortune. And, who else better than someone who didn't know her.

He wished, now, he'd told her the truth. A truth that would have complicated things at the time, but wouldn't have created the Gordian knot he now faced. If she married him merely for his title and fortune, he should be glad that's all there was. But, he wasn't. Instead, he wondered if she'd worn her necklace the other night expecting someone to recognize it.

Did that mean she regretted going against her great-grandmother's wishes?

℘

Three mornings later, Tina and Jay set out for an early morning ride in Hyde Park. The air was crisp, a hint of fall on the way.

Her mount, a glossy black mare named Star that Jay had purchased for her at Tattersalls, was frisky, tossing its mane and stomping its hooves impatiently once Jay set her on its back. She glanced over at him as he mounted Midnight.

"I'm sure Felicia is glad he's getting some exercise," she said, "but she misses him terribly."

Jay's grin caused her heart to miss a beat.

"Has she said so?" he asked as they headed in the direction of the park.

She nodded. "Her last letter asked if we had left him at Collingswood."

Jay acknowledged her response, but said no more as they rode through the streets. There were no carriages about at this time of the morning, only the hacks of tradesmen going about their morning rounds delivering goods. It had rained the night before and Tina breathed in the cool, fresh air, devoid of the usual earthly smells and odors that seemed to envelop the city streets.

Watching her husband's broad shoulders, encased in a dark riding jacket, Tina relived the previous night when she had explored every inch, marveling over the muscles, sinew, and bone that moved beneath the smooth skin of his shoulders and back. Even now a frisson of pleasure snaked through her at the thought. She was sure a more perfect specimen of manhood could not be found anywhere.

It was difficult keeping her feelings to herself. Understanding Jay's feelings about his father, she knew he viewed love suspiciously and was trying not to succumb to the same emotion. Despite that, she loved him more each day, finding those times when they were not together boring and flat.

Her thoughts went back to nearly a week ago. To the night she'd worn the pendant. She'd only done so because it seemed to go well with the gown she wore. Yet, for the entire night she'd viewed every man who approached her with suspicion, wondering if he would be the one to recognize it. When no one except Jay and the Earl of Weston commented on it, she'd been relieved.

Taking it off later than evening had felt as if she'd lifted a millstone from around her neck. She would not wear it again, she decided. Except for the waltz with Jay, she hadn't truly enjoyed herself that night at all.

Reaching the park and entering through the gates, Star surged ahead of Midnight. Tina laughed at the mare's antics. Just a little further and she and Jay would let the horses run—it was the reason they came out so early.

Glancing over at Jay as they reached the far end of the more sedate path, she said, "I think Star is up for a race this morning."

He laughed, his deep chuckles infectious. "I'll give you a head start to the count of five."

"You'll never catch us, then," she warned, and kicked Star into a gallop.

Tina was an excellent rider. Not quite the daredevil on a horse as her sister was, she nevertheless could easily hold her own on a spirited animal. As she sped across the grass, the wind whistling across her face and through her hair, she only hoped Milly had anchored the tiny hat with its ridiculous feather on well.

The feeling was wonderful and Tina knew what it felt like to fly. Glorying in her freedom, she was unprepared for the small movement of the saddle. It wasn't far, but it was enough to throw her off balance and cause her to try to rein in her mount. Star, however, had no intention of slowing down as they flew over the path, throwing up clumps of grass and dirt in their wake.

As she heard the sound of hoof beats behind her and realized that Jay was gaining, she felt her saddle slip again and knew a moment's panic.

Pulling sharply back on Star's reins, she tried to bring the animal under control. Reluctantly, the horse began to comply, but it was too late. The saddle suddenly seemed to give way completely beneath her and Tina knew she was falling.

Jay began to count as he watched Tina take off down the open area. *One*...Admiring her seat and the slim, green velvet clad silhouette she presented on the mare's back, he noted that she suddenly seemed off balance. *Two*...Midnight snickered, eager to be off. *Three*...There was something about the way she moved that struck him as not right. He sprang Midnight into a gallop. He hadn't given her to the count of five, but he didn't care. Something was wrong.

Giving Midnight his head, Jay watched Tina closely as they shortened the distance. This time he saw her tilt sideways on the saddle. His heart leaped into his throat. She was about to fall! He could see the saddle slipping.

Urging Midnight to greater speed, he could see now that she was trying to slow Star down, but the mare was having none of it. Midnight seemed to sprout wings, as if he understood the urgency driving his rider. They were closing in on Tina, but was it fast enough?

Star began to slow just a bit, but it was sufficient. Jay reached them just as the saddle slipped to the side completely. Tina kicked free of the stirrup as he reached her, her arms flung wide, enabling him to pluck her, literally, from mid-air— and possible death had she fallen to the ground.

Pulling up, he slowed Midnight gradually. The stallion eased into a canter, then a walk, finally stopping altogether, its sides heaving.

Jay looked down at Tina. She had lost her hat and her hair had come loose, flowing down over his arm. Her small hands clutched the front of his jacket, her knuckles showing white, and her face was buried in his chest. His own heartbeat pounded in his ears, yet he could still hear her gasping for air as her body shuddered against him.

"M'lord!" Jenkins reached them. His mount was as winded as he, but he had Star's reins. "What happened, m'lord? Is her ladyship hurt?"

"No, she's fine," Jay responded grimly. "It looks as if the cinch-strap came loose."

The groom looked puzzled, but he had no idea Jay was keeping his fury barely in check. Instructing the groom to take the mare home, Jay watched as the little man returned the way he had come, Tina's mare trailing behind him with the saddle sitting askew on its back, then looked down at Tina again.

She no longer had a death grip on his jacket, and her breathing seemed closer to normal. Lifting his hand, he tipped her head back so he could look down into her face—and assure himself she was still here and still his. He let out a breath he hadn't realized he was holding when she looked up at him through watery eyes.

"What happened?" he asked gently.

"I don't know." Her voice trembled slightly. "I felt the saddle slipping and tried to slow Star down. Then it felt like it all came loose and I thought I was about to hit the ground, and...well, you know what happened then."

Jay nodded, unable to stop himself from reliving the moment he realized she was about to fall from her horse at a full gallop. Suppressing a shudder, he tightened his arms about her, lifting her higher against his chest.

"Are you all right?" he parroted the groom, and when she nodded, he pressed, "You're sure?"

She let out a shaky laugh. "Yes," she assured him. Slipping her arms around his waist and resting her head against his chest, she relaxed in his arms. "Let's go home."

Jay pressed a kiss to her forehead, then gathered up Midnight's reins and turned the stallion back the way they had come.

Once back at the house, Jay would have insisted she go back to bed, but she was having none of that. She insisted she was fine now that the danger had passed. Besides she was meeting Lady Weston not long after breakfast to finish looking at the plans for the gardens being replanted at Westover House.

Jay watched her ascend the staircase, the knot in his gut only slightly less tight than it had been when he caught her as she fell from Star's back. Once she disappeared from view, he turned and headed to the stables.

Tina entered her room and sat at the dressing table. The person who looked back at her from the mirror was not the person she was used to seeing. She shook her head trying to dispel the image of wide aquamarine eyes in a ghostly pale face, surrounded by a cloud of raven curls, but the image remained. Her heart continued to beat erratically as she relived the morning's ride.

Closing her eyes, she recalled the moment Jay had tipped her head back to look down at her. For one unguarded second she had seen naked fear in his eyes and, despite the circumstances, hope had raised its head. Perhaps he did care for her after all.

Instinct warned her a declaration on her part might damage the bond growing between them, but now she wondered if she was brave enough to take the plunge. The emotion she had read in his eyes this morning heartened her, but was it too new? Too fragile? If she pressed, would he bury it and deny its existence?

Milly hurried into the room, interrupting her thoughts.

"Oh, m'lady, 'tis glad I am you aren't hurt," she blurted.

Tina shook herself from her thoughts and turned to watch as Milly disappeared into the dressing room, returning with a morning gown of rose muslin and laying it out on the bed.

"Everyone is saying how his lordship saved you," the maid continued. "Cook is planning on makin' a special cake just for him. Old Darby has been at all the stablehands about your saddle, and swears that he'll find out what happened."

Tina unbuttoned her jacket and slipped it off just as Milly turned toward her.

"Oh, your hair! I'll have it right as rain soon."

Tina allowed the maid to chatter all the while helping her to change out of her riding outfit into the gown. It was easy to let the young woman talk without responding for Milly rarely needed any response—especially on a morning like this when her chatter was from worry and anxiousness. Tina appreciated her caring.

CR

"What could he possibly hope to gain now?" Jon asked Jay two afternoons later as the two of them sat in the library at Thane House. "He" was Roderick Milton, the still-missing steward. Having come to the conclusion someone was trying to harm Tina, Jay had confided his concerns to Jon and the two of them decided Milton was the only possible culprit.

Tina was out with the Westover ladies at a garden party. Jay had been reluctant to let her go, but without coming right out and telling her what he suspected, he could not confine her to the house. He had, instead, instructed the footman who had accompanied the ladies, to keep her in sight as much as possible.

"I don't know," Jay answered now. "Has Pymm returned from the north yet?"

"He was due back a few days ago," Jon replied. "Let's hope the delay has yielded results."

Keyes knocked and entered the library moments later. "A Mr. Pymm to see you, my lord."

Jay sat up. At last!

"Show him in."

Mr. Rufus Pymm was a large man, intimidating in size and appearance. With a black patch over one eye and a dark beard in a swarthy face, he was the perfect picture of a pirate.

"I came immediately when I reached town, my lord. I will give you my written report later, but I thought you needed to hear this information now." He turned as he spoke, indicating a small, distinguished looking gentleman who had followed him in. "This is Mr. Stapleton of Messrs. Stapleton and Poole, solicitors. From Carlisle."

Jay invited them both to sit down, then turned to Mr. Stapleton, as it was obvious he was expected to speak first.

"My firm has represented the Mildens of Mildenwood Hall for a number of generations," he began. "My father was particularly close to Lord Richard two generations back."

Jon started at the name. "Damn!" he exclaimed. "Now I remember. He was my great-grandfather."

The solicitor looked at him. They had not been introduced in the detective's haste to have him tell his story. "Lord Wynton, I presume?" he now asked.

Jon nodded in response and wanted to ask how he knew who he was, but the solicitor merely nodded in acknowledgment and continued.

"When Lord Richard died in 1814, the bulk of his estate was left to his son, Ashton, however, there was an irregular bequest concerning a small portion of his holdings that, according to Mr. Pymm, concerns you—or rather, your wife—my lord."

Jay leaned forward in his chair behind the massive desk. "My wife? How?"

"It is somewhat complicated, but I will endeavor to explain as clearly as I can," the solicitor said. "Lord Richard apparently fathered a daughter, Shana. Her mother was a gypsy. Although Lord Richard had no antipathy toward gypsies—indeed, he was apparently on good terms with the small band he allowed to camp on his land year after year—he knew they had no use for money or land. He therefore left a large amount of money and a small estate to his daughter's oldest unmarried female descendant alive on January 1, 1850. The inheritance was to be hers upon her marriage and the subsequent birth of her first child, provided she did not marry a gypsy."

"What?" Jon clearly echoed Jay's thoughts.

"There is more," the solicitor continued. "If she dies without issue, the inheritance reverts back to the Milden family. Upon the birth of her first child, the inheritance becomes hers free and clear, regardless of whether the child survives."

The silence in the room was deafening. The ticking of the small clock over the fireplace seemed overly loud.

"There's your motive, my lord," the detective spoke into the silence.

"How so?" Jay asked. "What has Roderick Milton to do with a bequest from my wife's great-grandfather?"

"Er, beggin' your pardon, my lord, I got ahead of myself,"

the detective replied, picking up where the solicitor left off. "When Lord Richard died, his son, Lord Ashton ran his stepsister off, hoping she would return to her mother's gypsy band. Instead she met and married a Lord Tindale. Once the family learned of the marriage—and subsequent birth of a daughter—they thought the matter settled and the land lost forever."

"Lord Ashton Milden had three sons. Merrick, the oldest, inherited the title, Delbert, the second purchased a commission, and the third, Rodney, was to study the law," the solicitor began again. "When Lord Ashton died in 1852, his will, which I drew up for him in 1848, left that contingent piece of property to his youngest son should it return to the family. Lord Ashton would not have mentioned the property had I not brought it up, but I felt it was my responsibility to remind him that the status of the property was still unsettled."

"Rodney?" Jay asked. He and Jon exchanged glances, coming to the same conclusion at the same time the detective proffered his *piece de resistance*.

"As it turns out, Rodney Milden and Roderick Milton are the same person."

By the time the solicitor and detective left, the four had reasoned out most of the events of the last few years. The solicitor's admission that one of his clerks had allowed Mr. Milden to undertake to find Felicia and any offspring she might have had was the last piece in the puzzle of why no one had contacted Tina or Felicia before.

"God's blood, what a tangle," Jon exclaimed after they left. "We'll have to tell Tina. Besides it being dangerous for her not to know, she'll be furious if we don't and she does find out."

A sudden commotion in the entryway heralded the arrival of Tina and her two new friends. Glancing at the clock, Jay thought it was a bit early for the party to be over already. He fully expected Tina to burst into the library and launch into a recitation of her afternoon. A solemn duchess was admitted instead.

"I'm afraid there's been a small mishap, my lord," she began.

Jay was out of his chair instantly, his heart rising to his throat. "What kind of mishap?"

The duchess waived her jewel-bedecked hand at him. "Calm down, my boy. Nothing serious happened. Your lady only got a little wet, that's all. And, yes, thank you, I'll take a sherry, if you please."

Jay noticed Jon grinning as he marched over to the sideboard and poured the duchess a sherry. Handing her the glass and keeping himself severely in check, he managed to inquire in a level voice, "And, how did my wife get a little wet?"

"It was just an accident. We were strolling by the river's edge and managed to get jostled. She lost her footing and fell. Although the current was quite strong, she was able to swim almost to shore and pull herself out. Lord Northburn went in after her, and helped her out."

Lady Weston entered the library just then. "I left her in the care of her maid. She says she's just fine."

Her last words were lost to Jay, who bolted from the room, leaving three pairs of eyes watching the library door slam behind him.

Jon rose to his feet, a large grin on his face as he turned to Lady Weston and offered her some refreshment.

Jay took the stairs three at a time, surprising Keyes and the footman who happened to be in the front hall at the time. Nearly colliding with Milly, who was leaving Tina's room with an armful of wet clothing, he managed to stop long enough to ask her where Tina was.

"I left her in the bathing chamber, my lord. She was sore in need of a hot bath."

He barely heard the last of her comments as he rushed to the appointed chamber.

Tina was soaking in a tub of steaming rose scented water. Her head resting back against the edge of the tub, eyes closed, she could feel her muscles relaxing. It had been an exhausting afternoon.

Reliving once again the moment she had felt hands on her waist and the violent shove that had sent her into the water, she shivered. Someone had deliberately pushed her into the river. Thank God Papa had taught her to swim. He couldn't have anticipated she'd have to fight her way out of a strong current dressed in today's fashions. Corsets and petticoats were not designed for swimming. If not for Lord Northburn, she might not have made it at all. By the time he reached her, she had managed to pull herself partially out of the water, but the current and her heavy skirts had been dragging her back. She might not have had the strength to hold on much longer.

Hearing the door open, she said, "I'm fine now, Milly. When I get out, I think I will take a short nap. Would you find out if my husband is at home?"

"Your husband is very much at home, madam," came a tightly controlled voice from the door.

Water sloshed over the edge of the tub as she spun around and looked up abruptly. "Jay!"

Jay came further into the small room, his countenance grim, and seated himself on a bench beside the large tub. His dark eyes seemed even darker in the dimness of the room as they moved over her as if cataloguing her various parts. She felt a blush cover her chest and neck.

For a moment Jay studied her flushed face and overbright eyes, breathing deeply to calm his racing heart. He was incensed with himself, with her, and the whole world. He had nearly lost her. Regardless of what the duchess said, he did not believe for one moment she had been merely jostled. Yet, so as not to alarm her, he tried for levity in his next words.

"I should have warned you the river is no place for a swim. Especially at this time of the year."

Tina's eyebrows nearly disappeared into her hairline as she replied in an equally calm voice, "I did not go in voluntarily. I was pushed." Before he could say anything else, she continued, "I don't want to talk about it now. I'm too tired. Let me finish my bath, take a nap, and I will explain everything over tea."

Jay didn't understand why she wasn't in hysterics. Most women of his acquaintance would have been prostrate with fear by now. Did she not understand that someone was trying to hurt, or possibly kill, her?

"Very well. I will leave you to your rest, for now." He had seen for himself that she was still in one piece and none the worse physically for the experience. Rising to his feet, he leaned over the tub and gave her a hard, quick kiss on the mouth. "I'm glad you're safe," he said gruffly.

Then he left the room and headed back downstairs.

Chapter Fifteen

Tina finished her bath and allowed Milly to help her into a nightrail, then climbed into bed. She was exhausted from her exertions and wanted nothing more than to rest. Sleep, however, was elusive. Staring at the embroidered canopy above her head, her thoughts went over again the events of the last two weeks.

Someone was trying to kill her. The broken pin on her carriage wheel could have been an accident. The stone in her horse's hoof could have been mere happenstance. The runaway hackney on the street might have been a chance misfortune. The broken cinch strap on her saddle was none of those—she had seen it—it had been cut. And today she had been deliberately pushed into the river.

Why?

She knew of no one who might want her dead. Roderick Milton had tried to force her to leave Thane Park, but he didn't want her dead, did he? If so, why? What would he gain by her death?

"A small property on the west coast and a large bank account," Jay informed her over tea. "It's not much more than a small manor on a few acres of land, but it's in a good location and the land is good. And, of course, there is the money."

Tina was dumbstruck. "But, why me?"

"It wasn't left to you in particular," Jon told her. "You just happen to meet all of the requirements."

"If your great-grandfather had omitted just the 'unmarried' requirement, it would have been your mother, and the property would have already been out of reach before Milton found any of you," Jay added.

"Oh." Picking up her teacup and taking a sip, she put the cup and saucer down carefully before asking, "So, now what? How do we flush out Mr. Milton, or is it Milden?"

"Either, or both," Jay replied tersely. "But *we* are not doing anything. Jon and I will handle this."

"And how do you propose to do so without me, since I'm the one he's trying to kill?" she asked reasonably.

She knew Jay didn't want her to be right, but she knew she was. He and Jon could scour London for Roderick Milton, Rodney Milden, or whatever he was calling himself now, but if he was out to harm her, then wherever she was, was the most likely place to find him.

Jay didn't want it to be that way. He did not want her in danger. But how was he to protect her? Confining her to the house was not practical. She had already begun preparations for her soiree to be held at the end of the season in two weeks. Could they find him before then? They would certainly try. The detective was already out looking for him and they had contacted the Metropolitan Police as well. His brother, they'd discovered, had been posted to India a year ago and not returned. The oldest brother hadn't heard from him in over a year.

"For one thing, from now on you will not leave this house without Jon or myself as an escort," he told her now.

She shook her head. "That won't do. You and Jon have more important things to do than to trail around after me all day."

"Nothing is more important than your safety," Jon interposed before Jay had a chance.

"Now that I know, I will be very careful," she informed them. "I will never leave the house without a footman, at least." She was trying to be reasonable, but she could tell Jay did not want to be reasonable right now.

Jay's frown grew blacker with each word. She sighed. He was going to become difficult. She recognized the possessive streak in him, but it was more than that. He wanted to protect her. Yet, his method of protection would smother her if she wasn't careful.

"You will not leave this house without an escort," he repeated. "A footman alone won't do. Where was the footman who went with you today?"

Tina had no answer to that question. She knew he was thinking that servants, no matter how diligent, could not accompany her everywhere. Today had been a good example. Someone had insinuated themselves into the crowd strolling along the banks of the river. Someone who looked enough like a gentleman to pass inspection. If it had been Milton, neither the duchess nor Lady Weston knew him, so even if they had seen him, he wouldn't have attracted their attention.

"Then I will not attend any more garden parties without you or Jon—or any other outdoor activities."

"No." Jay's voice was implacable.

Sighing again, Tina rose to her feet. "If you are going to be unreasonable about this, then there is no use discussing it. But I will not become a prisoner in my own home again."

Then she turned and walked out of the room, closing the door quietly behind her. Two pairs of eyes followed her, one in stunned silence, the other silently applauding.

Now *that* was the sister he remembered.

Jay sat immobile as his wife left the room in the wake of a near ultimatum. It had happened again. How had he lost control of the conversation so soon? He had been so worried about her safety, he hadn't considered how she would feel.

'I will not become a prisoner in my own home, again.' He winced at those words. They were nearly the same words he had used to convince Felicia and Tina they needed to leave Thane Park. She had not liked them then—and she didn't like them now.

Yet, the fear he felt was very real. The need to protect her nearly overwhelmed him with its intensity. He would not allow anything to hurt her. And he knew he'd go to any lengths to ensure nothing did. She could not possibly understand the lengths Milton might go to in order to claim what he considered his. His thoughts brought him up short.

When had she turned his life upside down? When had she become more important than the title, the land, the inheritance? When had he stopped thinking of her as an enjoyable means to an end, and begun to see her as his wife. He would protect her by all means possible—but that didn't mean he loved her. Did it?

CR

Upstairs in her suite, Tina searched for and found the small case she brought with her from Thane Park. Although she had not expected to need its contents, she carried them with her when she left. Now she was glad she had.

Ringing for Milly, she set the small wooden case on her bed and opened the lid to reveal the two small pistols contained within. Jay's father had read about women in America who carried small pistols, called derringers, for protection and thought it an excellent idea. For some reason, he felt they were better than the small pocket pistols ladies had been carrying in England for years, so he had ordered two sets—one for her mother and one for her.

They hadn't necessarily needed them while at the Park, but Papa said he was taking no chances with their safety. She supposed now he might have thought they just needed some protection when he wasn't around. But it was more likely a whim brought on by reading—but who was she to argue? Especially since now the knowledge would be useful.

She and Felicia had discussed the best way to conceal them on their persons more than once. They had considered and discarded a number of ideas before hitting upon the idea of hiding one under their petticoats and carrying one in a reticule. A person finding the one in the reticule might not search further for a second one, they had reasoned, so an idea had been born.

When Milly arrived she found Tina sitting on her bed, a number of pairs of drawers spread out on the bed beside her. Swearing her to secrecy, Tina explained what she needed.

"I need you to cut and sew a pocket on these," Tina told her, holding up a pair of drawers. "It must be large enough to put my hand inside of, but tie closed at the top so that anything put inside will not fall out by accident." She knew that it was useless to tell Milly what she was going to put inside the pocket—it would only alarm her. "Eventually, I want this done to every pair, but for now, I must have one finished by tonight."

"Yes, ma'am." Milly hurried out with the bundle, and Tina turned back to the box.

Lifting out one of the pistols, she checked that it was clean, then checked to see how much ammunition she had left. She would have to ask Jon to get her some more. She had a feeling Jay would not necessarily be amenable to her plan, but she could not sit idle and feel vulnerable. She would not be a prisoner in her own home. It had been that way at Thane Park—she had been afraid to venture into the village. But now she couldn't stay inside the house day in and day out. She would go mad.

Putting away the pistols and box, she wandered into her sitting room. Settling on a chaise, she opened the book of sonnets she had borrowed from the library a few days ago. Trying to lose herself in the familiar writings of Shakespeare turned into a useless endeavor and she gave up to stare without seeing across the room.

Jay was only trying to protect her the best way he knew how. She knew that. But, having used that form of protection herself at Thane Park, she now understood it was pointless. Initially she had stayed in the dower house as a form of defense. If she didn't go out, she didn't have to subject herself to the hostile and accusing stares, and it became a habit to just remain in isolation. It occasionally grated on her, the forced seclusion, but she had come to accept it, understanding eventually it had to change.

That was then, in any case, and this was now. Having tasted the delights of the *ton*, she was not willing to absent herself from the social scene because a madman was on the loose.

She loved Jay dearly and she was beginning to suspect his feelings for her were deeper than he would admit. Why else would he seem frantic over her safety? Concern would be expected, but he was overreacting. Keeping her in the house or requiring that she only leave in his or Jon's company would not stop a murderer. It would only make him more desperate.

She would just have to be vigilant at all times. Even in the house. Jon and Jay might think they could protect her constantly, but she knew that was impossible. They could not plan for every eventuality. It was up to her to think of those things they overlooked. The household was one such place. Rising from the chaise, she crossed to the bellpull to summon the butler and housekeeper.

If Keyes or Mrs. Greaves were surprised at her request, they kept it to themselves. "I know this is somewhat out of the ordinary, however, at this time, I feel his lordship and I must insist on strict adherence. There are to be no new staff hired without our personal approval. This includes anyone for any reason, including stablehands."

The two servants exchanged quick glances, but said nothing.

"Also, if we have hired anyone new on in, say, the past fortnight, I would like to speak with them."

"We haven't needed to," Mrs. Greaves spoke up. "We'll be needin' to hire more footmen for your ladyship's soiree, though. We would have been startin' to send the notices 'round to the agencies next week."

Tina thought for a moment, then said, "I think we will have to wait on that. I will let you know when it should be done."

Although she knew she could trust the two standing before her to keep the secret, she did not feel comfortable revealing the reasons for this new directive concerning household hiring. She didn't know whether Jay would approve of them knowing.

Dismissing the two servants, she walked over to a window and stared out at the gathering darkness. A star twinkling overhead caught her eye, reminding her of the pendant Nona had given her. This might not have happened if she had waited for the person with the other half. But she could not imagine loving anyone else other than Jay. If the person with the other half of the pendant was her destiny, then why had she fallen so completely in love with Jay?

Was it possible Nona had been wrong? Or had she brought this misfortune upon herself by ignoring her great-grandmother's words? Did she truly love Jay—or had she merely taken the safe way out? What if Milton decided to kill Jay? Had she exposed him to a madman's vengeance needlessly? She had married him because it was the most sensible thing to do under the circumstances. It was what Papa had wanted. But had her guilt driven her decision—and would that decision now cost another of her beloved Papa's sons his life?

If the person with the other half of the pendant was her destiny, how had she fallen in love with Jay? The question bothered her more than she was willing to admit, but she wouldn't give it another thought if Jay loved her in return. She loved and revered her great-grandmother, but Nona was gone now and she had to live her own life. Nona was a part of her past, a beloved part, but nevertheless still past. She would always cherish the time spent with her great-grandmother and wearing the pendant would keep the memories dear, but she had to look forward. Someday she would pass the pendant on to her own daughter. The other half, might surface eventually, but she would not tell her daughter she should marry whoever possessed it.

CR

Tina dressed for dinner with care. Worried Jay would forbid her to attend the Wolverton rout that evening, she was pleasantly surprised when he did not.

Jay had done his share of thinking earlier that evening as well. He might have the authority to order her to stay home, but what would it accomplish? She probably would not accept the mandate with grace and he wasn't sure he wanted to experience Tina in a temper. Until recently he had considered her someone to protect, cherish, spoil, and generally shield from harm. He was rapidly coming to the conclusion, however, that he had woefully underestimated her ability to deal with difficult situations. Whatever reasons she had used to isolate herself at Thane Park would remain hers, but he knew that having observed her there, he had jumped to conclusions concerning her ability to face hostility. He had the feeling she would surprise him again before this situation was through.

In the carriage on the way to the Wolverton's, she informed him of her edict regarding the hiring of servants. Needless to say, it hadn't occurred to him to wonder whether someone could hire on inside the house and do her harm.

"But," she continued, "Mrs. Greaves informs me it is usual to hire on extra footmen for a large function such as my soiree. Notices would have gone out to agencies soon. I don't know how to handle that area at the moment. I'm not sure I want to interview another twenty footmen for one night."

Jay's initial instinct was she should cancel the soiree, but he suspected that idea would not be well received.

"Let me think on it," he promised. "Perhaps Jon and I can come up with something."

"Thank you." Looking across the interior of the carriage at him, she was reminded again how much she loved him. She wished she knew what he felt for her. Reaching out, she put her hand on his knee to get his attention. "And thank you for not insisting I remain at home tonight," she said softly.

She felt his muscles bunch under her hand and his eyes glanced down to where it lay. His voice was strained when he spoke. "You're welcome, madam. However, if you want to arrive in the same condition you left Thane House, you might want to remove your hand and not tempt me further."

Tina's eyes widened at the undercurrent in his voice and words. Snatching her hand back as if she had been burned, she could feel the blood flooding her face and neck.

"Oh. I—I didn't mean..."

Jay leaned forward and tipped her chin up so their eyes met. Even in the weak light from the carriage lamp, she could see flames leaping in the polished depths. For a long moment, he studied her face, then he smiled.

"Teasing you is too easy at times. I'm afraid I fall for the temptation too readily." Then he took her mouth in a brief kiss, breaking off just as the carriage came to a stop.

Once inside, Jay stayed beside her even as her circle of admirers began forming. Although a few of them cast anxious glances in his direction, none ventured any remarks to him. When Jon joined them and later, Lord Westover, the three men talked among themselves, yet Jay kept her in sight at all times.

He was being obvious, but if Milton happened to be present, he wanted him to comprehend Tina would not be an easy target. He wished he could think of a way to draw Milton out without involving Tina, but so far he hadn't come up with a plan.

"Between Teddy and I, we have spoken to every one of Aaron's friends we can find. None have seen Milton within the last month." Jon's voice was laced with disappointment.

"He has to be somewhere," Jay said. "And soon he will run out of coin. That may bring him out."

It brought Jay some satisfaction to know Rodney Milden had evidently not expected them to discover his real identity. He had put all of his stolen funds into a bank account under his own name. Jay, Jon, and the Metropolitan Police had convinced the bank manager to halt any activity within the account, with one exception. Anyone requesting funds from the account had to do it personally to the bank manager, and the bank manager conveniently had a new assistant, who also happened to be a policeman.

It was Teddy who stated the obvious. "It's possible now that he knows we know, he'll just drop everything and disappear. After all, even if he manages to do away with Lady Thanet, he would never be able to take possession of the property. He'd be a sitting duck."

"One would hope he has thought it that far through and would do just that," Jay responded dryly. "However, that would require he be a rational person. Murderers are seldom rational."

"Got a point there," Teddy conceded.

The final notes of the country dance were just dying when Tina felt a chill down her spine. Turning to her partner, her eyes met a pair of malevolent gray ones across the room. For a moment, she was motionless as his hatred enveloped her in a cold fog. Tearing her eyes away, she allowed Lord Exton to lead her off the floor. Once back in the small group, she moved to Jay's side and slipped her small hand into his large, warm one.

Trying to stay calm, she looked up at him, but still could not stop the small shudder that went through her. Just as before, she could feel Milton's hate like a tangible force. She needed Jay for strength, and she needed to stay calm. She knew Milton could do nothing in a crowded ballroom, but she was taking no chances.

He's just trying to frighten you, she told herself. *He can do nothing here.* Yet, he was succeeding. Despite her confidence he could do nothing in the crowded room, she was still afraid.

Jay looked down as Tina slipped in beside him and noticed her agitation. When she put her hand in his and he felt her shiver, he was instantly alert. Bending his head, he asked, "What is it?" His voice was low, and she responded in an equally low whisper.

"He's here. Across the room, by the balcony doors."

Jay nodded. Turning to Jon on his other side, he said in a low voice. "Turn toward me as if speaking and look toward the balcony doors. Tina says Milton is there."

Jon did as he was told. "I see him. Unfortunately, if either of us made a move in that direction, he'd be out the doors and gone before we even got a few steps."

"Is he speaking to anyone in particular?"

"No, but Martindale is approaching him. Damn! I hope Teddy told him not to mention we were looking for him."

Jay shrugged. "It doesn't matter. He must know we are on to him by now, unless he has not tried to withdraw funds from his account within the last few days. If he was the one who actually pushed Tina this afternoon, he has to have realized she knew the shove was deliberate."

Jon turned to Teddy. "What did you tell Martindale?"

"I didn't speak to him, Gerald did," he replied. "Why?"

"Because Milton is here. No, don't look directly, but he's over by the balcony doors speaking with Martindale."

Jay put Tina's hand on his arm and covered it with his own. He felt some of the tension leave her body as he said, "Come, let's walk. It's nearly time for supper, so we can head in that direction."

Over supper, Tina relaxed once Jon and Teddy joined them to report Milton had left. Once Jay and Tina had left the ballroom, Jon told them he had made it clear he had seen Milton by openly staring at him and pointing him out to Teddy. Milton had slipped out the balcony doors a few moments later.

The duchess and Lady Weston joined them and supper passed uneventfully. Staying just long enough to dance a waltz together, Tina and Jay took their leave not much later. Lady

Weston promised to call on Tina the next day.

"Will you tell her what is going on?" Jay asked her in the carriage.

"Should I?" she asked. "It would be nice to have another woman to confide in. But, I don't know how she'll react. I wouldn't want her to get hurt." She sighed. "Actually it would be nice to have Felicia here right now."

Jay could not stop the groan that escaped. "You do not know how glad I am she is not."

"Why?"

"Because the first time I laid eyes on her she was holding a pistol on Milton. She gave him quite a scare, and I don't doubt she'd try to finish the job if she knew what was happening now."

"What!" Tina looked up at him, dismayed. "When was this?"

"The first day I arrived at Thane Park. Just as I was greeting Keyes at the front door, I heard a shot and went to investigate." Relating the events he witnessed, he then added, "She was protecting you. She made it clear he had been tolerated only because he hadn't upset you too much. But, apparently your last encounter had left you shaken and she decided to take matters into her own hands."

Tina was shocked. "I thought I had been calm enough when I went back out to the garden to tell her what he told me. She was so excited to find out you had arrived in London. She has always seemed unreasonably hostile toward him, but it never occurred to me she might go so far." The blood drained from her face, leaving wide aquamarine pools in a pale face. "If you hadn't arrived, I shudder to think what Mr. Milton might have done in retaliation."

Her distress affected him more than he was willing to admit and he nearly reached out and pulled her into his arms. "It was because of that scene I sought her out to find out more about Milton, but then I was sidetracked because she didn't believe who I was."

"Because of the picture in the gallery. Your hair must have darkened as you aged because it's nearly the same shade as Aaron's in the picture."

He shook his head. "My parents paid the artist to lighten

my hair so Aaron and I would look more alike. I didn't want to look like Aaron. He might have been older than I, but I did not look up to him, nor did I want to be like him."

"Why not? I thought all younger brothers looked up to the older one. There was a time when Jon looked up to Aaron, but I don't think Aaron was very nice to him when Papa wasn't around."

"That's exactly it. Aaron was one person around our father, but a different person altogether out of our father's sight. The problem was that our father refused to believe me when I brought it to his attention. I was always the one in the wrong if there was a choice between us."

He couldn't put a name to the emotion that entered her eyes. At least it wasn't pity. He didn't need her pity. He'd dealt with Aaron and his father by leaving home and answering only to himself and his conscience.

Knowing how she felt about Aaron vindicated his feelings when it came to his brother, but he wasn't sure he would ever believe his father had changed so drastically.

"I'm glad you aren't like Aaron," was all she said as the carriage came to a stop.

Once inside, she sent a footman to find Milly and have her bring her a cup of tea, while she headed upstairs. Keyes informed Jay a message had arrived for him while they were out and he had left it in the library.

Tina was already asleep when he entered her room sometime later. The message had been Pymm's written report. He could have waited until tomorrow to read it, but once he started, he hadn't put it down until he had finished it. He would discuss its contents with Jon tomorrow, but at least for now, Tina was safe.

She turned into his arms as he settled into the bed beside her, curling up close against his side. He wished he could keep her this way forever—or at least until the threat passed. But he wasn't sure that would ever happen as long as Milton was loose.

He suspected Milton was beyond just wanting a piece of property. If he had to hazard a guess, he would say Milton somehow believed Tina responsible for everything that went wrong in his life. The dislike of gypsies was the foundation. It must have come as a shock to the family to lose the property—and to the descendant of a bastard gypsy-born daughter. For Milton, the loss was personal. If not for Tina, it would have been his. That Tina was unaware of the bequest and had not somehow schemed to get it was irrelevant. It was hers whether she wanted it or not. And for that, he could not forgive her. Irrational it may seem, but, as he told Lord Weston, murderers were seldom rational.

He tried not to think of how closely Milton's situation paralleled his own. Tina was unaware of the will, had not schemed to deprive him of his birthright, yet he still had regained it all under false pretenses. Even though it looked as if she'd married him for his title and fortune, could he really fault her for wanting security? Did he know any woman who would have acted any differently given the choices she had before her?

Perhaps the question he ought to be asking himself is whether he thought she would have acted differently had she known the truth? Would she have, as he assumed, preferred a season first? She'd said no, but she hadn't been in possession of all the facts. The knowledge that she had the other half of his medallion assuaged his guilt over not honoring his promise, but made him wonder if she'd worn her half because she regretted not following her great-grandmother's wishes.

His conscience accused him of using her ignorance, just as Milton had, to his advantage. Would she forgive him if she ever found out?

03

In the end, Tina confided in Lady Weston and the duchess. It wasn't that she planned to include the duchess, but she knew Jay had discussed Mr. Milton with Lord Weston as well as the duke. It seemed only logical the ladies knew what was going on as well.

In addition, Tina decided she was going to need some help in the plan she had begun to formulate. She knew Jay and Jon both would be appalled.

"I'm hoping he will make a move the night of the Thurston's masquerade," she told the ladies. "It would be very easy to slip in disguised and try something, and I plan to be an easy target."

"How do you propose to do that?" Lady Weston asked. "Once anyone finds out what your costume is going to be, you won't be able to lose yourself in the crowd. Everyone will know who you are."

"I plan on being something he won't be able to overlook. Very few others will identify me with a gypsy costume, but he will."

The duchess nodded in agreement. "You've got the right of it there, but how do you propose to get past that husband of yours? I can't see him letting you leave the house dressed as a sitting duck."

"I'm still working on it," Tina replied. "But I'll figure something out."

"Just what do you expect Milton to do once he sees you?" Lady Weston asked.

"I'm hoping he'll try to abduct me," she confided. "I don't think he'll try to do anything at a ball—too many people. But, a body has to surface sometime in order for people to believe I'm dead. So, he'd have to take me away to try to kill me."

"But surely you don't want to end up alone with him?" The duchess was horrified.

"Of course not." Tina replied. "Even though I don't want Jay to see my costume until after I'm there, I will suggest to him he have the detective he's hired at the ball to help him and Jon keep an eye on me." She thought for a moment. "Of course, I haven't worked out all the details yet, but I'm hoping the detective will be able to take Mr. Milton into custody, and out of our lives forever."

Lady Weston nodded. "It might work, if Milton reacts predictably. But what if he doesn't? Suppose all he does is draw you out into the garden and try to murder you there?"

"Jon and Jay, both, would say I was insane to try this scheme, but I've not gone completely mad. I won't be drawn out into the garden without an escort. I'm well aware that would be asking for trouble."

Both ladies were heartened by this declaration and pledged their support. The duchess, however, had the last word.

"It still remains to be seen whether you will be able to cozen that overprotective husband of yours into letting you arrive at the Thurston's at all without him in attendance."

CR

The next week proved to be the most stressful week of Tina's life. Although Milton did not appear at another function, she was constantly looking over her shoulder and jumping at shadows. It was, in short, nerve-wracking. Convinced, however, Milton would make a move of some sort the night of the masquerade, she moved forward with her plans.

The afternoon of the masquerade she and Lady Weston were at Westover House enjoying tea when their husbands joined them. The duchess was out to tea with one of her cronies, the duke having taken himself off to his club for the afternoon and early evening.

"You still have not told me what costume you are wearing this evening," Jay remarked to Tina during a lull in the conversation.

"I know," she responded, her eyes twinkling. "You will just have to wait and see."

Jay was obviously not pleased by her answer. "I take it by that you mean it is a closely guarded secret?"

"Of course. After all, if everyone knew what everyone else was, what would be the purpose of a masquerade?"

Although he attempted at least once more to find out her costume, she remained adamant he not know.

"Geri and I are getting ready here," she told him. "So you need not worry about me."

The statement was met by raised eyebrows.

"Besides, I thought you were arranging to have the detective and some others there tonight. If I come with Geri and Lord Weston, you can make sure your arrangements are in place. I will be perfectly safe with them."

Jay was unconvinced. "I'm not questioning Gerald's ability to keep you safe, mind you, but why do I suspect there is more here than meets the eye?"

"Perhaps because you are naturally suspicious."

Her nonchalance would have been charming, if it wasn't so irritating, he thought. But he wasn't about to argue over a costume with her. In any case, she was right, he needed to have some men there. He, too, had surmised the masquerade might be a good place for Milton to make a move and he was taking no chances. He would see her arrive with the Westons and would point her out to the men.

Once apprized of the situation, the Thurstons had been eager to cooperate and allow for a few extra "footmen" to be placed in strategic locations. Although Milton had not been invited, they understood it was nearly impossible to ensure only persons with invitations actually attended these affairs. Anyone could come in through the garden, for instance, once the fete was in full swing, and no one would be any wiser.

It would be nice to know ahead of time what she was wearing, but he had discovered women delighted in these doings and who was wearing what were closely guarded secrets. He would not quibble over her wish for secrecy. After all, a costume was a costume. She wouldn't stand out any more than any of the other women in the room.

Chapter Sixteen

"Are you sure about this?" Lady Weston eyed Tina's costume with no little trepidation later in the evening.

"Yes. Very sure," Tina replied, studying the ensemble in the mirror.

The white, off the shoulder, peasant blouse decorated with red embroidered flowers around the low neckline didn't reveal any more or less than most of her evening gowns and the bright red skirt, bolstered by four petticoats, reached completely to the floor, although most gypsies wore theirs at ankle length. Knowing she couldn't go barefoot, she was wearing stockings and slippers underneath, as well as a pair of her specially altered drawers. A black fringed shawl completed the ensemble, tied at her waist at one side and ending in a triangular point on the other side. For jewelry, a necklace consisting of gold coins matched the several bracelets she wore.

The costume wasn't risque by any means, but she knew Lady Weston was primarily concerned about her hair. Partially braided with coins woven into it, the rest was loose, falling in curling waves nearly to her hips. Even the black half mask she wore could not completely conceal her identity. But that was exactly what she was counting on.

"Then I suppose we ought to be going." Lady Weston sounded like she was headed for an execution, not a masquerade ball.

Tina couldn't help the giggle that escaped as the two women left the room to head downstairs. It had not escaped her, the contrast between the two of them.

"What's so funny?"

"I was just thinking how opposite we look together. I'm not sure that anyone will have ever seen a nun and a gypsy together before."

That made Lady Weston laugh. "I'm sure you're right," she said as they reached the entryway. "You had best put your cloak on while I go get Gerald. I'm not sure he'll let you out of the house if he sees you before we get there."

Tina had retrieved her cloak from the butler and put it on by the time Lady Weston returned with her husband and the duchess. The duchess looked at her closely, but said nothing.

Tina was quiet on the short ride there. As she had for most of the evening, she wondered what she would do if Jay took one look at her and decided to take her home. Making a scene would not solve anything, but she hadn't come up with any arguments in favor of him letting her stay. Her best hope was to already be enjoying herself by the time he found her.

She was learning fast that Jay enjoyed indulging her. He might not ever love her, but he was willing to spoil her and she was not above using that to get what she wanted. Tonight she wanted to enjoy her first masquerade ball and, hopefully, trap Milton at the same time.

Jon must have been haunting the door because he was at her side almost the moment she entered Thurston House. Dressed in plain evening clothes and wearing a black silk domino, she would have recognized those emerald eyes anywhere.

"I'm not supposed to know who you are," she whispered as she fumbled with the fastening of her cloak. For a moment, she wasn't sure she wanted to remove it. She wasn't sure she wanted to see Jon's reaction. He, at least, would recognize what she was doing—even if Jay did not.

Jon noticed her hesitation. "What's wrong?" he asked, "You're already nervous."

"Where's Jay?"

Jon cocked his head toward the ballroom. "I think I last saw him outside in the garden talking to Pymm, why?"

Gathering her courage, she removed her cloak and handed it to the hovering footman. "Just wondered."

Jon stared at her as if she had grown two heads. "Are you

out of your mind?" he nearly shouted.

"Shhh, keep your voice down. I don't want to draw too much attention."

Slipping her arm through his, she followed the Westons into the ballroom, dragging him along, a smile pasted on her face.

"He's going to kill you—and I'm going to watch—and applaud."

Tina tossed her head. "Then Milton won't have to," she countered.

They entered the crowded room and continued in the duchess' wake until she stopped and turned back to them. Her eyes were hard to make out behind the mask of her sky blue domino.

"Ahh, I see," she said and Tina couldn't tell whether her voice held disapproval or not.

"What do you see, Your Grace?" a tight-lipped Jon asked.

"What the shouting is all about, of course. Now, run along and see if you can find your sister and I something to drink."

Jon was not convinced, but did as he was bid.

"I hope you have a good explanation for your husband, my dear. Your brother might have expected something like this from you, but I'm afraid you may find the man you married has another side to him—especially once he sets eyes on you."

"Jon obviously didn't expect it from me, either. Except for my hair, I do not think there is anything wrong with the way I am dressed. It is just a costume after all."

The duchess chortled and patted her arm. "Let us hope your husband thinks so, too."

Tina was dancing when Jay entered the ballroom from the garden. He had not seen her come in, but he knew Jon was waiting by the door to keep watch for her. Pymm and four policemen were stationed throughout the ballroom and gardens to watch for anything untoward.

Now, he was free to find Tina. He had tried to guess what she might devise in the way of a costume. Knowing she had the help of the duchess and Lady Weston, he knew she could be any number of things. Surveying the dancers as he skirted the ballroom, he suddenly caught sight of a bright red skirt and raven-hued hair.

His blood chilled. She wouldn't, his mind screamed. She could not possibly be that naïve. Yet, he was sure he had found her, even though his thoughts denied the evidence before his eyes.

Jay watched the woman until the dance came to an end, then moved to intercept her and her partner as they left the dance floor. He reached them just as they reached the side of a woman in a sky blue domino. The woman's escort bowed over her hand and raised it to his lips, then left her to another man standing beside the woman in the blue domino. He recognized Jon.

As he approached, he heard her laugh. The sound enveloped him and settled somewhere in the vicinity of his heart. It lightened his mood somewhat, but only a notch.

"And then he asked me to tell his fortune," she was saying to her companions.

"And what did you say to that," the woman, whom he recognized as the duchess, asked.

"I told him I had left my crystal ball at home for the evening, but perhaps another time," Tina replied easily. She smiled as she sipped the lemonade Jon handed her.

Jay came up behind her, resisting the impulse to clamp his hands around her waist and anchor her back against him.

"Perhaps you should have offered to read the cards for him, instead," he said in a taut voice. He didn't trust himself to say more. He was still reeling from her costume.

How dare she openly challenge Milton to come for her? He expected she would wear a normal costume and be difficult to pick out among everyone else. But, no, not his wife! She had to blatantly advertise her presence. It would be like picking a blood-red rose out of a snowbank. He had underestimated her—again.

She spun around to look up at him, the laughter dying in her eyes at the sparks flying from his. His black gaze took in her features, alight with joy, before that light was extinguished with one look at his face. He knew he was scowling, but the more he looked at her, the blacker his thoughts, and the deeper the glare. His mood soured. The crowded ballroom faded into the distance, then disappeared.

"My lord?" her voice was tentative.

Good, he thought. *I ought to pack her up and take her home right this minute and to hell with Milton.* But, even as he considered doing just that, her next partner appeared as the sets were forming for a quadrille.

Tina escaped to the dance floor with her partner, breathing a quick sigh of relief. For the moment she was fine, but she still had to return to face Jay. What would she say to him to make him realize she knew what she was doing? How could she convince him she couldn't just sit still and let him and Jon try to handle this whole affair? She had done so at the Park, and Felicia had taken things upon herself she hadn't even known of. It would not happen again. She had to know what was happening and the only way to keep up was to take an active part.

She went through the steps of the dance without thinking, her feet moving to the music in the complicated pattern all on their own. Somehow she managed to smile at her partner, but she was grateful when the music ended. For a few moments, she knew she was out of Jay's line of sight, but paid scant attention to where her partner was leading her.

So deep in thought was she that she did not realize he was taking a circuitous route back to the duchess' side until it was too late and she found herself face to face with Roderick Milton.

"I would recommend you not make any sudden movements, my dear," he said in a low, silky voice her partner did not hear. "I have a pistol pointed right at you and there is another trained on your husband at this very moment." His smile under the mask of his black domino was malevolent. "Now, be a good girl and continue walking with me. One false move and the marquis dies right in the middle of the ballroom."

Tina felt the blood pounding in her veins, the blood rushing in her ears. Dear God, she had fallen right into a trap by being so distracted. Striving to calm herself, she turned and thanked her partner, managed to make an excuse that Milton was her next dance partner, then moved to his side and allowed him to lead her away. Once the young man disappeared into the crowd, Milton turned and led her into a side room where card tables had been set up. Unhurriedly they strolled through, and exited the room into a hallway on the other side.

Marshaling her thoughts and emotions, she tried to remember what she had planned if he made a move. Her reticule suddenly felt as if it contained a small elephant and her mouth went dry. Did he notice it was so heavy? How could he not? It was almost dragging her arm down, and her with it.

Milton grabbed her wrist in a hard grip and dragged her into another small room off the dimly lit hall. Flinging her into the room, he closed the door and leaned back against it, watching her as she stumbled, recovered her balance, then turned to face him. The room was dark, lit only by the moonlight streaming through the windows. Her eyes were enormous behind her mask in a face devoid of all color. A feral smile appeared.

"You should have married me." He levered himself away from the door and sauntered toward her. "You could have had anything you wanted. *We* would have had everything. That's what Aaron would have wanted. But you and your mother ruined everything."

Tina backed away from him as he moved closer, the sides of his domino parting to reveal he really did have a pistol. "If I had married you, you would have gotten just the property on the north coast. That's all there was."

He stopped then and stared at her incredulously. The moment, and her nerves, stretched taut as he stared at her in complete disbelief, then said in wonder, "You don't know?"

"Don't know what?"

He started to laugh. The sound grated along her nerves and pounded in her head until she thought she would scream. But he continued to laugh, the pistol wavering wildly.

Looking around the room, Tina wondered if she could escape through either of the two windows against the opposite wall. Backing slowly so as not to bring attention to the movement, she moved stealthily toward one of them.

"You were the wealthiest heiress in all England. I, at least, would have told you after we married. But, he just married you and said nothing at all," Milton said through his laughter. "Oh, that's rich." He ripped off his mask and shrugged out of the cape.

She reached the window and leaned back against it.

"What are you talking about?" For now, keeping him talking was her only plan.

"You!" he spat viciously, the laughter suddenly leaving his eyes. "You were so perfect, so calm, and so efficient. But you were nothing to Aaron except a means to an end. The old marquis loved you above his own children." An eerie expression crossed his face. "He made sure Aaron knew if he expected to inherit he had to marry you. Aaron only wanted back what was rightfully his, but I didn't want him to claim it all just yet. I needed him to promise me my family's property back first. But he wouldn't."

Tina slipped both hands behind her, searching for the catch on the window. Her fingers grew cold, and chills began to slither down her spine. First laughter, then cold determination. If Milton made a sudden move and the pistol went off, she might die before anyone found her.

"You'd do well to remember it was my family too, cousin," she spat. "If your father hadn't thrown my grandmother out, leaving her to fend for herself, perhaps the result might have been different."

His eyes darkened ominously. The hatred she read there was very real, nearly tangible. "She was a gypsy—the daughter of a whore."

Tina knew better than to continue to taunt him. He was obviously unstable and she would pay if he lost it completely—perhaps with her life.

The pistol in his hand suddenly stopped wavering and she looked up into cold, emotionless gray eyes. "Aaron didn't want you," he repeated. "But he had no choice, so I had to kill him. He said whatever he got for marrying you, he deserved. It was all his, after all."

"You killed Aaron?" she tried for appalled, but only managed horror.

"Of course," he boasted. "It was clever of me to tell everyone there had been a duel. Even that old bitch, Lady Bowen, believed he would die rather than marry a black-haired gypsy.

She wanted one of her girls to marry him. He didn't want them either, but she thought you had stolen him away from her precious little tramps.

"I had everything under control. Even Aaron's father couldn't stop me. He had to die, too. He finally figured out I had dipped into the coffers. But, I couldn't let him turn me off. I still hadn't figured out what to do with you yet."

Tina stared, openmouthed, at Milton. "Papa, too? But, why?"

"I had to. Don't you understand? I had to." Milton was falling apart right before her eyes and that scared her more than she would let show. "I had to stay close enough to you to decide what to do about you. Then the long, lost brother returned, and that meddling brat threatened me. He didn't waste any time marrying you, did he? He'd waited too long to return. He had to."

That got Tina's attention and, for the moment, she forgot about the catch she had finally found with her hands. "Had to?"

"Of course. The old bastard made sure he would. He wouldn't have inherited a farthing if he hadn't." At Tina's disbelieving stare, he continued. "After Aaron died, the previous marquis changed his will to say that if his other son didn't marry you within five years, you would inherit everything. All his son would get was the title." Milton's eyes burned with an accusatory flame. "He didn't have any choice. It was either marry you or lose everything, just like Aaron."

Tina's blood froze in her veins, goosebumps rose on her arms. "No," she whispered. "No! It's not true. You've done nothing but lie, cheat, and steal from the beginning—why should I believe you?"

His smile taunted her. "*I* would have married you to get what *I* wanted. After all, it wouldn't have been very hard to dispose of you after a reasonable amount of time." He began moving toward her again. "I would have made sure you never bore a child of mine. I wouldn't have wanted a gypsy half-breed brat."

Tina tried to assimilate everything she was hearing. It couldn't be true. Jay wouldn't have married her just for the properties, would he? But, even as her heart denied it, her mind went back over their short courtship. He had initially wanted to honor the betrothal contract, but when she had refused to hold him to it, he had proposed outright. Then there was the special license so they could marry quickly. So Felicia could go to her young ladies' academy and Jon would not have to worry about her. And all done before the fifth year anniversary of her stepfather's death.

She couldn't think. She didn't want it to be true, but her mind screamed it was. Why else would he have married her so soon after meeting her? He barely knew her. And she had fallen for it. She never suspected he had any other motives than fulfilling his father's wishes. And she had fallen in love with him along the way. Pain so intense she nearly screamed ripped through her. How could she have been so naïve? So trusting? He hadn't wanted her, he'd just wanted his patrimony back.

Just before Milton reached her, she managed to push the window open and slip one of her bracelets off. She heard it hit the ground and realized it hadn't fallen far. They must still be on the ground level. If only she could distract him long enough to climb through.

"Get away from that window!" he snarled, grasping a handful of her hair and pulling her away. She spun away and landed on a small chaise. Rolling off, she moved quickly to put the chaise between them. Her scalp tingled painfully and a throbbing began in her head.

"You know if you kill me, my brother and husband will hunt you down. You'll never have a moment's peace. You'll always be looking over your shoulder, wondering if the next person you see will be one of them."

She realized her mistake instantly. Bravado disconcerted some people, but not Roderick Milton. He had spent years making people, especially women, cringe before him. He recognized it when he saw it, knew it for what it was, and gloried in the power it gave him.

He laughed at her again, a strange light entering his eyes. He truly was mad, she thought. "Ah, but maybe I won't kill you, yet," he grinned. "There are worse things than death. Especially for a woman."

From behind the chaise, she watched him approach. Looking around, she spied a settee across the room on the other side of the fireplace to her left. If only. Glancing in the direction of the windows on her right, she made a move and watched him move to intercept her, then dashed to the settee, crouching behind it so only her head was visible. She reached up and tore off her mask, the better to watch him approach.

"You can run around this room all night, but I will catch you eventually," he purred. "Aaron promised you to me, and I will collect on that promise before this night is through."

"I'd rather die first!"

The chuckle that escaped him made her shiver. "Afterwards, maybe, but certainly not before," he promised. "Then I will send your husband to join you."

Tina tried to control her galloping pulse as her hands, unseen by Milton, extracted first the derringer from her reticule, then the one from her drawers' pocket. She knew it was possible she'd need two shots. If she didn't kill him with the first one, he just might shoot her before she got the second one off, but it was a chance she had to take. Regardless of her outburst, she did not plan to die this night, nor did she plan to just wound him. She would not allow him to go after Jay, too. He had already stolen one of Papa's sons, she would not let him have the other.

Ignoring the voice that reminded her she had gone against Nona's wishes, she would not allow another murder because of her. She would make it right—or die trying. Jay deserved more. He deserved to live his life free of the curse of her presence.

But, oh how she wanted to live. For Jay, and to find out the truth. Nona had promised her happiness, but only if she found the other half of the pendant. What had she done? Perhaps this was her punishment for not following Nona's edict. She didn't know whether it was or not, but she was leaving nothing to chance. He continued to stalk her, moving closer to the settee. She backed away from it slowly, keeping her hands hidden from view. When she came up against the fireplace, she knew she was trapped. Watching him approach, she fought hard to quell her rising panic.

"Such bravery," he crooned. "I will enjoy taming you. Aaron said it couldn't be done, but I taught him how."

Tina continued to inch along the wall, but she knew she was moving into a corner and could see no way out.

"Aren't you just a bit curious?" he asked. "Don't you want to know whether he learned his lessons well?"

Her chin rose. "He learned enough to frighten a sixteen-year-old into wishing him dead."

That stopped him momentarily. "Wishing him dead?" His eyes glowed menacingly, but he held the gun steady. "Interesting."

She reached the corner and knew it was all over. It was now or never. Steeling herself, she pulled one hand from behind her back and pointed the small weapon at him. "Don't come any closer," she warned in as strong a voice as she could muster, "or I'll shoot."

His attention snapped to the small pistol she held trained on him. His mouth dropped open fleetingly, then he grinned. "And just what do you expect to do with that toy?"

Tina did not answer him. As long as he thought the weapon could not possibly inflict serious damage, she knew he would not use his own. Allowing him to continue to think he had the upper hand would be to her advantage. She had to allow him to get a little closer. And she had to make her first shot count. There would not be another chance.

Sidling out of the corner with her back to the wall, she began beating on the wall behind her with her other fist. If there was anyone in the hall, she hoped they would hear and come to investigate.

For the rest of her life, she would never be able to recall the exact sequence of events that happened next. The muffled sound of footsteps, voices, and the gunshot all merged together. She vaguely remembered hearing someone in the hall, then banging on the door as someone tried to get in. Recognizing his voice, she screamed Jay's name just as Milton lunged for her. She moved quickly to avoid him, tripping over her own foot and falling to her left, directly into the marble surrounding the fireplace. As she fell, she saw Milton raise his pistol and she raised her own and fired. Pain exploded in her skull, then everything went black.

CR

Jay had been watching Tina and her partner while taking the duchess to task over his wife's costume.

"How could you let her leave the house with a target painted on her back? She may as well have come as herself and not bothered with the mask!"

He knew the duchess was not cowed. In fact, she was quite enjoying herself. "I'm afraid your lady has a mind of her own. I could not have stopped her even if I had wanted to. However, if you must know, I did not lay eyes on her costume until after we arrived. When Gerald and I met her in the foyer at Westover House, she was already wearing her cloak."

Jay fumed at her answer, but could not gainsay her. After all, he and Jon had not considered she would do something so outrageous, either. Watching her dance, though, he could not help but admire her poise. She seemed relaxed and confident. No one watching her would think she was trying to draw out a murderer.

Her hair swirled around her as she went through the turns of the dance and he unconsciously flexed his fingers as he remembered running them through its thickness just this morning. His body reacted to the images his mind conjured up and he had to tamp down his rising passion in favor of more sober thoughts. Like never taking his eyes off of his wife, who didn't seem to realize she wasn't really wearing a costume at all. It was like waving a red flag in front of a bull—or rather, swishing a red skirt in front of a murderer.

The dance finally came to an end, but Tina and her partner were on the other side of the room. He wanted to wade through the throng of dancers and retrieve her immediately, but he knew that would cause too much of a commotion. Besides, he could still see her and track her—couldn't he?

He lost sight of her momentarily among the crowd, then found her again. She and her partner were talking to another man in a black domino. A group of young people stopped right in front of him for a few seconds, then moved on. Looking over to where he had last seen her, he expected to see her and her partner moving toward their little group, but she wasn't there. In fact, he couldn't see her at all.

Trying not to overreact, he scanned the room completely. Impossible! She was nowhere to be found. She can't be hard to find, he told himself. She was the only gypsy in the room. Turning to Jon, he kept his voice calm as he said, "I can't see Tina. Let's circulate and see if we can find her. You go that way and I'll head in this direction."

Jon was instantly alert. Taking one look at Jay's face, he realized Jay was one step away from panic. He nodded and, giving the dowager an excuse, moved into the crowd in the direction Jay had indicated. Jay went the other way.

Ten minutes later, they still hadn't found her and dread was beginning to surface. Jay went out to check with Pymm in the garden and returned minutes later to say that she hadn't gone out there. She had to still be in the house. Jay questioned the four policemen dressed as footmen in the room. None of them had seen her leave. Unfortunately, since he hadn't had the time to point her out, they hadn't been keeping an eye on her alone.

Returning to the spot he had last seen her, Jay surveyed the area. It was near two card rooms set up for attendees who did not wish to dance. Of course, in the card room, identities were known, so they wasted no time stripping off the stifling dominos and began to question the card players. Finally, one remembered seeing a gypsy walk through with a domino-clad partner, and pointed them to the opposite door.

Summoning Pymm and two of the policemen, he and Jon headed for the door. The hall was dimly lit and lined with doors—all closed. Abandoning all pretense of subtlety, he and Jon began opening doors down the hall, the policemen rushing into each one in turn.

Jay was beyond panic by now. He had lost her. He had never felt so helpless before in his life. What if they did not find her in time? Suppose Milton had already smuggled her out of the house and the search of this hallway was for naught? What if Milton had already managed to kill her and all they would find was her body?

His blood turned to ice at the thought. No! He couldn't lose her now. Not now. Not ever. She was too important to him. She had become part of him. She had re-created a part of him he thought long dead, and filled it with her laughter and warmth. He would not lose that now. Her great-grandmother had promised him happiness and he intended to claim it. But, it depended on Tina for its existence. Without Tina there would be no joy, no happiness, no warmth, and...no love.

He nearly staggered at the force of his emotions. He loved her! He had not wanted to. Had not planned to, ever. All he needed to do was keep her happy and all would be fine. He did not want or need love. It was merely lust wrapped up in pretty phrases, after all. But he had been wrong and now he faced the truth. Without Tina, his life was worthless. Without Tina, he was only one-half of a whole. Without Tina, there was nothing left in this world for him, his life was over. They had to find her. He had to tell her how he felt.

He heard a sharp rapping on the wall beside him as he was approaching the next door. What would someone be doing to cause that kind of noise at this hour of the evening? Then it occurred to him it might be someone in trouble. Tina! Turning to the group behind him, he waved them to him and called, "This way," then bolted the last few steps to the door. The group followed.

Locked! Damn! Twisting the handle furiously, he called her name and banged on the door.

"Let me, my lord," Pymm came up beside him. Just as Pymm raised his foot and kicked the door, he heard Tina scream his name.

Pandemonium erupted. The door crashed open, he heard a gunshot, and his heart stopped. Then silence. Utter and complete silence—as if the world had stopped.

He rushed into the room, wildly scanning it while the policemen rushed in behind him. Someone lit a lamp at almost the same time he spied Tina.

She was crumpled against the fireplace, wedged beneath another body. For a moment, he couldn't bring himself to look and he watched in a daze as Jon rushed past him and rolled Milton off of her.

Pymm dragged Milton further away and knelt down to check him. "He's dead, my lord."

Jay forced himself to move to Jon's side and dropped down beside Tina. Blood was splattered across the front of her gown. Jon removed something from her hand and put it in his pocket. Then he did the same with the other hand, before turning to

Jay.

"She's still alive, but it looks like she's hit her head."

Jay couldn't remember the last time he cried, but the tears would not be held in check. Oblivious to the others in the room, he gathered Tina's limp, blood-covered form into his arms and cradled her gently as the tears streamed down his face.

Jon took control. He could see Jay was in no shape to do anything other than hold his wife. While relieved she still lived, he could tell she had hit her head, and head injuries were completely unpredictable. God alone, knew whether she would eventually wake up.

Chapter Seventeen

For the third night since bringing Tina home, Jay sat beside her bed and watched her sleep. He knew she was actually sleeping now as she had roused earlier in the day. She hadn't asked for him, but he was heartened to know she had awakened. Milly informed him she had complained of a headache, taken some willowbark tea and toast, then fallen asleep again.

His thoughts went back to the night of the masquerade and its aftermath. To the moment when Jon handed him two small pistols and told him they belonged to Tina. She had been holding both, he said, but only one had been discharged. She had only needed one shot. It had gone right through Milton's heart. His pistol had not been fired.

She had taken matters into her own hands and he had been none the wiser. Why hadn't she told him? Why hadn't he guessed? He had seen Felicia threaten Milton with a pistol. Why hadn't it occurred to him Tina would be just as proficient? Because he hadn't trusted her. He'd wanted to protect her himself. He wanted to be everything to her and believing she could actually do some things for herself did not fit well into that scenario.

She looked at him so often with complete trust and confidence he had begun to believe he was invincible. And, for her, he had tried to live up to the person he thought she wanted him to be. But, he hadn't trusted she might be able to handle some situations herself. If he'd known she was armed, would he have been so angry at her costume? Now he knew why she seemed to dance without a care, and enjoy herself without fear.

Dropping his head into his hands, he relived again the terror that enveloped him when he had burst into the room and heard the gunshot, Tina's scream still echoing in his ears. He thought he'd lost her. When Jon rolled Milton's body off of her and he had seen all the blood, he'd thought the worst. But it had all been Milton's blood.

Now, he kept vigil. Watching her sleep night after night. Tonight there was a little color back in her cheeks, but she was still far too pale. Milly had braided her hair into a long, fat, rope. It lay coiled beside her head like a snake. She was turned slightly to her side, her hand resting on the pillow in front of her face. He hoped when she awoke, she would want to see him.

The last time he had seen her in the ballroom, he had been so angry at her chosen costume he could barely speak to her. Indeed, he had remained silently censorious in the face of her laughter, until her partner had claimed her for the next dance. He regretted they had parted so. He wanted to see her smile again.

Resting his head against the back of the chair, his long legs stretched out in front of him crossed at the ankles, he closed his eyes.

Tina opened her eyes slowly. For a moment she saw nothing except shadows in the room. Laying still so as not to disturb her head, she let her eyes roam as far as they could. As they became accustomed to the gloom, she noted the chair drawn up near the bed. Jay sat, head back in a relaxed pose, eyes closed in sleep.

Silently, she studied him. He looked tired. Shadows had developed under his eyes, and she noted the stubble on his chin. The sharpness of his features were relaxed in sleep and her gaze touched them lovingly. Despite what Milton had told her, she still loved him. She suspected she always would. But would the betrayal she felt ever completely disappear?

She sighed aloud and Jay awoke instantly at the soft sound. For a long moment, he stared down into her eyes and relived the last moment he had seen them in a crowded ballroom. This time, however, instead of laughter, they contained a wariness he had never seen before.

Moving toward her, he asked softly, "How's your head?"

She moved and winced slightly. "Better than earlier," she murmured. "The pain is not as bad."

"Would you like anything?"

"No."

Jay sat gingerly beside her on the bed and cupped her jaw in his large hand. "You gave Jon and I quite a scare, you know. I'm sure in the space of thirty minutes, we both aged ten years. I don't know about Jon, but I didn't have those ten years to spare."

She smiled sadly. "I'm sorry. But, I had to do something." She stared up into his face for a moment. "What happened?"

Jay recognized the question behind her question. "Milton is dead. You shot him."

"Oh."

"What's the last thing you remember?"

"I remember calling you because I thought I heard your voice. Then Milton came at me and I fell."

"You hit your head on the fireplace, but apparently shot Milton before you lost consciousness. He landed on top of you."

Tina rolled onto her back and looked up at him. He was dressed in a black silk dressing gown over baggy silk trousers. Probably so as not to embarrass Milly, she thought. He usually wore nothing at all under his dressing gown.

She closed her eyes. She didn't want to remember. If Milton was dead, she didn't need to. She was free. Free to live without fear. Free to love Jay. Even her worry about disregarding Nona's edict faded into the distance.

Jay's touch was warm on her cheek and she turned her face into his hand. She needed his touch as much as she needed air. Despite her doubts, she would always need him.

Tiredness washed over her again and she shivered. Opening her eyes, she reached toward him. "Come to bed, please."

Jay noted the fatigue in her eyes and voice and understood what she wanted. Making love to her had not entered his mind, but he did want to hold her, to assure himself that she was still here, still alive, and still his.

Shedding his robe, he slid into the bed beside her and gathered her into his arms. Just as she had the night they returned to Kenwyck, she curled up against his side and relaxed completely. Within moments her deep even breathing told him she was asleep again.

"Sleep well, my love. You will always be safe here," he whispered tenderly, then allowed himself to relax and drift into slumber as well.

CR

Tina awoke the next morning feeling rested and hungry. When Milly entered the room in response to her summons, she found Tina sitting on the side of the bed, preparing to rise.

"Here, m'lady," she rushed to Tina's side. "You should not be up."

"I cannot stay in bed, Milly," she responded reasonably. "I need to be up and about. How many days have I been abed already?"

"It's been three days since his lordship brought you home."

"Three days! There is too much to do to stay abed." Her soiree was planned for two days hence. "I won't go any further than the downstairs drawing room," she promised her maid, "but I must get up."

Jay was surprised to see her enter the breakfast room a short time later. Urging her to sit, he filled a plate and set it before her, while a footman was sent for tea.

"I did not expect to see you this morning," he ventured.

"I just couldn't stand the thought of staying in bed all day. If Milly had her way, I would not be up for another week, then I would truly go mad."

"Another day wouldn't have hurt."

"I've already lost three days of planning," she told him. "My soiree is now only two days away. I've a lot to finish up."

He looked at her closely for a minute. "Are you sure?" he asked. "I don't think anyone would mind if you cancelled—considering the circumstances."

She looked up sharply, grimacing at the mild discomfort sudden movement still caused. "Don't tell me everyone knows what happened?"

"I'm not exactly sure what anyone knows—I do not listen to gossip. But, there are rumors out there. I suspect the duchess and Lady Weston could fill you in."

"Hmmm," she contemplated his statement. "I will send around a note and invite them both to visit this afternoon. But, that is all the more reason to continue planning the soiree. The *ton* must see that I'm fine. It will squelch any rumors that might hint otherwise."

"You should not care about the *ton*'s gossip mill," he told her firmly.

She did not answer him. He probably wouldn't understand she didn't care for herself, but she did not want him to be thought less of.

"I don't," she replied, then changed the subject. "I don't suppose you will see Jon sometime today? I'd like to see him and he's so hard to track down some days."

Jay sighed. "I might. Shall I inform him you command his presence?"

She looked up, laughter in her eyes. "Yes, please do."

Jay left shortly afterwards, heading for his shipping offices, but promising to be back for luncheon.

Tina spent the morning going over menus with the Cook, meeting with Mrs. Greaves and Keyes over the soiree preparations, and going over lists from the caterers and flower vendors. Jon arrived shortly before luncheon.

"How are you feeling?" he asked, holding her close for a hug. It wasn't the same as Jay, but the brotherly comfort was welcome all the same. "You gave Jay and I the fright of our lives, you know."

"I know. I've already told Jay I was sorry, and now I'll say the same to you. I'm sorry, but I knew I was the best person to draw him out. You would never have caught him otherwise."

Jon led her over to a small settee and the two of them sat down. "I will overlook your not letting me know what you were up to, but you should have let Jay know what you were doing."

She shook her head slowly, mindful of the dull headache she still had. "He would not have agreed. As it was, I didn't even dare let him know I had the pistols."

"Well, he knows now. I gave them to him after I took them out of your hands."

She looked at him in resignation. "I was hoping you would have just pocketed them and returned them to me."

"Too many secrets, Tina. It's not good for your marriage. You should have told him you were proficient enough with them. He might not have worried so."

"Just as he should have told me about his father's will?" she asked. He was a fine one for secrets. He probably knew about the will, too.

Jon was suddenly wary. "What about his father's will?"

"Are you telling me you don't know?"

"Know what?"

"That Papa conditioned Jay's inheritance upon his marriage to me?"

Jon's silence told her what she wanted to know.

"Don't prevaricate," she told him. "Just tell me the truth."

She noted the shuttered look that entered his eyes, the same look she'd seen in Jay's when he didn't want to tell her something unpleasant.

"What do you want to know?" The resignation in his voice told her much more than he likely intended.

She couldn't keep the hurt out of her voice. "Milton told me not only did he kill Aaron to keep him from marrying me, but he also killed Papa because Papa caught him stealing. Then he told me Jay had no choice but to marry me because he would have forfeited everything if he hadn't." The lump in her throat made it difficult to speak. "So, is it true? Did you know?"

She was confident Jon wouldn't outright lie to her.

"Yes," he sighed, "I knew. Mama didn't want you to know, so I promised not to tell you."

Confusion set in. "But, how? Why?"

"Jay's father created a new will shortly before he died—or was murdered, I guess. It required that Jay honor the betrothal contract within five years of his death or you would inherit everything."

"Me? Why not Felicia? She was his daughter."

"I know, but you were the one he promised Thane Park to. Felicia could not marry one of her brothers and keep the properties in the family, so I'm guessing he thought if Jay refused to marry you, the property might as well be yours."

Tina looked away, across the room, gazing sightlessly at the windows. "So Jay only married me to get back property he should have inherited anyway." Tears burned behind her eyes, but she refused to let them fall.

Jon didn't answer.

She turned back to him. "That was it wasn't it? That was why he wanted to marry me. Why he wanted the wedding to take place so soon. It had nothing to do with me at all.

"And I fell for it," she whispered. "I wanted it not to be true." Her eyes took in the room without seeing it. She couldn't look at Jon—it hurt too much. Betrayed by her own brother. "I didn't want to believe Milton. But I knew. I knew I should have been suspicious he wanted to marry me. But, I—I thought, foolishly, that—that—"

"Tina, don't do this to yourself." Jon's voice was strained. She looked back up at him, blinking rapidly to restrain the tears. "You didn't see him the night of the masquerade. He was frantic."

"That's only to be expected," she dismissed his words. "I'm his wife. To everyone else he has to at least pretend to care."

"Tina," Jon reached out and grasped her shoulders, "Tina, grown men do not cry, but I saw him." Tears spilled unheeded down her cheeks. "There was no one to put an act on for when we found you in that back room at the Thurston's. He was devastated. He picked you up and just held you and cried. I don't think the policemen knew quite what to do."

"Then why hasn't he told me the truth?" she sniffed. "Why didn't he trust me with the truth before we were married?"

Jon had no answer for that and his hands dropped from her shoulders. "I don't know," was all he said.

She searched her pockets for a handkerchief and found one. Blotting her eyes, drying her face, and blowing her nose, she regained her control and faced him again.

"Someone should have told me. Now I understand why Milton wanted me to marry him even though he hated me."

"What!" Jon sat up, his eyes glittering like cold emeralds.

"And I thought it was because he wanted to control Felicia. To control her inheritance somehow. I never dreamed it was because..."

"Tina, don't," he pleaded. "You're creating suppositions out of nothing."

She jumped to her feet, ignoring the discomfort in her head. "What is it about me that makes people leave things to me and then don't tell me?" she demanded, ignoring his words and pacing back and forth in front of the fireplace.

Jon didn't answer. The question was rhetorical. He was too busy scrambling for answers he didn't have. Why hadn't Jay told her by now? They'd been married for months. What was he waiting for?

"It's because I'm a woman and we are all supposed to be idiots who care about nothing except fashion and parties. Am I right?" she demanded.

Jon knew better than to jump in. She had left her hurt and pity behind and was now working her way to anger and beyond. He wasn't sure he wanted to be here when Jay got home. It had been a long time since he had seen her so animated about anything, but he remembered the explosive temper she'd once had as a child.

"Of course I'm right!" she declared. "You all think alike. You think women are nothing but pretty ornaments to be clothed in bright colors and given pretty things and displayed for public view. Even dear Papa, for all that he wanted me to have Thane Park, thought the same. But, heaven forbid we have an intelligent thought in our heads. If it wasn't for the fact we bear children, we would be useless to you."

Jon stopped listening. Damnation! Why hadn't Jay told her? He knew Tina would be hurt upon learning the truth. He realized she had fallen in love with her husband the moment he saw her upon her return from up north. That Jay hadn't trusted her with the truth now seemed an insurmountable problem. How would they ever get back—past those barriers?

He knew Jay had been reluctant to tell her. Jay wasn't sure what she would have done. Perhaps he suspected she might refuse to marry him, wanting to keep the properties. But, maybe...

"Tina." The sharpness in his voice brought her to a stop. "Tina, what would you have done if he had told you?"

"Done?" She was taken aback by his question.

"Yes. Tell me, what would you have done if he had told you the truth, then asked you to marry him."

The question hadn't occurred to her. "I—I don't know," she responded truthfully. "What would have happened if I had refused him?"

"I'm not sure."

Her forehead puckered for a moment as she mulled over this sudden turn in events. "Then maybe I had better find out." She moved toward a chair and dropped into it. "Who would know?"

"Probably his solicitor."

"Hmmm. The last time I spoke to Mr. Strate, he refused to tell me anything. Maybe if you make an appointment he'd be more forthcoming. I'm free this afternoon."

"Me?" Wariness was evident in his voice. "I don't think that is a good idea."

Tina looked up at him, her face set in stubborn lines. "And why not?"

"Don't you think you ought to discuss this with Jay first?"

"Why should I discuss it with him? He didn't see fit to discuss it with me. All I want to know is what would have happened if I had refused. It seems Mr. Strate would know that, wouldn't he?"

"Yes, I suppose he would. But, Tina..."

"If you won't take me, then I'll have to go myself."

Jon took in the determined look on her face and capitulated. He knew she would do just that. He sighed. He hoped Mr. Strate would tell her something to make her see reason. If he didn't...well, Jon didn't want to contemplate the results if the solicitor failed.

Jon was in the library, sampling Jay's whiskey and contemplating the fire when Jay arrived home for luncheon. He and Tina had sent off notes: his to Mr. Strate requesting an appointment in the afternoon for half past two, hers to the Westover ladies, postponing their afternoon meeting until tea time, after which Tina proclaimed herself tired and said she would take luncheon in her room and rest. Jay, she told him, would understand.

And so did he. Tina didn't want to face her husband over luncheon, having now confirmed he had only married her to retrieve property which should have been his all along.

Jay was not alone. With him was his partner, Brand, who had docked that morning with a ship full of spices, silks, cotton, and a variety of other delicacies.

Without Tina present, over luncheon the three talked business, with Brand regaling the two of them with his latest misadventures and triumphs.

"It was a close thing in the West Indies," he told Jay. "But, luckily, *Night Star* was there, too, and with both crews, we were able to finish our business and get out. Madsen was headed up the American coast to pick up another cargo before he headed back, so I suspect he will dock within the month."

Jay nodded. *Night Star* was another of their ships. Its captain, Adam Madsen had sailed for them for a number of years. He was a good man, familiar with the sea and its vagaries. He and Brand both knew if they were in a bind, *Night Star*'s captain was a good man to have in your corner.

"That will be good," Jay said. "Are you going to stay around for a while this time?"

"No," Brand replied. "I have a letter I will post just before I leave, but I'm not ready yet. I think we will head back to the Orient this time—perhaps make a stop in India."

"I see." Jay toyed with the stem of his wine glass. "And when are you planning on leaving?"

"By week's end," Brand said. He drained his glass and set it down. "There's nothing for me here right now. The letter will let him know I'm still alive, but it will be up to him to decide what to do about the rest."

Jay nodded. "I will keep an eye on things for you."

Jon did not understand the conversation, so kept quiet. But Jay enlightened him after Brand left to finish overseeing the unloading of his ship's cargo.

"I was hoping he would meet Tina, but perhaps tomorrow."

"Any particular reason?"

"I thought to get her opinion on whether he'll do for Felicia in a couple of years."

Jon grinned at the memory. "As I remember you promised Felicia a duke."

"So I did. And Brand will be one someday, if he doesn't get himself killed first." Jay chuckled at the question in Jon's eyes. "Brand is the Marquess of Lofton, but for now he chooses not to reveal his presence."

"Warringham! I knew I'd seen those eyes somewhere. They are quite distinctive."

"True," Jay agreed. "Which is why he chooses to stay out of England for now. Frankly, I'm hoping he will stay away long enough for Felicia to make her come out. I would like the two of them to meet. What happens after that is up to them."

"Matchmaking? You?"

Jay chuckled. "I find it fascinating myself. But, I wasn't leading Felicia on when I told her I would keep my eyes open. I just happened to already know of an excellent candidate."

They left the house together, Jon heading for his own town house while Jay headed back to his offices. Jon returned a short time later to find Tina waiting for him in the entryway.

"Are you sure about this?"

"Very sure."

He nodded and turned to escort her outside, where he helped her into his carriage. There was little use arguing with her when she'd already made up her mind. A short distance later, they stopped in front of a large brick-fronted townhouse. It looked much like Thane House on the outside, rising three stories high plus attics.

"Where are we and why are we here?"

"My house," he told her. "Welcome to Kent House." Ushering her inside, he helped her out of her sea green pelisse and handed it to his butler, before guiding her into the spacious library. Seating her before the fire, he ordered tea for her, then settled himself across from her.

"Why are we here, Jon?"

"Mr. Strate ought to be here momentarily." he answered. "I thought you might prefer to meet him on neutral ground, where it might not get back to Jay you had met with his solicitor without his knowledge."

"Oh." It had not occurred to her it might get back to Jay, but now Jon had mentioned it, she could see it could be a possibility. A clerk might have let it slip, or she might have been seen by an acquaintance who might have said something.

Mr. Strate arrived on the heels of the tea trolley. Apologizing profusely for being late, he then settled into the chair Jon indicated and accepted a cup of tea. "I must congratulate you, my lady, on your marriage. The previous marquis would be ecstatic to find that his plans had come to fruition."

Tina got right to the point. "It would have been easier had I known of those plans, would it not?"

Mr. Strate had the grace to look a little sheepish. "I am sorry about that, my lady, but his lordship insisted that I not tell you of the provisions of the will. I don't know if he expected your mother to tell you or expected you not to know, but I was given specific instructions in that regard."

Tina didn't know what to say to his admission, so she asked the question she'd brought him here for originally. "What would have happened had I refused to marry him?"

Setting his cup down, Mr. Strate turned sharp pale blue eyes on her.

"That depends upon the circumstances," he answered. "The previous marquis obviously didn't expect it to happen, so we did not discuss it in detail. However, it would be my opinion that had his lordship proposed and you turned him down, the provisions of the will would have been met."

"But didn't it require that he honor the betrothal contract?"

"Yes, yes it did. And, by proposing to you, he would have indicated his intention to do just that. If you had refused, he had no control over your actions. You, therefore, would have been the one in breach of contract, which, it could have been argued, would void the provisions of the will."

"In other words, if I had said "no", I would have lost everything."

"Possibly."

"Possibly?"

"You could have hired a barrister to argue before the court that by not marrying you, he did not fulfill the terms of the betrothal contract and, therefore, you were entitled to inherit. It might have been a long, protracted case, but there were possible compromises the court might have entertained."

"Such as?"

"Because the marquisate has extensive properties, a division might have settled the case."

"A division?"

"Yes. The court may have been amenable to awarding the family properties to his lordship, that is Collingswood and Thane Park, and the rest to you. The court might not have wished to deprive the marquisate of its hereditary properties. And since there were extensive properties beyond those, the court would not have felt it was depriving you of an inheritance."

"I see." Tina sat back in her chair. "But that would have destroyed Papa's intent in the end."

"I beg your pardon, my lady?" the solicitor was clearly puzzled.

"Papa, I mean, the late marquis, intended that I receive Thane Park. I'm not sure what he would have done with the rest, had he been able to specifically indicate who should receive what, but I know he wanted me to have the Park."

"That would have changed the tenor of the case significantly, had you evidence of that," Mr. Strate said. "He said nothing to me when the will was written. However, since it was not necessary to bring the matter before the court, I do not see why it matters at this point."

Tina stared off across the room. A long, complicated court battle would have drained them both dry. It would have been a losing proposition for both of them. Regardless of how she felt about his duplicity, their marriage was the only solution which made sense. Any other scenario involving solicitors and barristers might have easily left them with nothing—not even each other.

"No," she said softly. "At this point, neither do I."

After the solicitor left, she turned to Jon. "So what do I do now?"

"You are the only one who can make that decision," he replied somberly. "I know you feel betrayed, but perhaps you can work it out. He's a good man, Tina. I wouldn't want to see you two torn apart by this."

"I just wish he had told me," she said forlornly. "I don't know what I might have done, but I wish I hadn't learned from Mr. Milton that everything I thought I knew about my own marriage was a lie."

"It can't be everything, Tina." Jon's voice was a combination of regret and hope. "There have to have been things you two found enjoyable together. Some common ground."

Tina marshaled her thoughts for a moment. It wouldn't do to tell her brother she and Jay were compatible in bed. But, there were other things the two of them had in common. A love for Thane Park, Collingswood, and the other properties and the people on them. A sense of humor. An attraction to each other. She knew this was true. Even when they were separated, they seemed attuned to each other. The awareness she felt when Jay entered a room seemed reciprocated on his part.

Perhaps there was something to go on. But, what did they really have without trust? That was what worried her. He had not trusted her with the provisions of his father's will. But she hadn't trusted him either. She had taken matters into her own hands by trying to trap Milton and it had almost backfired.

Maybe that's where they needed to start. At least it was where she intended to start. She would trust him more and, hopefully, gain his trust in return.

Thoughts of the pendant intruded and she wondered again if she hadn't brought this entire debacle upon herself by disregarding Nona's wishes. Yet it was much too difficult to believe there was someone else out there who was her destiny. Jay completely filled her world. There wasn't room for anyone else, was there?

Jon returned her home shortly before tea time. She had spent a pleasant afternoon exploring his new home, much of it examining the portraits in the gallery. She had found one portrait particularly interesting. It showed their father in his uniform. Looking at the portrait brought back long buried memories.

They were hazy memories, but still she remembered her father as he had been in India. Tall, dark haired, with emerald green eyes—the very image of Jon now. And when he laughed, the room laughed with him. She closed her eyes and remembered the feel of being lifted in his arms and twirled around, the feel of the gold buttons on his smart red coat. She had loved her father, but he had left her life all too soon. Jay's father had filled the void and had given her mother a new happiness. For that she would always cherish his memory.

Chapter Eighteen

Geri and the duchess arrived for tea and, after briefly discussing the events of the night of the masquerade, settled down to finalizing the plans for Tina's soiree. She was certain Jay thought she was foolish for going ahead with the event, but it was her affair.

He wouldn't understand that she refused to let her investment go to waste. She'd spent quite a bit of time planning the perfect occasion. Besides, she wanted to be firmly established by the time Felicia made her debut and it wouldn't do to have to cancel her very first event.

On the duchess' advice, she'd kept it small. Instead of inviting everyone currently in the city, she, Geri, and the duchess had culled a list of over 300 to just over 100. She was grateful, now, she'd decided against dinner beforehand. That might have been too much in her current state.

She hadn't received RSVPs from everyone, but she planned as if everyone, plus a few extra, would show anyway. She was especially anxious about one invitation in particular. Unfortunately, thinking about that gave her a headache, so she pushed it away to worry about later.

"Well, if you're sure about this," Geri said, "I think you have everything well in hand."

The duchess agreed. "Despite losing the last few days, your staff is very well trained, so there should not be any problems."

"Thank you. I have already expressed my appreciation to Keyes for having the forethought to contact your butler regarding extra footmen. You must convey my thanks as well."

The duchess laughed. "Morton is a well-paid treasure. I will pass on your thanks."

All too soon, they were leaving, and Tina climbed the staircase to her chamber.

Still unsure of her own thoughts on her stepfather's will, she took the coward's way out and sought her bed. Jay would understand, she knew, and she would have some extra time to decide how to bring up the issue for discussion.

The next day was full of frenzied activity as Tina prepared for her soiree. She had little time to think of anything except the event that evening. Jay left her to her own devices once he realized he could not talk her out of it, but only retreated as far as the library, promising to be on hand should she need assistance.

Thankfully, the staff had been exceptionally efficient and there was very little to do except supervise as Mrs. Greaves gave direction. At luncheon, Jay emerged and insisted she stop and have a bite to eat.

"If you are going to insist on having this soiree," he told her, "I want you to be able to enjoy it."

Despite that she was still out of charity with him for the moment, she appreciated his caring and even heeded his advice to rest for the afternoon.

"You have done well," the duchess assured Tina when she arrived later that evening.

Tina smiled and looked around the ballroom. "Thank you, Your Grace. I could not have done it without you and Geri."

"Nonsense! We only offered a little advice."

Then she took herself off to mingle with the guests. Tina looked up at Jay, standing beside her. So handsome in his severe black and white evening clothes, he was the perfect foil for her this evening as she had chosen to wear the silver and white gown she had been married in.

She wondered if the tension she felt between them was one-sided, or if he felt the strain as well. Just as the betrothal contract had preyed on her thoughts when they first met, now his father's will made her question his motives. One more day, she told herself. Tomorrow she'd find time to speak to him about everything—including her pendant.

During a short break in the receiving line she took the opportunity to gaze out over the ballroom. She had taken her mother's suggestions and turned the room into one of understated elegance. Painted white, with gilt trim around the large windows, it was the perfect frame for the *ton*. The crystal chandeliers with their many candles threw light as if the sun were present, scattering rainbow prisms around the room. The parquet floor had been waxed to a shine and mirrored the kaleidoscope of ball gowns.

Jay was about to suggest they abandon their posts and have the musicians begin, when a late arrival entered. He stiffened at the sight of the dowager Countess of Wynton. Tina, sensing a change in his demeanor, turned just as her grandmother reached them.

Dressed in a gown of deep green velvet, her blond hair perfectly coiffed, emeralds and diamonds spitting fire from her ears and around her neck, she was a regal figure, even with the cane.

Tina stared into eyes the same shade as Jon's for a moment, then smiled. "I'm so glad you came," she said hesitantly.

The countess looked at Jay, then back at her. "Are you?"

"But, of course," Tina replied, sincerely. "I would not have sent the invitation otherwise."

"Then you must accept my apologies." The countess's hand went to her throat where the locket Jay had noticed before lay, suspended below the emeralds and diamonds by a thin gold chain. Looking up at Jay, she added cryptically, "You were right," she said crisply, "And I shall consider you in my debt."

A smile tugged at his lips as he raised her hand to them. "A debt that can never be repaid," he confirmed.

"Apologies for what?" Tina was puzzled at the exchange. "Whose debt?" Obviously there was something going on here that she was unaware of.

Her grandmother turned back to her. "For being a bitter, stubborn old woman. But we will talk of it later. For now, I am glad to see you unhurt." Turning to look out over the sea of color that was the ballroom, she asked, "And where is that brother of yours? I would speak with him as well."

"He is here, somewhere." Turning eyes bright with a sheen of moisture in them on Jay, her voice wobbled a bit when she asked him to find her grandmother a chair while she found Jon.

Jon did not believe her at first, when she found him. "Why would she want to speak with me?" he groused. "She ordered me out of her house the last time—the only time—I saw her."

"I think she wants to make amends." Tina's eyes widened at his snort of disbelief. "She apologized to me. I think she wants to do the same to you. Now, come on. And, be nice."

Jon allowed himself to be led to where Jay stood beside a chaise where their grandmother rested. The two men exchanged glances, but said nothing.

Leaving Jon with their grandmother, she allowed Jay to lead her out onto the floor for the first dance—a waltz—of the evening.

"I can't believe she actually came—and spoke to me," Tina's eyes were shining brighter than the candles overhead. "When I sent the invitation, I wasn't sure."

"Perhaps she has finally realized what she is missing. She cannot bring back her husband or sons, but you and Jon, you are all the family she has left."

"What did she mean by you being in her debt?"

Jay chuckled as he spun her into a turn. "I meant it originally as a joke, but, as I told her, it can never be repaid." Looking down into the puzzled blue-green depths, he explained. "I told her once I was in her debt for ignoring you."

Confusion warred with her conscience as color rose in her cheeks. When he looked down at her, his dark eyes brimming with warmth and tenderness, the cynic she'd become since the masquerade faltered. How could he look at her like that and not care for her?

"I will always wish I had hurried home when I first heard the rumor of Aaron's death. Then you would not have suffered at Milton's hands. But I will always be glad your grandmother did not take you under her wing."

What was he saying? Was he truly glad they'd married? As for her, she knew she would have spent more time looking for the other half of her pendant. Perhaps none of the events of four nights ago would have happened at all had she found it.

Later, she sat beside her grandmother and listened to her talk about her father. "He would have been proud of you—of the way you and Jon turned out. His letters home were always so lighthearted and gay. In some ways, I envied him. He obviously loved your mother very much. It just took me too long to see it."

"Jon showed me his portrait at Kent House. It looked very much as I remember him."

The countess nodded. "Jon looks very much like him. I'm afraid I've had so much loss in my life, I didn't recognize a lifeline when I saw it. Jon reminded me too much of your father."

Reaching up, she unclasped the locket she wore and, releasing the catch, handed it to Tina. Tina stared in awe at the miniatures within. One side held a picture of her parents while from the other side she and Jon beamed up at the observer.

Tina suddenly recalled a part of the letter Lord Enderly had given her. It had described the locket her father had sent his mother at the same time as the letter to his friend. She remembered wondering if the dowager had discarded it, but discovering she wore it always gave Tina the courage to forgive the past. It could not have been easy for her grandmother to swallow her pride and admit her mistakes.

"Nona said she didn't know if our grandmother would ever accept us," Tina told Jon later. "I wish I could have told her about tonight."

"I suspect Nona would have known, even if the cards did not tell her." He looked out over the crowd for a moment, then turned back to her. "Have you spoken to Jay about his father's will?"

She grimaced. "No. I've been too busy. Tomorrow."

"Putting it off won't make it any easier."

"I'm not trying to put it off, but this soiree is all I've thought of for the past two days," she snapped.

Jon merely looked at her for a few moments longer—long enough to make her uncomfortable—before replying, "Very well. I will stay out of it."

Guilt washed over her. "I'm sorry, Jon."

He shrugged a black-clad shoulder. "No need to be. It's your marriage and your life. I need reminding occasionally that you no longer need me to look after you."

She wanted to tell him that she would always need him, but held her tongue. Regardless of his words, she knew he would be there for her should she ask for his help.

CR

Tina slept away a large portion of the next day. Exhaustion had finally claimed her after the soiree and its attendant excitement. By the time she awoke, it was after noon.

Ringing for Milly, she requested a light meal, then went into the dressing room to peruse her gowns. She wanted tonight to be a new beginning. It was time to repair her marriage. Studying the rainbow of gowns hanging there, she finally selected a burgundy silk, decorated with black trim. Someone else might look at it as if it were a just-out-of-mourning dress, but she knew that its shade enhanced her own coloring. Her skin would look milky white against the black trim, accentuating her own raven hued tresses. With it she wore the pendant.

Just before she left her room for dinner, she handed Milly the case for her pistols and instructed her to place it on her husband's desk in the library.

Jay was not alone when she entered the drawing room. He had with him a tall, slender young man with golden hair and unusual eyes. He introduced him as his partner, Brand.

"Just Brand?" she inquired, accepting a glass of sherry from Jay.

"Just Brand, my lady," he confirmed, bowing over her hand.

His eyes locked on the pendant and, for a moment, she thought she saw recognition in his eyes. A frisson of apprehension slithered down her spine at his expression and she held her breath waiting for him to speak.

"Then you must call me just Tina," she insisted when he remained silent. "If we are to be friends, we may as well be informal."

"Will Jon be joining us tonight?" Jay asked, an odd tone in

his voice.

Tina looked over at him, noting the smoldering look in his eyes. "No. Not that I'm aware of. I think he's planned to dine at his club, then look in on one or two card parties."

"He is not expecting to see you at any of them, is he?"

"No. After last night, I'm giving myself another few days to rest before I attempt any outings."

"Good," he remarked, as Keyes announced dinner.

Tina turned to Brand, noting again his preoccupation with her pendant, and slipped her arm through his. "I'd love to hear more about your voyages," she began as she led him from the room, leaving Jay to amble in their wake. "You must tell me about some of the more interesting places you have been."

Tina set herself to be charming to their guest, although the last thing she wanted tonight was company. She didn't want to make small talk with his partner, she wanted to talk to Jay. But Jay told her Brand was leaving the next morning with the tide, so she told herself she could extend herself for one more night. It had already been two days since her conversation with Mr. Strate, and tonight was still young.

Drawing Brand out, just as Felicia had Jay that long ago night at Thane Park, she found herself amazed at his depictions of faraway places. Places she might only dream of visiting someday—if ever. Brand was a gifted observer and his descriptions of people, places, and animals were so real she could almost feel them. Never had she met someone who could tell a story so vividly. Jay's tales paled in comparison.

"I'm sure the West Indies or Caribbean would be lovely to visit, but I would settle for seeing Paris or Rome someday," she told Brand.

"Perhaps a Mediterranean vacation would be a possibility next year," Jay granted.

After Brand took his leave, Tina and Jay retired to the library. "I like him. Is he married?"

Jay looked up from his snifter of brandy. "No. Why?"

"I thought he might be a good candidate for Felicia. He wouldn't bore her to death after the first dance. I think they might get along quite well."

"And Jon accused me of matchmaking," he commented, drawing a glance from her.

"Matchmaking? You? Who?"

"I was also thinking Felicia and Brand might suit." He took a swallow of his brandy. "I promised her a duke, if you'll recall."

"She'll forget all that once she gets to know him," Tina predicted.

"Possibly." Jay did not sound convinced, but Tina did not want to pursue this topic for now. Felicia would take care of herself in a few years, but now she had better things to do.

Tina wandered over to his desk and spied her case. Lifting the lid, she looked up at him just as he drained the rest of the brandy from his glass.

"Jay?"

He put the glass down and came to her side. "Hmmm?"

"Jon told me he gave you my pistols the night of the masquerade." Looking down into the empty case, she continued, "Might I have them back?"

The silence in the room seemed to stretch for an inordinate amount of time. She didn't have the courage to look up at him. She was afraid of what she might see. Anger. Displeasure. She wanted, no needed, him to understand.

Jay crossed behind her and opened the top drawer of the desk. A moment later, he laid the two small weapons beside the case. Taking a deep breath, she raised her eyes to his. The look in his eyes nearly stole that same breath away.

"I wish you'd told me you had these." His voice held a note of regret. Was he really disappointed she hadn't confided in him? Or was he piqued to find out she hadn't needed his help? Either way, she knew what was really lacking was trust. He might not be able to put a name to it, but she could.

"I know I should have told you," she said as she picked up each weapon, checked it, then fitted it into its space within the case. "But, I was afraid you might not trust me with them." Glancing back up at his face, she continued, "I would not have felt as safe in public after I was pushed into the river, if I had not had them with me."

He turned her into his arms then. "You have been carrying

them since then?"

She nodded. "I had both of them on me every time I left the house—and one on me at all times, even when I was in the house." She glanced at the open case, at the two small pistols nestled within. "Felicia and I devised a way to carry both so if one was ever taken away, we would always have the second one."

He groaned. "Don't tell me that Felicia has a set, too?"

She nodded again. "The set she has used to belong to Mama."

"Where did you get them?"

"Papa gave them to me on my fourteenth birthday. He taught Jon and I both to use his own pistols."

"And Felicia?"

"Jon and I taught her. After Mama died we gave her Mama's set."

"Did Jon know you were carrying them?"

Tina understood the hidden question and wondered anew how they had come so far on the surface without trusting each other. But, perhaps it was because it was all they had. On the surface, their marriage was perfect. They seemed the ideal couple, both adoring and attentive, in public as well as private. Yet, it had taken a crisis to realize their marriage lacked depth. Thinking she might have confided in Jon could cripple the fragile bond she was trying to forge.

She shook her head. "No, although he may have guessed. He knows I have them."

His sigh of relief was not lost on her. But his next words were telling. "You should have trusted me."

The same way you trusted me? No, she would not accuse. She wanted a discussion, not an argument.

She moved away from him. For a fraction of a second, she felt his arms tighten, then he let her go and she crossed the room to the fireplace to warm her suddenly chilled arms.

"I couldn't," she said, her voice strained. "I couldn't take the chance you wouldn't trust me with them." She stood staring down into the flames for a long time before she continued. "Milton didn't believe I would shoot him. Even after his encounter with Felicia, he did not believe I would do it."

Jay was astounded. His father had become a different person after he left home. He knew he wouldn't have recognized him had he returned before his death. He still had difficulty reconciling the father he'd known with the stepfather she and Jon often spoke of.

He continued to watch her in silence. He could feel the tension in the air, could feel her confusion and pain. But he sensed there was more, so he waited.

"I should have only wounded him, so the policemen could take him into custody," she said in a voice so cold it could have frozen the fire she was standing before, "but he threatened you, and I was afraid we'd never be free of him."

Jay moved then. Striding to her side, he turned her toward him and tipped her chin up so he could look into her eyes.

"Are you telling me you shot him because he threatened me?"

"Yes. No. I just didn't want him to come back," she said in a quiet voice. "I could have just shot him and made him drop his pistol. He was close enough I would not have missed, but I—I killed him instead."

Her eyes had gone cold and dead. For a moment, he was at a loss. Once again she had surprised him into speechlessness. Yet, he did not blame her. He might not have been in the room, but he was certain that if she hadn't killed Milton, Milton would have killed her.

"Why?" he finally found his voice.

"For Papa," she answered. "He killed Aaron and it destroyed Papa. I couldn't let him take another of Papa's sons. I couldn't let him hurt you."

She was shivering now, even though she stood before a roaring fire.

"My father's dead, Tina. It would not have mattered to him," he said gently.

She closed her eyes and moisture began to seep from under her lashes. "But it would have mattered to me," she whispered, agony in every word.

The pain in her voice revealed how much she was

struggling. He was at sea. He wanted more than anything to help her, but he couldn't see how to assuage the guilt she was obviously feeling. He, personally, wouldn't have felt guilty at all if he'd been the one to shoot Milton. So, what was the point? "Why?"

She moved closer to him, seeking his warmth, and his arms automatically closed around her.

"Because I love you." Her voice was clogged with tears. "I couldn't let him hurt you. I couldn't let him win."

Jay barely heard the rest of her statement. She loved him! His heart swelled and his spirit took flight. Joy such as he had never experienced before flooded his whole being, opening up that small dark place inside him and filling it to overflowing. She loved him!

Her arms encircled his waist, her cheek pressed against his chest. "I know you don't love me, but I..."

"How do you know that?" he asked hoarsely. "What makes you think I don't love you?"

She looked up. The firelight on his face enhanced the sharpness of his features. "How could you?"

"How could I not?" he countered gently.

Her world tilted alarmingly. He couldn't possibly love her. He didn't even trust her. He didn't want her hurt. He didn't want her to suffer. But those were protective instincts. He was possessive, sometimes absurdly so. But that wasn't love. How could he love her when he didn't trust her?

She broke away from him again. "You don't love me," she whispered brokenly. "You only married me to get back Thane Park."

There. It was out. Despite her earlier resolve not to accuse, it came out that way after all. Moving slowly around him, she dropped into one of the chairs.

Jay froze at the tortured words. Turning slowly, he watched her crumple into one of the wingback chairs positioned before the fireplace, averting her face to stare into the flames.

She knew. He didn't know how she had found out. It was irrelevant now. What mattered was that he explain himself, something he rarely did. Since the day he left home at sixteen, he had been answerable to very few people. He had done as he pleased for the most part. Even in his shipping business, in his partnership with Brand, his was the final word, his decisions rarely questioned. But now, he owed her an explanation.

Dropping to his knees before her chair, he took her cold hands in his. "You're right," he told her and felt her stiffen. "I did marry you to reclaim what I felt was rightfully mine." Rubbing her cold hands, he took a deep breath and exhaled softly. "When Strate initially apprized me of the contents of my father's will, then the betrothal contract, I was furious. In his own way, my father had disowned me the only way he knew how. The only way I could regain what I considered to be my birthright was to marry someone I had never met and didn't know. He was still trying to control me, regardless of what I wanted to do with my life.

"So I procrastinated. I spent three weeks in London, putting off my arrival at Thane Park until I couldn't justify it any longer. I knew when I left London I probably had no choice." He looked up into her eyes. "I still don't know what I expected to find when I reached the Park, but I do know that you were not it."

He dropped her hands and, turning, sat on the rug at her feet, his back against the chair, one long leg stretched out in front of him, the other bent, with an arm resting on his knee.

"Then I had to return to London. It was a frustrating two weeks with Jon and I scouring London for Milton and coming up empty-handed. We finally hired a detective, and I went back to Thane Park while Jon headed for Yorkshire. One full day in your company and my decision was made, but I made a terrible mistake." He ran his hand through his hair, the gesture filled with frustration.

"Jon warned me to tell you the truth about my father's will, but I couldn't bring myself to. I was afraid you might decide to take your chances in London, rather than settle for me."

"There was a time when I wanted a season, but after Aaron's death I convinced myself that I didn't want to come to London." Her voice was hushed and he had to strain to hear her. "All I ever wanted was to stay at the Park. Papa promised me, but I knew after he died, it was possible it wouldn't happen. Still, when you came I was hoping you would honor the contract after all. I thought that as long as you didn't hurt me like Aaron had, I would be content."

Jay turned then and dragged her off the chair and into his lap. Cradling her against him, his voice was ragged as he said, "Aaron was a fool. I could never hurt you. Never!"

Looking up at him, she put her hand on his cheek. "I know. You are too much like your father," she began. He stiffened in denial. "I know you do not believe me, but your father was the warmest, gentlest, kindest, most loving man I've ever known and you are just like him."

Jay covered her hand with his and planted a kiss in her palm. "I don't know exactly when I fell in love with you, but I know when I finally realized it." She said nothing, only watched him expectantly. "It was when you disappeared from the Thurston's ballroom. I was so frantic I couldn't think straight. I knew then if anything happened to you my life would be over. Just the thought of living without you still has the power to send me into a panic. And the thought that I could have lost you continues to haunt me."

She sighed. "I think I realized at the same time that I'd married you under false pretenses, too. I had convinced myself that all I wanted was someone who wouldn't hurt me, but it wasn't enough." Her hand went to the pendant resting above her breasts. "I wanted you to love me as much as I loved you and I was afraid that I'd ruined everything by not telling you about—"

She lapsed into silence and Jay waited for her to continue. When she didn't, he lifted the pendant, feeling the warmth from her skin. "About this, perhaps?"

Her cheeks turned scarlet and tears gathered in her eyes. "My...my great-grandmother gave it to me and told me—"

"To only marry the person with the mate."

"Jon told you?" The guilt in her eyes sliced through him like a rapier.

He gathered her closer, burying his face in her hair for a moment to get control. When he loosened his embrace, he brushed a kiss across her forehead before replying, "No, love. Those were the same words Nona said to me."

Using one hand, he reached up and released the studs on

the front of his shirt before untying his neckwear and opening the garment to show her the medallion he wore.

Tina stared in amazement at the flat disk suspended by a chain. She knew without looking that the diamond star in the center would fit into the shape in the center of her pendant.

"How...how long have you had it?"

"Eighteen years." He reached up and stroked her cheek. "I made a promise once, long ago, that I would marry the woman I found with the mate to mine. I thought I was breaking that promise when I married you." He drew a deep breath, letting it out on a long sigh. "I nearly allowed the time to lapse because of it, because of my promise."

Tina shook her head. "But, how did you meet Nona?"

"She found me on the road to London on a summer night. I had left Collingswood after arguing with my father. Aaron had played another one of his pranks. This one involved dressing one of the stablehands up enough to look like me from a distance and sending him out on one of my father's prized horses. When I tried to explain it hadn't been me, my father wouldn't believe me. He told me if I couldn't own up to my own misconduct, I was no son of his."

Tina's eyes widened in surprise at this side to her stepfather Jay had often hinted at but she had never seen.

"You have to understand I was quite wild as a youngster. It's not that it wasn't something I would never have done, it's just I hadn't done it that time. I'm not proud of some of the things I did back then, but if I was caught out, I never lied about it. That my father refused to see that rankled."

One of Jay's hands moved up her back, dislodging her carefully arranged coiffeur. She could feel his fingers running through the thick mass of curls as he continued to speak.

"So, I ran away. I had a purse full of coins—enough to get me to London, at least. But, on the way, I was waylaid by a band of ruffians. When Nona found me, I was bruised and bleeding a bit. My pride was probably hurt more than anything else, but I was convinced she'd saved my life. She put me in her wagon and patched me up. Then she took me to London.

"Before she left me near the docks, she gave me this medallion and made me promise to never part with it until I found its mate. She said it would bring me good fortune and success as long as I kept it. In return, I promised to marry the woman I found with the mate. She specifically told me it would be her great-granddaughter, but I only recently remembered that small detail.

"When I discovered the coil my father left, I was angry. I didn't really wile away three weeks in London doing nothing. I tried to find Nona, but I didn't remember her name. When I tried to describe her, none of the gypsies I encountered knew who she was. I thought maybe she had died. Then I met you.

"I didn't want to renege on my promise. I had kept the pendant as I promised and now I was back, prepared to honor the second half of the promise, but I was torn.

"I went back and forth with myself over whether to continue looking for Nona or reclaim my lands. I also fell under your spell. After just a day in your company, I knew I had to have you. You were the one I wanted, not some nameless, faceless person wearing a diamond starburst pendant. So, I pushed it into the back of my mind and proposed."

Astonished at his tale, Tina felt the need to explain her own actions. "I thought all the accidents were happening because I'd disregarded Nona's words. When we were growing up she had us convinced that if we didn't follow the dictates of her cards, something disastrous would happen. But, when she wanted me to promise to wait, I couldn't do it. I think, even then, I knew that I would marry you if you asked. Then the accidents began after we returned to town. Even though you were sure that Mr. Milton was behind them, I still wondered if I had brought them upon us because I'd ignored Nona."

"Is that why you wore the pendant to the Loughton's rout?"

"Actually, I wore it on impulse. I'd left it at a jeweler's to be cleaned while we went up north and had just received it back that afternoon. It was so lovely, I couldn't resist putting it on. Then I spent most of the evening worried that someone would recognize it."

"Someone did, but I didn't know how to tell you without producing the other half."

She relaxed more fully into his body. "Oh."

"Is that why you haven't worn it again—until tonight?"

She nodded. "I wanted to ask you about your father's will and tell you about the pendant. Then Brand kept staring at it and I began to worry all over again."

Jay's chuckle shook both of them. "That's because he'd only brought me the other half earlier in the week."

"Earlier in the week?"

He nodded. "I think we were a bit superstitious about our good fortune in acquiring our first ship. We named it the Gypsy Star and kept this," he pointed to his medallion, "in the safe on board. When I realized you had the other half, I resolved to wait until he returned to retrieve it."

"So, it was mere happenstance that he returned this week?"

"Very much so."

They were silent for a long time. The fire crackling was the only sound in the room. The noise from the street was barely discernable. They could have been the only two people in London. The clock on the mantel chimed. Eleven-thirty. It wasn't very late, but it seemed as if they had been in the library for hours, though he knew Brand had left shortly after ten.

Running his fingers through her thick, shining mass of curls, he knew how it felt to touch perfection. "I was jealous the night of the masquerade," he confessed. "Watching you dance, I was sure every man in the room wanted a chance to run his fingers through your hair."

She looked up at him, shaking her head and dislodging more pins. "That is a privilege reserved for you alone, my lord." Her hands moved up around his neck and she pulled his head down to hers. Just before their mouths met, she whispered against his, "I love you."

Lips merged, breath mingled, and tongues danced as they clung to each other. For the time being all was right in their world. There were no doubts, no cares, no worries, only each other. Tomorrow would take care of itself, but tonight was theirs to savor.

Breaking the kiss, Jay rose awkwardly to his feet, still holding her in his arms. "It has been an eventful week. It's time for you to be in bed."

Her hands slid across his chest beneath the material of his

shirt. Half way up the stairs, he felt her lips on his neck and heard her murmur. "I'm ready for bed, but I'm not tired." He nearly lost his footing.

"Siren," he accused, opening the door to her suite.

She smiled gloriously. "Only for you."

Stopping beside her bed, he put her down on her feet. Then he slowly, teasingly, peeled each layer of clothing from her body, planting kisses on her bare skin as it was uncovered.

Tina was not as patient and he chuckled when he heard a rip as she hurried to divest him of his clothing.

He made love to her tenderly, worshiping her body with his hands and mouth. He had always been gentle with her, but tonight he took his time, caressing, stroking, and reveling in the tiny sighs and moans coming from her lips. He wanted nothing more than to lose himself in her and never emerge and for that one timeless moment when they became one, he knew he'd experienced an ecstasy many strive for but few achieve. He never wanted it to end.

Much later he gathered her close in his arms and rested his chin on the top of her head. He hadn't realized it all those years ago, but her great-grandmother had given him a treasure beyond price, and a reason to return home. He was sorry he had not been able to thank Nona properly, but he would do so for the rest of his life—by loving his wife.

Tina curled into his body with a sigh. Relaxed and boneless from their lovemaking, she was slowly drifting off to sleep when something sharp poked her bare shoulder. Reaching up, she unclasped her pendant and dropped it onto the pillow behind her, then did the same with Jay's. When he raised his head and looked down at her, she smiled and said, "I don't think we need to wear them any longer."

His laughter echoed around the room.

She smiled contentedly as she snuggled against him. Everything had turned out just as Nona said. She had found her destiny—and Papa's legacy would be preserved. It was enough.

Comfortable in each other's arms, neither of them noticed the two pendants slide off the pillow together, the diamond star winking in the firelight.

Epilogue

July 1871

Collingswood

The young girl stood silently beside her mother, watching as the carriage came bowling up the drive. It was hot and she wished they could have waited inside, but Mama always waited for Papa on the steps. So, today, she waited too, her white dimity dress spotless, chestnut braids gleaming in the sun, and large blue-green eyes following the carriage intently until it came to a stop at the bottom of the steps in front of them.

Five-year-old Andrew and the baby, Chrissy, were both napping upstairs under Nanny's watchful eye. She, at age 8, no longer needed afternoon naps and Mama had begun teaching her the keys on the pianoforte in the afternoons. They had been in the music room when Keyes informed them a carriage was approaching.

A footman hurried forward to open the door and a man stepped out. Letting go of her mother's hand, she launched herself at him as he approached the steps. "Papa!"

Jay caught the excited bundle of white ruffles, hugging her close before proceeding up the steps to greet his wife.

"It's good to be home," he said, brushing a kiss lightly across Tina's forehead.

The little girl giggled. "We're not at home," she chided. "It's only Collingswood."

Jay looked down at his oldest. Shana would someday be a real beauty, he thought, but, then again, he was biased. His smile encompassed them both as he replied, "Home is always where my family is."

Tina led them inside the cool interior. Ordering refreshments, she asked, "Did you get it?"

"Of course," he answered as the footman carried in a large package behind him. "Put it in the library," he instructed.

The package turned out to be a small table, once Jay fitted the legs on it. Glass topped, with a black velvet-lined compartment, Jay put it beside one of the chairs near the fireplace.

"Ooooh, how pretty, Papa," Shana cooed. "Can we open it?"

"I'm afraid not, poppet," he replied. "It's only for display."

Tina looked down at the contents of the table. The two pendants Nona had given them, now locked together as one, rested there, its double chain spread for display. The center diamond in the pendant seemed to wink at her.

"But why?" Shana asked.

Tina sat in the chair beside the table, drawing her daughter into her lap. "Come, I will tell you a story."

"I will change and rejoin you shortly," Jay said, then turned and exited the room.

"A story?" Shana asked.

Tina nodded and began, "Once upon a time there was a gypsy girl named Nona..."

About the Author

To learn more about Denise Patrick, please visit: www.denisesden.blogspot.com.

Send an email to denisepatrick@gmail.com or, to find out more about her upcoming releases, join in the fun with other readers on her Coffee Time Romance Forum at:

www.coffeetimeromance.com/board/forumdisplay.php?f=2 96.

Banished and disowned for saving a stranger's life...

The Importance of Almack's
©2007 Denise Patrick

In Regency England, lineage and vouchers to Almack's are everything, but Pamela Clarkdale has neither. After her father casts her out, she considers herself fortunate to have obtained a position as a companion to an elderly widow.

Kitt Covington has sworn off Almack's and marriage. Why attend one when he has no interest in the other? Guilt, however, is a powerful motivator. Knowing he caused Pamela to be thrown out of her home, he proposes a sham betrothal between them to ease his conscience.

Kitt's offer is tempting and Pamela agrees, with the caveat that the betrothal will disappear at the end of the season. But not only is Pamela refused vouchers to Almack's, her family is scheming to destroy her to protect a secret she doesn't realize she knows. When the twenty-year-old web of lies and deceit begins to unravel, will Pamela and Kitt discover that Almack's isn't really that important after all?

Available now in ebook and print from Samhain Publishing.

Enjoy the following excerpt from The Importance of Almack's...

Kitt watched her eat, satisfied with her appetite. His godmother confided in him that she hadn't eaten much over the last two days. A change of scenery was just what she needed. Although, why he'd brought her here, he didn't know.

To be sure, he loved this place—as long as he didn't allow memories of his mother to intrude on his enjoyment. He tried not to think of his mother very often; her defection still hurt despite her death nearly a decade ago. His memories of this place were of wandering the parkland, swimming in the pond and fishing in the stream. By the time he went off to school at nine, he was closer to his governess than either of his parents. Three years later, his mother deserted her husband and son.

"I think my father would have sold it, but he didn't want to displace his sister."

"His sister?"

"My Aunt Lydia came here to live shortly before I was sent off to school. She was an invalid due to a riding accident some years before. I believe she and my mother got along quite well, but once I went off to school, I did not see her much. Frisky stayed on as her companion because she had no other family and would have looked for another position once I no longer needed her. When my aunt died three years ago, Frisky was too old to go anywhere else."

As they finished lunch, Kitt asked Pamela if she'd like to stroll around the grounds. Dorie was summoned and sent for Pamela's bonnet, then the two of them set off. As landscaping went, it was very simple. The gardens boasted all manner of flowers, climbing vines, small trees, and two fountains. Once beyond the formal terraces, the parkland spread out before them in stretches of grass dotted with wildflowers and clusters of trees. All it needed, Kitt mused, was a woodland nymph or two.

He nearly laughed out loud. When had he become so fanciful? Glancing down at Pamela beside him, he couldn't see her face because of the brim of her bonnet, but he knew she was taking in everything around them.

"Do you hunt here?"

He shook his head. "No. It was once a hunting lodge, but some ancestor put a stop to it and no one has ever restarted the practice. Why do you ask?"

"I have seen a few deer and wondered if they were here because they felt safe."

"Possibly."

They came to the stream. An arched stone footbridge spanned the flowing water. Kitt's tread was firm over the uneven stones as he assisted Pamela onto the bridge. At its center, they stopped and looked down.

"It's so peaceful here." There was a wistfulness in Pamela's voice. "I could stay here forever."

Kitt slipped his arms around her, turning her toward him and anchoring her against his body.

"You could," he said, his fingers coming up to stroke her cheek. "You could come here to live if you wished."

Pamela raised her eyes to him, reminding him why he felt she belonged here. Her eyes blended with this place. The woodland, parkland and meadows were all reflected in the brown and green of her eyes. She was the nymph this place lacked.

"I could?"

"If I get a special license, we could be married by the end of the week."

Joy such as she had never known blossomed in Pamela's chest. Her heart soared on eagle's wings. Warmth raced through her veins, filling her with happiness.

Yes! Yes! Oh, yes!

The words were on the tip of her tongue but remained unspoken as Kitt continued. "You would no longer have to worry about gossip, or your sister and grandparents. No one would ever snub you again. You would have everything you ever wanted."

She crashed to earth with a jolt. *But what about love?*

The question went unasked. For she knew the answer. Kitt felt responsible for her. He felt sorry for her. But he did not love her. He would marry her out of a sense of responsibility, and to protect her. He would throw away his entire future on a misguided notion of honor. She could not let him do it.

"No." She dropped her eyes to his chest as she spoke, blinking furiously to keep back the tears.

Kitt stiffened. "Why not?" She couldn't tell from the sharpness of his voice whether he was angry or disappointed. When she remained silent, he asked, "Are you worried about what everyone will think?"

"No! Yes! Oh, I don't know!" She broke away, turning to stare off down the course of the stream. Kitt moved behind her and his hands slid up her arms, leaving gooseflesh in their wake.

"You shouldn't care." His voice was gentle, his breath stirred the tiny wisps of hair at her temple. "I don't."

She closed her eyes and leaned back against him. Oh, how she wanted to believe him. She wanted to believe the *ton* didn't matter. She wanted to believe his declaration that he didn't care meant he cared for her enough to brave society's censure.

But she couldn't. The *ton* was a world of its own. If you didn't play by its rules, regardless of your rank, you were shunned. That was the world Kitt had been born into, the only world he knew. She could not allow him to walk away from it because of her. He would never be happy, and he would eventually come to resent her. It would destroy him.

"It doesn't matter. I can't let you make such a sacrifice for me. I'm not worth it."

She was not prepared for his anger. His hands tightened on her shoulders and he spun her around to face him. "Not worth it?" he thundered. "What the hell is that supposed to mean?"

Pamela would have backed away from him had the bridge wall not been behind her, forcing her to stand her ground. Blue fire blazed from his eyes. Inside, she cringed. Drawing on the courage she had used to face her stepfather, she confronted him bravely. "I will not be a charity case. I might consider your proposal if you loved me, but—"

"Love!" he spat with such vehemence she winced. "What in the name of all that's holy does love have to do with this?"

"Very little to you, obviously." Her anger rose to match his. "Nevertheless, I refuse to marry without it."

Kitt's mouth worked for a moment, as if he would say something more. Then, with a last blast from searing blue eyes, he spun on his heel and stalked away.

GREAT CHEAP FUN

Discover eBooks!

THE FASTEST WAY TO GET THE HOTTEST NAMES

Get your favorite authors on your favorite reader, long before they're
out in print! Ebooks from Samhain go wherever you go, and work with
whatever you carry—Palm, PDF, Mobi, and more.

Samhain
Publishing Ltd

Printed in the United States
127519LV00004B/211-225/P